BEASTS &
BARBARIANS

A Sword and Sorcery Savage Worlds setting

BY UMBERTO PIGNATELLI

CREDITS

ADDITIONAL IDEAS AND MATERIAL: Jonathan M. Thompson, Piotr Koryś and Tomasz Z. Majkowski.

EDITING: Dave Blewer, Mike Slabon, Bartek Kowalczyk, Jordan Trais, Jeanne Trais

COVER ART: Tomasz Tworek

DREAD DOMINIONS MAP: Justin Russell

INTERIOR ART: Magdalena Partyka, Tomasz Tworek, Rick Hershey andJehremy Moler (Empty Room Studio), T. Jordan Peacock, Claudio Pozas, Mario Zuccarello, Maxwell Song, Bradley K McDevitt, Kuźnia Gier, William McAuslands (Outland Arts), Cobra-Games © Weyns Peter, Some artwork copyright Michael Hammes and Philip Reed, used under license. www. roninarts.com

LAYOUT: winnicki art studio (winnicki.pro)

PLAYTESTERS: Daniele Bonetto, Luca Coero Borga, Maner Samuel, Paolo Boiero, Pierpaolo Ferrari.

SPECIAL UMBERTO'S THANKS TO: Francesca Viarengo, Marta Castellano (my wife) queen of all the Amazons, Massimo Campolucci (my uncle), for being the first, real Dhaar, Simone Ronco and Polliotti Yoshi (my friends) for fighting alone against the Valk' demons.

SPECIAL PIOTR'S THANKS TO: And to Justyna and Marysia. For making the dream come true.

SPECIAL PINNACLE ENTERTAINMENT THANKS: for allowing the use of the analyze foe, draining touch and legerdemain Powers, originally appeared in the Fantasy Companion.

ADDITIONAL THANKS TO: Shane Hensley, David Jarvis and Sean Preston. Without you, it wouldn't happen.

TABLE OF CONTENTS

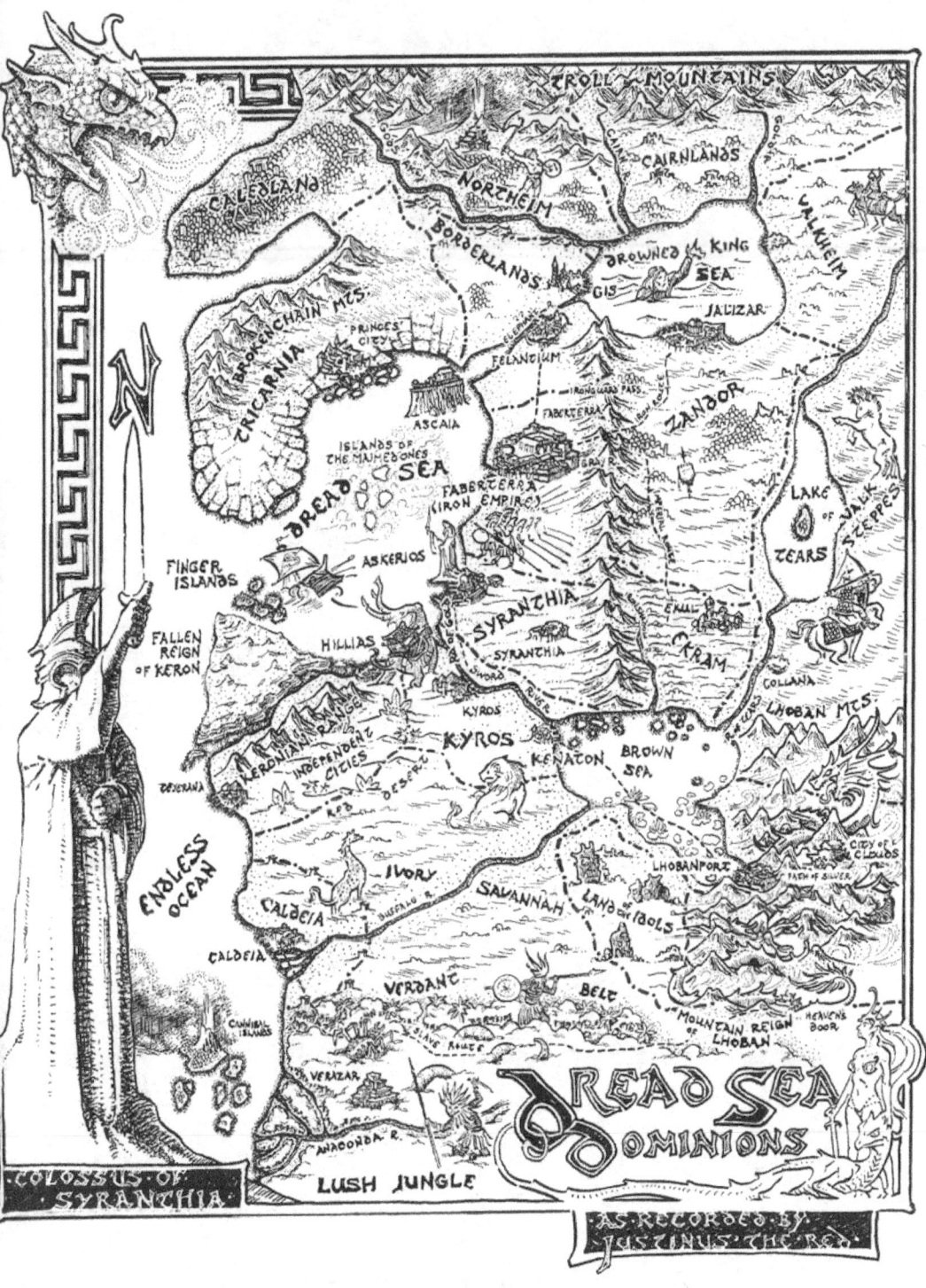

TROLL MOUNTAINS

CALEDLAND

CAIRNLANDS

NORZHEIM

VALKHEIM

BORDERLANDS

DROWNED KING SEA

GIS

JALIZAR

BROKENCHAIN MTS.

PRINCES CITY

TRICARNIA

FELANCIUM

ZANDOR

ASCAIA

IRONGUARD PASS

FABERTERRA

ISLANDS OF THE MAIMED ONES

DREAD SEA

GRAYR

LAKE OF TEARS

FABERTERRA (IRON EMPIRE)

WALK OF THE STEPPES

FINGER ISLANDS

ASKERIOS

SYRANTHIA

EMIL

CRAM

FALLEN REIGN OF KERON

HILLIAS

SYRANTHIA

COLLANA

LHOBAN MTS.

KERONIAN RANGE

KYROS

KYROS

KENATON

BROWN SEA

TRICARNIA

INDEPENDENT CITIES

RED DESERT

CITY OF CLOUDS

LHOBANPORT

PATH OF SILVER

ENDLESS OCEAN

IVORY

BUFFALO R.

SAVANNAH

LAND OF FOOLS

CALDEIA

CALDEIA

VERDANT

BELT

MOUNTAIN REIGN OF LHOBAN

HEAVEN'S DOOR

CANNIBAL ISLANDS

SLAVE ROUTE

VENZAR

ANACONDA R.

LUSH JUNGLE

DREAD SEA DOMINIONS

COLOSSUS OF SYRANTHIA

AS RECORDED BY JUSTINUS THE RED

*S*hangor looks suspiciously at the dark jungle in front of him. Born in the forests of the savage north, he is usually at ease in the woods, but there is something strange amongst these unfamiliar, vine-covered trees. His nose is full of the ripe smell of corruption — and of ancient evil. His skin crawls, as if unseen eyes were watching him.

His hand instinctively caresses the hilt of his axe. The contact with the wood, polished by use, gives the massive barbarian comfort. He crouches down to examine the tracks in the mud. Five men, at least, went this way, carrying Korala, the daughter of the caravan master, whom they took several hours ago. The prints of bare feet are noticeably smaller than those of a full-grown man.

"Pygmies!" Shangor curses, thinking of the stories he has heard about these vicious, elusive savages. Tales of silent blowpipes loaded with poison darts, promising a painful death, and of kidnapped maidens, sacrificed to bestial gods. Yet, Korala's beauty — and her father's gold — drive his worries away.

As he follows the tracks, he soon becomes aware of a low, thudding noise — sacrificial drums, and not far away. His sharp ears lead him unerringly towards them, until he finds himself in front of a strange, forbidding ruin of huge size.

His hesitation gone, Shangor immediately readies his axe, smiling grimly. As always, thought and action are one and the same in his barbaric, uncivilized mind.

The light of the moon shines on his massive muscles while, clad only in a loincloth, he sneaks through the dark jungle, as silent as a leopard...

WELCOME TO *BEAST AND BARBARIANS*, Gramel' setting of sword and sorcery! In the

following pages you'll find all you need to create powerful barbarians, courageous

amazons, cunning rogues, or mysterious warlocks and venture across

the Dread Sea Dominions!

Now grab your sword, flex your mighty muscles and let's get started.

about this book...

THIS IS THE EXPANDED EDITION of the latest *Beasts and Barbarians Savage Worlds*

setting. In this book you'll find the Player Guide which lets you create a sword and

sorcery hero using the *Savage Worlds* rules so you can start playing right away. Also

included is the Game Master Guide which includes all the information you will need

to run short tales, long adventures and whole campaigns in the Dominions!

In the next few months, Gramel will publish several additional modules, each providing

a complete adventure, an expansion to the Book of Lore, in-depth descriptions of the

various regions of the Dread Sea Dominions, deeper background details,

and much more!

PLAYER'S GUIDE

CHAPTER 1:
THE BOOK OF LORE

*I*n the year of the Burning Phoenix, the twenty-fourth year of reign of his majesty Emperor Domistan — tenth of his line, Ruler of the Iron Empire, Lord of the Dread Sea, Guardian of the North, Heir of the Eastern and the Western Empire —, I, Velastios of Syranthia, write this chronicle, so that all my knowledge, gathered throughout a lifetime at the humble service of the Library, will not disappear when Hulian, Smith of Words, finally calls me to his side in the skies...

The world described in this setting is called the Dread Sea Dominions, by the name of the massive body of water at its center, where the most important modern civilization, the Iron Empire, has flourished and now is slowly, but unstoppably, decaying under the pressure of its own size and of the barbarians pushing on its borders.

This is an age in which a brave warrior and his sword can carve his name in history.

A BRIEF HISTORY OF THE WORLD

THE DREAD STAR

Almost two thousand and five hundred years ago, where the Dread Sea stands now, there was a great plain where a magnificent civilization flourished - the Keronian Empire. They were a noble race of magicians, astrologers, and priests, and under their domination the world knew marvels that today are almost impossible to imagine. Despite their powers, they were not fair minded people, and some scholars say they were not even humans.

The strength of the Keronians came from their slaves — thousands of dark-skinned men who constructed their marble and alabaster cities, raised their observatory temples, and died on the altars of their ancient gods.

In that age, the primitive white men lived in caverns in the north, and took great care not to come near the borders of the Keronian Empire, because the Keronian gods were always thirsting for blood, no matter what the race of the sacrificial victims was.

But one day, in a single moment, the Keronian Empire ended. A massive mountain of fire falling from the skies hit the very center of the empire, destroying it and leaving an enormous crater, soon filled with the waters of the Endless Ocean.

The stories call the falling mountain the Dread Star, and the newly created body of water took the name of the Dread Sea, because, even today, its waters are of an intense red color.

The philosophers and sages debate about why the Keronians, mages, and astrologers failed to foresee the destruction that was upon them and they did not leave the empire in time. Someone says they foresaw the cataclysm, but only too late; others say that the Dread Star was a punishment sent by the gods for the many evils committed by this cruel race.

The impact of the Dread Star raised a massive cloud of dust. For many years, the light of the sun was dimmed all over the continent and most of the few survivors died of famine, pestilence, and even worse afflictions.

Then strong winds took the red dust south over the northern part of what today are the Lush Jungles. The trees died, their trunks calcified, and the whole area became the so-called Red Desert. Further south the situation was better, but the jungle was forced to recede becoming the Ivory Savannah that still exist today.

Climate changes were not the only effects of the Dread Star. The thin dust filling the air transformed the world in many strange ways. Beasts of all types started to appear, such as white and black-striped horses in the Ivory Savannah, and massive flying snakes known as Lhoban Dragons, in the south east, among the highest cliffs of the continent.

Mutations caused by the fallen star did not spare the humans either. Many of them started to become brutish, feral beings, and the most unfortunate, the primitive people from the mountains of the north-east now turned into the hulking beasts known as Trolls.

With the passing of time, these abominations became rarer, but they never entirely disappeared. In remote, unpopulated areas, the monsters dwelling in the old Keronian ruins still howl at the moon today...

HERO'S JOURNAL: THE LOTUS

One of the most mysterious changes after the fall of the Dread Star was the diffusion of the Lotus. It is a strange plant with flowers of intense colors: red, white, purple and many other. The Lotus appeared all over the continent in several different forms. In the Caledlands the Green Lotus grows, like mistletoe, on the branches of ancient oaks. In the Ivory Savannah, flowers of Gray Lotus blossom from the top of tall weeds. In the Brown Sea, the Purple Lotus closely resembles water lily. Whatever its form is, the Lotus has great magical powers, but it is also very dangerous. If eaten fresh,

it is toxic and might lead to death but, if processed and mixed with other ingredients, it can create fantastic essences, poisons, and so on. Each type of Lotus has a different effect depending on the color of the plant and the ingredients it is mixed with. Lotus masters are an exclusive sect of alchemists specializing in the study of this remarkable plant. Their recipes are handed down from a master to a disciple in the utmost secrecy and Lotus masters are ready to kill to learn the recipe of a rival sect member. The greatest Lotus masters are the Alchemists of the Free City of Gis.

THE DAWN OF CIVILIZATION

The centuries passed and the climate slowly stabilized. The Dread Sea, for some unknown reason, is quite warm, and this made the surrounding areas temperate and comfortable. No longer fearing the Keronians, the white men of the north started migrating south, to the warmer regions. Some of them abandoned their primitive way of life and discovered agriculture. The first small villages appeared all around the fertile shores of the Dread Sea.

Another migration happened in that remote era. The olive-skinned slaves of the Keronians, who had survived the cataclysm because they lived on the outskirts of the empire, took to the road. They were following a primeval urge to go as far as possible from the land of their masters. Some of them reached the vast woodlands of the north-east peninsula of the Dominions and became known as the Caleds, while the southern ones, of a smaller stature, reached the Lush Jungles and became the progenitors of the present-day Pygmies.

Despite their different appearance and the enormous distance between them, the two olive-skinned races still share many common features. They are both primitive, very reclusive and isolationists, and always live in the forests, perhaps because the constant sight of the sky reminds them of the day when the Dread Star fell onto the world.

But let us return to the fertile shores of the Dread Sea, the cradle of civilization. In the space of a thousand years, the small villages became cities which soon expanded their boundaries and became small, autocratic city states. Their numbers were growing and, in a few centuries, they started to compete for more fertile areas. Many small-scale wars were being fought in those days, but no city was strong enough to conquer the others permanently.

Then Fabron, a priest-smith from the small town of Faberterra, the follower of a minor deity named Hulian, discovered a way to melt the strange stones of the Gray River.

Thus, iron was discovered.

THE IRON EMPIRE

The dwellers of Faberterra were farmers who used to work together plowing large fields. The working crews provided the basis for the Iron Empire's war machine: the phalanx. The Iron Priests of Hulian were the first generals of the armies; they led their troops in Hulian's name, but they swore loyalty to a Council of wise citizens.

Thanks to their iron weapons and armor, Hulian's followers conquered all their immediate neighbors. In a few generations Faberterra became a large state along the eastern coast of the Dread Sea. Yet, these men were conquerors, not pillagers: any city surrendering to their might was spared. After swearing loyalty to the Council of Faberterra, the city was permitted to join the Empire, first as vassal and, after a period of twenty five years, as a rightful member of the Confedera-tion.

This was the fate of the city state of Syranthia which became the biggest center of learning of the Confederation.

The Iron Confederation, as it was then called, continued to expand toward the north and south for two hundred years until it faced two major threats: the northern Reign of Tricarnia and the southern Autarchate of Kyros.

Tricarnia was a huge reign created by some bastardized survivors of the cataclysm that hit the Keronians. Two thousand years of breeding with lesser races made them more humanlike in appearance, but they maintained the ancient Keronian way of life. Tricarnia's massive estates, cultivated by slaves, were governed by small hierarchies of corrupt Priest Princes, worshippers of ancient Keronian gods and powerful sorcerers.

Slaves also formed the bulk of the Tricarnian army. Although they did not know how to use iron, the sheer numbers of their slave soldiers, combined with the arcane knowledge of the Priest Princes, were enough to stop the advances of the Iron Empire toward the north. Many battles were fought, but the dark magic of the Tricarnian sorcerers awoke creatures not seen in the world for eons, and pestilence and misfortune tormented the invaders.

In the end, the mighty Iron Phalanxes of Faberterra were forced to withdraw.

It was not just a political and military defeat, but also a spiritual one. The Tricarnians went into battle with the standard of their main Goddess, Hordan, Lady of Darkness, and they took no prisoners because they sacrificed them all on the altars of their evil deity. In the end, the lost war shook the faith of the Confederation: Hulian was accused of being a false god, the Iron Priests were lynched and, in the end, the popularity of the cult faded.

In the south the situation was not any better.

The Autarchate of Kyros was a big state with access to two seas, the Dread Sea and the Brown Sea. It was ruled by an absolute monarchy and it managed to stop the expansion of the Iron Confederacy.

Kyros had a tradition of war against the black people of the Ivory Savannah. It was a constant struggle between two opposite ways of living: the nomadic herders of the Ivory Savannah Tribes against the farming communities of Kyros. Through contacts with the Savannah people, Kyros acquired a powerful weapon, the bane of the Iron Confederacy: elephants. They were the only beasts in the world capable of standing against the Buffalo Riders of the Savannah.

The Iron Phalanxes of the Confederacy fled in front of the mighty charge of the armored pachyderms, and, after a couple of disastrous battles, the generals of Faberterra were again forced to retreat.

Meanwhile, a minor but quite important event happened: the insular city of Ascaia, an early conquest of the Confederation, revolted against the local governor. It would be viewed as one of the strangest rebellions in the history of the Confederation. This rebellion was motivated, not by politics, but by the gender of those doing the rebelling. The women of the city, tired of being oppressed by their men, took to

arms. It was a very bloody war and, within a week, no man was left alive on the island. At the head of the rebels were Galla, the wife of the former governor, and Ilenya, a female gladiator of the arena. They became the first Sister Queens of Ascaia.

This was the founding of the Amazon Reign. The Confederation tried to regain control of the island, but Ascaia is surrounded by dangerous reefs, with only one, easily defendable port, and its agriculture is self-sustaining. So, the Amazons resisted all the attacks and, in a few years, their reign became a grudgingly accepted reality.

After these three blatant failures, the Confederacy languished for twenty years.

Then, senator Domestan was elected Masterarkos, High General of the Iron Confederacy Armies. A former veteran of the Tricarnian wars, he was a top tactician and a skillful politician. He made a truce with the Tricarnians and, at the same time, he allied himself with Khmeros, the younger brother of the Kyros Autarch, supporting his claim to the Autarchate's throne.

Kyros was shaken by a civil war and, in the end; the Iron Confederacy crushed the two factions, annexing the Land of the Elephants to its domains.

Domestan used this success to force the Iron Council to give him absolute power. This was the end of the Confederation and the start of the Iron Empire, with Domestan I as the first Emperor.

The reasons for the following decisions taken by Domestan are unknown. It is rumored that the High Priests of Hulian came out of the isolation they had been in since being defeated by the Tricarnians; they visited the Emperor and revealed to him a prophecy, which said that Tricarnia and her evil goddess would be destroyed, if fought with an army led by a single man.

The Emperor recognized the figure in the prophecy as himself and, with a unified kingdom under his command and the might of the Kyrosian elephants on his side, attacked Tricarnia again.

A series of terrible battles were fought in the north, the most famous being the Battle of the Elephants River, where two hundred of these mighty beasts died. But, in the end, the Iron Empire crushed the bulk of the Tricarnian army. Then, the Phalanxes entered Tricarnia and started pillaging the land, with the priests of Hulian spurring them to burn down the unholy temples and observatories dotting the country.

But Tricarnia was never truly conquered. In the towers of the City of Princes, the capital, the Priests Princes devised a plan to save their reign and turn defeat into victory.

An ambassador, accompanied by a hooded figure, arrived at Domestan's camp. He offered the instant capitulation of Tricarnia and annexation of the northern reign to the Empire but asked for the pillaging to be stopped at once. The Emperor was very doubtful but the ambassador said there was more, and removed the hood of his traveling companion. Thus, Domestan first set eyes on Princess Salkaria of Tricarnia who was to become his bride. Salkaria was one of the most beautiful women in the Dominions.

Domestan was utterly bewitched by her beauty.

Despite the firm opposition by the priests of Hulian, the peace treaty was signed, the conditions accepted, and the new state of things ratified by the marriage between Emperor Domestan and Princess Salkaria. From that moment on, the infected blood of the Tricarnians entered the imperial bloodline. Rumors say that Salkaria—a witch of great power—totally subjugated his Imperial Majesty and from then on the skilled politician and general was only a puppet in the hands of the Priest Princes. But this version of the story appears only in the secret chronicles of the High Temple of Hulian.

Indeed, misty Tricarnia joined the Empire but preserved a great degree of independence, becoming more an ally than just a vassal country. The Priest Princes retained their titles and all their slaves.

Empress Salkaria soon became an important figure especially on religious matters. She granted her protection to Tulemar, chief of a minor faction of the clergy of Hulian, and in a few years they developed a new religious doctrine in which Hulian and Hordan became a single god with two faces called the Divine Couple.

The true priest-smiths of Hulian called it heresy but the Emperor ratified the Divine Couple as official god of the Empire and the Hulianites were forced to go into hiding.

The imperial act was called the Salkarian Reformation, and it marked the start of the Imperial Age. The Salkarian Reformation also introduced a new calendar — the Reformed Salkarian Calendar, which is still used today.

Since its alliance with Tricarnia, the Iron Empire has been experiencing a constant growth. It expanded toward the north taking lands from the savage tribes of Northeim, conquering a vast area as far as the Godaxe River.

The Empire achieved this goal by using a mix of brute force and cunning politics. Its generals often allied themselves with certain Northlander clans against other Northlander clans and then, after eliminating the common enemies, they subdued their former allies.

Nonetheless, they have never tried to enter the Caledlands. The Caleds are reclusive and very dangerous. Their naked spearmen are armed with simple bone tipped lances but they are capable of tremendous feats of savagery, and the powers of their tattooed druids are feared even by the Tricarnian Priest Princes.

In the same period the Iron Empire also expanded eastward, beyond the Iron Mountains. On the other side, they found a temperate land populated by a race of farmers and herders living in a handful of city states. Their territories were vast and bordered only by the Drowned King Sea to the north, the Lhoban Mountains to the south and the Tears River and Lake to the east.

The most powerful of these city states was Jalizar and its territory was named Zandor.

In only two hundred years the whole of Zandor was conquered with weapons, cunning politics and the occasional subtle use of Tricarnian black magic.

The Iron Empire reached its apogee which continued for two hundred years.

But that age of peace was not fated to last.

THE VALK INVASIONS

Three hundred years ago the Iron Empire saw the face of its mortal enemy: the Valk.

They came from the endless, unexplored steppes eastward of the Tears River. The Valk were short, bowlegged men but they were the best riders in the known world. Their ugly ponies were sturdier even than the white thoroughbreds of Kyros and able to travel for a whole day without getting tired. Hence, the Valk were highly mobile mounted archers, not slow, heavy impact troops like the cataphracts of Syranthia.

They used stirrups and curved bows made of bone with a range unmatched in the west.

The Valk were demon worshippers led by female priestesses, the Valkyrie. It seems that their invasion started because of a collective vision the Valkyrie had.

In that vision, Sha Mekri, the most ancient demon god of the Valk ordered them to conquer the west. This is an unconfirmed rumor but the reality was that in ten years two million Valk moved west from the eastern steppes.

The first to be invaded were the Cairnlords, a barbaric culture living north of the Drowned King Sea. They had long been the bitter enemies of the neighbors, the Northlanders.

The Valk displaced the Cairnlords, who were forced to invade the lands of the Northlanders. The Northlanders did the same with the Empire which, for the first time in centuries, was forced to face an attack on its borders.

At the same time, for unknown reasons, the Caleds came out of their forests and started a ferocious guerrilla war against the Tricarnian territories of the Empire

showing that the former slaves still hated their ancestral masters as much as ever.

But the Empire no longer had the impressive military force it had once boasted. The Iron Phalanxes had not been used in real wars for three centuries and were but a shadow of their former selves.

They fought as best as they could but the Empire lost most of the Northern provinces and was not able to reach Tricarnia which, left alone to fight against the Caleds declared its independence from the Empire.

Many stories are told of the Tricarnian-Caledan wars. Terrible sorceries were used by both sides and since then the woods of the Caledlands have been even darker than before. In the end the Caleds withdrew to their woods but Tricarnia was wounded so deeply that, even today, most of the reign is reduced to ruined shells which are inhabited only by phantoms and dark creatures.

In the meantime, the Northlanders and Cairnlords swarmed south pillaging and destroying. They reached the borders of Faberterra before the joint efforts of the Phalanxes and mercenaries coming from the south threw them back in the battle of Felantium, a few miles from the Elephants River.

But this was only the beginning of the Empire's decline

Taking advantage of the Empire's weakness Kyros, where a new dynasty of Autarchs had seized power, declared its independence. Faberterra's central government wasn't able to react.

Fifty years later Syranthia, the economic center of the Empire, also declared its independence and was ruled by a group of rich merchant lords. However, Syranthia still bore formal respect to the Imperial government.

Yet, the Valk invasion was to bring more terror and destruction. A hundred years later the mounted barbarians reached the plains of Zandor, the eastern part of the Iron Empire.

DECLINE OF THE EMPIRE

At this point the Iron Empire was forced to choose: defending the northern territories from the Northlanders and Cairnlords or use all its forces in defense of Zandor and the rich east.

They tried to save both which proved an ill-fated choice.

To stop the barbarians from taking over in the north, the Emperor created a vast area named the Borderlands including the parts of the Empire raided by Northlanders.

The Borderlands were small, independent reigns, in the hands of capable warlords allied with the Empire.

These warlords and their people were now civilized descendants of previously conquered Northlanders. Yet, they were too civilized to be real barbarians and too barbaric to be rightful citizens of the Empire.

Large parts of their territories were in the hands of the marauders and their rule was often only theoretical. However, the Borderlanders, as they were named, had their own forces, mercenaries fighting under their banners to keep their ancestral brothers at bay.

A lengthy, bloody war was fought, but in the end the Borderlanders managed to drive the barbarians away and a semblance of civilization appeared again in these lands.

The Iron Empire could only send a token force. Emperor Domistan XII, doubtful of the Borderlanders' actual chances of winning the war and fearing an assault from Kyros, didn't want to leave Faberterra unguarded.

Therefore the eastern part of the Empire faced the impact of the Valk invasion alone.

In a show of disdain for the Emperor's cowardice his brother Ornestan, Governor of the East and Prince of Jalizar, declared independence from the Iron Empire and the new kingdom of Zandor was born with the barbarians at its doorsteps.

Zandor lasted for less than twelve years. The Valk invaders crossed the Tear River, razed the border city of Collana and swarmed into the reign.

They were lead by the Valkyrie and by the great warrior chief Dhaar, worshipped as the incarnation of Sha Mekri, a man who managed to gather under his command countless clans of the steppe.

The Valk don't conquer. They are nomads and herders: they raze, pillage and burn what they cannot take away. The armies of Zandor, despite having been the best in the Iron Empire, could not withstand the speed and hit and run tactics of the nomads. In a few years, the Zandorian armies were forced to retreat to the cities and to protect very small areas around the major centers, while the barbarians triumphed everywhere else. The Valk brought with them their unholy cult of demons and whole villages were sacrificed to Sha Mekri and other demons.

Centuries of civilizations were wiped out in a few seasons. The ruins of razed cities soon dotted the landscape of Zandor and, despite their treasures; they were infested by Valk demons.

In truth, the Reign of Zandor ended when the armies retreated to defend their cities. Each of them became once again a city state standing alone against the demon worshipping nomads.

In the end, Dhaar and his horde reached Jalizar and besieged it.

The siege went on for three years and Ornestan II, king of Jalizar and nephew of the founder of the kingdom, was ready to surrender to Dhaar when the unexpected happened: the Valk leader died.

Strange stories are told about how the mighty nomad ruler passed away and about a ship full of treasures that set sail from Jalizar to Gis, Free City of the Alchemists, and came back empty, just three days after Dhaar's death.

Whatever the cause, the death of the incarnation of Sha Mekri had a tremendous impact on the Valk invasion. For a long period, the Valkyrie went totally mad. They babbled incoherently and many of them committed suicide or disappeared in the steppes.

Taking advantage of this situation, Dhaar's three sons started a tremendous fratricidal war to gain power over the horde. In the end, Tukal, the eldest, went north with his followers and settled in the vast are today known as Valkheim. Juggu, the second brother, remained in the north of Zandor, while Eku, the youngest, moved south and created an independent monarchy in the city of Ekram, where he learnt the western customs and became a civilized and decadent man.

So, this takes us to the present. The Empire is dying, its customs are in full decadence and the barbarians are ready to quench their thirst for power from the sweet cup of civilization.

The Borderlands people have been keeping the Northlanders and Cairnlords away from the heart of the Empire so far, but their threat is ever present.

The construction of a line of forts on the Godaxe River has kept the situation under control, but almost every year the Northlanders attack a fort to test the Borderlands' defenses. It is only a matter of time before one of them falls and the barbarians swarm again into the lush lands of the south.

The landscape is dotted with ruins of ancient palaces where strange beasts and phantoms of past ages roam freely. The will of local tyrants is often the only law and, in the shadows, evil priests pray to their dark gods so that this troubled era may end as an even worse one may start.

This is the era of Beasts and Barbarians.

Note that this isn't the full history of the world, a great number of events are left out and many lands of minor importance in the Empire's history aren't even mentioned. Further information on the history of the Dread Sea Dominions will be available in the Gazetteer Chapter and in the Book of Lore, parts of the series's future installments.

TIMELINE
Every civilization refers to a different calendar to date historical events but, for ease of use, the Reformed Salkarian Calendar is adopted in this manual. It calculates all dates starting from the presumed year in which the Dread Star fell (AF = After Fall, BF = Before Fall).

3000 BF	Apogee of the Keronian Empire
0 AF	Fall of the Dread Star. End of the Keronian Empire.
600-700	The dusts of the Dread Star start to dissipate.
600-610	Survived Keronian Princes found the Tricarnian reign in the north.
700-800	Migrations Era: the Caleds and Pygmies go to the forests. The white man occupies the shores of the Dread Sea.
997	The Great library of Syranthia is discovered.
1000	Foundation of Faberterra.
1000-1300	War of the city states around the Dread Sea.
1224	Fabron, Smith Priest of Hulian, discovers iron.

1300	The Iron Confederacy is created.
1397	Syranthia is annexed by the Iron Confederacy.
1525–1526	First Faberterra-Kyros war.
1528–1529	First Faberterra-Tricarnia war.
1528	Ascaia's rebellion. Foundation of the Amazons Reign.
1532	Domestan becomes Masterarkos of the Iron Confederacy.
1535–1538	Second Faberterra-Kyros war.
1540	Kyros is annexed by the Iron Confederacy. End of the Confederacy and creation of the Iron Empire. Domestan I crowned Imperator.
1545–1550	Second Faberterra-Tricarnia war.
1551	Tricarnia capitulates and is annexed by the Empire.
1551	Princess Salkaria of Tricarnia marries Emperor Domestan I.
1560	Salkarian Reformation. Legitimate priests of Hulian go into hiding.
1562	Death of Domestan I. Domestan II, his son, takes the crown.
1570–1650	The Iron Empire expands to the north, conquering various barbarian tribes.
1660–1860	The Iron Empire expands eastward. Conquest of Zandor.
2060–2300	Empire's apogee. An era of peace. Reduction in the Iron Phalanx forces.
2327	Start of the Valk invasion. Cairnlands invaded.
2330	The Valk push the Cairnlanders westward of the Gold River.
2332–2350	Northlanders and Cairnlanders, driven away by the Valk, attack the Iron Empire.
2334	Numerous Caleds war bands attack Tricarnia.
2335	Tricarnia declares independence from the Iron Empire.
2333–2340	Caled-Tricarnia war.
2350	Battle of Felantium. The Iron Empire armies stop the Northlanders a few miles south of the Elephants River.
2355	Emperor Domestan X founds the Borderlands.
2370	Restoration of the Autarchate in Kyros. Kyros seceded from the Iron Empire.
2420	Syranthia peacefully detaches from the Iron Empire.
2425	In the Valk Steppes, Dhaar, son of a minor Valk war chief, is born.
2450	The greatest Valk horde seen in history, led by Dhaar, crosses the River of Tears, attacking Collana. The invasion of Zandor begins.
2451	Ornestan, Governor of Zandor, asks the Iron Empire for support. Domestan XII, the Cautious, refuses it. Zandor faces the invasion alone.
2452	Ornestan declares the independence of Zandor from the Empire. Start the Twelve Winters Reign.
2464	Zandor fights the Valks on its own soil, but the Zandorian armies are divided and slowly driven back year after year.
2464–2467	Siege of Jalizar. Ornestan II is King of Zandor.
2467	Death of Dhaar. The Valk horde shatters.
2470	Tukal, first son of Dhaar, founds Valkheim.
2470	Juggu, second son of Dhaar, dies. The Valk clans in Zandor are independent.
2471	Eku, third son of Dhaar, marries Yasmine of Ekram. Foundation of the Ekul kingdom.
2510	Today.

CULTURES OF THE DREAD SEA DOMINIONS

IVORY SAVANNAH TRIBES

'Ivory Savannah Tribes' is a collective name used by the Imperials to define all the black populations living south of Kyros, from the actual Savannah nomads to the farmers of the Verdant Belt and even the feared Cannibals of the Cannibal Islands.

There are great differences among them but they all have black skin. They tend to be of average height and build and quite strong, but these aren't universal features. Many Savannah nomads are as tall as the Northlanders while some of Verdant Belt

dwellers, due to occasional breeding with Pygmies, are quite short.

The Savannah people have harmonious bodies and their women especially are very attractive. A common saying claims that a Savannah tribe dancer can melt the heart of a man with the beauty of her dance and make him die on the spot, if she wants to.

Sadly, their physical qualities and their lack of technology made them very appreciated as slaves. Caldea, in particular, a minor white men reign in the south, has an economy based on capturing and selling Savannah slaves to foreign states, while Kyros often launches slave raids through the Ivory Savannah.

The Ivory Savannah Tribes have no common cultural identity and fierce rivalries exist among different tribes. This is definitely an advantage for slave traders. They don't even need fight for slaves, they sim-

IMPERIAL   TRICARNIAN   CAIRN LORD   VALK   JADEMAN   NORTHLANDER

IVORY TRIBESMAN   PYGMY

ply buy war prisoners sold by rival tribes in exchange for cheap weapons. This practice has been going on for centuries.

Ivory Savannah Tribes men and women wear pelts and simple wool cloths. They like strong colors, like red and yellow, and are particularly fond of feathers and strange headgears. Women usually are bare-breasted.

Typical Ivory Savannah Tribes names are short and contain many labials. For example: Eba, Utu, Ushul, Ngoba, Talindi, Malima.

CAIRN LORDS

Cairnlords or Cairnlanders are tall and muscular, with grayish skin and usually black or gray hair.

They are a truly remarkable — and slightly disgusting — race because, well, they are tomb dwellers. Their land was once a powerful empire, even more ancient than the Keronian Empire, but even its name is forgotten today.

The only remnants of that distant past are the massive Cairns, artificial hills containing the tombs of the so-called Ancestors. Some of the Cairns are so large that they can be considered true necropolises.

The Cairnlanders inhabit them, sleeping, eating, mating and generally living side by side with the ancient dead ones. They also bury their relatives in the Cairns, so the Ancestors' numbers are always growing.

For a Cairnlander the difference between life and death isn't that big, or that important. He sees them as two only slightly different states of existence. Even after death, he continues to stay with his fam-

ily, and his skull may become a relative's favorite pot, his femur a war club or some other useful tool.

They are convinced that the spirits of the Ancestors speak to them, leading and protecting them. Controlling a large Cairn grants great power, not only because of the ancient treasures buried within (the Cairnlanders' metalworking techniques are primitive and almost all their metal comes from the Cairns), but also because of the protection granted by the newly-acquired Ancestors.

The kingdom of the Ancestors was once so vast that some Cairns are within the boundaries of the Northlanders' territories and even of the Iron Empire. However, this does not stop enemy Cairn Lords from fighting savagely to gain control of the major Cairns, near or far though they might be.

The Cairnladers are organized in clans, ruled by a chief or a king. They live off hunting, herding, very primitive agriculture, and pillaging.

They usually wear pelts and ancient rags or armor they found in their Cairns. Almost all of them also wear an amulet or some other object belonging to an Ancestor, in the belief that it will grant protection.

Moreover, they tend to have self-imposed names, more similar to nicknames than to standard, civilized names. Some examples are Whispering Ears, Goatpaw, Brokensword, Seven He Killed, Bride of the Dead One, Skeletal Horse, etc.

IMPERIALS

The Imperials are the broadest and, therefore, most difficult civilization to define within the Dread Sea Dominions. The name applies to all the civilized populations once under the rule of the Iron Empire.

The typical Imperial, living in Faberterra, Syranthia, or northern Kyros, is of average build and has tanned skin. Manual workers and farmers tend to have a darker complexion, while aristocrats and merchants are fairer, but this is only due to the different lives they lead.

Their hair can be of any color, but brown is the most common, and they usually have dark eyes. Depending on their status and wealth, they can have a well-tended beard and mustache but the military always shave, a tradition coming from health regulations imposed on the Iron Phalanxes centuries ago.

They wear long and short tunics, sandals and cloaks made of wool, cotton, or, in the hotter lands, of imported Tricarnian silk.

Imperials tend to be sophisticated and civilized. They shun many other races whom they see, sometimes with good reason, as barbarians. Centuries of conquests and the accumulation of riches have made them fat, arrogant and with a passion for pleasures, an aspect of their culture mostly deriving from their contacts with the Tricarnians.

However, they can be dangerous enemies. Civilized people tend to be schemers and plotters and a concealed dagger can be more dangerous that an openly shown barbarian axe.

On the bright side, Imperials are cosmopolitan, quite tolerant of other cultures and religions, generally curious of the world, and open to new ideas.

The current ruling system of the Empire is an absolute monarchy but the Emperor is far away, in Faberterra, so the various parts of the Empire are ruled by governors. In addition to this, with the progressive decadence of the Empire, many Imperial lands have become independent and have reverted to their previous forms of government, monarchy, oligarchy and, in some cases, democracy.

Imperial names generally include a first name and a patronymic or family name, such as Tellario Voleskos, Domitio Antiokan, Marika Eleucorikos, Irenya Berenantios, etc.

JADEMEN

The Jademen are of average build and tend to be quite small, though not as small as the Valk. They have pale yellow or jade green skin, black hair, and almond-shaped eyes.

Their ancestral home is Lhoban, a bleak territory of tall mountains — the highest peaks in the known world —, so cold that only a few animals, like the yaks, can live there.

For this reason, the Jademen usually dress in wool garments. Weaving is very important in their culture, and the wool cloth from Lhoban is among the finest and most finely decorated in the world. They have very little facial hair, and sporting a beard is always seen as a sign of maturity and wisdom.

Lhoban is a particular form of theocracy ruled by monks. Their leader, the Enlightened One, is a sort of semi-divine figure who provides spiritual guidance to the whole kingdom from his secluded monastery in the City of Clouds. The lesser monks travel the land and ensure that his will is carried out.

The Jademen aren't religious in a traditional way, but their philosophy is based on the concept of perpetual reincarnation and progressive improvement toward final Enlightenment. This doesn't mean they don't believe in the supernatural — in fact, the opposite is true. The Lhoban monks are aware of the supernatural threats looming over the world of men — demons, alien gods, and so on — and one of the tenets of their philosophy is fighting against these abominations. In particular, they have been fighting a long war in the Lands of Idols (see page 48).

Due to Lhoban's very harsh environment, many Jademen left and established large communities in the Dread Sea Dominions, principally in Ekum, Kyros and in Gis, the City of the Alchemists.

The Jademen are very polite and respectful, even ceremonious, but this must not be mistaken for cowardice. They can be deadly warriors, and many of them are trained in deadly fighting techniques unknown in the rest of the Empire.

Their names have a Tibetan flavor, as Akar, Amrita, Dhargey, Gu Lang, Jimpa, Lasya, Sangmu.

NORTHLANDERS

The Northlanders are by far the largest and toughest people in the Dread Sea Dominions. Many of them are taller than seven feet and strong enough to wrestle an ox barehanded.

Both men and women wear their hair long, and married women usually plait it. Men tend to have long beards but, especially among the southern tribes, they shave, mainly in order to tell their brothers apart from their enemies in battle.

They dress primarily in furs and roughly-woven wool clothes. The men often walk around bare-chested, even during cold winters, because this is seen as a sign of strength while women are dressed in a more traditional way with a long gown.

The Northlanders are fascinated by metal. They are just starting to learn the art of melting iron and blacksmiths are held in high esteem.

They are proud, stubborn and bold, but they fear and loathe the supernatural.

Their world view is plain and simple: the strong prevail over the weak, like the wolf over the deer, and there is nothing strange about it. The world of nature works like that, just like that of men.

They are organized in large families or clans, usually led by the oldest male members, and they live off hunting and foraging. Quarrels and feuds with neighbors are fairly common and often end in bloodshed.

The Northlanders are very individualistic and only a few times in their history a charismatic leader has managed to unite them under one banner usually to fight a major threat, as a Cairnlanders' attack or an Imperial invasion.

Typical Northlanders names are short and sharp-sounding, as Shangor, Torm, Uma, Verrik, Gorn, Targar, Beren.

They don't use patronymics, except in very official situations. For a Northlander it is a man's sword, not his father, that makes him important.

Tricarnians

Tricarnia is inhabited by two different races: the High Tricarnians — who are nobles, priests, top military personnel, merchants, and so on — and slaves , who form the bulk of the nation.

Tricarnian slaves are a mix of other races, captured in raids or bought from pirates and slave traders in Caldeia, Kyros or in the Independent Cities.

The High Tricarnians aren't fully human, because the blood of the old Keronians runs in their veins. They are mostly very tall and slender, with pale or rarely jet-black complexion. They have very smooth skin and no body hair, a feature which other cultures find a little repulsive. Despite this detail, many of them are very beautiful, with elongated and sharp features. Some say that the High Tricarnians have found a way to extend their lives beyond the limits of the other races, but no evidence has ever been found to confirm this rumor.

They usually wear long, elaborated garments of silk, a fairly ordinary commodity in Tricarnia, since it is produced in the local silkworm farms, a relic from the region's Keronian past. In battle they used to wear exquisite armor made of bronze, replaced now by iron, and pointed helms.

The Tricarnians tend to be cruel, a natural instinct to them, like that of a cat torturing a mouse. They consider other races inferior, worth using only as slaves, as victims on the altars of their alien gods, or as guinea pigs in gruesome experiments.

They brought decadence to the Iron Empire, but the worst vices of the dissolute Imperial nobles or merchants appear quite ridiculous if compared to what happens daily in the citadel of a Priest Prince of Tricarnia.

The other two distinctive traits of this civilization are slavery and sorcery.

As said before, the whole economy of Tricarnia is based on slavery. Being only a fraction of the total population, the High Tricarnians alone cannot keep the masses of slaves under control, so various levels of slavery exist.

The most unfortunate are the humble rice field workers, the slave miners, and the leech catchers (the medicinal use of leeches is a common practice among High

Tricarnians). Just above them are the slave warriors and guards, who live in better conditions. They control their inferiors and are the bulk of the army. At the top of the slaves' social ladder are the eunuchs, a caste of castrated men who are the elite warriors and administrators.

Sorcery is common. Almost all true-blood Tricarnias have some knowledge of sorcery which is necessary to survive the scheming and plotting of their equals, eager to enhance their power and social standing. Various forms of sorcery are practiced, but corrupting magic and the evocation of dark creatures are the most widespread. Lotusmastery and drug use in general are common and encouraged, also among the slaves. The reason is obvious: a drugged slave is easier to control.

Tricarnia is divided in Principalities, each of them totally independent and governed by a single noble family. Scheming, plotting and open warfare among the Princes are common. The capital of Tricarnia, the City of Princes, is considered as a neutral ground, and no open act of war can be committed there. It is also the seat of the High Prince, the ruler of Tricarnia.

Tricarnians deeply hate (and secretly fear) the Caleds, the descendants of their ancient slaves, who still seek revenge for thousands of years spent in slavery.

Typical high Tricarnian names have an ancient ring to them and are always preceded by title, like Princess Salkaria, Price Hoolon, Priest Tokariel, and so on. Omitting the title when addressing a Tricarnian noble is considered a mortal insult, except among family members.

Valk

The Valk are the shortest of the common races, with the exception of the Pygmies. Most are slightly over five feet tall and a Valk surpassing six feet is considered a giant.

They have black or brown hair, with the exception of the Valkyrie, their priestesses, who always have white or blonde hair (usually dyed). The warriors use long braids, and cut them only in case of dishonor. The longer the braid the most powerful and brave the warrior. They have little or no beard, because one of their rites of passage, the Blood Offering, consists in

self inflicting wounds to the cheeks, thus preventing the growth of facial hair.

The Valk are dressed in leather and both sexes use trousers and boots, the most practical garments for a race of horse riders. They learn to ride even before being able to walk and are incredibly skilled on their ponies.

The basis of Valk economy, in times of peace, is herding sheep, cows, and, naturally horses. Horse milk and goat meat are their staple and they are particularly fond of fermented milk spirits, which all the other races find disgusting.

They are organized in clans, led by warlords, who share the power with the Valkyrie. Except for the priestesses, who are respected and feared, Valk women have a very low standing in society, so much so that marriage is rare and a warrior simply keeps in his tent the women he wants, in a condition of semi slavery. Only after the birth of a son, the father becomes responsible for supporting the woman.

The Valk religion deeply influences their way of life. They are demon worshippers and see demons in many manifestation of the natural world, such as thunder, the steppe winds, and the terrible plagues that often decimate the cattle and bring famine onto the clans. They don't fear the demons, at least not openly, but recognize and respect their supernatural powers.

Valk names are throaty and with many consonants: Dhaar, Khull, Dakka, Rigga, Throgg, Vulkat are all good examples.

Hero's Journal:
Caleds and Pygmies
These races are reclusive and xenophobic, so they are not a good choice as player characters. In addition, very little is known

about them except for some rumors reported below.

The Caleds are a primitive people living in the Caledland. They don't know metalworking, but among them there are very dangerous sorcerers, called druids. They rarely leave their woodlands and, when this happens, it is usually bad news, since they are waging war against someone.

The Pygmies are very short people of the Lush Jungles. They are primitive, and very skilled in the use of blowpipes and poisons. They worship cruel gods that periodically ask for the bloody sacrifices of human victims usually chosen from among non-Pygmy invaders.

The players will discover more information about these races during their adventures.

WAY OF LIFE

TECHNOLOGY

Differently from other fantasy worlds, the Dread Sea Dominions aren't dormant. In a few thousand years, they have evolved from the stone age to the current iron age. Yet, this isn't true for all the Dominions, since certain populations (like the Caleds, the Pygmies and the tribes of the Ivory Savannah) are still primitive.

It is hardly possible to provide a comprehensive description of all the technologies of a certain world, so the following list includes the major scientific achievements of the Dread Sea Dominions.

Alchemy: This field overlaps that of magic. The Lotus masters (see sidebar on page 13) are experts in drug and poison making, but only from the Lotus plants. The Alchemists of Gis, instead, are true scientists and know how to use Greek fire, acids, and similar things. Their con-

coctions are very costly and seldom sold outside the city. Kyros, Syranthia and the Independent Cities know glass.

Currency: Coins made of metals are used in civilized lands, but their value is determined by the trading value of salt. Barter is widespread in the remote, uncivilized areas along the borders of the Empire. The Empire adopted the Syranthian Moon as official currency, and this roughly circular coin is now common in all the ports and markets of the Dominions.

Entertainment: Since literacy is rare, minstrels, musicians and taletellers are very important as they are actors and mimes. Especially in the southern lands, dancing is a very common form of recreation. Many enjoy the "blood sports", originally from Tricarnia: shows in the arena where gladiators slaughter (or get slaughtered by) massive beasts and other desperate warriors. These violent games are appreciated by both the nobility and the commoners alike, especially in big cities where the games in the arena and the distribution of free food keep the masses at bay and ease the burden of living in a decadent Empire.

Food Production: Agriculture is the main source of food in the Empire but outside its boundaries (and in the most depressed areas, like the Borderlands) hunting and harvesting are by far the most common way of surviving. In the Savannah and among the Valk herding is widespread. In the past, several populations knew how to use the iron plow but, in the current period, few have retained this skill, since iron must be used for weapons and armors, not for farming. Crop rotation is still unknown.

Ground Travel: Most folks travel on foot, while the rich have horses or carriages. Many paved roads, named Imperial Roads, were built in the past but today they are generally abandoned and infested by bandits. The Valk always ride; a Valk that cannot ride is abandoned and left to die by the rest of his tribe. The Cairnlords also uses carriages, sometimes pulled by rams, and the top warriors of the Iron Savannah ride the impressive and savage war buffalos.

Government: The most advanced form of government is the oligarchy of the merchant lords of Syranthia, but various forms of monarchy are the standard government in most lands.

Literacy: ninety percent of the population cannot read and write these days. The most educated lands are Syranthia, Tricarnia (limited to the nobles), Caldeia, Faberterra, Kyros and Lhoban (limited to the monks).

Medicine: Outside the largest cities, witchcraft, superstition and midwifery are the closest things to medical science while in the cities there are medics and barbers. Syranthia also has an academy of medicine where the anatomy of man is studied. Anatomy is also well known in Tricarnia due to the traditional use of tortures.

Metallurgy: At the height of its power, the Empire and all its subjects knew the use of iron and even started experimenting with a better, lower-carbon league called steel but today it is very rare. The barbaric Northlanders, Cairn Lords, and the Savannah Tribes know only bronze, but they can acquire better metal weapons through trading and pillaging. The Caleds and the Pygmies don't use any metal.

Sea Travel: The ships of the Dominions are quite primitive and usually sail close to the coast. The biggest vessels are the Tricarnian galleys but the most maneuverable are the Syranthian merchant ships, which can be seen in all parts of the world. The Amazons too are very skilled sailors, and they use a particular type of sail unknown to the other cultures.

Warfare: Nowadays, the strongest warriors are Valk mounted archer with armor of boiled leather, a composite bone bow and a saddle with stirrups. Second bests are the fully-armored Syranthian cataphracts knights, and in third place there is the irregular barbarian infantry. The terrible war elephants of Kyros have almost disappeared today and the Iron Phalanxes are reduced to less than ten legions.

HERO'S JOURNAL: LANGUAGES OF THE DREAD SEA DOMINIONS

The common language spoken almost everywhere is Imperial Syranthian. Almost all lands have a national language and dozens of dialects, but very few are recorded in writing. The major languages of the Dominions are:

Alchemists' Code. *The Alchemists of Gis developed this strange language, in truth more of a secret code then a real mother tongue, to protect the secrecy of their discoveries and potions. The Code is taught only to initiates and requires a certain mathematical ability and decryption skills to understand it. So, only characters with Smarts d8 or more can learn this language. It exists only in written form.*

Barbarian Languages. *The Northeim people, the Caleds and the Cairnlords speak three different languages (Northern, Caled, and Cairn Tongue). Out of these three, only the Cairn Tongue is written using a runic alphabet.*

Ivory Savannah Tribes Languages. *The Ivory Savannah Tribes speak an impressive number of different dialects that are all quite similar. In gaming terms only one language is considered: the Savannah's*

Tongue. In certain parts of the Verdant Belt the most advanced tribes speak a bastardized form of Caldeian called Slavers' Tongue, used mainly for contacts with Caldeian slavers. Both languages lack a written form.

Imperial Syranthian. *Imperial Syranthian, or simply Imperial, is a simple and rather regular alphabetic language, originally from Syranthia. Every playing character can speak it, and, depending on her background, might be also able to write it.*

Tricarnian and Ancient Keronian. *Tricarnias and Caldeians are the descendants of the ancient Keronian Empire. They speak a common version of the language in the daily life (Tricarnian) but use a ceremonial, ancient language during religious rites and in sorcery (Ancient Keronian). These are considered two different languages.*

Lhoban Secrets. *The Jademen speak a mountain dialect, but the secrets of the*

are lengths of ropes, with particular knots. Looking at the size of the knots, their distance from each other, and other parameters, the monks can read and communicate their Secrets.

Pygmy. *The Pygmies speak their own tongue. It is very difficult to learn this language, due to the strong isolation of these diminutive people.*

Valk. *The Valk speak a very weird, totally unique language. Its peculiarity might be due to the very different origins of the steppe nomads, but there is a theory among the Syranthian sages according to which Valk isn't a human language. A creepy fact supports this theory: the demons speak Valk. No one knows whether a written form of this language exists.*

RELIGION

Religious practices vary greatly across the Dominions and literally hundreds of cults exist, many of them on a local basis. In this paragraph only the most important religions are detailed.

Before the Salkarian Reformation, the Empire was very open-minded on matters of religion. As long as a land or a city paid the taxes, it was free to worship whatever god it wanted.

monks must be preserved with great care, so a "written" form of communication was devised, called Lhoban Secrets. The Secrets

With the Reformation a new divinity was introduced, the **Divine Couple**, Hulian and Hordan, the artificial fusion of

Hulian, the smith god of Faberterra, and Hordan, the female goddess of Tricarnia. They are seen as the two faces of the same divinity: Hulian is the male principle, who governs over logic, fire, science and the written word. He also symbolizes the day. Hordan, instead, is the feminine principle: she is the goddess of emotions, water, and the spoken word. She also protects love, births, seasons, and the arts. She symbolizes the night. Statues of the Divine Couple feature a single head with two sides: a handsome blonde man (Hulian) and a striking black-haired woman (Hordan). The statues are never anchored to the ground, and it is the priests' duty to rotate them at dawn and dusk, to show the face of the divinity currently in charge in a given moment of the day. In the Great Temple of the Divine Couple in Faberterra (the former High Temple of Hulian), an ingenious water mechanism slowly rotates the statues in a shown of technology that always impresses the commoners.

In truth, the Divine Couple is an artificial divinity, created to unify two very different people, the Tricarnians and the Imperials, and usually only lip service is paid to them.

In secret, because it is highly illegal, the Iron Priests still worship **Hulian Lord of Fire** in the catacombs of Faberterra and in other parts of the Empire. In this more real version of the cult, Hulian is the Smith god, He Who Turns the Darkness Away, lord of the Word, and protector of humanity. The priests of Hulian are aware that alien gods and their servants are still walking in the world, and it's the priests' sacred duty to fight them. It is not a secret that they are losing, but they will continue until the last fire burns out. Hulian Lord of Fire is represented as a lion-headed man, tall and muscular, with the sun painted on his chest and a smith's hammer in his right hand.

Although the Imperial Law forbids it, in Tricarnia, **Hordan Mistress of Darkness** is still openly worshipped by the Priest Princes and their minions. Hordan is an ancient demonic creature adored since the times of the Keronian Empire. She is the goddess of darkness, pain, and unholy appetites. Despite her human appearance, Hordan is completely alien, ever thirsting for blood, violent sex, and other depraved acts.

She is usually represented as a busty barechested woman of otherworldly beauty. But a closer inspection reveals her demonic origin: her long braids end in tiny snake heads, her open mouth shows a snakelike tongue, and her nipples are deadly stingers.

Hordan is a generous goddess — as long as she is satiated with constant sacrifices. Otherwise, she feeds on her own followers' bodies and souls.

The Northlanders have a rather cold relationship with the divine. They mainly worship the **Lord of Thunder**, a distant god who simply watches the mortals from the skies and shows his rage and power during thunderstorms. The Lord of Thunder intervenes only when a child is born, blowing into the lungs of the infant, giving him strength. What the human will do with his gift does not concern the god.

The Ivory Savannah Tribes have a very complex theology, with many minor divinities, but they mainly worship **Etu, the Mother**, a female divinity presiding over rains and births, and **Uletu, God of Strength**, represented as a lion or bull, either as a beast or in hybrid human-beast form.

The Valk worship demons, the most important of which is **Sha Mekri**, an expression that in their language simply means "the King". Sha Mekri is the incarnation of warfare and destruction. He is usually represented as a blaze (as sometimes happens in autumn in the steppes), or as a massive black stallion with a fanged mouth, whose hooves leave a trail of fire. In very rare cases, he is portrayed as a massive man, dressed in metal armor full of spikes and riding a metal stallion.

The Cairnlords worship the **Ancestors**, the dead ones. Many of them don't need to be depicted, because they still exist, in embalmed form, in their necropolis. Sometimes, they aren't even truly dead. The Northlander warriors who return from incursions in the Cairns tell wild stories of emaciated figures dressed in ancient rags, who were obviously dead and yet they walked and commanded the living ones.

As mentioned before, the Jademen don't worship a god, though they recognize the existence of supernatural creatures, some of them good but mostly flawed and evil. Instead, they believe that every being can reach divinity through self-improvement and meditation following the **Path of Enlightenment**. Death is but a transition within this process: a creature reincarnates in another being, lesser or higher, depending on how it behaved in its previous life. The monks are at the higher stages of the process and the Enlightened One has almost completed it.

What is there beyond? It is a secret that will be revealed only to those who reach the divine.

This philosophy, exported by the Jademen who left their country to live in the Dread Sea Dominions, slowly blended with the western rites and was adopted by many sects, like the Stylites of the Land of Idols, eremites who lives in constant meditation on the top of tall columns.

The divinities of the Caleds and of the Pygmies are unknown.

CLIMATE

The Dread Sea Dominions have not been charted in an exact way (today the science of geometry is practiced only by some scholar of the Syranthian Library), so it is difficult to estimate their actual size, but they certainly have a very wide range of different climates.

The northern reigns including the Caledlands, Northeim and the Cairnlands are cold, with winters lasting as long as six months and wide expanses of forests. The Troll Mountains, usually considered the northern boundaries of the world, are in the grip of ice for most of the year.

On the other hand, the lands facing the Dread Sea enjoy by far the best climate. Faberterra, Syranthia and Kyros have a temperate, Mediterranean climate with warm winters, long autumns and springs and generally hot summers. They have plants of all species including olive and fig trees, and the harvest there is always generous.

Tricarnia differs slightly from its neighbors. Despite being in the north, it is protected from the cold winds by the Brokenchain Mountains, so it has a temperate climate but it is quite damp. It has large, half-flooded rice fields that give the nation the aspect of a massive swamp which is always shrouded by thick fog.

Going south, the climate gets hotter. The area called the Horn, comprising the Fallen Kingdom, the Red Dunes Desert and the Ivory Savannah is scorching all year round, and the highest temperatures are reached in the desert. With the exception of oases, the vegetation mainly includes palms, cacti and other resilient plants. In the Ivory Savannah the main vegetable is the Bone Grass, a sturdy type of herb that in the summer takes on a pale color resembling that of bones.

Thanks to its position around the mouth of the Buffalo River, Caldeia enjoys a mild climate and its vegetation is similar to that of Kyros and Faberterra.

Going further south, the Lush Jungle and the Cannibal Islands have a tropical climate. Plants of every type and size grow in these snake-infested lands.

Moving east, Lhoban is an area of high mountains; it is quite cold with short, hot summers. Except for some lichens, very few plants grow in these lands but the valley bottoms are fertile, enjoy a mild weather, and yield excellent crops.

The old kingdom of Zandor, comprising Ekul, Jalizar and Valkheim, has the most varied climate.

Ekul is a cold, windswept desert with small oases. Here nothing stops the winds blowing from the Valk steppes. The only exception consists in the coastal regions, witch are very fertile.

Jalizar has a continental climate which gets milder and good for the agriculture on the shores of the Drowned King Sea.

Valkheim, actually a part of the steppe, is always exposed to the winds and except for a short, hot summer, it is frozen all year round.

GAZETTEER: THE DREAD SEA DOMINIONS TODAY

Here follows a brief description of the most important areas of the Dread Sea Dominions as they are today. A brief summary is presented for every nation, as an example of what the Book of Lore (featured in the future installments of the series) will contain.

ASCAIA, AMAZONS ISLAND

Ascaia is a small island, not far from the mouth of the Elephants River. It has tall reefs and a single port, but the weather is very good and the land fertile making it an excellent place for growing crops and breeding horses.

In the years before the foundation of the Empire by Domestan, the local female population rebelled and eliminated all the males from the island. The leaders of the rebellion were Gella, the wife of the former governor, a very cruel man, and Ilenya, a female gladiator of the local arena. The two women became the first Sister Queens of Ascaia. Since then, very few men have been allowed onto the island, which is now known as the Amazons' Island.

The Amazons' Island is very easily defended and has wide terraced fields; the island is fairly self-sufficient, only lacking one fundamental resource for their survival: men.

For the purpose of mating, the Amazons choose slaves, war prisoners and occasional lovers they find while on missions on the mainland. When an Amazon gives birth to a child, if it is a female, she can join the Amazons. If it is a male, he is immediately separated from his mother and sent to his father, if possible, or a foster family is found, but he cannot stay on the island longer than seven days after birth.

The Amazons have a martial culture (a necessity to avoid being re-conquered by males) and they have become skilled sailors, excellent mercenaries and, under some Queens, dreaded pirates and slave hunters. Luckily, it is no longer this way, at least officially. The current Queens signed an agreement with Emperor Domestan XII accepting to patrol the Elephant River and to actively hunt the Pirates of the Fingers, a task which they are carrying out the most efficiently. But there are always some independent Amazon captains who, while on the open sea, raid and sink merchant ships. As long as they are not spotted, nothing happens and the Sister Queens usually turn a blind eye because such deeds bring wealth to the island and help preserve its fearful reputation.

Amazons' Code. The Amazons' code of honor (see sidebar) implies that Amazons must help other women in distress but experience has taught them not to push this too far. Outside Ascaia, the world is not ready to accept an independent woman, and the Amazons face constant mistrust without even looking for trouble. But one principle is constantly respected: if a woman, whatever her status is, reaches Ascaia and asks to join the Amazons, her request must be put to the Sister Queens.

HERO'S JOURNAL:
AMAZONS' CODE OF HONOR
Amazon characters have the Code of Honor (Amazons) Hindrance. The principles of the Code are as follows:

† *You are free. No man will ever chain you.*

† *No man will defend you. You have your wits, your strength and your sword. You will defend yourself.*

† *Aid women whenever you can, but a woman must first help herself.*

† *Ascaia is your holy land, your mother and your refuge. You will give your life to protect it.*

† *Any woman can ask you to be brought to Ascaia and join the Amazons. Accepting or refusing is not your task. You must bring her to the Sister Queens.*

OTHER AMAZON CULTURES
Sword and Sorcery worlds are very male-centered and women are usually only seen as prizes for the winners or objects of pleasure. An Amazon can be an interesting character to play as. Ascaia's Amazons are the most famous, but they certainly aren't the only group of independent females in the Dread Sea Dominions. The Valkyire are another famous example and in the barbarian lands it could be that a woman takes up her father's sword and shows the world what stuff a heroine is made of.

BORDERLANDS
"The Borderlands people know the barbarians well because they are of the same breed", as the ancient saying goes. And it is at least partially true. The Borderlands were once part of Northeim but were taken by the Imperials with war, treachery and cunning diplomacy and their inhabitants slowly mixed with the Imperials, thus becoming the Borderlands people. These people have the better of the two cultures: the knowledge and rationalism of the Imperials and the energy and vitality of the barbarians. When the true Northlanders attacked the Empire, the first people to withstand them were the Borderlands people.

It was clear that the Imperial Phalanxes would not be enough to defend the land and the Borderlands people did what they usually do — they defended themselves against their savage cousins from Northeim.

In the end, the Empire lost its authority over this area, and some small, independent kingdoms were established and called the Borderlands. Although they are under the formal protection of the Emperor of Faberterra, they are on their own, fighting to preserve what they created with such great effort. The biggest Borderland is Felantium, ruled by a count, the nephew of the man who, many years ago, stopped the barbarians from invading the Empire in an epic battle fought in front of the city gates.

The border between the Borderlands and Northeim is the Godaxe River, where a line of forts manned by soldiers from the Borderlands stands. These forts are vital since every year the Northlanders, Cairnlanders or Nandals launch violent attacks on them but, so far, no fort has fallen. When this happens, the barbarians invade Borderlands again and it becomes a grim day for all the civilized populations.

There is another nightmare that haunts the lords of the Borderlands — the fact that one day the Drowned King Sea might freeze as far south as the Godaxe River which would pave the way for a massive invasion of the south.

The Price of Blood. Though the Borderlands are divided and ruled by different laws, one rule is applied everywhere: if a man volunteers to defend one of the forts and serves for at least five years, he is rewarded with a piece of land in his Borderland and receives an additional plot for every extra five years. This rule is called The Price of Blood and it is only fair compensation for what the soldiers must endure defending their land. However, it is also a way to lure colonists from the south. In the Borderlands, capable men can carve out a future for themselves.

CAIRN LANDS

The Cairn Lands are a vast, wild area of deep forests and rolling hills. No city or other civilized settlement is visible because many of the seemingly natural hills are in truth artificial mounds built by the ancient dwellers of this region. The Cairn Lords, today's inhabitants, live in the Cairns which make for excellent houses, stables, and fortresses, if you don't mind living side by side with your dead ones, whom they call the Ancestors.

This is no wealthy region and the Cairn Lords are not an advanced people. They live off hunting, herding, and occasional raids on nearby lands. But when darkness falls, the Cairnlanders enter their underground tunnels and lock themselves in, since during the night a strange fog appears and wicked things, best left undisturbed, emerge from the oldest, still unexplored Cairns.

The mounds called Cairns do not exist only in the Cairn Lands, although this region has the biggest concentration of them. Many are found in Valkheim, the Northlands and the Borderlands. During the long, cold winters, the northern part of the Drowned King Sea freezes, giving the Cairnlords access to the Borderlands and Valkheim. This is the best time for raids in the south, to look for a bigger home or simply to stay away from their haunted lands, which in winter become even more dangerous.

The Legend of the Drowned King. There is a story about a powerful king of the Cairn Lords who refused the traditions. He did not want to live in a Cairn but desired to dwell in a palace, as the southerners do. But he needed slaves and many riches to build such a thing. So, ignoring the teachings of the Ancestors, he ordered his men to build a large fleet. He meant to use it to raid Jalizar and the City of the Alchemists and to use the spoils to build his palace. When summer came, the fleet was ready and his army sailed south. But during the first night at sea, a terrible storm caught the fleet by surprise. All the ships sank and the whole army, including the king, drowned. From then on, during stormy nights a ghost fleet has been haunting the sea of the Drowned King, the man who refused to live in the Cairns.

HERO'S JOURNAL:
CAIRNLANDERS' TALISMANS

The Cairnlanders are very superstitious, and most of them always carry a relic of their Ancestors. It might be a piece of bone, a tooth, an amulet and its function is to protect the wearer. If the Game Master agrees, a Cairnlander character can take a single background Edge (as Luck) even after creation or take a single Edge, ignoring rank limitations. This Edge is linked to the Ancestors' relic and works only if the hero has his Ancestor's relic with him.

CALDEIA

Caldeia is a city state around the mouth of the Buffalo River. It has one heavily defended city, Caldeia of the tall towers, and some smaller fortified settlements in its surroundings. Caldeia was founded several centuries ago by an exiled Priest Prince of Tricarnia, Caldaios the Cruel, and today it is still a monarchy, de facto ruled by the nobles and a cast of priests.

Remarkably, Caldaios the Cruel is still formally the King of Caldeia. He should be more than four hundred years old now, but nobody has ever announced his death and, though he hasn't appeared in public for at least three centuries, there are rumors he still lives in self-imposed reclusion in the royal palace of Caldeia City.

Caldeia is very rich because it trades the two most precious goods produced in the south of the world: Khav and slaves.

The fertile area of the Buffaloes River's mouth boasts the world's largest plantations of the insidious drug, also known as Lesser Lotus. This cheap and very addictive drug is produced and refined in Caldeia and then sold across the Dominions. The Khav plantations are tended by slaves who are all heavily addicted to Khav. Many of them die, but Caldeia's flesh markets have plenty of replacements.

Slaves are the second most traded good in Caldeia. Raiding parties depart monthly from the Caldeian settlements and venture deep in the Savannah to surprise black tribes and capture large groups of slaves who are then dragged in chains to Caldeia and sent to the plantations or sold to foreigners. Many of the slaves in the northern kingdoms and Tricarnia come from here.

Raids in the Savannah are not the only method the Caldeians use to capture slaves. Caravans of slavers periodically travel the infamous Slave Route, a road that goes from Caldeia, across the Verdant Belt, to the far mountains of Lhoban. Along the way, the slavers trade with the Ivory Savannah Tribes and other barbaric reigns of the Verdant Belt, bartering cheap weapons and Khav for slaves. These slaves are often members of the same population they are bought from, who are made prisoners during bloody feuds among clans. The Caldeian slavers make sure they support different tribes, even rival ones, so that no unity can be achieved among the Ivory Savannah Tribes.

Khav Wars. In the last few years, there have been attacks on the least protected Khav plantations, causing heavy economic damage to Caldeia. The raiders are Ivory Savannah Tribe warriors and mercenaries from the north. They also free slaves and enact guerrilla tactics on Caldeian soil. Caldeia's answer has been strong and violent, but it is hard to defeat such an elusive enemy: the raiders generally attack along the borders and then rapidly retreat to the Ivory Savannah, hiding their tracks. The remarkable thing is that they don't take away any of the precious Khav, but they simply burn it. Someone thinks that the White King of the Ivory Savannah is behind these attacks, but no proof has been found so far because, until now, the Caldeian army hasn't managed to capture any raider alive. The matter is further complicated by the fact that independent, non-Caldeian Khav sellers have appeared in the northern lands. They have very competitive prices and they gain a greater share of the market every day. A drug war is about to break out…

HERO'S JOURNAL:

Khav Addiction Khav addiction is a Major Habit. In addition to the standard addiction rules, Khav has the following effects: it causes –2 to all Spirit and Smarts based rolls and eliminates the sense of fatigue. A Khav addict does not receive penalty for Fatigue, but he actually feels it. It is not unusual for slaves addicted to Khav to work to death. The price of Khav varies depending on its purity: a dose may cost from half a Moon to twenty Moons. It is common throughout the Dread Sea Dominions, especially in slave-based nations.

CALEDLAND

Let us be honest: no one has ever explored Caledland. It is a vast, ancient forest inhabited by primitive savages, the Caleds. The only ones who dared enter the forest were the Tricarnians, during the war, and some Imperial Phalanxes, when the Empire was so strong that it considered conquering the Caledlands. Yet, none of them ever came back. The Caleds aren't invincible — after all they are only naked, tattooed barbarians, who fight with stone-tipped spears — but their strength lies mainly in their druids, a caste of very powerful sorcerers. During the Tricarnian-Caledian Wars, many acts of foul sorceries were committed by both parties and the part of the Caledian forest bordering Tricarnia is now an accursed place, where terrible abominations lurk in the shadows of ancient trees.

War Drums. The Caleds periodically leave their woods and raid the nearby regions. They do not seek spoils, but a single commodity: humans — who are brought to Caledland and never seen again. Immediately before such expeditions, the sound of rolling drums comes from the forest. This means that the Caleds are going on a hunting spree. Nobody knows what the captives are used for, they are probably sacrificed to the gods or, as many say, they are eaten. The strange thing is that the Caleds' raids do not seem to follow any logic: they are willing to travel hundreds of miles, to some remote village in Northeim or a farm in the Borderlands, to kidnap a single person. The reason why they go to so much trouble to capture a single unlucky individual, while simply butchering everyone else, is one of the many mysteries surrounding the Caleds.

CANNIBALS ISLANDS

The Cannibal Islands are a group of medium-sized landmasses not far from the Lush Jungles. The first travelers who came here thought they had found a true paradise with pleasant weather, strange fruit plants, colorful birds and crystal-clear water full of fish.

In truth, these islands are home to one of the most ferocious people in the world, the black cannibal tribes. These primitive men attack and eat any stranger they meet, and the first explorers, caught by surprise, ended their lives in the greasiest of ways.

In addition, a couple of times a year, they sail in their long war pirogues to the mainland, to hunt their favorite quarry: man. They usually set ambushes around the mouth of the Anaconda River or along the Verdant Belt, but a few times they have gone as far as the Independent Cities.

Cannibals' God. Some lucky mariners who have managed to escape the Cannibal Islands tell stories of a giant monster that is the god of the Cannibals. Most of the human prey they catch is sacrificed to appease the monstrous divinity. Yet, the nature of the god is unknown and these stories might be only a legend or a tale to hide some disturbing truth.

EKUL

Ekul, the southern part of former Zandor, is mainly a desert. The industrious population always fights to farm the scarce good soil, and great resources are spent in reclamation and irrigation. Thanks to this enlightened policy, Ekul is now a fairly pleasant place to live and enjoys good trading relations with Kyros, Syranthia and Jalizar.

In truth, Ekul it is a very young nation. This land suffered the first, tremendous impact of the Valk invasion; many of its cities were destroyed and the population killed. Then, luckily, the Valk moved north, toward the richest lands. After the death of Dhaar, leader of the Valk, his third son Eku, with a large number of clans went south and invaded this land once again.

Rather than facing another war, the locals willingly submitted. They opened to Eku the doors of their main city, which was renamed Ekul, and offered him the hand of Yasmine, daughter of the former Imperial Governor.

Eku was still young, and a very curious and attentive person. He took up his residence in the ex Imperial Palace. He was truly fascinated by the way of life in the southern lands and soon became a civilized man.

Not all his followers were pleased with his behavior, so he was forced to crush a good part of them. His remaining followers adapted to a semi stantial life. Ekul is a vast territory, but only a small part of it, the coastal region, is farmed. The rest can only be used as pastures, and these were the lands assigned to Valk.

After the disaster of Collana (see below), Eku abandoned the traditional Valk religion. All the Valkyrie were forced to leave the kingdom or face execution, which caused great anger among Eku's followers and attacks from the Valk of the north. Yet, Eku's supporters were ready to face them and came out victorious. Ekul enjoys very friendly relationships with Lhoban, and the king himself has embraced the strange philosophy of the Jademen. Ekul today is home to the greatest community of Jademen in all the Dominions.

But all good things come to an end, and Ekul's age of enlightenment does not seem to be destined to last. King Eku is ninety years old now and his only heir is his granddaughter. When he dies, a civil war will certainly break out: several Valk clan chiefs as well as many noble families of imperial origin are ready to claim the throne. At the same time, both Kyros and the still uncivilized Valk hordes of the north mean to attack the country even before Eku's body grows cold.

The Cursed City of Collana. Collana, the gem of the kingdom, was the center of trade between the western reigns and the Far East. It was also the first city to face the might of the Valk hordes. They not only crushed, burned and razed it, but the Valkyrie did *something* there — an unholy rite of tremendous power that summoned a legion of demons. Yet, when such a terrible force is awakened, it cannot be controlled, so the Valk were forced to leave Collana in the hands of demons. Some years ago, when Eku was already king, several Lhoban monks, experts in battling these evil abominations, asked permission to try and stop the demons from expanding further. King Eku gave his permission gladly, and now the monks are doing their best to control Collana, but they are losing their battle. Year after year, the evil things dwelling in the city multiply and grow stronger and, at night, strange terrors infest the roads and the grasslands of the reign.

FABERTERRA

Faberterra was the heart of the Iron Empire, the place where the destinies of very far countries were decided. Today, Faberterra is only a shadow of its former glory. The rich countryside, full of large estates and prosperous farms, is slowing decaying, because the landowners spend more time indulging in personal pleasure than looking after their properties. Commerce is still prosperous, but only because Faberterra is at the center of the world. The tide is turning and more and more ships choose Askerios to dock.

"Life is short and the Empire is fading. We are doomed. So, let's enjoy ourselves".

This is the common way of thinking in Faberterra. So far, the state has never been invaded, but no one can forget that the barbarian hordes were recently stopped at Felantium, which isn't that far. So many Imperials have decided to spend their last days indulging in orgies, feasts and other exotic entertainments, while others regularly visit the temple of the Divine Couple and pray for the Empire and their own soul.

Yet, their prayers seem to go unanswered.

Certainly, Faberterra is still the capital of the Empire and its people are haughty, but it is nothing more than a habit. The mighty Phalanxes are reduced to a few units, and their loyalty isn't always certain. The Emperor protects his palace with a force of mercenaries, while the Phalanxes are assigned to patrol the borders. Many believe that sooner or later a Phalanx commander will try to overthrow the Emperor and seize the crown.

Gladiators Games. Faberterra City is the biggest settlement of the known world: almost a million people live there — and the situation is growing tenser by the day. Bad news from the north, less commerce and a stagnating economy cause turmoil among the people, whom the Emperor tries to appease by distributing free food and organizing great shows of gladiators in the arena. Today the Arena of Faber-terra is greater than the one in the City of Princes in Tricarnia and its gladiators are real celebrities — all of which has been achieved by almost depleting the Emperor's coffers. Many wonder how much longer the situation can hold out.

FALLEN KINGDOM OF KERON

The Fallen Kingdom of Keron was that part of the Keronian Empire that, being quite far from the center, wasn't directly affected by the terrible impact of the Dread Star and its high location on a plateau protected it from being flooded.

Yet, this doesn't mean its people survived.

The consequences of the cataclysm, clouds of dusts, earthquakes, famines and pestilences wiped the local population away, and Keron is now only an arid place full of crumbing ruins. The Fallen Kingdom is believed to be haunted. The mariners sailing near its coast report seeing strange lights at night and hearing the sound of spectral songs. For no reason will a captain dock on these cursed shores.

The Fallen Kingdom is separated from the mainland by the Keronian Range, a very recent group of mountains created during the cataclysm. Crossing it to reach the Fallen Kingdom is very difficult, because its peaks are lofty and there are only a few passes. In addition, the area is still affected by intense seismic activity, another good reason to stay away from them.

Kiramas Folly. A hundred years ago, Kiramas, one of the most powerful Priest Princes of Tricarnia, decided to explore the Fallen Kingdom. His intention was to find ancient relics of the Keronians and, if possible, to create a new Tricarnian base in the south of the world. It was a great expedition, with a large numbers of ships, slaves and beasts but, once they entered the Fallen Kingdom, they disappeared. Scouts were sent to investigate but they too didn't come back. Any further attempt to locate Kiramas was suspended and all that is now left of his expedition are the hulls of his ships rotting on the shore.

FINGERS ISLANDS

The Fingers of the Dead Ones, or simply Fingers' Islands, are a group of islands north of the Fallen Kingdom of Keron. They were once part of the Keronian Empire, but the Dread Star disaster separated them from the mainland. The islands, surrounded by treacherous shallows, are dotted with ancient Keronian ruins engulfed by the jungle. They owe their name to the common practice on Tricarnian galleys to cut off the pinkie of lazy oarsmen, and "fingers" is usually the nickname given to mutineers.

The Fingers' Islands are indeed a base for pirates, who from here launch attacks on merchant ships and raid the Iron Empire or Tricarnia. The navies of civilized states have often tried to wipe them off, but getting to their base has always been extremely dangerous and costly. The Fingers' Islands are just a few days' voyage from the Independent Cities, the perfect place where to sell stolen goods and spend one's looted coins. They are also very close to the Fallen Kingdom of Keron, but the pirates avoid that haunted land.

The Cove. There are rumors of a hidden bay on the Fingers' Islands which hosts a true piratical city, where crews find refuge and ships are repaired. This place is called The Cove. The exact location of The Cove is kept secret. Only pirate captains and the most trusted helmsmen know how to reach it avoiding the shallows. It is a secret for which many military authorities would be willing to pay a lot of gold.

GIS, FREE CITY OF THE ALCHEMISTS

There is a legend saying that the day Fabron, the Iron Priest of Faberterra, discovered iron, on the shores of the Drowned King Sea a wandering warlock built the first hut of what, centuries later, would become Gis, the Free City of the Alchemists. The initiators of the Alchemists were a group of foreign mages, probably from Lhoban. Today, life in Gis revolves around the business of the supernatural. Cairnlord relic sellers have their stalls next to those of the Caldeian Lotus masters, and Valk prophets of the steppes offer their visions side by side with black-skinned dancer witches, worshippers of Etu. There is only one law in Gis: all magic is possible, as long as it doesn't harm anyone and isn't detrimental to the business, of course.

Of the many forms of magic practiced in the city, the most common is alchemy. The Alchemists, also named Master Alchemists, are the rulers of Gis. Their skills are far more powerful than the knowledge of Lotus mastered by Lotus masters. They can produce fire that burns on the water and cannot be extinguished, magic oils that make a barren land fertile again, and many other wonderful things. But their services are very costly and only kings and nobles can afford them.

The Alchemists are a very reclusive corporation. They live in great mansions which they also use as laboratories, protected by their servants and apprentices, and they rarely give audience to common people, unless, of course, a large pile of gold is involved.

The identity of the Alchemists is not made public. They always wear long robes, special metal masks and gauntlets that bestow them great powers. The Master Alchemists have always been twelve and their number cannot change, because only twelve metal masks exist. The rules for succession aren't very clear. Some say that, when an old master alchemist dies, the other eleven choose a successor from among his apprentices. He will take the mask and continue to rule the mansion laboratory. Yet, others believe that the Master Alchemists are immortal.

Gis is a place of wonders, but it is also full of supernatural dangers.

The Battlefield of Greenmelt. Gis was born as a free city and no foreign power, not even the Iron Empire, has even tried to subdue it. None except the Valk. After Dhaar's death, rumors claimed that the mighty warlord had been killed by the Alchemists' magic. A great number of Valk clans gathered outside the City of the Alchemists, ready to destroy it to avenge their lord.

But that very night a strange, greenish fog spilled from the mouths of the metal statues along the walls of Gis. The fog silently sneaked into the Valk's camp and everyone enveloped by it died in a horrible way, his flesh melted, as if burnt by an incredibly powerful acid. At dawn, the Valk camp was a cemetery. But the fog never went away. Still today, dozens of years later, there is a large area of green fog, called the Greenmelt, where the half corroded shapes of the Valk encampment can be seen. Nobody knows if the air is still poisonous, because nobody is foolish enough to venture there.

Independent Cities

The first Independent Cities were founded by the Syranthians in an attempt to avoid the taxes imposed by Kyros on the goods coming from the south of the world. They were far more successful that the Syranthians had expected. Desert nomads, Ivory Savannah Tribes and, occasionally, Caldeian merchants started to visit them, selling goods from the south and buying products from Faberterra,

Tricarnia and other northern reigns. In a few years the Independent Cities increased in number and grew in size, going from small trading posts to large cities. This happened also thanks to the adventurers and other shady individuals who came here from all over the Dominions, lured by the prospect of easy money to be made.

In the end, distant Syranthia lost control over these fiercely independent cities.

Today, a dozen Independent Cities exist, but the most important are Hillias, on the Dread Sea, and Teyerana, on the shores of the Endless Ocean. The first is ruled by a merchant league, similar to Syranthia's, while the other is a monarchy, governed with an iron fist by Korr, a former pirate from the Fingers' Islands. The other cities are either on the coast or in the Red Desert. They are not united and often fight with one another — a state of things that Kyros, Caldeia and Syranthia are very happy to support.

Mercenary Life. The Independent Cities are excellent places for any individual who is able to wield the sword. The various city lords are always looking for good fighters to join the city patrol, protect caravans, and, occasionally raid enemy cities. The hierarchy in the mercenary militia is usually very mobile and a skilled swordsman can start the day as watchman of the local latrines and go to bed as Captain of the King's Guard. But remember: life is always dangerous in the Independent Cities and, no matter how high a man climbs, he can suddenly fall equally low.

ISLANDS OF THE MAIMED ONES

This archipelago in the centre of the Dread Sea is usually avoided by all mariners. The ground here is red as dried blood and the waters are hotter than in the rest of the Dread Sea. The islands are covered in a thick jungle, as lush as that of the Pygmies' lands, home to strange beasts unknown in the rest of the Dominions and to weird mutations of common animals. Some very primitive barbarians live here. They are hideous to look upon — their bodies full of disgusting mutations and their minds twisted and deranged. There is no reason to willingly visit this accursed place, ex-

cept to capture some savage beasts, which fetch a handsome price if suitable for the games in the arena.

Fragments of the Dread Star. The sages say that the Islands of the Maimed Ones are a fragment of the original Dread Star, and this is the cause of the strange mutations of its dwellers. Many centuries ago, wondering what type of ore could be extracted from this otherworldly ground, a smith priest of Faberterra built a fort and a mine on one of the islands. The local barbarians were enraged and both the priest and his followers were butchered before a single piece of ore could reach Faberterra. Today, the mine is still there, abandoned.

IVORY SAVANNAH

The Ivory Savannah is an endless land of rolling hills and flat plains. It owes its name to a very common herb that takes on a particular gray color while drying in the autumn. The Savannah is a savage place inhabited by lions, gazelles, the striped horses named zebras, and even stranger beasts. Despite what strangers may think, the king of the savannah isn't the powerful lion or the mighty elephant; it is the gnu, a particular type of buffalo.

The gnu herds migrate north during the hot summers, reaching the grasslands bordering the Brown Sea, while in the autumn they migrate south, following the Buffalo River, to the borders of Caldeia.

The Savannah Tribes, who are mostly herders or hunters, follow the migrations of the herds that provide them with food. They are organized in clans, some of them small (four to ten members), others as numerous as five hundred strong. The clans are led by local chiefs and are usually independent, though it isn't uncommon for several clans to team up for big hunting raids or on similar occasions. The Savannah Tribes are constantly fighting the populations of the Verdant Belt and their relationships with Kyros are even colder. In fact, the very fertile lands between the Sword River and the Buffalo River are coveted both by the Kyrosian farmers and by the Savannah herders. The latter take their herds to feed on the Kyrosian crops, while the Kyrosians not only fight the trespassers but also attack peaceful Savannah Tribes to catch slaves. Caldeia does likewise in the south.

The White King. The Ngobi Tribe, one of the most powerful of the savannah, has a tradition of taming and using the buffaloes as battle mounts. These mighty beasts are feared even by the Kyrosian army. Through endless generations of tribe wars and wise political treaties, the Ngobi have subjugated or made alliances with all the major tribes of the savannah, achieving a leading position. But it is only under the rule of a charismatic leader, the White King, which they have managed to bring all the clans together. Very few strangers have seen the White King in person, and they say he is white and not black. Under the guide of their new leader, the Ngobi have also built a new capital of the reign somewhere in the heart of the Savannah. They call it the City of Elephants, and rumors say it is a marvelous place. Until now the White King hasn't waged any war but both Caldeia and Kyros are very worried about what the unified tribes can do in the south of the world.

KYROS

Kyros enjoys an excellent position in the center of the Dominions as a gateway between south and north, and east and west. It is an ancient land with imposing pal-

aces and well tended gardens. In days of yore, before the Iron Empire, Kyros was ruled by an Autarch, a monarch with absolute power.

In that era, Kyros had the might of elephants on its side which made the Ivory Savannah Tribes of the Ivory Savannah tremble and kept the ironclad Phalanxes of Faberterra at bay.

Sadly, those times are long gone and now very few war elephants survive in Kyros.

The central government has been fighting an eternal war of attrition against the Ivory Savannah Tribes. All the Kyrosian rulers, first the Autarchs and then the Imperial Governors, have coveted the rich lands south of the Buffalo River, as they are the most fertile, but the Savannah tribes have always fought back to retain control over them.

The Kyrosian army constantly patrols the disputed lands, where fortified farming villages exist, but the Ivory Savannah Tribes' clever guerrilla warfare seems to be unbeatable. Most likely, if Kyros had surrendered these lands to the nomads and focused on trade, it would now be the wealthiest kingdom in the world. But, as things stand today, profit from trade and farming is barely enough to support the great Kyrosian army and numerous mercenary forces.

A Psychotic King. The Autarchate was restored when Kyros became independent from the Empire. The first rulers of the second dynasty of Autarchs were men of worth. Sadly, Ganymedes II of Kyros, the current Autarch, isn't. He is quite young, not older than thirty summers, yet he is as mad as a hatter. He murdered his three older brothers to seize the throne and barely escaped an attempted poisoning in the troubled times before he took power. Since then Ganymedes has become paranoid. He thinks that the merchant princes of Syranthia have launched a secret trade war to impoverish and conquer his lands. He also believes that Kyros's border will be attacked by King Eku of Ekul, although Eku is an agonizing ninety-year-old man. But his worst fear is the White King, the legendary ruler of the Savannah Tribes. Ganymedes is convinced that the Tribes will invade Kyros, raze his city and kill him. He constantly babbles about removing that threat somehow. In the mouth of a common madman, these words would be of no interest. But, spoken by the king of one of the strongest states in the world, they mean only one thing: impending doom on the horizon.

LAND OF THE IDOLS

The Land of the Idols is an area west of Lhoban, dotted with ancient ruins of unknown origin. The remnants of palaces and roads abound, but the most common are the stone idols — columns shaped to resemble statues, from fifteen to fifty feet tall, representing humanoids, real and fantastic beasts and, in some cases, wholly alien creatures. Nobody, not even the sages of Syranthia, knows who built these idols and why.

The land is very spooky and animals don't like it, except rats, snakes, and bats. People generally avoid it, because there are stories of caravans that took a shortcut to Lhoban through the Land of the Idols and never reached their destination.

The Stylites. The only inhabitants of the Land of the Idols are the Stylites. "Stylus" is an ancient Syranthian word meaning column and the Stylites are hermit monks, usually from Lhoban, who spend their life meditating on the top of an idol column. The Stylites are very wise and sometimes can answer questions nobody else can, but their trance is often so deep that they even forget to eat and drink. The reason behind their unusual meditation practices is unknown and, if asked, the monks just say: "we are protecting the world".

LHOBAN

Lhoban is a land of high mountains and deep valleys. Crossing it isn't easy, because very few passes are open, especially in winter, and only the local guides know them. Basically, Lhoban is a land of mountain men who live in small villages and lead a simple, hard life, tending yaks and goats.

In truth, there is much more to Lhoban. First, in the low valleys the climate is milder and terraced farming is extensively practiced. Second, Lhobanmen love trading and their two main border cities,

Heaven's Door and Lhobanport, are bustling with activity. Lhobanmen produce excellent wool and their weaving techniques are the best in all the Dominions.

Third, Lhoban is a land of high spirituality. Although each village is ruled by a council of elders, the monks are the true ruling class, as well as the cohesive force of this wide country. Lhoban monks (as explained on page 34) are basically philosophers who follow a doctrine of self-improvement and enlightenment. They live in secluded monasteries, but often visit the villages, protecting the commoners from dangers and bringing the word of their master, the Enlightened One, the true ruler of the country.

Indeed, Lhoban has its fair share of strange creatures (among which the elusive Lhoban Dragons) and dark creatures that only the spiritual powers of the monks can stop. In addition, many valleys are isolated or still unexplored, so nobody truly knows what lurks within them.

Seekers of the Black Light. Several centuries ago, a new philosophy spread among the monks: true enlightenment cannot be achieved through spiritual purity, but only through its opposite, perpetual evil. According to this belief, only in deepest chaos can the true adept find his real self. This new sect of monks became the mortal enemy of the traditional one, following the path of darkness and trying to unleash the forces of evil onto the world. Naturally the good monks rose against this abomination and a terrible war was fought. In the end, the Order of Light, as the monks following the true philosophy are called, triumphed, and the Seekers of the Black Light were defeated. But evil is resilient and, like bad weeds, the evil monks survived and regained strength. They are now a secret order, living in hidden monasteries, walking among the common people or, even worse, hiding among the good monks to spread chaos, corruption, and disorder. Rumor has it that their evil schemes are extremely far reaching and even involve faraway states.

LUSH JUNGLE

The Lush Jungle is an enormous tropical forest that marks the southern border of the known world. Nobody has explored it completely, because it is a very dangerous place. Mortal diseases and beasts like snakes and spiders of any size and degree of venomousness are only some of the dangers lurking under its trees.

The Lush Jungle is the ancestral home of the Pygmies, a primitive race of dwarfed men who withdrew to the shadow of the mangroves shortly after the fall of the Dread Star. According to the Syranthian sages, they are the descendants of Keronian slaves, who came here to find their freedom.

Whatever the reason, they are very reclusive and possessive about their land. The Pygmies are deceitful, just like the spiders they love so much. They let you go deep into their territory and then they attack you with venomous blowguns, traps, and so on. Very few of those going on expeditions into the Jungle make it back.

Why would a civilized man want to go to this wild land?

The reason is simple: greed. The bed of the Anaconda River, the main stream crossing the jungle, it is said, is littered with gold, ready for the taking by those so bold to dive into it, despite its crocodiles and giant water snakes. The mountains are even more appealing, as they are full of precious ore.

These rumors have lured adventurers and desperate rogues from all over the Dominions.

There is also a city, Verazar, founded fifty years ago by a drunken prospector. It is a place full of diseases, whores, and the scum of the world. It is also the starting point for mining expeditions into the jungle. Actually, although a certain quantity of gold can be found, the expeditions aren't worth the trouble. Even if someone was lucky enough to find a huge amount of gold and come back to Verazar, avoiding the dangers of the jungle, the cutthroats of the city would rob and kill him in no time.

But greed makes people optimistic and many are willing to try their luck.

Aurica and the Anaconda Springs. After a few shots of cheap liquor in a tavern in Verazar, many adventurers will start talking of a city entirely made of gold hidden deep in the jungle. It is deserted, because its inhabitants died centuries ago, and it is waiting to be found by a lucky prospector! Those who have detailed information claim that Aurica — that's the city's name — is located near the fabled springs of the Anaconda River, which no one has ever found. Many expeditions set off to find Aurica, but nobody every returned.

NORTHEIM

The lands of Northeim are full of deep valleys, wild rivers and ancient forests. Northeim is mostly uninhabited, because the Northalders live in isolated clans and don't farm on a large scale.

The Northlanders aren't the only dwellers of this immense area. The Cairnlanders, the Nandals, and the few inhabitants of Imperial outposts call this place home.

Northeim is a wild land: wolves, bears, mountain lions and many other creatures roam the land and only the strongest of men can endure life in this harsh place. It is also rich in natural resources, such as wood and excellent stone, but also copper, iron and gold. Yet, the Northlanders are too uncivilized to be skilled in the use of metals. They can barely work them and have no idea about how to build a decent mine. It is easier for them to buy or steal metal weapons and tools from the southerners, although some of them are slowly learning the secrets of metalworking, that fascinates them.

Mount of Fire. The Smoking Mountain, or Mount of Fire, is a big volcano in the heart of Northeim. Fifty years ago, a group of Imperials came here and built a strange temple, called the Monastery of the Hammer. The Northlanders attacked it, thinking they would find only weak priests defending precious artifacts. But they were wrong. The temple was inhabited by a horde of metal-clad warriors, who slaughtered the barbarians. Now the Northlanders grudgingly respect their neighbors and some friendly relations are budding. The temple dwellers have revealed themselves as the true followers of Hulian, the Smith God, and are teaching the Northlanders a lot of things, among them the secret of forging iron!

RED DESERT

The sages say that the Red Desert was created by the dusts raised by the fall of the Dread Star and it had once been a great forest. Seeing it today, it is hard to believe the sages. Rocks and thin reddish sand stretch for hundreds of miles in every direction, interrupted only by the occasional oasis. Despite its appearance, the Red Desert hides several treasures and marvels, like great forests of petrified trees, plains lined by veins of precious ore and dotted with gems surfacing from the ground and, finally, the Red Lotus, a very precious variety of Lotus that lives as tiny spores on the stone petals of desert roses. It is also a dangerous place, inhabited by deadly beasts. Besides scorpions and snakes of small to giant size, there are Skull Jackals, very dangerous predators, and the dreaded Ulatisha, The Being That Digs in the Sand, a semi-mythological monster.

For what concerns its civilizations, the Red Desert hosts some Independent Cities and is home to nomads and tribes of herders, the only people capable of surviving in this harsh land. They are divided in clans, usually recognized by the color of their capes. Brown and green nomads are quite peaceful, but the red-caped ones aren't.

Red Nomads. These desert dwellers aren't a friendly people, except when they expose the face, which happens very rarely. Then, they are jovial and amicable. But, if their faces are covered by the kballa, a sort of heavy veil, they are ready to assault you, rob you of all your belongings, and leave you to die of thirst in the desert, without remorse or good reason. Some say that the Red Nomads descend from the survivors of the Fallen Kingdom of Keron, because they speak a strange language and worship desert spirits called Djinns. The Red Nomads sometimes trespass into the Ivory Savannah and engage the Ivory Savannah Tribes in bloody battles.

Syranthia

Syranthia is a land of low, rolling hills and fertile plains. Agriculture is widespread and it produces mainly vegetables, fruit and grapes (Syranthia's wine is famous

throughout the Dominions). This is why Faberterra conquered Syranthia many years before the Empire.

Its two main cities are renowned for different reasons. Syranthia City, the capital of the reign, owes its fame to the Library, the greatest collection of books, scrolls and tablets in the known world. Legions of scholars spend their lives studying such wealth of knowledge and the city is a place of learning and trade.

Askerios, almost as old as Syranthia City, is the most important economic center of the Empire and the biggest port in the known world. Slaves from Ascaia, timber from Northeim, and Water Lotus from the Brown Sea are only some of the goods that can be found there.

Syranthia is ruled by a council of merchant princes, who managed to become independent from the Empire without any bloodshed. In truth, Syranthia still pays tribute to Faberterra, but it is only a very small percentage of its huge riches and certainly a worthwhile investment, if it helps Faberterra in fighting the northern barbarians.

Despite being mainly farmers, merchants and scholars, the Syranthians know how to defend themselves. Their military fleet is impressive and, on the mainland, they boast a tradition of cataphracts cavalry, the heaviest mounted troops in the Dominions, usually made up of the younger sons of the merchant elite.

Secret Cults of Syranthia. Syranthia represents civilization in its most opulent form. Syranthian merchants are fat and greedy, their women snobbish and full of jewelry. Many upper class Syranthians indulge in strange pleasures coming from the south, or even follow the unholy Tricarnian religion. The latter use the arts of mages and warlocks to gain an advantage over their competitors. Seemingly rich and happy, Syranthia is actually home to much evil.

HERO'S JOURNAL:
THE SEA GUARDIAN OF ASKERIOS

Askerios is famous for its massive Sea Guardian, a fifty-yard tall bronze statue of a man holding a torch. The statue is hollow and doubles up as a lighthouse: its torch is the light that leads the ships to the haven of Askerios. There are various stories about the origin of the Sea Guardian. Some say it was built by an ancient king of the city and represents a now forgotten divinity, others say it is a gift from Hordan, fallen from the sky along with the Dread Star. A third theory claims that it is a Keronian relic, found while digging the city's foundations. The Askeronians, however, usually believe either of the first two theories. Whatever its origin, the Askeronians know that, as long as the Sea Guardian protects its port, Askerios will be prosperous. Another strange fact about the statue is that, after centuries of being exposed to the elements, it is still intact, with no trace of rust on its smooth surface.

TRICARNIA

Tricarnia is a land of vast plains, crossed by a web of small rivers. The climate is mild and the crops abundant. As said before (see Tricarnians on page 27), Tricarnia is divided in Principalities, each ruled by a Priest Prince, although the day-to-day business is usually supervised by eunuch slave-bureaucrats.

Tricarnians have greatly developed their farming techniques. In the last few centuries, they have used the many rivers of their land to create a great network of irrigation canals for their main food production: rice fields.

The rice crops are so abundant that they can feed the masses of slaves who live in this land.

Tricarnia is what is left of the great Keronian Empire and the Priest Princes think with the grandiosity of their ancestors. Their cities, usually quite small, have such beautiful and complex architecture that even the best masons of Faberterra cannot imitate. However, the center of all important decisions is the Prince's palace, which includes all the most important parts of the city. So, for example, the merchant houses are located in the courtyard of the palace, like the temples and other major facilities. This is something that strangers must be aware of: entering a Tricarnian city means entering the Prince's palace. Everything in it belongs to him and is only temporarily used by the slaves and servants.

The two major social classes are nobles and slaves, but a very small group of middlemen exist. They are freed slaves or the children of freed slaves and work as traders and specialized artisans. They are called freemen and their freedom is by no means guaranteed — they can easily be forced back to slavery.

Tricarnia has faced quite a number of harsh wars on its land, mainly against the Iron Empire and the Caleds, but also the Northlanders have occasionally attacked its borders. This is why large parts of it are not inhabited and crumbling ruins dot the land.

Brokenchain Mountains. Not all the slaves are content with their condition, but for many of them there is no other choice. The few who manage to escape from their cruel masters go north, crossing dangerous deserted areas, and take refuge in the mountains, where free communities of runaway slaves exist. Here life is hard for the former slaves, but they do not mind because here they can be masters of themselves. The Tricarnian Princes know of these communities but do not destroy them. The reason is simple: free men are

usually stronger and more intelligent than the average slave and the mountains are a good source of manpower. Every now and then, a Tricarnian Prince takes his army and goes hunting for men in the Brokenchain Mountains. This is both business and pleasure, because few things excite the Tricarnian nobles more than hunting men. But lately something has changed. The runaway slaves of the Mountains don't simply flee, they fight. Someone has taught them how to defend themselves and, even worse, has given them weapons. The army of last Priest Prince who went to the Mountains to hunt for slaves was butchered and the Prince himself barely managed to escape. This outrageous behavior cannot be tolerated and will be harshly punished.

TROLLS MOUNTAINS

The Troll Mountains mark the northern border of the world. What lies beyond these tall, snowcapped peaks is a mystery even to the sages of Syranthia. What lurks among the mountains, instead, is well-known: Trolls — big furry creatures, with a really bad attitude and a taste for human flesh. Many other incredible beasts live in the Trolls Mountain, such as giant bears, elks, and vicious snow vipers.

When the winter is harsh and hunger torments their bellies, the trolls leave the mountains and go hunting for men in Northeim and the Cairnlands.

There are two species of trolls. The great trolls, or true trolls, are five-yard tall hulking brutes with razor sharp claws and they require dozens of fearless warriors to be stopped. Luckily, they are barely smarter than animals and clever tactics, complemented by a lot of luck, are enough to deal with them.

The small trolls instead, also named Nandals, are a race of primitive cavemen. The shape of their throat makes them unable to speak; they can only emit low sounds and grunts, so they are named Nandals, which in the Northeim language means 'mute'. Despite being smaller than true trolls, the Nandals are more vicious, because they are gifted with brutish force and a certain degree of intelligence. They usually hunt men for food or kidnap women to mate with them.

The Nandals are less geographically stable than great trolls. When they migrate, entire clans come down from the north, sometimes as far as the Borderlands or in the Iron Mountains. A Nandal invasion is always a major threat to a civilized race, because the cavemen don't parley and don't give quarters. They simply kill, pillage, and rape.

Ancestors of Men. It is said that the Nandals were once common white men, who had the misfortune of being exposed to massive amounts of the dusts from the Dread Star, which mutated them into the aggressive creatures they are today. Some Northeim warriors who ventured into the Troll Mountains to hunt or simply to show their courage claim to have seen ancient paintings representing white men in the caves inhabited by the Nandals.

VALKHEIM

Valkheim is the new home of the Valk. The clans faithful to Tukal, first son of Dhaar, followed him here and established a new Valk reign.

Valkheim is a land of grassy plains and rocky hills. It is largely uninhabited, except for some villages of fishermen and farmers on the shores of the Drowned King Sea. This population is a mix of Cairnlanders and more civilized men from Zandor and, generally, they are pacific and quite superstitious. Shortly after coming to Valkheim, the Valk warriors, full of rage over the death of their leader, razed these villagers and butchered their inhabitants. After a while, Tukal, who wasn't a fool, understood that these people could be used as slaves by the Valk, so he spared the lives of the survivors. The Valk call them "the Cows", since they aren't able to fight.

The Cows are fairly good craftsmen and can build boats, which the Valk are not familiar with. Tukal's idea was to create a fleet of ships to transport his men and horses to the Borderlands and invade Faberterra, the heart of the Empire. But this was a short-lived dream: the boats were too primitive, had room for no more than a dozen horses each, and could not sail too far from the coast.

So the plan was abandoned, but the Cows were allowed to live in independent communities and pay tribute to the Valk lords. Today, the Valk live in the eastern part of the country, leading their traditional, nomadic life, while the Cows continue to live on the coast. The Cows are quite content with the situation: the Valk are harsh masters but protect them from the Cairnlanders, who periodically raid their lands.

The Valk threat is still looming. Rogal, son of Tukal and current leader of the Valk, is using Valkheim to gather men whom he summons from friendly clans out of the deep steppe. When he has a big enough army, he plans to invade the Dread Sea Dominions again to finish the work of his grandfather.

Dhaar's Tomb. On a hill, deep in the steppe, the Valk made the Cows build a massive stone construction. It is the tomb of Dhaar, the greatest ruler of the Valk.

His body lies within, perpetually tended by a special group of Valkyries. For unknown reasons, the corpse is still intact, as if the mighty warrior were asleep and not dead. The Valkyries believe that the spirit of Sha Mekri dwells in Dhaar's body and that, sooner or later, he will wake up to lead the Valk horde once more.

VALK STEPPE

This land is only the first, little chunk of the Far East, where whole hordes of Valk clans and other strange populations live. Very little is known about them.

VERDANT BELT

The area of the Verdant Belt could be a true paradise on earth. It is a fertile land, where farming is easy and the climate mild.

But it is surrounded by vultures.

It is threatened from the north by the Savannah Tribes, who often trespass into the Belt with their herds. To the south there are the dark Lush Jungles, from where the Pygmies and other dark things occasionally come looking for prey. But the greatest evil comes from east in the shape of Caldeian slave traders, who travel down the Slave Route ending in Heavensdoor, in Lhoban. They smile a lot, and bring drugs and precious metal weapons, but in exchange they want a huge amount of slaves.

The Verdant Belt is inhabited by farmers of the Ivory Savannah Tribes. They mainly grow bananas, the basis of their diet, and live in fortified villages. They use a particular farming technique called "fire and plant": they burn large parts of the rainforest and then cultivate the de-forested area for four-five years. After this period, the soil is depleted, so the area is abandoned and a new village is founded somewhere else.

The Verdant Belt tribes are fiercely independent, but in the last few years some of them have been subjugated by the White King of the Ivory Savannah. They pay tribute in exchange for the King's protection and are starting to trade vegetables for cattle, a business that is mutually profitable. Obviously, Caldeia doesn't look kindly on the new peace spreading across the Belt and, wherever possible, it tries to bring war to the area.

Flesh Eaters. There is a legend among the Belt Tribes about a cursed race of Jaguar Men, who live in the thick of the Lush Jungles and leave only to hunt the Ivory Savannah Tribes. There is no evidence of their existence, but lately entire villages along the border have been found empty of their inhabitants. Is the legend true or is something even darker stretching its fingers over the Belt?

ZANDOR

Zandor is the rotten remnant of what was once the flower of the eastern Iron Empire. Before the Valk Invasion, Jalizar, its capital, was the biggest city in the world, rivaling Faberterra in beauty and riches. During the Empire, the Governor of Jalizar had a power greater than that of most kings.

Then the Valk arrived and destroyed everything.

The immense region of Zandor — once full of prosperous towns, rich villages and well tended fields — is now a mass of crumbling ruins, inhabited only by coyotes and by the unholy beasts summoned by the Valkyries. The fields have reverted to forests and rocky plains, only good as pastures for the Valk's herds, and twisted trees grow in the deserted palaces.

At the death of Dhaar, the Valk warlord, the clans faithful to Juggu, Dhaar's second son, remained here, believing they could conquer the whole land in a few months.

But Juggu wasn't a lucky man. He died after three months of an infected wound and the various clans, driven by age-old rivalries, soon lost their short-lived unity.

Today, the Zandorian Valk are too divided to conquer the whole region, but they are strong enough to be a constant threat, so control over the land is virtually shared. The Zandorians live in isolated, independent settlements, with a strong militia and draconian laws, and they can only protect the nearby territories. The Valk, instead, wander the region freely, following their nomadic customs.

In truth, nobody is capable of ruling over Zandor.

Jalizar, City of Thieves. The city Jalizar was the best at withstanding the Valk invasion. Its mighty walls stopped the nomads, but its citizens suffered greatly. Famine, theft and all types of crimes were common during the three-year siege.

Today the situation isn't much better. The city has undoubtedly recovered some of its order and still is the major trading center of the northeast. Heavily guarded caravans arrive from and depart for Faberterra and Ekul weekly, while massive ships transport their cargo across the Drowned King Sea. But the wealth isn't evenly distributed: the immensely rich merchants control all the revenues from trade, while the masses starve. Even the King of Jalizar, nicknamed the Ragamuffin King, is forced to beg the merchants for gold to preserve a semblance of order in the city.

Besides the merchants, the major force in the city is the thieves. At least three major guilds of criminals exist, and they exert strong control over the territory. Even the merchant houses are forced to do business with them. Life in Jalizar is corrupt and almost everything, love and faith included, is for sale. But it is also a place of great opportunities for those with a sharp mind and a quick sword.

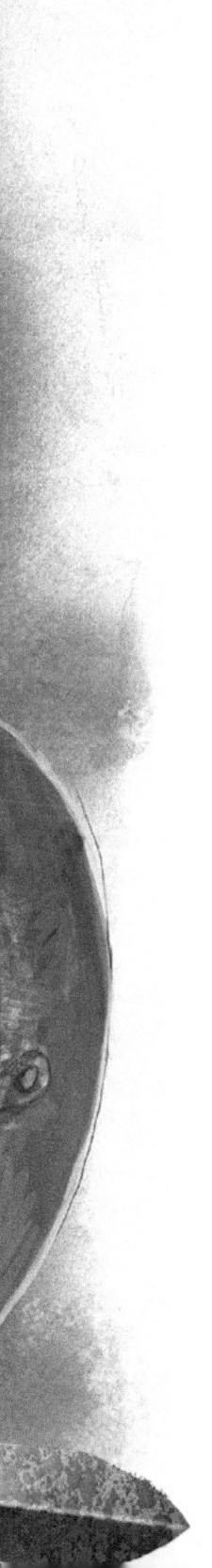

CHAPTER 2

CHARACTERS

HEROIC CONCEPTS

The world of *Beasts and Barbarians* is full of interesting characters, but you might be a little overwhelmed or simply out of ideas, so here is a list of character types you can use or tweak to create your outstanding hero.

Adventurer. The typical jack-of-all-trades, an adventurer comes from all walks of life and has abilities in various fields. He can be a treasure hunter, a traveler with great wanderlust or a clever scoundrel. Whatever his past, adventures are his daily business.

Amazon. The Dread Sea Dominions are a very chauvinistic world and women are usually seen as objects for pleasure or, even worse, as breeding machines. An Amazon is a woman who has emancipated herself; she fights and lives exactly like a man. The Ascaian Amazons are the only Amazon culture of the Dread Sea Dominions, but also outside Ascaia a courageous woman can leave her place in society, take up the sword and prove her worth.

Assassin. An Assassin can find employment in any place and among any culture. He might be a shady lone wolf, a member of the powerful assassin guild of Jalizar, or an executioner following one of the dark cults in the decadent cities of the Iron Empire. Whatever his background, this individual is very skilled in one task: killing.

Bandit. The Empire, the law, and civilization itself are crumbling, and the world is full of wolves ready to take advantage of the situation. This character is one of them. He usually earns his living sacking, pillaging and stealing. Most Bandits are ruthless bastards, but the more sympathetic ones steal from the rich to give to the poor. These individuals are usually liked by the commoners and become the subjects of stories and ballads.

Barbarian. Barbarian literally means "one who stutters" and the word identifies all the people who don't speak the Imperial language fluently. Today the term refers to all the uncivilized populations beyond the boundaries of the Iron Empire. Traditionally, barbarians have been represented in two ways: as hulking brutes with none of the traits of civilized people, living only by the law of the sword, or as good savages, living peacefully in communion with nature — an ability that the civilized men have lost. Most barbarians don't perfectly fit either archetype, but are a mix of both.

Courtesan. A courtesan can be an exotic dancer at the court of a prince, or a simple tavern wench. Whatever her origin, she is usually beautiful and, besides her erotic skills, she is quite capable of manipulating the stupid males with her beauty.

Entertainer. Poets, bards, acrobats, mimes and every type of showmen are common in the Dominions. They tell stories, report news and entertain people with their performances. Some of them, as court poets, can be firmly rooted in a single place, but many are wanderers, taking their songs and show wherever they can find an audience.

Gladiator. Gladiators are fighters who combat in the arena for the delight of the crowds. They can be rich celebrities, at whose sight women sigh and faint, but there are also desperate toughs who wrestle with rabid dogs in back alleys for a few copper coins. In many places gladiators are slaves, though they usually lead a better life than a free man, constantly pampered and well nourished by their master. At least until they meet their end in the arena.

Lotus master. Skilled alchemists, poisoners and healers, these feared individuals know how to use the Lotus to heal a wound, kill a man in a horrible way, or summon strange visions from the air. They are a reclusive sect and very jealous of their secrets.

Mercenary. Some fight for an ideal and some for self defense, but a mercenary fights only for loot and money. Usually, but not always, he is a skilled warrior. A big mouth and impressive appearance might be the only weapons a mercenary possesses and it is difficult to understand before the battle if the man you hired is a real fighter or just a windbag. But remember, regardless of his skill, a mercenary is first and foremost loyal to his purse.

Monk. Monks are people in search of enlightenment and self perfection. Through meditation and contemplation they learn how to perform amazing feats impossible for the common man. Some of them can endure thirst and hunger for months, while others can kill a man with a single bare-handed blow. The most famous monks come from faraway Lhoban, but several other monastic groups exist, like the Stylites of the Land of Idols. Some of them are pacifists, philosophers, sages, and men of knowledge, while others, usually martial artists of great prowess, actively fight the evil of the world.

Noble. Decadent princes of Tricarnia, merchant lords of Syranthia, Northlander tribe chiefs, all these people are nobles, born to rule the people, and responsible for their subjects' safety. They mostly lead a stable and pampered life, but some of them decide, or are forced, to choose the path of adventure.

Nomad. Nomads are constantly on the move. Some of them, like the Valk, are herders, so they are forced to move to let their beasts graze, while others are hunters that follow the migrations of their quarries, like the Ivory Savannah Tribes hunting gnus in the Ivory Savannah. Some nomads move on foot but a great part of them have horses and are excellent riders.

Pirate. The scourge of the seas, these men don't know any lord beside the captain of their ship, and hunt and prey on any vessel they find. Some of them still possess a glint of honor and humanity, but for the greatest part they are only a bunch of criminals.

Priest. There are many gods in the Dread Sea Dominions, hence a great number of priests. Despite sharing the same name, there are many differences among them. A depraved priest of Hordan, for example, is very different from a pious Sheppard of the Divine Couple or from a midwife priestess of Etu. Remember that, in the Dread Sea Dominions, priests have no supernatural powers. If they want them, they must devote themselves to sorcery, a very dangerous path.

Sage. Although the world is in the hands of warriors, barbarians and other men of the sword, there are some who actively seek, protect, and preserve knowledge, in all its forms. These individuals are Sages. They might be archivists at the Library of Syranthia or enlightened aristocrats with a passion for books. Whatever their origin, knowledge is what they seek and protect.

Sailor. A wanderer of the seas, a sailor feels more at his ease on the deck of a ship than on solid ground. He has seen a lot of places and kissed women of very different complexions, and he wants more of both. He isn't against a little piracy if it keeps his purse fat, but mainly he is a traveler and an adventurer.

Slave. Sadly, slavery is very common, so it is no surprise if a hero is born in chains or made a slave. Slaves come from all social classes, and a slave, or an ex-slave, can be a very motivated character and have a very wide array of skills. He can be a lowly servant, but also a warrior slave of the Tricarnian army, or a sage or a scribe kept alive for his unusual abilities. Remember, anyone can fall into slavery.

Sorcerer. Magic is a dangerous business that requires constant application and a strong mind. The very soul of the practitioner is involved in the dark rituals necessary to bind the arcane forces to the caster's will. So mages of all types must be aware of the risks they run when they whisper their forgotten spells. A sorcerer is a generic term for all those wizards, warlocks and petty practitioners involved in magic. Although many of them are only charlatans, the few individuals truly gifted with magical powers are among the most powerful, and most dangerous, individuals of all the Dominions.

Thief. Wherever there is wealth, there is someone ready to snatch it. A thief is an expert in stealing property, and no safe, wall, or guard can stop him. She can be a member of a powerful thieves' guild, like those of Jalizar, or a freelance, but her skills are not in question when it comes to stealth and break-ins.

Warrior. The sword rules the world in this troubled age. This individual can be a clan warrior from the savage north, a slave fighter of Tricarnia, an elegant cataphracts knight of Syranthia, a member of the Iron Phalanxes, a simple caravan guard or whatever you want, but his main feature is his ability in the art of war.

TWEAKING AND MIXING CONCEPTS

Characters, like real people, have a past and are the result of their past experiences. This is particularly true for sword and sorcery heroes.

So you can create a more vivid hero by mixing and tweaking the concepts. For example, by merging together a Monk and a Bandit, you can create a hero that, brought up as a monk in faraway Lhoban, has become corrupted by vice while traveling in the western countries and turned to bandit life to satisfy his new needs. He could be trying to regain his former purity or fully enjoy his current state.

Whatever his choice, this hero can make for an interesting character.

Similarly, you can combine a Barbarian and a Slave. Your hero is a former Ivory Savannah Tribe barbarian who was captured by Caldeian slave hunters and sold as a slave in Tricarnia. When the adventure starts, he has just managed to free himself and is trying to return south to his land…

When you grasp the technique, it is easy to create interesting characters in no time.

CHARACTER CREATION

The creation of a playing character for *Beasts and Barbarians* follows the standard Savage Worlds rules. All the playable races are humans, so the heroes begin with a free Edge.

Normally, *Beasts and Barbarians* heroes are more experienced than standard fantasy adventurers and start the game at Seasoned Rank (20 Experience Points).

LITERACY, LANGUAGES AND REALITY CHECK

The Dread Sea Dominions are a very illiterate world. So, as per the standard game rules, almost all the characters should have the Illiterate Hindrance. Yet, this would cause a generic flattening of the heroes. Hence, the Hindrance is ignored and each player is allowed to decide if his hero knows how to read and write or not (depending on the hero's background). Illiterate characters have an extra Skill point, to be spent on a Smarts based skill.

Characters can become literate during the game by spending a leveling option.

A hero starts the game knowing a number of languages equal to half his Smarts die, plus his native tongue as per the Multiple Languages setting rules. New languages can be acquired through advancements.

SKILLS

The following skills are modified or extended to fit the setting.

KNOWLEDGE

The following are the most useful areas of knowledge Skills in this setting.

Arcana. It covers the vast field of magic, the occult and the supernatural.

Battle. Useful for mass combats.

History. It covers the knowledge of the past.

Legends and Lore. From common folklore to knowledge of myths and fantastic creatures and places.

Religion. It covers all the religious matters. In some cases, it can also be used, with a penalty, to cover Arcana, Legends and Lore matters.

Specific Area. Its focus can be the Empire, North Dominions, South Dominions, Eastern Lands, or a specific city or country.

PILOTING

This skill isn't used.

DRIVING

This skill is used to drive chariots, carts, and other similar vehicles.

STEALTH

Beside its other uses, Stealth is used to deliver venom while going unnoticed. Pouring poison into a tankard while no one is looking, for example at a feast or in a crowded tavern, requires a Stealth roll. In case of failure, someone notices the attempt. In a one-to-one situation (like two people drinking together) or when someone is explicitly paying attention, delivering poison requires an opposed roll between the poisoners's Stealth and the observer's Notice.

FORBIDDEN HINDRANCES

The following Hindrances aren't used in this setting: All Thumbs, Doubting Thomas, and Illiterate.

MODIFIED HINDRANCES

POVERTY (MINOR)

Besides starting with half the amount of money, a Poor hero also halves his Savings (see page 104).

NEW HINDRANCES

Some new Hindrances are available in this setting.

CAROUSER (MINOR)

The hero usually puts himself in danger while relaxing and feasting. Whenever he decides to draw a card for the After the Adventure Events, he draws two cards and the Game Master chooses which of the two is to be considered (usually the worst).

DAMSEL IN DISTRESS (MAJOR)

The world of *Beasts and Barbarians* isn't inhabited only by muscular warriors, witty rogues, or powerful sorcerers. It is also a world of beautiful women who, sometimes, put themselves in danger and are hopefully saved from such perils by valiant heroes.

A Damsel in Distress is one of these unfortunate women. She is totally unable to defend herself, so she has –2 to Fighting, Fear rolls and to resisting Test of Wills. She appears very vulnerable and this makes her a favorite target for slave hunters, evil magicians and other bad guys, who have in mind a "fate worse than death" for her. Hungry monsters might also attack her to satiate their craving for human flesh.

Conversely, neutral or good characters like her and feel protective toward her tender body. For these reasons, she gains +2 to Charisma and receives an additional Bennie. This Bennie can be used as normal or, once per session, she can freely give it to a friend (as for the Common Bond Edge).

A Damsel in Distress can learn how to cope with the harshness of the world. Every time she gets an advancement she is allowed a Spirit (−4) roll. In case of success, she loses one of the three penalties above. Once all the penalties are removed, she loses the additional Bennie and the possibility to share it but retains her Charisma bonus.

Damsels in Distress are generally females, but nothing prevents a male from taking this Hindrance, except for the constant mockery by his companions.

IRASCIBLE (MINOR)

The hero cannot stand insults of any kind and is ready to react to them. Besides effects on role playing, he also suffers −2 resisting Taunts or Smarts based Tricks. As partial compensation, a hero with the Berserk Edge can apply a −1 to the Smarts roll to go into the berserk state.

FEAR OF MAGIC
(MINOR, MAJOR)

Magic is always mistrusted in the Dread Sea Dominions, but the hero is a particular case: he truly dreads it. He tries in every way to avoid the supernatural and even friendly magic. In case of the Major Hindrance, his revulsion also prevents him from using magical objects, Lotus potions included. Whenever forced to face or use magic, the character must make a Fear roll.

FORBIDDEN EDGES

These Edges aren't used in this setting: Adept, MacGyver, Mentalist, Mr. Fix It, and Wizard.

MODIFIED EDGES

ACE

This Edge is slightly modified to work on chariots (Driving), ships (Boating) and mounts (Riding). Each of these "vehicles" requires a related Edge (to be taken only once). Said Edges are: Charioteer (Driving), Quartermaster (Boating), or Born in the Saddle (Riding).

A hero with one of these Edges adds +2 to Driving, Boating or Riding rolls. In addition, he may also spend Bennies on soak rolls for any vehicle, vessel or mount he controls. This is a Driving, Boating or Riding roll at −2 (canceling the usual +2). Each success and raise soaks a wound and any critical hit that would have resulted from it.

ARCANE BACKGROUND

Three new arcane backgrounds are used in *Beasts and Barbarians*: Lotusmastery, Sorcery, and Enlightment. All the other arcane backgrounds are banned. See the Arcane Background chapter for further details.

CHAMPION

Requirements: Novice, Arcane Background (Enlightment), Enlightment d6+, Spirit d8+, Strength d6+, Vigor d8+, Fighting d8+

Apart from the different requirements, it works as usual.

HOLY/UNHOLY WARRIOR

Requirements: Novice, Arcane Background (Enlightment), Enlightment d8+, Spirit d8+

Apart from the different requirements, it works as usual.

NOBLE

See Rich and Filthy Rich for monetary changes. For the rest, it works as usual.

SOUL DRAIN

Requirements: Novice, Arcane Background (Sorcery), Sorcery d8+, Knowledge (Arcana) d8+

Apart from the different requirements, it works as usual.

RICH AND FILTHY RICH

For adventuring heroes, these Edges grant respectively five times and ten times the starting funds, but they bestow no regular income. For NPCs they work in the customary way.

NEW EDGES

BACKGROUND EDGES

BRUTE

Requirements: Novice, Strength d6+, Vigor d6+

This Edge represents the bad side of barbarism (while Savage represents its good side). This hero has the strong, feral attributes of a beast and looks with open disdain at the decadence of civilization. His philosophy is simple and clear: the strong survive, the weak succumb.

In combat, he unleashes his primitive nature; this causes all melee attacks to be made at an additional +1 to damage rolls, +2 if he hits with a raise.

BUFFALO RIDER

Requirements: Novice, Riding d6+, Vigor d6+, Ivory Savannah Tribes origins

This hero is one of the feared Buffalo Riders of the Ivory Savannah. He begins the game with a War Buffalo and a Buffalo Lance. Usually Buffalo Riders are Loyal to their life companions. The Buffalo is a Henchman and a Buffalo Rider can spend advancement, at Veteran Rank, to promote his mount to full Wild Card status. If the buffalo dies, it isn't replaced unless bought again from the Ivory Savannah Tribes.

FALLEN NOBLE

Requirements: Novice

A staple of heroic fantasy is the fallen noble, an important man or woman who has somehow lost his or her birthrights. This is a reworked version of the Noble Edge, to be used with this type of background.

A Fallen Noble has +1 Charisma. He has a certain amount of social importance, but not as much as if he occupied his rightful position. In addition, he can choose one of these three advantages.

Follower. A servant of some type accompanies the hero. He can be a faithful retainer, a sworn defender, a teacher or whoever the character wishes. He is a Henchman and his stats are set by the Game Master. If the follower dies, he isn't replaced. When the hero reaches the Veteran rank, he can promote the follower to Wild Card status by spending advancement.

Bag of Gold. The hero has lost his privileges but he has saved some money, at least. He starts with three times the standard amount of funds.

Heirloom. The hero owns a minor relic, decided by the Game Master.

If the Fallen Noble manages to regain his status, this Edge is replaced by the standard Noble Edge, but the character maintains the follower, money, or heirloom he chose when taking this Edge.

FORMER GLADIATOR

Requirements: Novice, Agility d6+, Fighting d8+, Intimidation d6+

The hero is a veteran of the sun scorched arenas of the Dread Sea Dominion – he doesn`t know the meaning of the words "fair fight", but he knows how to scare opponent's to death. If he succeeds in an Intimidation test against an adjaced opponent, he receives a free Fighting attack. This attack does not incur a Multiaction penalty.

GHOULBLOOD

Requirements: Vigor d6+, Must be a Cairnlander

During long and moonless nights, Ancestors sometimes visit the beds of young Cairnlander women. Children born of these strange unions have grayish complexion and are not totally human. They have +2 to any rolls against undead magic powers and undead creatures don't generally threaten them, unless attacked. In gaming terms, a Ghoulblood hero can make a Reaction roll when meeting an undead. With a Neutral or better result he isn't attacked. In addition, a Ghoulblood

hero tends to heal very fast. He is allowed a Natural Healing roll every two days.

HOPLITE TRAINING

Requirements: Novice, Strength d6+, Vigor d6+

The hero spent a long time wearing heavy armor. Maybe he trained as a Hoplite, the phalanx soldiers, or in a similar military corp. When calculating encumbrance, he considers only half of the weight of the armor and shield he wears.

In addition, he has +2 to Vigor rolls to resisting fatigue caused by long marches and by wearing armor in hot environments.

SAVAGE

Requirements: Novice, Survival d8+

This hero was either born in the bitter mountains of north, or lived in the Ivory Savannah or in the insidious Lush Jungle. Whatever his origin, he is the typical "noble savage", perfectly at ease in the nature. He perceives incoming danger by smelling the air, climbs cliffs and tall trees with the agility of a monkey and instinctively recognizes the right herbs to cure wounds and diseases.

While in a natural environment (so this Edge doesn't work in ruins, cities or underground), he has the two following advantages when using the Healing, Notice and Climbing skills.

First, if his skill is lower than his controlling attribute, he can roll using the attribute value instead of the skill value (so Agility instead of Climbing and Smarts instead of Healing and Notice). If the skill is equal or higher than the controlling attribute, he gains +1 to the skill roll.

Second, he never suffers penalties for lack of equipment on these skills.

Combat Edges

Armor Use

Requirements: Wild Card, Novice, Fighting d6+, Vigor d8+

This hero is very skilled in using armor to absorb the impact of blows. Before rolling to soak a wound, he can activate this Edge. In this case, the current Armor value is added to the Soak roll. To keep the game fast, furious and fun, the torso armor value is always considered, regardless of called shots targeting specific body parts of the character.

This rough treatment ruins the armor and it loses one Armor point after each use of this Edge, but a warrior considers it a good bargain, if it helps him stay alive!

Damaged armor can be fixed with a Repair roll. Each roll requires 1d4 hours and returns a single Armor point, two with a raise.

Armor dropped to zero Armor Bonus becomes useless junk and cannot be repaired.

Distract

Requirements: Novice, Fighting d8+, Smarts d6+, Taunt d4+

This fighter knows how to distract an enemy during melee, at the cost of temporarily decreasing the effectiveness of his attacks. Once per round, before attempting a Fighting roll against an opponent, he can make a free Trick against the same opponent. It doesn't count as an additional action, but it causes −2 to all

the hero's damage rolls until his next turn (so the penalty applies also if he uses First Strike or other similar Edges before his next turn). This Edge cannot be combined with a Wild Attack.

Loincloth Hero/Bikini Heroine

Requirements: Wild Card, Novice, Agility d8+, Vigor d6+

Comics, movies and books always depict bare-chested barbarians fighting hordes of enemies without suffering the slightest scratch. They also show scantily dressed amazons engaging in savage melees with bug-eyed creatures and finishing their fight with no more than tousled hair.

This Edge allows you to emulate this cinematic way of fighting. A hero or heroine with this Edge can make a free soak roll for each wounding attack as long as they are unarmored. To get the bonus, a character must have no torso armor on (shields are allowed). If he wants, he can wear bracers, greaves or a helm, but these are only cosmetic, granting no armor bonus. A hero can not have this Edge and the Iron Jaw Edge.

Loincloth God/Bikini Goddess

Requirements: Wild Card, Heroic, Dodge, Loincloth Hero/Bikini Heroine, Vigor d8+

While bare-chested, your hero is rarely threatened by minor attacks. As long as unarmored, the sheer power of his cool, barbaric appearance raises his Wild Die by one step when soaking wounds (usually from d6 to d8). In addition, once per session, he can add his Charisma, if positive, to a single Soak roll.

ONE HAND AND A HALF

Requirements: Seasoned, Agility d6+, Fighting d8+, Strength d6+

Your heroine has mastered the technique of fighting with a one-handed weapon using two hands. This versatile fighting style allows her to strike harder blows or perform nimble defenses. When fighting with a one-handed weapon at least of medium size (Str+d6 damage or greater), she can use it two handed. In this case, she cannot use a shield but gains one of the two following benefits: +1 to damage rolls *or* +1 Parry. The character can switch from a bonus to the other with a free action, but she must decide this at the beginning of her turn.

STRONG ARM

Requirements: Seasoned, Strength d6+, Shooting d6+ or Throwing d6+

Your character has an exceptionally powerful arm and this influences how far he can throw spears, sling projectiles, daggers, and other muscle-propelled distance weapons. This Edge applies to every ranged weapon that deals damage based on Strength, as a throwing axe or a sling. It doesn't work with fixed damage weapons, like bows.

It increases the range brackets of these weapons by 50% (round fractions down).

To keep the modified ranges consistent with the other weapons, first calculate Short range and then multiply it by 2 and by 4 to obtain Medium and Long ranges. So, a throwing axe (Range: 3/6/12), used with this Edge will have range brackets of 4/8/16, not 6/9/18.

TOOTH AND NAIL

Requirements: Veteran, Nerves of Steel

No matter how hard you punish this hero, each wound inflicted is only another reason to stand up and grin. The character receives +1 to damage rolls for each Wound he currently has, up to +2.

POWER EDGES

BEING LIKE WATER

Requirements: Novice, Enlightment d6+, Fighting d6+, Spirit d8+

For monks and other Enlightened individual the practice of martial arts is a true meditation technique that allows them to focus their inner powers at best. A few individuals reach a particular state in which certain fighting moves perfectly blend with one's inner concentration. Monks call this condition Being Like Water. A character taking this Edge must choose a particular Monk Weapon (unarmed attacks are considered a weapon for the purposes of this Edge) and a single Power he knows. When the hero is wielding this weapon and he scores a raise on the Enlightment roll activating the chosen Power, he reduces by one the cost of Power Points (as for the Wizard Edge).

If he wants, every time the character gets an advancement, he can choose to change the affected Power or weapon for free (but not both at the same time).

BINDING RITUAL

Requirements: Heroic, Knowledge (Arcana) d10+, Sorcery d10+, Smarts d10+

Through long incantations, a sorcerer with this Edge can make the effect of a spell of his choice permanent. He must choose a spell that can be retained, like *summon ally*, *armor* or *boost trait*, and then perform a Sorcery (−4) roll to successfully cast and bind the spell. He pays twice the basic cost of the spell. Casting such a spell is a very long procedure, requiring one hour per Power Point of the spell. Also, if the caster is interrupted, he must start from scratch.

The bound spell is considered permanent until the caster dies or decides to drop it. It isn't dropped when the caster loses concentration, falls unconscious or sleeps. As long as the Ritual of Binding is active, the caster doesn't recover the Power Points used to cast the spell. A sorcerer can have only one actively bound spell at any given time.

CHEMICAL TRADITION

Requirements: Seasoned, Lotusmastery d8+, Knowledge (Arcana) d8+, Smarts d6+

For many, Lotusmastery is an art, like painting, poetry or cooking, and the real master knows how to make each potion different.. A chemist, instead, follows the opposite approach, using accurate amounts of ingredients and a precise procedure that allow for a more standardized product and less wasted material. When scoring a success on a roll to make a potion, the Lotus master can create two batches of a Power, spending the Power Points only once. This cancels the additional effects of scoring a raise, unless the Lotus master scores two raises, in which case he creates two batches, both with the raise effect. To regain the Power Points spent, both batches must be used.

Example. *Kurasta, Lotus master with the Chemical Tradition Edge, creates a lotus concoction imbued with the Healing Power. He rolls 7, so he creates two concoctions ca-pable of healing a single Wound. Later, he tries again, rolling 8 and scoring a raise. This time too he creates two concoctions curing a single Wound.*

Several months later, thanks to the bonus granted by a laboratory, he produces another healing potion, rolling a mighty 13! Two raises! This time Kurasta produces two batches of healing Lotus, each of them capable of curing two Wounds.

DEMON HUNTER

Requirements: Seasoned, Enlightment d8+, Holy Warrior

This character is devoted to fighting the undead. He has learnt ancient techniques to defeat spirits and to imprison a defeated demon, so that its energy can be used against other creatures of the same type. For this reason he receives +2 to Knowledge (Arcana) and Knowledge (Religion) rolls, on demon-related topics.

In addition, whenever a Wild Card with the Undead or Demon Monstrous Ability dies within 6" of the Demon Hunter, as a free action, he is allowed an opposed Spirit roll between his own Spirit and the creature's Spirit. If the Demon Hunter wins, he manages to capture the demon's soul and store it inside an object (usually a weapon, an amulet, or something similar), called the Vessel. The Vessel can be used by the Demon Hunter or sold to someone else.

The owner of the Vessel gains a special Bennie that can be used only against creatures with the Undead or Demon Monstrous Ability. This Bennie is conserved between sessions, until it is spent. Once the Bennie is spent, the trapped demon's energy is used and the vessel loses all its supernatural powers.

A Demon Hunter can bind a single imprisoned soul at any given time, plus one every two Ranks above Seasoned (so, two souls at the Heroic Rank).

IMPRESSIVE AURA

Requirements: Seasoned, Sorcery d6+, Spirit d6+

Sorcery is widely feared in the Dread Sea Dominions and the simple threat of evoking the dark forces is often enough to make a strong warrior tremble.

A character with this Edge can let her magical powers emerge for a brief moment, in order to scare an enemy. For example, her eyes might glow or she might cast a curse in the name of old, forbidden gods. The character is encouraged to describe how her magic nature surfaces and how she uses it to scare others.

In gaming terms, whenever she wants, she can use Sorcery instead of Intimidation but, if a 1 is rolled on the skill die, regardless of the Wild Die, the action costs 1 Power Point. Note that the skill substitution only refers to actual rolls, it doesn't affect Edge requirements. So, if an Edge requires Intimidation d6+, the character must have that Intimidation skill level in order to take the new Edge.

IMPROVED IMPRESSIVE AURA

Requirements: Heroic, Impressive Aura, Sorcery d8+, Spirit d8+

The curses of the sorcerer and the sheer force of her malevolence are now strong enough to affect the world and to actually harm enemies. When winning an Intimidation-based Test of Will with a raise, the Shaken result inflicted is considered as actual damage (so two Shaken results cause a Wound). The use of this Edge always costs a Power Point, but only if she manages to win the opposed roll with a raise (or rolls 1 on the Sorcery die, as per the Impressive Aura Edge).

LOTUS RESERVE

Requirements: Seasoned, Knowledge (Arcana) d6+, Lotusmastery d8+, Smarts d8+

Once per session, a Lotus master can spend a Bennie and declare that he has "just the right potion" for the situation. In gaming terms, it means he can create a Lotus concoction as a free action and ignoring the normal preparation time. In story terms, he has prepared the potion before and he only has to take it out of his bag.

He performs the arcane roll when activating the Edge and, if the Power doesn't work or he fumbles, the effects are applied immediately (the potion seemed good when prepared, but it turns out to be faulty or dangerous when used). The hero spends no Power Points for the potion and the Power only has the basic duration. This Edge cannot be combined with the Chemical Tradition Edge.

PROFESSIONAL EDGES

AMAZON

Requirements: Novice, Fighting d6+, Notice d6+, Strength d6+, Must be female

A woman is usually physically weaker than a man and this is why she is underestimated by men in close combat. This is the first lesson an Amazon learns, and the most important one: be opportunistic and turn your apparent weakness into strength, using all the opportunities your opponent gives.

An Amazon has +1 Parry and, whenever an opponent attacking her rolls 1 on the Fighting die, regardless of the Wild Die, she is entitled an immediate free Fighting attack against him. The additional attack can only be used once per round.

These advantages only work against male opponents and this Edge can only be taken by women.

The GM has the final judgment on when this Edge applies. For example, it can work against a giant ape but not against a man-shaped living statue, because the statue isn't a real "male" and doesn't consider women as being weaker.

DANCING WITCH/WARLOCK

Requirements: Novice, Agility d8+, Arcane Background (Sorcery), Vigor d6+, must be of Ivory Savannah Tribes origin

Rhythm runs in the veins of the black people from the south of the Dominions. A dancing witch (or warlock) is capable of fueling her magic with the rapture of her savage dance. In gaming terms, instead of paying the Power Point cost of maintaining a spell, she can dance. In this case, dancing counts as an action (causing a multiaction penalty to every other action performed in the meantime) and adds the "the caster must dance" trapping to the Power. A Dancing Witch can only dance to maintain a single Power at a given time. The dance can last indefinitely but it is usually very tiring, so a Dancing Witch must make a Vigor roll when she stops dancing and for every hour of continuous dancing. In case of failure, she suffers a level of Fatigue. When she becomes Exhausted, the spell is obviously broken.

LOWLIFE

Requirements: Novice, Smarts d4+, Streetwise d6+, Stealth d4+, Persuasion d4+

This character is a professional criminal. He can be a thief, a beggar, a smuggler, an assassin or whatever other type of criminal. He always knows where to find the right people, information, or pieces of equipment in the shady world of crime. He gains +2 to Streetwise and Persuasion rolls in a criminal environment. In addition, he can look for two additional Rare Items instead of one between sessions (see Gear section).

MONK

Requirements: Novice, Enlightment d8+, Spirit d8+

Monks are men of faith and humble followers of the Path of Enlightenment. They take vows of poverty, so a character taking this Edge automatically acquires the Poverty Hindrance. Monks are usually respected, gaining +1 to Persuasion rolls.

Monks can embrace either the contemplative philosophy or the militant philosophy. A character taking this Edge must choose a philosophy and cannot change it later.

Contemplative. To these monks violence is the last resort of the incompetents and they shun it in all its forms. They automatically receive the Pacifism (Major) Hindrance. If duly followed, their beliefs give them strong and pure souls. Contemplative monks gain +2 to the *dispel* and *banish* Powers. Their deep wisdom also allows them to use Spirit instead of Smarts for Common Knowledge rolls and Spirit instead of Vigor for Soak rolls.

Militant. A militant monk is more involved in the world than his contempla-

tive counterpart. He is a skilled martial artist and spellcaster. The militant monk can activate a Power with range Self without suffering a multi-action penalty. A militant monk may only attack with bare hands or a Monk weapon (see Gear chapter on page 89) to apply the effects of this Edge. Militant monk's Powers with Range Touch are considered Range Self instead.

PRIEST/PHILOSOPHER

Requirements: Novice, Knowledge (Religion) d8+, Smarts d6+, Spirit d6+

Priests are ministers of the gods. They are very different, depending on the divinities they worship. A wicked priestess of Hordan, for example, has nothing in common with a pious follower of the Divine Couple or a militant Iron Priest of Hulian.

A character must choose a specific deity when taking this Edge. The deity can be one of the major gods described in the Book of Lore or a minor one invented by the player. In the latter case, the player must provide the Game Master with a brief description of the cult, but this is only background information, as the type of god doesn't affect the Edge's mechanics.

A follower of the Path of Enlightenment can also take this Edge. He doesn't worship a specific deity but is a sincere disciple of the ancient doctrine. He is called a Philosopher and his Edge works in the same way.

Whatever faith they follow, priests share some similarities. They are well versed in theology, so they have +2 to Knowledge (Religion) rolls and, as they are respected figures, they have +1 to Persuasion rolls.

As said before, the gods don't grant their worshippers supernatural abilities. To possess such abilities, they must take the dangerous path of sorcery. Yet, prayer itself might prove useful. Maybe the gods really exist and sometimes hear the pleas of their followers or, even if they don't exist, the act of praying brings consolation and inspiration to the mortals.

As a free action, a Priest can pray his god for help. This requires a Spirit roll. In case of success, he is rewarded with a Bennie. This can be done as many times as the caster wants, but every attempt after the first, in the same session, suffers a cumulative −4. If a 1 is rolled on the Spirit die, regardless of the Wild Die, the gods are annoyed by the prayers: the character immediately loses a Bennie and cannot use this Edge again during the current session. Also, the gods don't forget: if the hero has no Bennie left and owes the gods one, he starts the next session with one Bennie less.

POISONER

Requirements: Novice, Healing d6+, Smarts d6+, Stealth d6+, Streetwise d6+

This character isn't a real Lotustmaster but he studied alchemy enough to be able to make poisons. He can use the *poison* Power with Smarts as arcane skill, and has a number of Power Points equal to half his Smarts die plus 1/Rank. So, a Seasoned hero with Smarts d8 has 4+4=6 Power

Points, which can only be used for the *poison* Power.

SAGE

Requirements: Novice, Scholar, Investigation d8+, Smarts d8+, must be literate

This hero spent years studying in the Great Library of Syranthia or another great center of learning, where he read a lot of books and became acquainted with various fields of knowledge, including very obscure ones.

When fighting a creature, he can make a Common Knowledge roll to remember one of her Special Abilities.

In addition, once per session, the player can invent a useful piece of knowledge, remembered from her studies, that helps her or the group in the current situation. This knowledge cannot contradict the consolidated background.

If the piece of information is accepted by the Game Master and doesn't disrupt the plot, it grants a bonus of +4 to a single roll or automatically solves a specific problem (GM's decision). Particularly good ideas should be rewarded with a Bennie too.

Example 1. Clamides of Askerios, a Sage woman, is in the thick of the jungle with her close friend, Shangor the Barbarian. Shangor is Incapacitated, due to various wounds suffered while fighting a giant snake. Clamides has a meager Healing d4 skill and no adequate equipment, so she fears she won't be able to patch up her friend up.

This is the time to remember some useful knowledge. Martha, who plays as Clamides, states that her heroine has spotted a patch of violet mushrooms, that, as she remembers from her past studies, are perfect for healing

wounds. The Game Master accepts the statement, and Clamides receives +4 to a single Healing roll.

Example 2. Clamides and Shangor are travelling in the southern deserts, when some hostile Red Nomads appear on the horizon. There are a dozen of them; surely too many even for the mighty barbarian. So it is time to make another statement. Martha declares that Clamides knows that Red Nomads consider blind men holy figures. So the learned woman quickly tells Shangor to tear a piece of his loincloth and cover his eyes with it, pretending to be blind. The Game Master deems the stratagem worthy of resolving the situation, avoiding a dangerous fight that isn't fundamental for the plot. The nomads approach the heroes and, spotting an apparently blind man, leave an offering of water and food, before departing quickly. Martha receives a Bennie too.

TREASURE HUNTER

Requirements: Novice, Agility d8+, Notice d6+, Lockpicking d6+, Smarts d6+, Streetwise d6+

This hero is an expert in exploring ancient ruins to retrieve precious artifacts and other valuables, so she knows how to avoid the terrible traps put in place to guard these treasures.

She gains +2 to Notice rolls to spot traps, to Agility rolls to avoid them, and to rolls to disarm these dangerous mechanisms. In addition, she always knows how and where to sell her loot, obtaining better prices than others. Hence, her maximum Savings are increased by 25%.

TRAINED THROWER

Requirements: Novice, Agility d6+, Shooting or Throwing d8+, Vigor d6+

Crossbows aren't a common weapon in the Dread Sea Dominions, so the standard ranged troops are bowmen, slingers, and javelin throwers. The effective use of these weapons requires long and intensive training and can be usually learnt only by professional militaries.

A character taking this Edge must choose from among a bow, sling or javelin, which from now becomes his professional weapon.

His training is intensive, so his muscles are perfectly used to the task they must accomplish: stretching the bowstring, swinging the sling or delivering the javelin. The character's Strength is considered a step higher in relation to the minimum requirements of his professional weapon, but this doesn't affect damage.

A Trained Thrower keeps his cool even in the direst situations. He knows that, when his arrow breaks in his hand and the charging cavalry is only one hundred paces away, the right thing to do is to take another arrow and shoot it — not to escape and die trampled by the enemy's horses.

For this reason, when using his professional weapon, whenever he rolls 1 on the Shooting die, regardless of the Wild Die, he can freely reroll the Shooting or Throwing die (but not the Wild Die).

In addition, the character receives the following free gear: leather armor and his professional weapon (a bow, a war sling, or 5 javelins). Characters who want a composite bow or a Valk bow must pay the difference.

WEIRD EDGES

HELPER

Requirements: Seasoned, Notice d8+, Persuasion d6+, Smarts d8+

Some people are particularly good at helping, supporting and coordinating others. As an action, this character observes a friend within 6" and makes a Notice (–2) roll. If successful, she gives her fiend a useful hint. The next Trait roll of the friend, if performed before the end of the next round, receives a +1 bonus. This Edge cannot be used on arcane or knowledge skill rolls, unless the Helper also possesses that skill.

If the Helper rolls 1 on the Notice roll, she gives bad advice or simply her clever remarks unnerve the friend, who has –2 to his next action.

In addition, a Helper always gives +1 to the lead character in cooperative rolls (if she isn't the leading hero).

TEMPTRESS

Requirements: Novice, Charisma 4+, Persuasion d8+, Smarts d8+

There are women who make empires fall with their beauty and who can make a man's blood boil with a single glance from their long-lashed eyes. Your heroine is one of these striking personalities and has no remorse in using her beauty to influence others.

In gaming terms she has the *boost/lower trait* Power but can use it only on members of the opposite sex, friends or enemies.

She uses Persuasion as arcane skill and has Charisma + 1/Rank Power Points. So a Seasoned Temptress with Charisma +4 has 4+2=6 Power Points.

This isn't true magic, but only the effect of the temptress's behavior on others. She can make a man feel like a god or a worm, influencing his ego, so her power doesn't register as magic, but it can be dispelled with the *dispel* Power. The Temptress must

be visible and interact in some way with her target: speaking or giving him a long, eloquent look is enough.

This Edge is usually taken by women but nothing prevents males from choosing it.

WATCH YOUR BACK!

Requirements: Novice, Agility d6+, Notice d6+, Spirit d8+, Pace 6+

This heroine is used to being chased. Maybe she is an Outlaw with the city guards permanently at her heels, or she is running from a powerful Enemy. Whatever the reason, when the situation requires the character to get away quickly, she knows what to do.

At the start of every Chase sequence, regardless of whether she is pursuing or being pursued, she receives a free Bennie.

As a professional fugitive, she has also developed a knack for finding the nearest exit of a building. When she is in a labyrinth, dungeon, ruin, cavern, house or any enclosed area, she is allowed a Spirit (–2) roll to instinctively find her way to the nearest exit. Be warned: the shortest path is necessarily the safest. The ability to find a way out doesn't work outdoor.

CHAPTER 3:
MAGIC

The magic of *Beasts and Barbarians* isn't of the high fantasy type. In the Dread Sea Dominions you won't find wizards throwing fireballs or turning into dragons. Magic tends to be more subtle, and usually dark, but by no means less powerful.

In this section you'll find all the rules you need to create a Lotus master, a sorcerer, or a follower of the Path of the Enlightenment. In addition, a new Power, specific for this setting, is described.

Powers and creatures marked with a (N) are new, and they are found later in this chapter.

GAME MASTER'S ADVICE: A SWORD AND SORCERY WORLD

Beasts and Barbarians is a setting that leans heavily on swordplay. Magic is powerful and feared, and must cause wonder when used. For this reason, each party should include no more than a single hero with the Arcane Background.

Magic can be very powerful but the true masters of the mystical arts are sorcerers and monks, who are several hundreds of years old and more suitable as adversaries and patrons of the party rather than as playing characters.

Heroes can certainly be mages, but they are practitioners, not real masters. This is why the New Power Edge is limited and can be taken only once per Rank.

If you want to create more traditional fantasy stories, feel free to ignore these restrictions.

ARCANE BACKGROUNDS

LOTUSMASTERY

Arcane Skill: Lotusmastery (Smarts)
Starting Power Points: 10
Starting Powers: 3

Available Powers: *barrier, blast, blind, boost/lower trait, burst, confusion, detect/conceal arcana, dispel, entangle, environmental protection, fear, healing, invisibility, light, obscure, poison (N), puppet, slow, slumber, smite, succor, stun, warrior gift, zombie.*

Lotus masters are skilled men who spend their life studying the incredible effects of Lotus, the strange plant appeared in the Dominions after the fall of the Dread Star. Many Lotus varieties exist: Gray, Red, Green and so on. The color usually identifies a particular type, but different parts of the plant (flower, root, pollen and so on) are used in potions to achieve different effects, allowing a virtually endless number of combinations.

The Lotus cannot be used in its pure form: it is toxic and, in some cases, even lethal. Instead, it must be refined and mixed with other ingredients, and special rites and spells must be recited to produce a batch of powder, a vial of elixir, pills, or other alchemical concoctions.

To create a concoction, a Lotus master needs his Lotus bag, a sort of miniature lab containing raw materials and basic tools. The process requires one hour per Rank of the Power he wants to imbue (so a Seasoned Power requires two hours of work).

At the end of the preparation time, the Lotus master rolls on the Lotusmastery skill and pays the necessary Power Points. These

Power Points aren't recovered until the potion is used or destroyed (burnt, dispelled and so on). Then, the Lotus master regains his Power Points at the normal rate.

If the skill roll is successful, a Lotus potion is prepared. It lasts indefinitely, until used, can be taken by any living being with an action. So a Pearly Lotus of Relief, a sweet potion that cures wounds, works exactly as the *healing* Power, while a Gray Lotus of Hollow Dreams, a powder with terrible hallucinogenic effects, induces *fear* in the individual targeted with it.

Raises work as normal, increasing the effects of the Power.

Before a scenario starts, a Lotus master can choose to prepare as many Lotus potions as he wants, ignoring time requirements. It is assumed he had enough time to prepare what he wished.

Range: The Lotus must come into contact with the target to work. So spells with a range of Attribute (as Smarts x2), Sight, Self or Touch require the Lotus to be ingested, injected, or delivered with a Touch Attack.

Ingestion is self explanatory: the potion must be drunk or eaten (not necessarily as a voluntary action).

To inject a Lotus potion, the target must be at least Shaken by damaging attack (a dagger scratch, or something similar).

Touch needs a Touch Attack (+2 to the Fighting roll).

Despite being more difficult to accomplish, ingestion or injection are more potent, especially for offensive Powers. The skill roll receives a +2, but only on opposed rolls.

The exact mode of administration is decided by the Lotus master upon creating the concoction.

Powers with range brackets mean that the Lotus must be put into a vial to be thrown at the target. It is done with a Throwing roll and the ranges are reduced to 3/6/12. Alternatively, a concentrated quantity of Lotus can be delivered with a blowgun dart (a Shooting roll using the blowgun ranges: 5/10/20).

Duration: Extra Points can be spent as usual to increase duration.

Laboratory: A Lotus master with access to a good laboratory, something bigger and better stocked than his basic Lotus bag, gains +2 to his rolls. Access to an even bigger facility, like the House of an Alchemist of Gis or another fully equipped workshop, grants a +4 bonus.

Backlash: A Lotus master rolling 1 on the skill die during the creation of his concoction inhales dangerous fumes or poisons himself in some way. He suffers an automatic Wound.

HERO'S JOURNAL:
LOTUS CONCOCTIONS

The Pharmacologia Segreta, the traditional book of Lotus recipes studied by every Lotus master, states the names of concoctions according to the standard convention: "Color Lotus of Something", e.g. Orange Lotus of the Phoenix, Violet Lotus of the Wailing Widow, and so on. This is the common way to define Lotus potions, but several outstanding Lotus masters deliberately give non-standard names to their elixirs to leave their mark. So there might be potions called Giscamon's Vendetta or Food for the Orphans.
Savage Worlds' use of trapping lets you create a virtually limitless number of Lotus potions. Here are some examples but the players and Game Masters can obviously create their own.

Mode of Delivery. *Ingestion, injection, and touch are the most common ways. See the Lotusmastery description for further details.*

Inhalation. *An inhaled power must be breathed in. It affects all targets in a Small Burst Template. Holding your breath is usually enough to avoid it, so opposed rolls to resist it have +1.*

Venom based. *Venom based concoctions are very subtle, but don't affect non-living targets. For example a venom based Blast can't be used to destroy door.*

Explosive. *A Lotus concoction can be explosive, dealing +1 damage or acquiring the Heavy Weapon Special Ability. However, it is quite dangerous to handle. If a roll is required to deliver it (for example a Throwing roll for a vial) and a 1 is rolled on the skill die, regardless of the Wild Die, the concoction explodes before use causing damage to the user.*

EXAMPLES OF LOTUSMASTERY TRAPPINGS USE

Smite **(Yellow Lotus of the Demons).** *When poured onto a weapon's blade, this foul-smelling liquid covers it in a persistent flame.*

Burst **(Purple Lotus of Pain).** *This dangerous powder, made to be thrown at targets, is a strong acid that, when in contact with the skin, lungs or other organic material, corrodes it.*

Dispel **(Gray Lotus of Panacea).** *This sweet potion can eliminate almost all the effects of other Lotus concoctions and foul magic, if drunk in time.*

Lower trait (Smarts) **(Wine of the Merchant).** *An odorless and tasteless liquid. The merchants from Jalizor mix it with wine and give it to potential customers during transactions.*

Warrior gift **(Berserk)** *(Blood Lotus of the Savannah Warriors). A foul-tasting potion made by the Lotus masters of the Ivory Savannah Tribes before a major battle.*

SORCERY

Arcane Skill: Sorcery (Smarts)
Starting Power Points: 10
Starting Powers: 2

Available Powers: *armor, barrier, beast friend, blast, boost/lower trait, bolt, confusion, darksight, deflection, disguise, drain power points, draining touch(N), detect/conceal arcana, divination, entangle, fear, havoc, intangibility, invisibility, obscure, puppet, slumber, smite, speak language, stun, summon ally.*

Sorcery is a very dangerous type of magic. The sorcerer, through arcane invocations and unholy rites, asks the intervention of forgotten divinities and powers that man isn't meant to know. These entities are usually generous toward the sorcerer, but they also very demanding. Many of those who meddle with dark magic end up with their minds destroyed and their souls eaten by creatures of unimaginable horror.

Evil entities are always eager for nourishment, so a sorcerer can decide to willingly give them a little of his living energy in exchange for extra power. This is done by self inflicting a Wound to gain 2 Power Points or +1 to a Sorcery roll. These wounds represent energy sacrificed to dark powers, cannot be Soaked and can only be healed naturally. The penalty caused by these wounds applies *after* the Sorcery roll they are inflicted for.

Sorcerers also have access to the Soul Drain Edge, with lower requirements than usual.

Backlash: A sorcerer who rolls 1 on the Sorcery die regardless of the Wild Die, has somehow displeased the evil entities he works with to gain his powers. He must roll on the Sorcery Critical Failures Table to discover what happens to him.

SORCERY CRITICAL FAILURES TABLE (D20)

1	**Evil Twist.** *The character's body is permanently twisted. His nails become long and claw-like, his teeth elongated and sharp, or whatever the Game Master decides. He permanently loses 1 Charisma point. On the plus side, his unarmed attacks deal +1 damage from now on. If the hero is exposed to this effect more than once, he only loses another Charisma point, but receives no further damage bonus.*
2-4	**Dark Energies.** *The caster's body is overwhelmed by an otherworldly force. He is Shaken for 1d6 rounds and loses one step of the Sorcery die for 24 hours.*
5-8	**Energy Sap.** *The caster must make a Vigor roll or be Incapacitated. Even in case of success, he suffers a level of Fatigue, which is recovered after an hour.*
9-12	**Not For The Human Mind.** *The caster has a brief glimpse of what the entity he is contacting REALLY is, and this can shatter the hardest of minds. He must make a Fear (−4) roll.*
13-15	**Devils' Joke.** *The spell works as if cast with a raise, but the evil entities change target: a positive spell affects an enemy; a negative one affects the caster or an ally.*
16-18	**Manifestation of Unholy Gods.** *The evil gods appear in all their terrible might, releasing a wave of pain and terror! Put a Large*

Burst Template on the caster. Whoever is within the template, caster included, suffers 3d6 damage and must make a Fear roll.

19 **Satiate My Hunger!** *One of the evil forces the sorcerer is contacting decides to take away some of the character's living energy. His Vigor die drops by one step. Every week the sorcerer is allowed a Vigor (–4) roll to regain it. In case of critical failure on one of these rolls, the loss is permanent.*

20 **Soul Drain.** *A part of the sorcerer's soul is snatched and devoured by evil entities. His Spirit die drops permanently by one step.*

HERO'S JOURNAL: THE ART OF SORCERY

Sorcery powers, usually spells or incantations of some sort, tend to be quite different from one another, depending on the source of the magic. A Tricarnian demon evoker's bolt, for example, is quite different from the bolt of a Ivory Savannah Tribe dancer witch. For this reason, trappings are very important in defining sorcery spells.

Always consider the basic rule of sorcery: the evil entities that grant their power to the warlock ask for something backing return (adoration, pain, entertainment or sacrifices) and their gifts always have a hidden cost.

As a rule of thumb, every sorcerer knows a single trapping for each of his spells.

New trappings for known spells are good rewards for sorcerer player characters. A hero can master a new trapping of a spell he already knows with a Smarts roll, if he finds a teacher or a book of some sort explaining it.

Here are some examples of trappings fitting the sword and sorcery style as well as related rule modifications, when needed. You should feel free to add others of your creation.

Dark Taint. *The power is inherently evil and somehow corrupts the recipient. In addition to the normal effects, the target suffers a Minor Hindrance for the duration of the spell.*

Fearful. *Simply seeing the spell in action can make a strong man tremble. The target and all those witnessing the spell suffer −1 to Spirit rolls for the duration of the spell.*

It is Only a Clever Trick. *For primitive cultures, as those of the Dread Sea Dominions, anything unknown is classified as magic. This is why ventriloquism, hypnosis, higher technology and very good sleight of hand are usually considered supernatural powers. A power that is only a clever trick usually has a weak point of some type.*

Object Required. *The power is linked to an object of some type. The object must be quite easy to replace (maximum cost: 10 Moons/Power Rank) and without it the spell cannot be cast. As compensation, spells that require an object have their basic duration increased by one round.*

Verbal. *The magic requires the caster to speak. So, the spell cannot be used if the sorcerer cannot speak or wants to remain inconspicuous.*

EXAMPLES OF SORCERY
TRAPPINGS IN USE
Here follow some examples of Powers with their trappings.

Summon ally (**Call of the Eaters**). *This evil spell requires the sorcerer to blow into a horn made with the bone of a beast* devoured by insects. The air from the mage's lungs turns into a swarm of hungry locusts (a small Swarm).

Boost/lower Trait (**Corrupt**). *The sorcerer can temporary infect the target with the dark taint of the supernatural creatures he serves. Every boosted or lowered trait manifests itself as a horrid physical mutation (such as bulging muscles for raised Strength, suckers on the hands for raised Climbing, festering wounds for lowered Vigor, and so on). This causes the target to receive the Ugly Hindrance while under the effect of the spell.*

Entangle (**Hands of the Dead**). *The sorcerer encourages the spirits of the dead to bring the poor victims of this spell to their dark kingdom. Cold arms surface from the ground and grab the targets, restraining them. Their touch is so cold and terrifying that the victims suffer an additional −1 to Spirit rolls for the duration of the spell.*

Deflection (**I am not here!**). *The sorcerer using this spell seems to have been hit by his enemy's blow but he is actually a yard away, staring at the attacker with magnetic eyes. It is a sort of hypnotic suggestion that prevents the attackers from hitting the target. After each failed attack, the target can freely move 1" away from the attacker. As a drawback, the power has only a Self range and can be avoided by simply closing one's eyes (so, the Blind Hindrance applies). As it isn't a "real" Deflection, the defensive bonus doesn't count as armor bonus against area attacks.*

Fear (**Unspeakable Name of Hordan**). *The caster knows the real name of the evil deity Hordan, so abominable that hearing it is enough for the people to fall into an abyss of primeval fear. If the caster cannot speak or the name cannot be heard, the spell doesn't work.*

PATH OF ENLIGHTENMENT

Arcane Skill: Enlightment (Spirit)
Starting Power Points: 15
Starting Powers: 1

Available Powers: *analyze foe(N), armor, banish, boost trait, darksight, deflection, detect arcana/conceal arcana, dispel, environmental protection, farsight, fly, invisibility, legerdemain(N), pummel, quickness, smite, speed, telekinesis, wall walker, warrior's gift.*

The followers of the Path of Enlightenment are usually monks from the far country of Lhoban. Through discipline, intensive training and meditation, they are capable of incredible feats. They maintain that their powers aren't truly magical and any man, with the right training and true devotion to self improvement, can achieve the same abilities.

But, in truth, many years of training are necessary to follow the Path of Enlightenment. That's why very few of these skilled individuals exist.

The Path of Enlightenment Powers usually manifest themselves as personal abilities, not as true spells. So, all the powers, except *banish*, *detect arcana*, *dispel* and *pummel* have a range of Self.

Backlash: An Enlightened One who rolls 1 on the Enlightment Skill dies, regardless of the Wild Die, temporarily loses his spiritual balance. He is Shaken and all his Enlightenment rolls suffer −2 for an hour.

HERO'S JOURNAL:
THE WAY OF LIGHT

The followers of the Path of Enlightenment usually gain powers consisting of incredible martial art techniques and amazing feats of the mind, achieved through endless hours of concentration and careful training.

Here are some examples of trappings adequate for the Path of Enlightenment.

Increased Awareness. *Perception is the key to this power. The Enlightened One is capable of seeing and manipulating very subtle energies. A power based on an increased awareness trapping grants +1 to the first Notice roll made during the duration of the spell.*

Martial Moves. *This Power is linked to a special combat move that must be performed by the caster in order to activate it. The Power requires the caster to be able to move freely; so, in certain cases, it cannot be activated in an inconspicuous way.*

Meditation Required. *The Enlightened One needs to be deeply focused to awaken this power. It means that the Power requires a round of intense concentration before it can be cast. As minor compensation, the character receives +2 to avoiding loss of concentration while maintaining the Power.*

Past Lives. *The source of this Power is the inner, unconscious knowledge gained by the character during his past lives, which are usually inaccessible. If the character scores a raise casting the spell, he sees a glimpse of his past incarnation, gaining +1 to Smarts and Smarts based skills in the current and next round.*

EXAMPLES OF ENLIGHTENMENT TRAPPINGS IN USE

Here follow some examples of Powers with their trappings.

Fly **(Move of the Air Warrior).** *Through this ancient technique the Enlightened One is capable of violating the laws of gravity, performing incredible jumps and similar feats, but at the end of the round he must always be on solid ground. As minor compensation, if attacking an enemy on the ground from a flying position, he gains +1 to Fighting rolls.*

Boost Trait (Healing) **(Gentle Pressure).** *The Enlightened One is capable of perceiving the altered flow of energy in a wounded being and to refocus it with the simple touch of his hands, thus helping the healing process. The altered state of perception caused by the Power also grants +1 to Notice rolls.*

Warrior gift (**Memory of the Past Lives**). *Each life is only the prosecution of a past life, through an infinite chain of reincarnations that end only with the final Enlightenment. Most cannot remember their past lives but the Enlightened One can, and through this power he "awakens" an ability possessed in one of his previous incarnations. If he scores a raise on the activation roll, he gains +1 to Smarts and Smarts based skill rolls in the current and next round.*

Pummel (**Stomp of the Master**). *Through the sheer strength of his soul, the Enlightened One can make the ground tremble by simply stomping his foot. Before releasing this terrible blow, the Enlightened One must concentrate for a full round.*

MODIFIED POWERS

Summon Ally
Rank: Novice
Power Points: 3+
Range: Smarts
Duration: 3 (1/Round) or Special
Trappings: Evocation, burning herbs, sacrifices.

This Power allows the caster to summon a powerful Extra loyal to him. In *Beasts and Barbarians* this power works in a slightly different way from to the one in the *Savage Worlds Deluxe*.

On a success, the ally is placed at any point within the range of the power. On a raise, the ally is more durable and is a Henchman.

A summoned ally acts on the initiative card of the caster and gets an immediate action as soon as it is summoned.

A character may learn this spell while of Novice Rank, but he cannot summon more powerful allies until he attains the appropriate Rank. The cost in Power Points depends on the type of ally the character wishes to summon. Use the Summon Ally table as a guideline for unlisted creatures. By taking this Power, a caster learns the ritual to summon a single type of creature, and automatically learns another one each time he achieves a new Rank. Rituals for evoking additional, very powerful creatures are usually contained in ancient, forbidden tomes, and finding them might be the goal of an adventure.

A caster of sufficient Rank to summon more powerful allies may choose to summon additional lower Rank allies instead, at the same cost. For each decrease in Rank, he gains one additional ally. For example, a Veteran caster could spend 5 Power Points to summon one Veteran-Rank-allowed ally, two Seasoned-Rank-allowed allies, or three Novice-Rank-allowed allies. Allies summoned by a single casting must all be of the same type.

A Backlash on the Summon Ally Table, in addition to the roll on the Sorcery Critical Failures, causes the creature to be evoked, but it is free from the caster's control and usually malevolent toward the sorcerer. In this case, the evoked creature doesn't disappear when the spell ends and it must be killed or *banished*.

Special: When not in combat, the caster can summon an ally and ask it to perform a single, non-combat task. The task must be related to the creature's nature or abilities. So, a Shadow Bat can be asked to act as a mount, a Twisted Servant to dig a passage through a blocked tunnel, a Demonic Mastiff to track someone, and so on. The task cannot take more than a day per caster's Rank to be completed. When the task is accomplished, the creature disappears and the spell ends. Casting the spell in this way requires five minutes per Rank of the creature summoned, and costs double the basic cost. The spell doesn't need to be maintained, but the caster doesn't recover the Power Points spent until the spell ends.

If during the task the creature is forced into combat, the spell switches to standard mode and the caster must pay the maintenance cost for the rounds of combat the creature is involved in.

Summon Ally

Cost	Rank	Ally
3	Novice	Fighting Bird (N), Keronian Imp (N), Twisted Servant (N), Wolf
4	Seasoned	Dire Wolf, Spirit of the Betrayer (N), Snake (Venomous), Swarm
5	Veteran	Ancestor Ghost (N), Demonic Mastiff (N), Snake (Constrictor), Giant Spider
6	Heroic	Fanged Ape (N), Shadow Bat (N), Bear
7	Legendary	Giant Worm, Singer Demon (N)

NEW POWERS

ANALYZE FOE

Rank: Novice
Power Points: 1 – 2
Range: Smarts x 2
Duration: 3 (1/round)
Trappings: Mystical sense, spiritual advice, gestalt knowledge.

Knowledge is power. Being able to judge the strength of a foe before engaging him in combat can be highly advantageous.

The character makes an arcane skill roll opposed by the target's Spirit. On a success, he gains a +1 bonus to Trait rolls to directly affect the target, and the target suffers a –1 penalty to Trait rolls to directly affect the caster. With a raise, the effect is increased to +2 and –2 for both. In addition, for 2 Power Points, a success allows the caster to learn of a single Immunity, Invulnerability, or Weakness of the target (if one exists), and a raise allows the knowledge of two.

DRAINING TOUCH

Rank: Seasoned
Power Points: 3
Range: Self
Duration: 3 (1/round)
Trappings: Dehydration, poison, black crackling energy around hand, disease. Mages have more ways to kill a foe than blasting him with balls of fire. The most insidious mages can kill with a casual touch.

This spell makes the touch of the caster deadly. After casting the spell, the mage delivers his draining touch on a successful touch attack (+2 Fighting). Victims must make a Vigor roll (at –2 if the mage scored a raise when casting) or suffer a level of Fatigue. Normally, these Fatigue levels recover at one per 5 minutes, but if the target rolls a 1 on his Vigor die, regardless of the Wild Die, he must recover as "normal" based on the trappings of the power (dehydration requires water, poison/disease may require healing, and so on). If the trapping has no specific recovery, it takes one hour to recover a Fatigue level.

LEGERDEMAIN

Rank: Novice
Power Points: 1
Range: Smarts
Duration: Instant
Trappings: Mimicking action, briefly summoned spirit, astral bi-location.

Legerdemain allows the character to perform a single action at range he would normally be capable of doing in person. If the action would require a Trait roll, then the caster rolls the lower of that Trait or his arcane skill to both activate the power and determine the results of the action. If the action does not require a Trait roll, then his arcane skill is used normally.

Casting *legerdemain* is a normal action, but the action performed through the use of it is considered a free action (existing free actions like speaking are unchanged). However the caster is still limited to not duplicating the same action in a round, so it is impossible to cast another spell via legerdemain.

The power does not create or duplicate the effects of any gear or magical effects upon the caster, but in all other ways, the action is treated exactly as if the caster were performing the action himself at the location.

For example, a Fighting attack does his normal unarmed Strength damage, even if the caster is holding a dagger with *smite* on it.

POISON

Rank: Novice
Power Points: 2 or more
Range: Self
Duration: Special
Trappings: Lotus potion.

Poisons are the most notorious and probably most insidious weapon of the Lotus masters. A poisoned target must make a Vigor roll, opposed to the Arcane Skill of the poison maker, for every Time Interval (see below). If the Arcane skill roll is higher, the victim suffers a Wound and, in case of a raise, he suffers two.

If the victim wins the roll, he suffers no damage but the venom continues to work and he must repeat the procedure for the next Time Interval. If he wins with a raise or more, he manages to defeat the poison, which ceases to cause damage.

Time Interval: This is the frequency of the roll to check for the poison's effect. It can be Very Fast (1 round), Fast (1 minute), Normal (1 hour), Slow (1 day), and Very Slow (1 week). The poisoner assigns a Time Interval to his concoction when he creates it.

Mode of *Administration:* The most common ways to administer venom are ingestion, touch, or injection (see the Lotusmastery Arcane Background description on page 78 for their effects). Other methods (such as inhaling) can be used but they cause −4 to the Arcane Roll to create the poison, double the Power Points cost, and must be approved by the Game Master on a single case basis.

Non lethal poisons: The caster can decide that the poison is non lethal, causing Fatigue instead of a Wound. Fatigue is recovered as normal.

Healing: A skilled medic can help a poisoned friend. First, he must recognize the venom used, with a Lotusmastery or Healing (−4) roll. If he is successful, the rolls to contrast the poison can be made using the highest between the victim's Vigor and the medic's Healing skill.

Example. Kurasta, wicked poisoner with Lotusmastery d10, decides to create a powerful poison to kill his hated cousin. He wants to be sure that nobody can blame him for the man's death, so he prepares a concoction with Very Slow Time Interval, which must be ingested to take effect (+2 to opposed rolls).

It costs him 2 Power Points.

Then he puts the concoction, the Black Milk of the Widow, into his poisoner's ring and goes to a banquet with his hated relative. He spikes his cousin's wine and, seven days after, when Kurasta is far away, his cousin starts feeling ill. A few weeks later, he dies of a mysterious fever, leaving Kurasta the only heir of the family's wealth.

GEAR

The common currency of the Dread Sea Dominions is the Syranthian Moon. A Moon is equal to $1, so you can pick items from the Savage Worlds core rules without any need to do mathematical conversions.

The characters start with 500 Moons, plus 100 for every rank above Novice.

After the equipment has been purchased, all the unused money goes into the characters' Savings (see Setting Rules). During the creation phase, the players can ignore the Rare (see below) feature, as long as they justify strange items with their background.

This section presents the pieces of equipment available in Beasts and Barbarians. It isn't a comprehensive list. You can always refer to the Savage Worlds core rules for missing items.

Here follows a brief description of the special abilities and features of the gear in Beasts and Barbarians.

Monk Weapon. This type of weapon is traditionally used by monks, characters with the Monk Edge who receive a particular ability when using them (see the Monk Edge on page 71 for details). For non Monk characters they have no other ability. They are readily available only in Lhoban, while in other lands they are Rare.

Rare. A rare item isn't available unless the hero makes a Streetwise (−2) roll. As a rule of thumb, each hero can try to locate a single rare item between a scenario and the next. The roll can be cooperative.

MELEE WEAPONS TABLE

Type	Damage	Wgt	Cost	Notes
Unarmed				
Iron Fists	Str+d4/+1	1	25	See notes, may be a Monk Weapon
Poisoner Glove	Str	-	100	See notes
Blades				
Amazon Blade	Str+d6	4	900	+1 Parry, see notes
Caldeian Dagger	Str+d4	2	350	+1 Parry, see notes
Dagger	Str+d4	1	25	
Great Sword	Str+d10	12	400	Parry −1, 2 hands
Lhoban Sword	Str+d6	6	900	Monk Weapon, +1 Parry, see notes
Long Sword	Str+d8	8	300	Includes scimitars
Short Sword	Str+d6	4	200	Includes sabers
Axes and Mauls				
Axe	Str+d6	2	200	
Club	Str+d4	2	5	
Battle Axe	Str+d8	10	300	
Great Axe	Str+d10	15	500	AP 1, Parry −1, 2 hands
Maul	Str+d10	20	400	AP 2 vs. rigid armor, AP 1, Parry −1, 2 hands
War Club	Str+d8	12	200	
Warhammer	Str+d6	8	250	AP 1 vs. rigid armor
Exotic Weapons				
Combat Net	Special	2	200	Allows Tricks at Reach 2, see Notes
Whip	Str+1	1	100	Allows Tricks at Reach 2
Flails				
Three-Piece Rod	Str+d6	8	200	Monk Weapon, Ignores Shield Parry and Cover Bonus
Pole Arms				
Barbed Spear	Str+d6+1	5	250	+1 Parry, Allows Tricks at Reach 1, 2 hands, see notes
Buffalo Lance	Str+d8	10	300	AP 2 when charging, allows Tricks at Reach 2, 2 hands when used while dismounted
Moon Blade	Str+d8	12	400	Monk Weapon, allows Tricks at Reach 1, 2 hands

Staff	Str+d4	8	10		Monk Weapon, +1 Parry, allows Tricks at Reach 1, 2 hands, see notes
Sorcerer's Staff	Str+d4	8	500		+1 Parry, allows Tricks at Reach 1, 2 hands, see Notes, Rare
Spear	Str+d6	5	200		1 hand: allows Tricks at Reach 1, 2 hands: +1 Parry
Whispering Staff	Str+d4	8	400		Monk Weapon, +1 Parry, allows Tricks at Reach 1, 2 hands, see notes

RANGED WEAPONS TABLE

Type	Rng	Dmg	Cost	Wgt	Str	Notes
Amazon Blade	6/12/24	Str+d6	900	4	d8	AP 2, see notes
Atlatl	Special	-	200	2	d6	1 action to reload, see notes
Axe, throwing	3/6/12	Str	75	2	-	
Blowgun	5/10/20	Special	50	1	-	See notes
Bow	12/24/48	2d6	250	3	d6	
Combat Net	1/2/4	Special	50	4	d6	See notes
Composite Bow	12/24/48	2d6	500	5	d8	AP 1
Valk Compos. Bow	15/30/60	2d6+1	300	6	d8	AP 1, see notes
Chakram	4/8/16	Str+d4	100	1	-	See notes
Javelin	6/12/24	Str+d4	100	1	-	
Knife/Dagger	3/6/9	Str+d4	25	1	-	
Severed Head	4/8/16	Str+d4	200	2	-	See notes
Sling, hunting	4/8/16	Str+d4	10	1		
Sling, war	8/16/32	Str+d6	100	1	d6	
Spear	3/6/12	Str+d6	200	3	d6	1 hand: Reach 1, 2 hands: +1 Parry

AMMUNITION TABLE

Ammo	Weight	Cost	Notes
Arrow	1/5	1/2	-
Sling stone	1/10	1/20	Stones can also be found for free with a Notice roll and 1d10 minutes
Sling bullet, lead	1/5	1/2	AP 1
Sling bullet, hollow	1/3	5	−2 to Shooting rolls, see notes

ARMOR TABLE

Type	Armor	Weight	Cost	Notes
Bikini/Loincloth	0	-	0	See notes
Gladiator Armguard	0	5	100	+1 Parry, Str+d4, see notes
Light Armor Suit	+1	15	50	Covers Torso, Arms, Legs
Light Armor Shirt	+1	7	30	Cover Torso
Light Armor Bracers/Greaves	+1	4	10	Covers Arms or Legs
Medium Armor Suit	+2	25	300	Covers Torso, Arms, Legs
Medium Corselet	+2	13	200	Covers Torso
Medium Bracers/Greaves	+2	6	50	Covers Arms or Legs
Heavy Armor Suit	+3	60	800	Covers Torso, Arms, Legs
Heavy Corselet	+3	34	400	Covers Torso
Heavy Bracers/Greaves	+3	13	200	Covers Arms or Legs
Pot Helm	+3	4	75	50% vs. head shot
Half Armor	Special	-25%	-25%	See Notes
Reinforced Armor	Special	+50%	+50%	See Notes, Rare
Shields				
Small Shield	-	8	25	+1 Parry
Medium Shield	-	12	200	+1 Parry, +2 Armor vs. ranged shots
Tribal Shield	-	12	250	+1 Parry, +2 Armor vs. ranged shots, see notes
Large Shield	-	20	300	+2 Parry, +2 Armor vs. ranged shots

MUNDANE ITEMS TABLE

Item	Cost	Weight	Note
Special Adventuring Gear			
Armorer Kit	100	10	
Healer Kit	50	3	
Lock Picks	200	1	
Lotus Concoction	200/Rank	-	Rare
Poisoner Ring	300	-	Rare
Refined Lotus	50/PP	-	Rare
Silk Rope (10")	50	1	Rare
Tiger's Claws	200	2	Rare

Lotusmaster's Bag	100/Rank	-	

Animals and Tack

Horse, Cheap	150	-	
Horse, Common	300	-	
Horse, Good	750	-	Rare
Fighting Bird	500	-	Rare
Fighting Bird's Barding	200	-	+1 Armor, for Fighting Birds
Fighting Bird's Talons	200	-	+1 damage, for Fighting Birds
Mule or Donkey	100	-	
Saddle, Common	10	-	
Saddle, Elaborate	200	-	
Steppe Pony	500	-	Rare
War Buffalo	Not Sold	-	Rare

Special

Alchemical Laboratory	1500/300	50	Rare

VEHICLES TABLE

Vehicle	Acc/TS	Tough.	Crew	Cost	Notes
Cart	1/5	10(2)	1+6	500	
Chariot (2 horses)	5/15	8	1+1	1K+	
Chariot, war (2 horses)	5/10	10(2)	1+1	3+	
Scythed wheels	-	-	-	+1K	See Notes
Rowboat	1/2	8(2)	1+3	500	
Small Merchant ship	2/10	13(2)	4+10	20K	
Large Merchant ship	2/8	15(4)	8+10	80K	
Trireme	2/8	19(4)	20+100	150K	Heavy Armor
Amazon Hawk ship	2/16	15(4)	10+50	100K	Heavy Armor

WEAPONS DESCRIPTIONS

Amazon Blade. A twenty-inch wide Chakram (see below) with several metal spikes protruding from the borders. It is a very dangerous melee weapon, and if you have the strength to throw it, it can deals terrible damage at distance. It is a very old gladiatorial arm, also named spiked Chakram, even if today is always called Amazon Blade. The origin of this name date to the Ascaia rebellion: one of the two first Sister Queens, Galla the gladiator, is always depicted using this weapon, so it is common believed it was her weapon of choice. For this reason, it is only issued to high rank Ascaian Amazons (must have the Noble Edge). An Amazon seeing an Amazon Blade in the hands of someone different from an Ascaian noble suffers −4 to reactions. It is Rare outside the boundaries of the island of the Amazons.

Atlatl. An Atlatl or spear thrower is a clever device that uses the principle of leverage to throw javelins and spears at amazing distances and with incredible strength. It consists of a piece of wood or bone, as long as the thrower's forearm, with a cup or a spur in which the butt of the projectile rests. It is held near the end farthest from the cup, and the projectile is thrown by the action of the upper arm and wrist. In gaming terms, it grants the Strong Arm Edge to the user. If the thrower already has this Edge, the effect is increased and the ranges are incremented by 100%.

In addition, the wielder's Strength is considered a step higher for the purpose of damage calculation. Placing and properly balancing the javelin is a long task, hence the increased reload time. It is a Rare weapon outside the Ivory Savannah and the Verdant Belt.

Barbed Spear. This particularly vicious weapon is used by the Cairnlanders and is usually stone or bone tipped. For this reason, it automatically breaks when the user scores a 1 on the Fighting or Throwing roll. It is Rare outside the Cairn Lands.

Blowgun. A hollow pipe, up to three feet long, used to shoot small darts. The projectiles are too small to deal any real damage and are normally used to deliver poisons or other Lotus concoctions, where a mere scratch is enough to poison the target. Hence, a Shooting roll is enough against an unarmored target to deliver the poison (no damage roll is required), while against armored ones (+1 armor or better) a called shot (−4) is required to pierce exposed skin, but also in this case no damage roll is needed.

Buffalo Lance. This bronze-tipped heavy spear is used by the feared buffalo riders of the Ivory Savannah as they charge their enemies. It is quite cumbersome in dismounted combat, so it must be used with two hands.

Caldeian Dagger. This thin, twisting dagger, is exclusively built in Caldeia, and has a strong religious meaning and is usually used in sacrifices and other ritual situations. It is also a wicked and very maneuverable blade, very good for parrying incoming blows. Given its slenderness, it must be forged in iron or stronger metals, otherwise it will break. These blades are always engraved with powerful symbols of power and prayers to the dark gods of Caldeia. In the hands of a character with the Arcane Background (Sorcery) or Priest Edge, dedicated to an evil deity, it also grants AP 1. It is a Rare item.

Chakram. A Chakram is a flat hoop, from five to twelve inches wide, with a sharp edge. It is usually made of metal, but bone and polished wood are also used. It is both a weapon and art object. The women of the Ivory Savannah Tribes often wear engraved Chakrams as bracers, so that they are always armed against the unwanted attentions of potential suitors. It is mainly a throwing weapon, used like a Frisbee, but it can also be used in melee with −1 to Fighting rolls. In the hands of a skilled user, it can be thrown with an arced trajectory to hit targets concealed around corners or behind partial cover. Hence, when used by a character with Throwing d8 or more he can ignore up to 2 points of Cover modifier, as the disk hits the target from an unusual angle. It is Rare outside the Ivory Savannah and the Verdant Belt.

Composite Bow. The composite bow is usually made of laminated wood and sinew, and it is stronger than the common bow known in the western countries. Composite bows are actually copies made by the civilized races of the Valk Composite Bows but they are by no means comparable to the traditional weapon of the steppe nomads. They are Rare in all the Dominions, except in Ekul, Valkheim, and Zandor.

Combat Net. This heavy net, usually fitted with tiny metal hooks and little weights, is a gladiatorial weapon. It grants +2 to Grapple rolls and it is usually used off-hand, with a trident (treat as a spear) in the main hand.

Iron Fists. This definition includes brass knuckles, cestus, the infamous Elephant

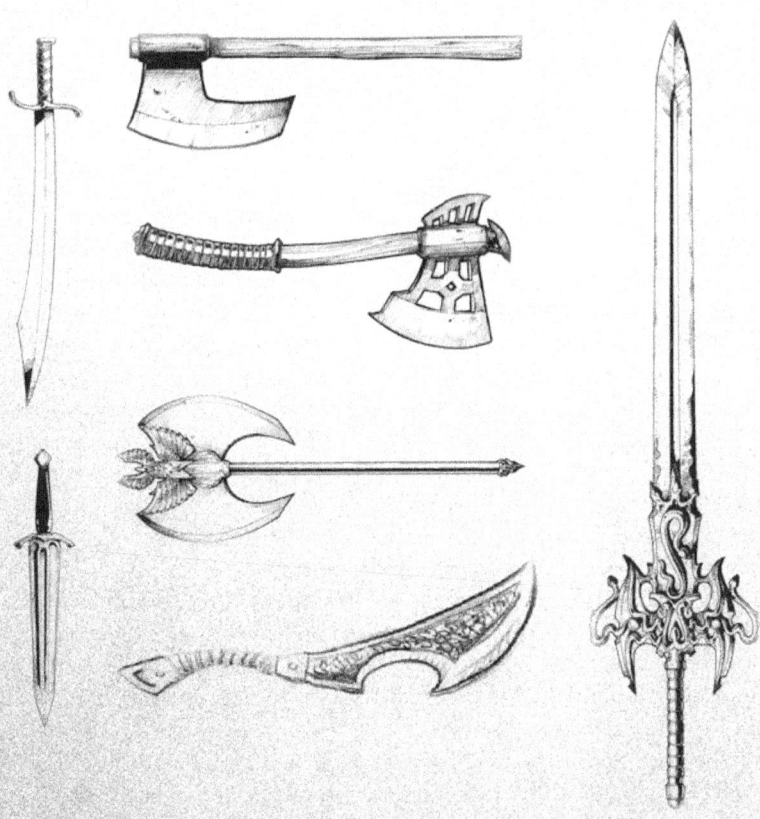

Horn used by Syranthian gladiators, and any other similar weapons for unarmed combat. It also includes special fist weapons used by Monks, like metal prayer beads (in this case, the item is considered a Monk Weapon). Characters with the Unarmed Warrior Edge granting Str+d4 damage add +1 to their unarmed damage. Fist weapons deal lethal damage.

Lhoban Sword. This highly decorated sword is typical of the monk warriors of Lhoban. It is made with particularly flexible metal that makes it ideal for parrying blows. It is very Rare outside Lhoban, and Streetwise rolls to locate it suffer and additional –2.

Moon Blade. A staff ending with a long, moon-shaped blade. This elegant weapon, something in between a spear and a halberd, is also called the Blade of the Maiden, for reasons unknown in the western countries.

Poisoner Glove. This heavy leather glove is usually coated with poison, and is used to deliver Lotus concoctions by touching the target. The wielder is considered to be armed when dealing Touch Attacks.

Severed Head. One of the wickedest habits of the Cairnlanders is to cut the heads of their fallen enemies. These prized trophies are then mummified and several metal spikes are stuck through them, turning them into spiked balls, used with a length of rope to hurl them. They are usually thrown at enemies to provoke fear. Besides damage, hitting someone with a Severed Head allows a free Intimidation

roll. Luckily, these items cannot be found outside the Cairn Lands, where they are fairly common.

Sling, War. This weapon is a longer version of the typical hunting sling and it is used in battle. It requires more strength than a normal sling but, in the hands of a skilled user, it is potentially deadlier than a bow.

Spear. This entry applies to spears, tridents, and other similar weapons. You can use a spear one handed, taking advantage of its long reach, or you can use it two handed for enhanced defense.

Sorcerer's Staff. These staves are usually carved and decorated in strange ways. Some of them are topped with skulls, gems, or other weird amulets. Each is crafted in a peculiar way — for example from the wood of an ancient tree and soaked in the blood of a virgin during a moonless night — which explains its very high price. When it is bought, the player must invent a background story for the staff in order to obtain it. It has minor magical power: in the hands of a character with the Sorcery Arcane Background it can deliver a Touch Attack, exactly as if the caster touched the target with his bare hands. Sorcerer's staffs can also be shorter, in which case they are called rods (treated as a club).

Staff. A long wooden stick, the most humble weapon a man can imagine. Given its length, in Beasts and Barbarians, a staff wielder is considered as having two separate weapons dealing Str+d4 each. It means he can use his staff for two attacks, one with his main hand and the other with his off hand, as per the standard rules, but in this case he loses the +1 Parry bonus.

Three-Piece Rod. This peculiar weapon is made from three pieces of reinforced wood, connected by two lengths of chain. It was originally a farming implement used to beat grain, but the monks found a martial application for it.

Valk Composite Bow. The main weapon of the Valk nomads. This curved bow made of bone, sinews and wood is the best ranged weapon in the known world. Young warriors construct their bows with their own hands, usually under the guidance of an uncle or another relative skilled in this craft. A Valk bow is stronger and has a greater range than any other compossite bow. They cannot be bought and losing one's bow is always considered shameful (−2 to Charisma), inferior only to losing one's horse. Valk bows are always Rare outside the Valk tribes. The listed cost is for a Valk character and refers to the raw materials rather than to the finished product. The Valk never sell them and buying one from third parties costs three times the listed cost. Only Valk heroes can start the game with a Valk Composite Bow.

War Club. This nasty weapon is a heavy club reinforced with sharp pieces of wood, stone, or even metal. It is as effective as a battle axe in the right hands, but considerably cheaper and heavier. It is usually found among the Ivory Savannah Tribes warriors, the most primitive Cairnlander clans, and the Nandals.

Whispering Staff. This strange weapon, only used by trained monks, is a fighting staff with two carved fissures at both ends. Quickly moving the staff produces a strange sound, like a whisper. Those skilled in wielding this weapon (must have Fighting d8+ or the Monk (Militant) Edge) can produce an intense, high-pitched sound that stuns nearby enemies. It counts a Smarts Trick affecting all the targets in a Small Burst Template centered on the wielder of the staff.

Ammo Descriptions

Sling Bullet, Lead. Metal sling bullets are very deadly because they deform on impact without losing their momentum.

Sling Bullet, Hollow. These peculiar bullets are made of very thin earthenware and can hold a single dose of a Lotus concoction. They are used to deliver poison from a distance. They are only produced in Gis and are issued to the Red Slingers, the elite mercenary troops protecting the City of Alchemists. They are quite big, so the shot tends to be less precise (−2 to Shooting rolls). They are Rare items. A Streetwise roll allows finding a batch of five.

Armor Descriptions

Armor can be bought in full suits (a faster option) or in parts, for players who want to choose their gear more accurately. Usually the sum of the parts is equivalent, in price and weight, to a full suit.

Gladiator Armguard. This item is bronze or hard leather material made with curved and overlapping metal segments or plates, fastened to leather straps, conceived to protect one of the arms of the warrior, usually the off-hand one. It is the trade-

mark protection of many gladiators, especially the Tricarnian ones, and for this reason is sometime called Tricarnian Gauntlet or Hordan Arm: for efficiency reasons, in fact, these items are usually made with exactly fourteen metal segments, cleverly linked, and the legend says that each of them represents a syllable of the secret name of the cruel Tricarnian goddess.

In game terms it grants +1 to Parry, and can be used offensively exactly as an Iron Fist. No other shield or armor can be equipped on a limb protected with a Gladiator Armguard.

It allows the use of the Loincloth Hero/Bikini Heroine Edge. It is a Rare Item outside arenas and other places where gladiatorial games are common.

Half Armor. To avoid being too encumbered or simply to save some money, many warriors choose to use a stripped down version of a suit of armor. It is a common option among many gladiators. They may choose to wear only the front part of a cuirass or armor that covers only the parts of the body not protected by the shield. Half armor costs and weighs a quarter less than a standard armor but, if the character is hit with a raise, he is considered to have −1 Armor. Only armor suits can be bought as Half Armor.

Heavy Armor. This armor is entirely made of metal, usually bronze or iron. It was the standard gear of the Iron Phalanxes and other heavy infantry troops, but today it

has almost fallen in disuse, given its cost and the training required to use it without collapsing from the weight (see the Hoplite Training Edge). It is a Rare item.

Light Armor. By far the most common armor in the Dread Sea Dominions, this broad category includes leather armor, gladiator outfits, Valk cuirasses of boiled skin, and many other types.

Loincloth/Bikini. A minimal piece of cloth or animal skin that protects no more than the wearer's modesty. It allows the use of the Loincloth Hero/Bikini Heroine Edge.

Medium Armor. So many types of armor designs exist in the Dread Sea Dominions that it's impossible to list all of them, so broad definitions are used here. Medium armor usually has a layer of leather, stiff cloth or, more rarely, wood, covered by plates or disks of metal, usually bronze. It is the most common armor among professional soldiers.

Reinforced Armor. Armor can have extra layers of protection, additional plates and so on. It costs much more and is more cumbersome to use, but it has its advantages. If a character doesn't have the Armor Use Edge, he can use the Edge once for free. After the use, the armor deteriorates as usual. Only if the Repair roll to patch up the armor is made with a raise, the free Armor Use Edge is restored, otherwise it is lost forever.

A character that already possesses the Edge has more advantages from the reinforced armor. The first time he uses the Armor Use Edge, its use is free and doesn't reduce the Armor value of the cuirass. Every following use is handled in the normal way. As for the untrained use described before, if the roll to Repair the armor scores a raise, the free use of the Reinforced armor is restored. Every type of armor suit can be bought in the Reinforced version. Armor cannot be both Reinforced and Half Armor. Reinforced Armor is a Rare item.

Tribal Shield. The members of the Ivory Savannah Tribes are used to painting and decorating their shields with demon faces or even with the skins of their enemies. Alternatively, some of them use the hides of the fiercest beasts they hunt (usually lions or rhinos). A tribal warrior can choose how to paint his shield. It gives him a +1 bonus to one of these rolls: Intimidation, Taunt or Persuasion. The modifier is decided when the shield is built. This object is Rare outside the Ivory Savannah and the Verdant Belt.

MUNDANE ITEMS DESCRIPTIONS

Alchemic Laboratory. It is a well equipped laboratory, which grants +2 to Lotusmastery rolls to prepare concoctions. The first price refers to buying the lab, the second to renting it for three days. It is a Rare item.

Armorer Kit. A basic assortment of smith tools to fix armor. Trying to patch up some armor without this basic equipment causes −2 to Repair rolls.

Healer Kit. Depending on the culture and type of healer, it can contain bandages and some rudimentary surgical tool, or dried leaves and amulets (good luck with that!). Trying to heal a wound without this basic equipment causes −2 to Healing rolls.

Lock Picks. The tools of the trades of every respectable thief. Trying to force a lock without lock picks cause −2 to Lockpicking rolls.

Lotus Concoction. A Lotus potion, imbued with a Lotusmastery Power. They are always Rare Items and the Game Master can limit their availability at his discretion.

Lotus master Bag. This is the bag that every Lotus master carries to brew his potions. A character with the Lotusmastery Arcane Background has it for free, and can replace it for free between adventures. It must be bought only if the character loses it during a scenario and wants to replace it before the start of the next one.

Poisoner Ring. This hollow ring can store a single dose of an alchemic concoction, and can be opened with light pressure or some other nimble movement. It grants +2 to Stealth rolls to deliver poisons. Rings are the most common form of these devices, but other items can be crafted to store poisons, granting the same bonus. It is a Rare item.

Refined Lotus. Doses of ready-to-use Lotus. Each dose can be used by a Lotus master instead of spending a Power Point. They are normally sold in batches of 2d6 doses. They are a Rare Item.

Silk Rope. Another tool of the trade of expert burglars, this rope is very light, but extremely resistant. It can be made in silk, or other exotic material, like women's hair. It is a Rare Item everywhere except in Jalizar.

Tiger's Claws. These peculiar crampons are used by Jalizar thieves to climb up walls. They give +2 to Climbing rolls, and are considered Iron Fists. They are Rare items.

ANIMALS

Fighting Bird. The habit of hunting or even fighting with hunting birds is very old, dating back to the Keronian Empire. In the Dread Sea Dominions various types of birds are used for these tasks, such as hawks, giant crows, and certain species of vultures.

Fighting Bird Barding. This light but protective harness covers the bird's throat and chest, granting a little extra protection.

Fighting Bird Talons. These minuscule, sharp metal talons are usually applied onto the fighting bird's own talons to deal extra damage. Fighting birds are trained from birth in using these special "gauntlets".

Horse, Cheap. A standard horse, with the same stats as a common horse, but Vigor decreased by a die step, or −2 Pace, or a single Hindrance decided by the Game Master. Identifying a cheap horse requires a Riding roll.

Horse, Common. A standard riding horse, as for the Savage Worlds core rules.

Horse, Good. A worthy beast. It can be a War horse or a common horse with +2 Pace, Vigor increased by a die step, or a useful Edge.

Steppe Pony. An ugly, furry pony of Valk breeds. It might not be very pretty, but it is gifted with incredible stamina (see page 152 for stats). It is a Rare item outside Valk controlled lands.

War Buffalo. A mighty buffalo trained as a mount for combat (see page 155 for stats). It is only available in the Ivory Savannah and it is never sold. A hero must have the Buffalo Rider Edge to own one of these mighty beasts.

VEHICLES

All the Dread Sea Dominions ships are designed to sail inshore, except the Amazons' ships (see below). So, when a ship is forced to sail in open sea, it suffers −2 to Boating rolls. The Amazons, an island population, are skilled mariners and have developed a particular type of sail, which allows them to sail in open sea without problems. Very few sailors except the Amazons know how to effectively use the "Amazon Sails".

Amazon Hawk Ships. The common Amazon warship is long, thin and with reduced draft, so that it can navigate in shallow waters, like rivers. The figureheads of these ships usually resemble a bird of prey, and the bow is painted to resemble a bird's plumage. Amazon Hawk Ships are very maneuverable, don't suffer penalties in open sea and generally grant +1 to Boating rolls to the helmsman.

Cart. A common farmer's cart or, for a higher price, a noble's coach.

Chariot. A fast vehicle used by rich aristocrats for recreation, by imperial couriers, and generally by those who need great speed in traveling. It is usually pulled by two horses, but four or six horses can also be used —or even eight in races in the arena. For every two additional horses the vehicle gains +5 Top Speed. A chariot with six or more horses is less maneuverable, causing −1 to Driving rolls. A chariot with eight horses doubles the Acceleration value. Horses aren't included; they must be bought separately.

Chariot, War. A chariot built for battle. It is driven by a charioteer and has space for a passenger, usually an archer or a slinger. War chariots follow the same rules as chariots, but they usually don't have more than four horses. When a horse pulling a chariot is killed, the driver must immediately roll on the Out of Control table. Ranged attacks from a chariot suffer the Unstable Platform modifier but, if the driver has both the Steady Hands and Charioteer Edge, the Steady Hands Edge applies to the passenger too. War chariots are commonly used in Syranthia, Kyros and among the Cairnlanders (where they are pulled by trained goats instead of horses).

Galley. The biggest ship of the Dread Sea Dominions, propelled by oars. The most common ones are triremes, so called because they have three rows of oars. Galleys are very common and used mostly as slave ships. The most impressive fleets of galleys are those of Tricarnia and Syranthia, followed by those of Caldeia and Kyros. Many galleys are armed with catapults, ballistae, or similar weapons.

Merchant ships. The most common type of ship, used by sailors all over the world. It usually has a lateen sail.

Scythed Wheels. A chariot can be fitted with a set of two scythed blades. On the tabletop, any target within 1" of the chariot suffers 2d8+1 damage unless he makes an Agility roll. When using the Chase rules, a scythed chariot gains +4 to Force attempts (in truth, it is only skimming the enemy chariot).

HERO'S JOURNAL:
QUALITY OF MATERIAL
In the Dread Sea Dominions the science of metallurgy is still in its infancy and many cultures use primitive materials to build weapons and other tools.

The most common materials, in descending order of hardness, are: steel (see below), iron, bronze, stone, bone, wood.

Iron weapons and armor are common only in the Iron Empire (Faberterra, Syranthia and Zandor). In the other lands they are Rare and cost double.

Bronze is common in the most of the Dominions. Only in the Caledlands, Lush Jungle, and Ivory Savannah it is Rare and cost double.

A character buying a tool made of a material weaker than the current standard in that land (so, for example a bronze dagger in Faberterra) pays 20% less.

The effects of having weapons of different grades of hardness are the following:

When a fighter rolls 1 on the Fighting Die, regardless of the Wild Die, and his opponent is using a weapon, shield or armor of harder material, the fighter's weapon breaks. The Game Master should not abuse this rule and use it only when it fits the story.

HERO'S JOURNAL:
THE MAGIC OF STEEL
Steel, in truth high-carbon iron, is the magical metal of Beasts and Barbarians. Steel was produced in small quantities at the height of the Empire by the priest smiths of Hulian, but the technique to smelt it is lost today, especially because very few forges can achieve the necessary temperatures. So, steel objects are prized relics and treasures.

A weapon made of steel has AP 2, while armor gains +1 Armor and weighs 25% less. They are almost priceless but, as a general guide, steel weapons and armor cost from ten to twenty times their standard cost, provided that the hero can find some for sale.

CHAPTER 5

SETTING RULES

I n this section you'll find the specific rules to make *Beasts and Barbarians* a setting of real sword and sorcery action. This setting use Blood and Guts, Born a Hero and Joker`s Wild rules from *Savage Worlds Deluxe*.

HENCHMEN AND RIGHT HANDS

Some characters — such as the right hand of a powerful sorcerer or the captain of the Priest Prince's guard — are stronger than Extras but they don't qualify for the Wild Card status, hence they are classed as Henchmen or Right Hands.

Henchmen are more resilient than Extra and they have three Wounds levels, exactly as Wild Cards, but neither Wild Die nor Bennies.

Conversely, Right Hands are more skilled and for this reason gain a Wild Die, but have a single Wound as Extras and no Bennies.

AFTER THE ADVENTURE

A word of advice: despite fitting the setting well, the following rules might not be suited to all groups of players. They can be ignored and the Game Master will simply reduce the loot of the various adventures to keep the game's economy balanced.

SAVINGS

Sword and Sorcery heroes usually find enormous riches in their adventures — and dilapidate them just as fast. At the start of their next adventure they are often almost penniless and desperate enough to embark on another mission.

To simulate this cliché, after replenishing their basic equipment (repairing armor or stocking up on arrows — note that buying a lost weapon is free), the characters are supposed to spend all the money on booze, courtesans or other recreational activities suited to their background (even books for learned characters!).

They only keep a small sum for emergencies and for purchasing new equipment, i.e. their Savings. The Savings are usually 100 Moons multiplied by the hero's Rank, but the GM can change the amount as he sees fit.

Logically, Savings cannot be higher than the money the hero earned in the previous adventure. So, if a Seasoned character only gained 30 Moons in his last adventure, that is what he owns — and he will likely be very sad, since he has no money to spend on courtesans and wine...

Savings can be stashed between adventures, unless an After the Adventure Event interferes (see below) or something happens during the game (e.g., the heroes are robbed).

AFTER THE ADVENTURE EVENTS

After calculating her Savings but before making any purchases, each player can draw a card from the Action Deck to check how she has passed her time after the last adventure, by consulting the After the Adventure Events Table.

Note that drawing a card is purely optional and the player is free to decide whether to draw it or not, since it might bring some useful advantage or some unwanted misfortune.

The table is willingly very generic. The Game Master, or the players themselves, should invent a brief, entertaining story of what has happened in the meantime. Very colorful descriptions or hilarious ones should be rewarded with a Bennie at the start of the next session.

Alternatively, the Game Master can use the results of the table to create a nice introduction to the next scenario.

At the Game Master's discretion, some characters, or even the whole group, can decide to share the same card and face the same consequences, but this decision must be made before drawing the card.

After the Adventure Events Table

Card	Effect

2   **Ouch!** The hero was arrested, imprisoned, robbed or something similar, but he managed to save his skin and escape. He loses all his money, including his Savings, and all his equipment except one item per Rank. As partial compensation, he is *very* enraged now, and this gives him +1 to Soak rolls for the entire duration of the next adventure.

3   **A Life of Excesses.** The hero has had too much of booze, food, Lotus, courtesans or whatever pleasure he prefers. Reduce by half the hero's Savings. If the card is red, the effect of all his partying is positive and the hero has +1 to Toughness for the next adventure. If the card is black, all the carousing has given him a bad headache or another similar consequence, and he starts the new adventure Fatigued. This fatigue lasts for the entire first session after this event.

4-6   **Carousing.** The hero has indulged in the usual adventurer's things: drinking a lot, meeting courtesans, and so on. But, besides wasting money, nothing particular has happened to him.

7   **So Booored!** The hero hates being idle. She has become so bored that she has taken up a distraction of some type. If the drawn card is red, the distraction is positive and constructive, like training, and she gains a temporary Edge of her choice, respecting all the requirements. If the card is black, she has acquired a bad habit or gotten into trouble. She gains an additional Minor Hindrance. Alternatively, she can take a Major Hindrance, gaining an extra Bennie as compensation. Both the Edge and the Hindrance last till the end of the next adventure.

8   **Enemy/Friend.** The character has done something that has earned him the friendship or hate of someone. If the card drawn is red, the hero has acquired a new friend. He gains the Connections Edge, limited to three uses. If the card is black, he has displeased someone and suffers the Enemy Hindrance, in the Minor version, for the next adventure.

9   **Item.** The character has managed to put her hands on a valuable object or, alternatively, lost a precious possession. If the card drawn is red, she acquires a single mundane item (taken from the Gear section) that can cost no more than twice her current Savings. It can be a Rare item. Note that she acquires it without spending any money. If the card is black, the hero has lost the most valuable item in her possession, with the exclusion of Valuable Possessions (see the Joker entry) and Trademark Weapons. Recovering them might be the aim of an adventure.

10   **I Am Rich!** Strangely the hero has managed not only to keep his saving but also to increase them. Maybe he has had a stroke of luck at the gambling table or wisely decided to invest them in some lucrative business. Whatever the reason, the hero immediately doubles his total Savings!

J   **Blessed/Cursed.** The hero has, willingly or unwillingly, done something that has displeased or appeased the supernatural powers. Alternatively, he has received a particularly good or bad omen. Whatever the way, this affects his destiny. If the card drawn is red, the effect is positive and the character gains the Luck Edge for the next adventure. If it is black, a malevolent curse of some type lingers on him and he suffers the Bad Luck Hindrance for the following adventure or until he manages to lift it during the game.

Q   **Fame.** Thanks to his heroic feats during the last adventure or in the downtime, the hero has acquired a certain reputation. If the card drawn is red, his reputation is positive, granting him +2 Charisma. If the card is black, his reputation is negative and he suffers −2 to Charisma.

The modifier lasts for the entire duration of the upcoming scenario.

K **"I have heard of you."** A follower joins the hero. It may be a slave the hero has freed, an old friend or relative or even an animal companion. It is an Extra and its stats are decided by the Game Master. When this card is dealt, the Game Master draws another card and doesn't show it to the players. If it is red, the follower is truly loyal to the character; if it is black he has a hidden agenda or brings some danger with him. To avoid having too many followers, if this card is dealt when another follower is already in the group, the player who draws it can choose to use it to promote a current follower to Henchman status or to give him a free advancement.

Ace **Taken a Break.** The hero has temporarily quit the adventuring life. He might have married, gone through a religious crisis, or simply decided to get another, more stable job for a while. But adventure runs in his blood and so, in the end, he comes back to action in the incoming scenario. He gains a free d4 in one skill of his choice or can raise one of his skills by one step, up to d6, to represent the experience he has gathered in his sabbatical period. But, on the flipside, his adventuring skills are quite rusty. The GM picks up to one skill per Rank of the hero and marks it with a dot on the character sheet. Until the player spends a Bennie on a roll on that skill, he doesn't have the Wild Die on it.

Joker **A Worthy Possession.** The hero has invested all her money (so his Savings drop to zero) in an exceptional product. Depending on the character's Rank and background, it can be a weapon, a set of clothes, a horse, a ship, a laboratory or even a minor magical relic, decided by the Game Master. She is totally enamored of it and persuaded of its goodness. The object is actually good and bestows +2 to one of the following: an attribute roll, a skill roll, Damage, Armor, Pace or Charisma. Alternatively, it grants +1 to Toughness or Parry, or a free Edge!

Example. Shangor the Barbarian, a Seasoned hero, finished his last adventure with a bag full of opals (2,000 Moons value). After finding a replacement for his trusted battle axe, lost during a battle (for free), he decides to relax for a while in Kyros City, to get a taste of the fabled pleasures of civilization.

Daniel, Shangor's player, decides to draw a card for the After the Adventure Events table and picks the Eight of Diamonds.

The Game Master informs him that Shangor earned a Connection Edge that can be used up to three times.

Daniel decides that Shangor met and fell in love with Symiria, the favorite courtesan of a powerful noble. He spent all his money on gifts (except a single opal well concealed in his right boot, value: 200 Moons) for the capricious girl and, in the end, his manly charm won her over.

Symiria will use her connections to get favors for her new barbarian lover, but she is a very fickle girl, so this romance will not last for very long.

Symiria is a new NPC that the Game Master can use. For example, he might decide that the next scenario starts with the kidnapping of the fascinating courtesan…

GAME MASTER
GUIDE

CHAPTER 6:

RUNNING BEASTS AND BARBARIANS

This chapter and the following ones contain hints and tips for the Game Master to run *Beasts and Barbarians*. Players should stop reading now, lest the foul Gods strike them blind!

SETTING THE MOOD

Beasts and Barbarians is explicitly a Sword and Sorcery setting, quite different from the standard high fantasy worlds. Here follow some keywords related to the main features of this world.

PULP

Bare-chested heroes fighting ugly, multi-eyed monsters! *Beasts and Barbarians* is a setting that falls squarely into the pulp genre, complete with larger than life heroes. It should be visual and colorful.

HEROIC

Pulp worlds and characters tend to be magnificent, with great dangers and equally great rewards. So the heroes don't explore a small goblin cave to find 12 copper coins. Instead, they venture through an ancient, moss covered temple, where frog-shaped worshippers of a forgotten god guard a gold idol big enough to pay the ransom of a king! It can be worth 10 thousand Moons, but it really doesn't matter: the characters will spend most of their money on booze, so there is no need to be stingy.

GRITTY

Beasts and Barbarians is a harsh word. So, don't be soft on your heroes: slavery, treachery and being stripped of everything are common occurrences.

FEARFUL MAGIC

Beasts and Barbarians isn't a world where you buy a magical sword from the local smith. Magic is present, but it is hidden, rarely fully understood and, most importantly, it must not be trusted. Even a skilled sorcerer must feel shivers down his spine as he summons an otherworldly creature.

NOT ONLY COMBAT: CHASES

Fighting monsters is important in Sword and Sorcery, but it must not be abused. There are a lot of other interesting things to do, while remaining focused on the action.

Think of action movies: the actual fighting scenes are only a small part of the story, but the heroes are pursued by enemies, risking their life running at breakneck speed on unstable bridges, trying to get away from impossible-to-beat creatures, or chasing elusive acrobat thieves across the city's rooftops.

Savage Worlds has an excellent chase system. Use it to spice up a scene and give your players an adrenaline rush.

NOT ONLY COMBAT: EXPLORATION

Many places the heroes will visit are extremely dangerous: temples full of traps, deep jungles, merciless deserts, haunted forests, and so on. Exploring and understanding them is a nice thing for many players and sometimes finding water and food in a desolate place or avoiding a lethal trap with skill and brains is more rewarding than bashing monsters with sword and bow.

NOT ONLY COMBAT: INTERACTION

The world doesn't include only people who kill and people who sell weapons. The heroes should meet at least one interesting personality in each adventure. And remember, these characters have their motivations and feelings. For example, a prince who hires the heroes to stop a bandit lord will not be happy at all if, when the group comes back with the severed head of the outlaw, he discovers that the bandit chief is in truth his son, bewitched by evil magic. He might condemn the heroes to death, creating an unsuspected twist in the adventure.

Swords and Sorcery personalities tend to be excessive: an evil tyrant is *extremely* evil, a charming courtesan is *incredibly* fascinating, a vengeful warrior is *obsessively* vindictive.

In addition, don't forget the characters' background: sometime an NPC coming back from the hero's past can add a lot to the story.

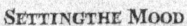

Similarly, don't forget to use the NPCs the players create during the After the Adventure phase and, if you think your players are responsible enough, give them some control over their NPCs.

Combat! Combat! Combat!

When combat breaks out, it must be interesting. Even if you don't use miniatures (but we suggest you do it), try to put a twist in every fight.

No combat should happen in an empty, colorless space. Let the players invent cool props for tricks, but try to always include in the scene something to inspire them. For example, a fight in a jungle ruin will have vines which the characters can use to jump and half broken columns that they can let fall onto their opponents, and so on. Try to be open to the players' ideas and don't be shy with Bennies, if it helps to keep the game cinematic.

Also remember that not every combat must be won, and not all victories come from pure strength in battle. Some monsters have immunities the heroes must discover, or must be tricked in some way to be overcome.

Minimal

The scenario doesn't necessarily have to involve saving a kingdom or destroying a powerful demon. Some good stories have a very humble beginning and setting and are very limited in space and time. Imagine the heroes stopping at an inn in a remote area. One of them chats with a boy, the local stable hand. During supper, a terrible scream is heard coming from the stable. The innkeeper, customers and heroes run to the stable and find that some rotten planks broke, revealing an old well, into which the young boy has fallen. Nobody knew about it. The boy is wounded, but still alive. The heroes are about to fetch their ropes to save him when the lad screams in terror! What is happening below, in the darkness?

It is a very humble and minimal situation, but nevertheless interesting.

Non Linear

There is nothing more boring than re-playing the same adventure over and over again. If the last scenario was a fight to defend a village from Valk raiders, don't propose a second battle adventure, unless there is a strong hook in it, but try something different. So, for example, if the Valk raiders were successfully driven out, start the next adventure with the heroes taken prisoners by a Valk warlord, who ambushed them as they were leaving the village.

To punish them for interfering with his campaign, the evil warlord leaves the party chained and stripped of all their equipment in an old ruin by the sea, which is flooded by the tide every day. Then, with an evil laugh he bids them farewell and leads his horde to the village, to finally destroy it. The heroes must free themselves before the tide rises and run back as fast as possible to save the village once again.

Also, if you feel the players are annoyed by the Savings rule, allow them to keep all the money after an adventure and propose a very strange purchase, such as a merchant ship or a remote estate, totally changing the mood of the campaign.

Whatever the way, try to be non linear.

Group Size

The best number of players to play a RPG is usually between four and six players with a Game Master, and four is often seen as the "perfect" number. If you play the scenarios proposed in the next installments of this series, you'll find they are designed for a group of four characters, but easily scalable for bigger or smaller groups, because the number of opponents is usually presented in the "X bandits per hero" format, where X is a number.

Nonetheless, very small groups require a little more tweaking, detailed below.

THE HEROIC DUO

Sword and Sorcery works very well with only two playing characters. To keep the game balanced but heroic at the same time, if your group includes only two heroes, you might consider doing the following:

1. The heroes begin their career with 10 extra Experience Points (usually 30 Experience Points)

2. The heroes automatically benefit from the Common Bond Edge

3. Use the Heroic Healing rule (see sidebar on page 113)

If you use these rules for published scenarios, consider the group as made of four characters in order to determine the number of opponents.

THE LONE WOLF

The lone barbarian hero is a staple of many heroic fantasy stories. So, a Game Master and a single player can play a satisfying game even in a one-to-one situation, with the following rule changes:

1. The Lone Wolf begins his career with 20 extra Experience Points (usually 40 Experience Points).

2. The Lone Wolf starts each session with an additional Bennie.

3. Halve (rounding down) gang up bonuses against the Lone Wolf.

4. Use the Really Heroic Healing rule (see sidebar on page 113).

If you use these rules for published scenarios, consider the group as made of three characters in order to determine the number of opponents.

ALTERNATIVE HEALING RULES

The following Healing rules should be used only in really cinematic games or when the size of the group is very small.

Heroic Healing. *After a fight, each hero is allowed an unmodified Vigor roll. With a success, he recovers a Wound (or a Fatigue level, player's choice), two with a raise. This represents the character "shrugging off" wounds and acts in addition to the normal Healing rolls.*

Really Heroic Healing. *Like the Heroic Healing, but the character automatically recovers one Wound with a failure, two with a success, and three with a Raise. Only with a critical failure he recovers no wounds.*

HEROIC INCAPACITATION

Heroes of sword and sorcery are rarely maimed and are usually back on their feet really fast. So, for a more pulpish game, apply the following modification to the incapaci-

tation rules. What follow is only meant for Wild Cards.

Injuries are never permanent. *Broken bones are back in shape when all the wounds are healed. The only exception is that a player can willingly accept a permanent injury. In this case, as a compensation he gains a free Edge at the start of the new adventure, if he justifies it storywise.*

Faster Natural Healing. *Cut all the natural healing times by half. So a hero does a natural healing roll after two days. If you apply this rule, remember to apply it also to related Edges: so a character with Ghoulblood (natural healing after two days) if this rule is applied rolls every day.*

EXTREME ACTIONS

The Dread Sea Dominions are a place where heroes die with a sword in the hand and a curse on their mouth.

When a hero is Incapacitated, do the usual Vigor roll and apply the results as normal, then the player can choose one of following options.

Given the power of these options each player can use this option only once per session.

Avenge me, my friend(s)! *The hero can distribute all his Bennie (minimum one) to his allies within his command radius (usually 5").*

Last Breath. *Even if the hero should be dead, the sheer force of his will allows him to act as normal for another round, ignoring all the wound penalties. At the end of that round he automatically passes out, as for failing on the Vigor roll on the Incapacitation table, or dies (if the previous roll indicated such a destiny).*

The Curse of a Dying Man. *The hero can throw a terrible curse to his opponent before going down. Unless the GM states differently, it is a lower trait spell, cast using the Spirit score of the incapacitated hero as Arcane Skill. If the hero is actually dying, he receives +4 to the Spirit roll, and the curse*

is permanent. Each hero can only use this option once each rank.

TWEAKING THE SETTING

If played "out-of-the-box", *Beasts and Barbarians* is a dark Sword and Sorcery world, with low magic. If you want, you can tweak the setting to fit your party's taste and gaming style. Here are two examples of how to tweak the setting.

LAW OF THE SWORD

This is the "hardcore" mode of *Beasts and Barbarians* for players who like a hard game and dark, pseudo-horror stories. The main difference is magic. No playing character is allowed to take Arcane Backgrounds and the pure sight of magic — good as well as evil — is so strange and alien that the heroes must make a Fear roll every time they witness a spell or other supernatural act. In this version of the game the Brave Edge can be taken even after character creation.

HUMOROUS GAME

This is the most lighthearted type of gameplay. It is mostly a question of setting and general attitude: evil characters aren't that evil or, if they are, they have very stupid reasons for being so. The Imperials are lazy and snobbish, while the barbarians are rowdy fellows who only like drinking a lot and mixing with women of ill repute. The Amazons are hysterical ladies and the wizards are lecherous old coots.

With these small modifications you can play the game as it is, or you might consider adding a couple of "silly" Edges that set the mood of the campaign, like the ones listed in the sidebar.

SILLY CAMPAIGNS EDGES

The following are example Edges only used in Humorous Games. There is no need for a full plethora of silly Edges; a couple are usually enough to set the mood of a campaign.

Barbarian Belch
(Combat Edge)
Prerequisite: Novice, Vigor d8+

Many barbarians have a soft spot for alcohol, but this hero is a true professional at swallowing enormous quantities of booze. This causes him some digestion problems, but also grants him a powerful belch, very similar in sound and intensity to the love call of the Northeim elks. As an action, the hero can belch at a nearby enemy, stunning him with the powerful fumes of his alcoholic belly. This is an opposed Vigor roll, and if the hero wins the enemy is Shaken. The hero has +2 to the roll if he drank at least a tankard of alcohol in the last ten minutes.

Running in High Heels
(Combat Edge)
Prerequisite: Novice, Agility d8+, Charisma 1+

This Edge is the female warriors' favorite, since they always want to look their best. And what looks better than exploring dangerous ruins in high heels? The character gains +1 Pace and +1 to the running die but, if she rolls 1 or 2 on the running die, she trips and falls. In addition, she can make nasty kick attacks dealing Str+d4 damage.

RELICS

The world of *Beast and Barbarians* isn't of the high magic type, so true magical relics should be rare and precious.

But, besides true magical items, a hero can find various minor objects, such as trusted swords, masterwork armor, and so on.

Not every relic is magical — sometimes it is only a very peculiar object. The players won't find relics easily; ideally, a single relic for each rank of the hero is enough. Remember, the real stars of *Beasts and Barbarians* are the heroes and their mighty muscles, not the shiny trinkets they wear!

After these general guidelines, let's look at some basic rules for relic creation.

Relic Idea

You should start with a general idea of the item, and of what its peculiarities are. Is it a sword, a book, a hat? Write a brief description of what it looks like and of its powers and background story.

Relic Rules

One or more of these bonuses can be applied to a relic:

† +2 on an Attribute or Skill roll
† +1 Parry or Toughness
† +2 Pace
† +2 Charisma
† +1 Armor Penetration
† +1 Damage
† One additional Edge
† One or more powers, used with arcane skill of d6 and 10 Power Points
† A single ability devised by the Game Master

The listed bonuses are more or less equivalent, except the unique ability invented by the Game Master. When creating a weak relic choose one bonus, two for an average relic, three or more for a very powerful item. Remember that Savage Worlds is a low numbers system, so a +2 modifier is a very good one, and +4 almost secures automatic success, so it should be avoided. When you create relics, try to give them circumstantial bonuses (so they work only in certain cases) or give them low bonuses in different fields. The table below shows some examples of relics suited to a *Beasts and Barbarians* campaign.

Cursed Relics. Magic is inherently dark and evil. So, it is no surprise that, instead of granting advantages, some magical items limits and hinders a character by giving her a penalty (use the same list before changing the sign of the modifiers).

You can push this concept further and decide that certain relics give the wielder a positive modifier in certain fields and a negative one in others.

Give Them a Twist

Relics, especially powerful ones, should not work like mass-produced high tech gadgets — after all they are imbued with magic. So, give them a twist, an interesting trait, or a narrative feature that makes them unique.

Relic Examples

The following table lists some relics that you can use as ideas for your own devices. Otherwise, roll on it when you need a quick item to be given to the heroes. Some of these objects are actually magical, others are simply remarkable.

Roll a d20 and read the following table:

1. **Helm of Koramos.** This elegant metal helm is very ancient. It belonged to Koramos, a famous general who died in a terrible way, and now his spirit haunts this relic. The possessor constantly hears the general's voice whispering in his mind, providing advice and teaching. It grants the Knowledge (Battle) skill at d8, Command, and another Leadership Edge (Game Master's choice). But, in stressful situations, the possessor can be overwhelmed by the strength of the general's mind and experience flashbacks of Koramos's memories. Whenever the character is dealt a deuce from the Action Deck, he must make a Spirit (−2) roll or be Shaken.

2. **Blood of Kalephon.** A legend says that a rider went from Kenaton to Kyros City in a single day to warn the king of an attack by the Ivory Savannah Tribes. The rider's name is

forgotten, but not that of his incredible mount: Kalephon, the white horse of the Savannah. This horse (cannot be a pony) has some of Kalephon's blood in its veins and gallops like the wind. It receives +2 Pace and its running die is increased by one step. In addition, the rider can spend Bennies for the horse, as for the Beast Bond Edge.

3. **Blood Tear.** This strange deep red crystal comes from the Red Desert. When held in the hand, in contact with bare skin, it seems to come alive and emanates a faint, red luminescence, as for the *light* spell. The strange glow lasts indefinitely until the crystal stays in contact with the skin. Every hour of use, a Vigor roll is required and, in case of failure, the individual holding it suffers a level of Fatigue.

4. **Holy Quipus of Lhoban.** These strange ropes full of minuscule knots, were made with the hair of old, sage monks and are true books, written in the strange secret language of Lhoban. They contain aphorisms, metaphors and religious teachings that are always a point of meditation for monks. An Enlightened character, with Smarts d8+ and capable of reading them, gains the Rapid Recharge Edge when wearing these Quipus.

5. **Noble Garment.** This remarkable piece of clothing, typical of the higher echelons of the society, makes its wearer (man or woman) look very fine. It grants +2 to Charisma as long as the character behaves in a way appropriate to his standing.

6. **Ring of Xaladu.** This beautiful ring, with a black stone encased in it, belonged to the famous Syranthian lord Xaladu, also known as the Bane of the Alchemists, for the ruthless repression enacted against practitioners of Lotusmastery during his reign. This ring grants excellent protection from poisons. The wearer gains +2 to Vigor rolls when contrasting the effects of poison, both natural and magical. As a minor drawback, the wearer receives −2 to all Lotusmastery rolls.

7. **Lucky Money.** A very ancient coin which has passed through so many hands that is impossible to discern the engravings on it. It isn't an obvious magical object, so a Spirit roll is required the first time a character puts her hands on it. If the roll is successful, the character perceives something particular in this object; otherwise she discards it as worthless junk. She receives an additional Bennie as per the Luck Edge, which can be kept between adventures. When the Bennie is spent, the money disappears.

8. **Imp's Mandible.** This scary mandible bone full of strange, sharp teeth, belongs to Xarigas, one of the most powerful Keronian Imps of the past. While in possession of this item, a sorcerer gains the *summon ally* power, cast with Sorcery d8 and 15 Power Points. The power only allows summoning a specific Keronian Imp, Xarigas, a Wild Card. Characters that already know the *summon ally* power can choose, instead of Sorcery d8, a +2 to the arcane roll to summon Xarigas. When Xarigas is *banished* or killed, the mandible crumbles to dust.

9. **Cup of Sacrifice.** This old cup of polished bronze belonged to an old Cairnlander priest. Once a month, the owner can spill some of his own blood into the cup and drink it as a sacrifice to the Ancestors. If he does so, he can use the *divination* Power, with arcane skill d10. The only cost of the spell is the spilling of blood, which cause a Wound that cannot be soaked and heals only with natural recovery.

10. **Armor Plate.** This ancient and sturdy metal plating, engraved with strange runes, can be added to an individual's armor with a Repair roll. The user of the armor can decide to add +4 to a Soak roll. The decision can be taken after the roll. After one use, the armor plate breaks and becomes useless.

11. **Steel Short Sword.** This old, plain sword is made of the strongest material

civilized men know: steel! It deals Str+d6+2 damage and has AP 2.

12. **Tome of Forbidden Secrets.** This ancient book of lore contains magical knowledge (usually a single Power from the Sorcery arcane background list). A mage reading it risks his very soul, because the dusty pages hold secrets not intended for a human mind. He must devote at least a full day to studying the book to gain some advantage. At the end of this period, he must make a Fear (–2) roll. If successful, he is allowed a Smarts roll. If he succeeds in this roll too, he learns the Power contained in the book. If he fails any of the rolls, he is allowed to try again once he gains a new Rank.

13. **Metal Scales Bikini.** Nobody knows who crafted this strange metal bikini but, although all barbarians say it is completely worthless, warrior women with Charisma 2+ can wear it, gaining +2 Armor, without renouncing the use of the Bikini Heroine Edge.

14. **Ring of the Mastiff.** This ring is made of a strange bone and has bizarre engravings on it. After a few days, its wielder feels his senses, especially smell, becoming sharper. In gaming terms, an Extra gains the Wild Die on Notice rolls, while a Wild Card has his Wild Die increased by one step. But this item is cursed! It is made with the tooth of a Demonic Mastiff (a Wild Card beast, see page 145) that wants it back! Every time the user rolls 1 on the Notice roll, the GM can let the Mastiff appear and attack him within a week. Even if the mastiff is killed, it continues to appear and, at every additional apparition, it brings along an additional Mastiff (an Extra). The curse stops if the wielder gives back the ring to the Mastiff.

15. **Colorless Lotus of Past Dreams.** This transparent Lotus concoction is one of the most feared, as well as sought-after, potions in the entire world. It has the power of letting a person remember his past lives! The drinker falls into a strong lethargy that leaves him unconscious for three days, after which he wakes up and makes a Spirit roll. In case of success, the past memories aid him by permanently increasing an Attribute by one step. In case of failure, his mind is broken and he permanently loses a Spirit die step.

16. **Bronze Staff.** This fighting staff is made of bronze and its construction dates back to a very ancient era. It has passed through the hands of many Lhoban monk warriors who have used it to defeat demons and other terrible creatures. It has the same stats as a standard staff but deals Str+d8 damage. It is very heavy (40 lbs) but in the hands of a character with Enlightenment d8+ it weights like a normal staff.

17. **Valkyria's Bowstring.** This bowstring was made with the hair of a Valkyria, Raksa, who was believed to be the daughter of a demon. When the bowstring is pulled, it sometimes cries with the voice of the dead Raksa, terrorizing the enemies. A character whose bow is fitted with this string can use the *Fear* power, with arcane skill d8 and 5 Power Points. The first time the character rolls a 1 on the Shooting die, regardless of the Wild Die, the bowstring breaks.

18. **Maneater's Cloak.** This impressive cloak was fashioned from the hide of one of the foulest beasts in the Savannah: an old lion that, too old to chase gazelles, developed a taste for human flesh. The wearer gains +2 to Intimidation and Fear rolls while wearing it, but he also receives the Habit (major) Hindrance of always craving human flesh. The Habit persists even while not wearing the cloak. The cloak must be destroyed and *banish* or *dispel* must be used on the character to free him from the curse.

19. **Snake Bracer.** This beautiful, ornamental bracer is made to resemble a coiled snake. In truth, dark magic animates it and the bracer can turn into a Venomous Snake (see *Savage Worlds* core rules). It counts as the *summon ally* Power, cast with an arcane ability of d8 and 5 Power Points. The snake is a creature of Novice rank. A legend says that this bracer somehow always manages to kill its owner.

20. **Mark of the Smith.** The Smith Priests of Hulian used to put a flame-shaped mark on weapons made to fight evil. This weapon (of the Game Master's choosing) bears the mark and grants the Holy Warrior and Champion Edges to the wielder. But Hulian can't leave such power in mortal hands for long: if the weapon is used against a demon, the Mark wears off at the end of the adventure.

TEMPORARY ITEMS

Non-permanent items are usually a good idea. Lotus concoctions that heal or give the hero a temporary boost are ok, because they can be easily controlled by the Game Master. Also, the Game Master should consider giving the heroes a very powerful relic only for some time.

CHAPTER 7:

ADVENTURE GENERATOR

Sometimes a GM might need inspiration for an adventure. The following pages introduce an Adventure Generator that will allow you to devise, in no time at all, amazing swords and sorcery plots for the entertainment of your players. You only need a deck of cards, a pencil and a piece of paper to jot down your story as it takes shape.

Are you ready? Then, let's go!

DECK PHASE

Draw four cards from the deck. Place them one next to the other in the order they are drawn. The suit and value of each card will create your adventure. More specifically, the suits will give you a *plot*, while the values will determine the *presentation*.

The plot is the raw structure of your story, basically "who does what", while the presentation is the way in which you narrate it to your audience, the players. Remember that even a simple story can be very enjoyable if told in the right way, using the right techniques, and peppering it with some nice twists.

Take some notes during the process, so that no important pieces of the puzzle will be missing at the end.

PLOT

Now, starting from the first card, the adventure's Setting, Adversary, Conflict and Reward will be determined.

FIRST CARD'S SUIT – SETTING

Pulp stories, and sword and sorcery ones are no exception, are heavily influenced by their location. Deciding where to set the main part of your adventure is the first step. Remember that this is only the core setting; other locations can be added as needed. For each type of setting you will find a list of iconic locations particularly suited to sword and sorcery adventures in the Dread Sea Dominions.

Spades – Urban. The adventure is set in a city, town, or other civilized location. Remember that a city is a place where a large number of individuals live together, so there are rules, laws and guards. It is also a place of religion, since the main temples are usually in cities. Economy is another important element: most merchants live in cities. And, where riches abound, there are always plenty of shady individuals ready to take advantage of the situation. Finally, the city is the place of the common man, where artisans, laborers and slaves work side by side.

Iconic urban locations: noble palaces, bazaars and marketplaces, temples and libraries, arenas and theatres, squares, large avenues and dark alleys, sewers and aqueducts, towers, prisons, city walls.

Hearts – Countryside. The adventure is still set in a civilized location but beyond the walls of a city. The heroes will move in a natural but not inherently dangerous environment, and their troubles will be caused by man rather than by nature. Remember that a countryside setting can

easily turn into a Wildlands setting if the heroes wander away from the civilized areas.

Iconic countryside locations: farms, inns, roads, villages, fields, well tended woods, navigable rivers, rural temples, encampments.

Diamonds – Wildlands. The adventure is set in a hostile natural environment. The Dread Sea Dominions are mostly wild and untamed by man and all the unsafe areas are collectively known as "Wildlands". The heroes will come up against bad weather, the risk of getting lost, predators, barbarians, and an unforgiving nature. Depending on the adventure, the Game Master should feel free to add natural threats besides those posed by the Adversary (see second card). Note that a countryside or urban setting can easily become a Wildland setting under certain specific climatic conditions (for example: a city during a pestilence, a village during a tornado, and so on).

Iconic Wildlands locations: sun scorched deserts, bayous and swamps, deep forests, insidious jungles, mountain ranges, steppes, frozen lakes, areas hit by tornadoes, floods, earthquakes.

Clubs – Ruins. A ruin is a place with limited human presence. Naturally, this does not mean it is safe. Ruin settings are grouped under two main categories. A "background ruin" does not feature the presence of man but has many remnants of the past. Examples of this setting are the Fallen Kingdom of Keron, or The Land of Idols. "Dungeon ruins", instead, are a totally different matter: they are enclosed spaces, full of monsters, traps and treasures, in which the heroes should be particularly wary.

Iconic ruins locations: caverns, cemeteries, old temples, sunken ships, abandoned mines, haunted castles, Cairns.

Joker – Weird. A weird location means that the adventure unfolds in a very strange location, such as a magical prison, or it is entirely set in a dream one of the characters has. If you are short of ideas, you can always draw two additional cards and try to mix them. For example, if you draw a heart (Wildland) and a club (Ruins), you can decide that the adventure is set in a military camp located among the ruins of an old city.

THE GOLDEN RULE

The most important rule you should remember when using an adventure generator is: "Stop whenever you want."

The generator is only a tool to help you sharpen your ideas. See it as a gym where you can develop your creative muscles. If you think you have devised a suitable plot only by considering the cards' suits and not their values, that will do just fine and you can stop. If you think one of the cards "ruins" the plot, ignore it or draw another. The generator is also quite robust, allowing you to change the number and/or meaning of the cards without affecting the rest. If you want to create an adventure with Two Adversaries and no Reward, you can do it. You are in charge!

Remember, the goal of the generator is to help YOU create an adventure. Use it, don't be used by it and feel free to experiment.

SECOND CARD'S SUIT – ADVERSARY

A sword and sorcery adventure needs a strong villain. This card tells you something about the nature and behavior of the heroes' main enemy. This doesn't obviously mean the enemy is alone: depending on his nature, he can have a whole horde of minions and servants under his command. Remember that this card doesn't tell you exactly *who* the adversary is but *how* he acts. For more specific examples, see the description of each type.

Spades – Brute. The adversary mainly relies on violence and sheer brute force. Subtlety and cunning aren't his weapons of choice; he prefers a more direct approach. If he controls magic and the supernatural, he uses them in a coarse way. He is very likely to have an army of followers ready to obey him and he keeps them at bay through fear and threats. Brute adversaries tend to be physically very strong.

Iconic brute adversaries: bandit and pirate lords, massive beasts and forgotten creatures, barbarian tribes, bloodthirsty shamans, stupid but incredibly strong monsters.

Hearts – Schemer. A schemer is someone who loves plotting. He will never step in directly, but will try to outwit and cheat the heroes. In many cases, the party won't discover his identity until far into the scenario, and uncovering his plots will be the main focus of the story. This dangerous individual might even present himself as a friend. A Schemer often has hireling and minions, whom he uses as pawns for his evil purposes.

Iconic schemer adversaries: corrupted courtesan, treacherous counsellor, secret worshipper of evil forces, spy-master, lone serial killer.

Diamonds – Power Lord. A power lord is defined by the great resources available to him. He isn't personally strong like a Brute or cunning like a Schemer, but he is charismatic, rich and socially prominent or has an army of followers under his command. A power lord is usually obsessed with power itself and will do anything to preserve or increase it. Minions and followers are very important to a Power Lord and their loyalty stem from various roots: fanaticism, duty, or even physical dependence.

Iconic power lord adversaries: power-hungry nobles, prophets or other religious figures, fallen heroes, leaders of demonic cults, generals, revolutionaries.

Clubs – Abomination. An Abomination threatens the heroes simply because he is too alien to follow the human way of life. He simply doesn't understand (or doesn't care about) morality, good and evil. Weirdness and fear are his main features. Some abominations are driven by lust,

hunger or needs so different from the human ones that the heroes will never truly understand them. An encounter with an abomination will always be a little scary.

Iconic abomination adversaries: demons, undead creatures, age-old sorcerers, ty-rants and rulers so detached from human life to be emotionless.

Joker – Special. A special opponent often has a peculiar background. He can be a re-luctant enemy or someone who unwitting-ly does something evil (like a farmer who unleashes a curse upon himself and his village by finding a cursed relic). Otherwise, he can be a mix of the other categories. In this case, draw two additional cards and mix them. For example, if you draw a spade (brute) and a club (abomination), the opponent might be a powerful gladiator who was killed in the arena and has comes back from the dead to murder innocent people and feed on their vital energy.

A MATTER OF SCALE

You can use the Adventure Generator on very different scales: you can work with it to create the general outline of an entire campaign, a single scenario, or an additional session of an already existing campaign. All you have to do is change scale.

While designing a campaign, you must consider a very long time span. The Adversary of a campaign won't probably appear for quite some time. He might have a number of hirelings, some of them important and others much less so. The Setting of the campaign will be broad, like a sort of background music which will permeate the various adventures, connecting them. The same is true for the Plot, the Conflict and the Reward.

Conversely, when you are designing a single adventure of the campaign above, a hireling of the main Adversary might be the Adversary of the current adventure. The creative process is the same but on a smaller scale. Your scenario will have its own Setting (although the campaign's Setting will still be present in the background) and a specific Adversary (with his own personality but connected to the main Adversary of the campaign). The same will be true for the Conflict and the Reward.

Third Card's Suit – Conflict

The previous cards referred to the *where* and *who* of the scenario, while this card tells you about the reasons behind the Adversary's actions. Alternatively, you can use the card to determine the party's motive for challenging the Adversary. In this case, you need a particularly good hook (see Getting into the Action below).

Spades – Passion. The enemy is driven by a strong emotion. It might be hate, revenge, or even love. The target of his passion and the reasons for his feelings must be determined. Is the target an NPC or one of the heroes? A mix of passions can be good, too. For example, a villain in love with a non-player character is rejected and his love turns into hate, leading him to seek terrible revenge. A passion is usually stirred in the mind and does not concern physical objects (for the latter, see the Desire entry below).

Iconic passion conflict: hate, love (reciprocated or not), honor, revenge, piety, desperation, lust, madness, justice.

Hearts – Desire. The reason behind the Adversary's (or the heroes') actions is the wish to obtain something, usually physical. The object of their desire depends on their nature. For example, a powerful sorcerer may covet a dark artifact, a despotic king may want to conquer a disputed land, an ugly demon may crave a pretty girl to eat or some human sacrifice.

Iconic desire conflict: wealth, knowledge, powerful items, status, love interests.

Diamonds – Survival. The Adversary (or the party) is driven by the sheer need to survive. Note that survival has a very broad meaning; for instance, it might refer to preserving the status quo. The king's most trusted counsellor might decide to murder the new, pretty queen, if he feels she is influencing her royal spouse too much. Similarly, a tribe of barbarians tormented by hunger may decide to assault a peaceful farming outpost. It most certainly isn't fair, but this is the unforgiving nature of the Dominions.

Iconic survival conflicts: food, self-esteem, vital resources or necessary drugs, survival of the species, mating.

Clubs – Nature. Some creatures are inherently dangerous. Monsters, predators and even humans try to impose their will or harm the heroes simply because it is in their nature. A monster or an abomination will do it out of instinct, but other motives may drive civilized humans. Why does a powerful prince with a harem full of gorgeous girls decide to kidnap a humble farmer's daughter? For no reason, except that he can, so he does. Sadly, evil needs no reason.

Iconic nature conflicts: innate cruelty, curiosity, instinct, education, sense of superiority.

Joker – Complex. Sometimes, conflicts have very complex reasons or no reason at all. For example, the whole thing might be a misunderstanding and the heroes have been wronged or involved in it by mistake. You can also draw two cards and try mixing them. For example, if the Adversary is a corrupt Tricarnian Prince, a spade (passion) and a club (nature) may mean that the lord is obsessed with perfect looking girls, and he kidnaps them to embalm and preserve them forever.

MATCHING CARDS
You can get additional help in the creative process if you find matching cards, i.e. two (or more) cards sharing the same suit or value. The presence of a match should make you concentrate more closely on the synergy created by the cards, and this will add flavor to your story.

If, for example, you draw a diamond for both the Setting (Wildlands) and the Adversary (Power Lord) and you decide that the Adversary is the rebellious governor of a remote province of the Empire, you can devise a plot in which the Adversary has made a pact with the local cannibal clans and, in exchange for monthly human sacrifices, the man-eaters will submit to his authority.

FOURTH CARD'S SUIT – REWARD

This card gives you an idea of what the heroes will gain if they manage to complete the adventure. Note that this is a double-edged sword: killing a powerful enemy or becoming extremely famous is not always a good thing.

Note: the Reward is purely optional. A Game Master should tailor the Reward of his stories based on the characteristics of the group. If no Reward is included, this card might provide an extra Setting for the adventure.

Spades – Saving your Skin. Sometimes, the heroes have to be content with getting home in one piece and having a story to tell their grandchildren. Note that this might not satisfy certain players, in which case you can add a minor reward (wealth or fame below) to make them happy.

Iconic life rewards: bare survival, no gain and no loss, missed opportunity.

Hearts – Wealth. The party will receive a large amount of money, which they can spend in the After the Adventure phase, precious items, or a permanent possession. Note that wealth often attracts unwanted attention.

Iconic richness rewards: money, jewels, ships, horses, castles, houses, slaves and servants, titles.

Diamonds – Fame. The heroes have become famous. Tales of their deeds have spread across the Dominions and their faces are recognized by the common people. But fame comes with its pros and cons. For instance, if the heroes are famed slayers of Cairnlanders, the Borderlands farmers will praise them but the Cainlanders will seek to eliminate them.

Iconic fame rewards: monster slayer, great warrior, just man, fearsome pirate, wise sage, best thief in town.

Clubs – Relationships. The party doesn't earn any material wealth but the support of some influential individual or group. This might involve receiving a simple favor or a much more important and permanent relationship, like being adopted by a tribe, a blood pact or a marriage.

However, remember that in gaining the friendship of a man you gain also his enemies.

Iconic relationship rewards: love interests, favors, introduction at court, recommendations, high rank in the city guards or army, marriage proposals, blood pacts.

Joker – Power or Mixed Blessing. The heroes have the chance to put their hands on something very powerful, such as a magical item, or they learn some important information, such as the secret location of a treasure. Otherwise, as above, you can draw two additional cards and mix them. For example a spade (Saving your Skin) and a club (Relationship) can be combined to create the following story: at the end of the adventure the heroes kill the monster and, although its enchanted gold turns to dust, they manage to save a damsel in distress who, along with her gorgeous sisters, will show the party her gratitude.

PRESENTATION

At this point, you should have a clear idea of what the structure of the adventure will be. Now, you need to consider the best way to tell your players the story. So, go back to each card and look at its value.

FIRST CARD'S VALUE – GETTING INTO THE ACTION

The start of a story is the most crucial part, along with the end. Just think of how many books, comics, or movies you have put aside simply because the starting pages or scenes didn't grab you. Hook your players from the very beginning and you'll certainly enjoy a memorable game.

Deuce – Mistaken Identity. A classic in certain types of fiction, this beginning can be very funny if used in moderation. One or more members of the party are mistaken for someone else. This can be an advantage or a disadvantage. It is an advantage if the heroes are mistaken for powerful heroes, noblemen and so on; it is a disadvantage if they are believed to be villains. In both cases, the mistaken identity triggers the adventure.

Three or Four – Wrong Place and Time. A very common but good way to start an adventure. By pure chance, the heroes find themselves in a place where they get involved in something interesting (active role). Otherwise, fate throws them into an unexpected situation (passive role). In the first case, the heroes have to *act* to begin the adventure. For example, they witness a murder attempt, and the beginning of the adventure depends on their will to intervene. In the second case (passive role), they might be forced to react when attacked by a group of bandits on the road. Both approaches are good.

:MOHLER 05:

Five to Seven – If the Pay is Good… The party has been recruited to complete a mission. This classic beginning has many advantages. Firstly, you clearly have three key points to work on: the patron who commissioned the job, the mission to be completed, and the reward (the reason that leads the players to act). You should also decide if the adventure starts with the patron making the proposal, so the heroes are allowed to refuse, or if they have already accepted the job. The first approach creates a freer but somewhat slower game; the second is more appropriate if you want to throw the players directly into the action.

Eight or Nine – Lucky Break. The heroes make a remarkable discovery and this triggers the adventure. For example, they find an ancient map or someone tells them an interesting story they want to check. You can also use rewards from a previous adventure to start a new story. For example, the heroes have recently acquired a precious idol made of gold. Then, they discover it is a fake, but where is the real idol?

Ten – Reluctant Heroes. The heroes are not keen on the adventure but they are forced to act by someone or something. Maybe they have been taken prisoners and must escape, or their ship has been wrecked and they must survive, or a devious patron has made them drink wine with a slow poison and will give them the antidote only if they complete a certain quest for him. Whatever the situation, this type of hook introduces a double motivation: the party must both accomplish the main task and get out of their raw deal (for example, by getting revenge on the poisoner).

Jack – Close and Personal. Each hero has a long personal history, probably full of enemies, grievances, curses, and so on. Well, it is time to put this to good use in a story. The character you have chosen is the focus of the adventure and the other heroes will help him out of friendship, or because he pays or forces them. If you use this hook on a regular basis, try to choose a different hero each time.

Queen – A Friend Is a Friend. A friend or a patron of the party asks for help. He can be an NPC the heroes met in a previous adventure or some long-forgotten acquaintance. Alternatively, the heroes need something and a friend intervenes to help them, which leads to the start of the adventure.

King – In the Thick of Things. This is more of a narrative technique than a real hook. Simply start the adventure in the

thick of things, or even toward the end if you prefer. Choose a climax point and run the story from there, giving the players very little information about what happened before (you can use a brief flashback). When the current scene is completed, you can start the adventure from the beginning, revealing the events that have led to the climax. When the two parts join, continue the story till the end. Note that this technique has a downside, since the heroes cannot die in the flashback (consider them as having the Improved Tough as Nails Edge). However, you can penalize them by taking a Bennie every time you have to save them from certain death. If you want to add another hook to the story, draw an additional card.

Ace – "Do You Remember When…?" Similar to In the Thick of Things, this hook allows you to create a quick adventure as part of a bigger one. Something a party member sees or does triggers the memory of a past adventure, which is then played. This hook is great when you are in the middle of a campaign and, for some reason, many players miss a session. You can play the past story while keeping the main campaign on standby. As in the case above, the heroes cannot die in the past but can be imprisoned, robbed, or saved by someone, so that at the end of the adventure they are alive but receive no Experience Point.

Joker – Weird. The joker means something really weird, like an adventure within a dream (or nightmare) of one of the heroes or a situation in which the players play other characters, as you see in certain horror movies in which a group of people is killed by the monster before the real stars come into the story. Otherwise, you can always draw two cards and combine them. For example, with a Ten (Reluctant Heroes) and an Ace (Do You Remember When…?) you can have a story about a time, years ago,

when the heroes were captured by pirates and eventually managed to escape.

THE IMPORTANCE OF FLAVORING

Once you have a basic plot, you should spend some time "flavoring" your adventure, i.e. rooting it into the Dread Sea Dominions environment. *This basically means providing more background. Don't underestimate the importance of details, like the names of the exotic beverages the heroes drink at the tavern or the description of the paintings they find in an ancient palace. Your players must think that everything their heroes see, hear and smell has a reason to exist.*

It is incredible how some minor details can add major realism to a story. You can always use the background found in this manual but, if you have some time, you might want to read an introductory anthropology text. The history of human civilizations will provide plenty of inspiration. When you are defining the background and general "feel" of a Beasts and Barbarians scenario, the following list of keywords might help you get into the right mood:

† *Iron Age*
† *Ignorance and superstition*
† *Barbarians on the borders*
† *Beautiful courtesans*
† *Decadent empires*
† *Sharp blades and strong arms*
† *Age-old civilizations*
† *Lotus plants and mutations*
† *Sweat and blood*
† *Slavery and wealth*
† *Law of the sword*
† *Exotic lands*
† *Drums in the savannah*
† *Demon-worshipping cults*
† *Sandals and bare breasts*
† *Elephants, tigers and dangerous beasts*
† *Barbarians are brutes*
† *Forgotten knowledge*
† *Barbarians are noble savages*
† *Merciless nature*

SECOND CARD'S – VALUE ATMOSPHERE

The value of the second card provides information on the mood of the game and general theme of the adventure.

Deuce – Horror. The general feel of the story is dark and spooky. You can achieve this by slightly altering the setting or by making the villain just a little bit scarier. Remember, subtlety is the best way to achieve a horror effect. For instance, a simple "find the kidnapped girl in the slums" plot can turn into a truly blood-chilling story if the slums are plagued by a terrible pestilence.

Three or Four – Mystery. A mystery of some sort is the main theme of the adventure. This can be achieved in two ways: the identity of a character (the patron, the villain) or the purpose of a mission is kept secret at the beginning of the scenario; otherwise, an element of the plot is different from what it seems. In both cases, the purpose of the adventure is to unravel the mystery.

Five to Seven – Journey. In this classic setting, the heroes must travel from a place to another. There can be different reasons for the journey. The party might be escorting someone, have to deliver a message or be driven by a dream or vision. The journey itself, with its many dangers, is the theme of the adventure, and it can be either a physical journey or a metaphorical one.

Eight or Nine – Hunt. The heroes must pursue or find someone or something. Alternatively, they are pursued and must shake off their enemies. Examples of Hunt are the classic "quest" for a magical item, tracking down a dangerous bandit to collect a bounty, or shadowing an opponent to locate his secret lair. But remember, if the heroes are discovered, the hunters can easily become the hunted...

Ten – Crime. The adventure's theme is a criminal action. The heroes are forced to do something outside the boundaries of the law, like committing treason, a theft, or a murder, or simply lying and cheating. This means that, besides fighting their enemies, they have to worry about guards and law enforcers. Alternatively, they can be on the side of good and they must stop a criminal of some sort.

Jack – Defenders. This situation gives the heroes a mainly passive role in the story. Don't worry, it can be very entertaining! They must either defend something or prevent someone from doing something. They might be guards hired to protect a person or property, or they might be entrusted with defending an outpost or fortification from the enemy hordes. The defenders are sometimes doomed to fail, but this will only lead to a new twist in the adventure. For example, if they are asked to protect a precious artifact from theft, and the object is stolen, the story turns into a Hunt or Crime and the party will have to retrieve the stolen item.

Queen – Romance. Ah, love, mover of souls and shaker of empires! The story's theme is the oldest and most basic in the universe: love. It can be passionate, pure, immortal, unreciprocated, true, or insincere. Remember that the worst things are done and the greatest sacrifices are made for love. The plot might involve a character's sentimental life: one of the heroes falls in love with someone or an NPC is attracted to a party member. Or else, it can be the story of an impossible love, doomed to turn into tragedy.

King – Intrigue. Similar to Mystery, the scenario's theme is a web of deceit around the heroes. They must act with cunning, stealth and deviousness to unravel it, or just deal with the situation head-on. Alternatively, they might be unwilling pawns in the villain's plan. Whatever the nature of the intrigue, remember: no one is telling the truth and no one should be trusted!

Ace – Big Event. The story is set during a very big event, or a part of it. This is an excellent way to make the players discover a little more about the world in which they are playing. First, the exact nature of the event must be determined: does the story happen during a natural catastrophe, like a flood or tornado? Is it set in the middle of a terrible war? Or is it about a happy occurrence, like a royal wedding? What is the heroes' part in the event? Are they impotent spectators (like during a natural catastrophe) or does everything depend on their bravery (the royal bride has gone missing and the heroes must bring her back before the wedding)?

Joker – Mixed. The Joker indicates a major mood change, like a comical story during a more serious campaign, to ease the tension a little, or a serious story during a light-hearted campaign. Or it may be something even stranger, like the heroes losing their memory at the start of the story. Finally, you can also draw two cards and mix

them. For example, if an Eight (Hunt) and a Queen (Romance) are drawn, the party may be hired to track down a reluctant bride who has run away with her lover.

MAPPING OR NOT?

Note: in this paragraph by "maps" we mean "exploration maps". Combat maps fall into the props category.

One of the most time-consuming activities during the preparation of a game is drawing exploration maps.

We love maps, no kidding, but in certain cases there is simply no time, or no reason, to have a map. Think about classic sword and sorcery fiction. The heroes often explore crumbling ruins and ancient palaces, full of strange shadows and monsters, and they constantly risk getting lost or falling into a ravine. However, the author never provides a detailed map of the locations, since a vague description increases the feeling of wonder and mystery, which would disappear if a complete map was available.

If you decide to use a map-less approach, you can adopt one of the two systems below.

Locations as Encounters. *Simply ignore the mapping side but detail the encounters as you would do in an outdoor scenario. Put them in an order of your choice or connect each of them like the old choose-your-adventure books did. For example, from location 1, the door to the right takes you to location 2, while the corridor leads to location 3 and so on.*

Abstract Navigation System. *This system is particularly useful when the heroes are trying to reach a specific location (for example, the main room of the unholy temple where a human sacrifice is about to start) and must do so in a limited time. First, choose an Advancement skill, like Tracking if they are following a path or Smarts if they are navigating a labyrinth. Then, determine the duration of the exploration rounds in real world terms (i.e. five minutes, an hour, half a day and so on). For each* *exploration round, the party makes a group roll on the Advancement skill. For each success and raise, they receive an Advancement Token (usually, maximum 2 per round) and draw a card from the action deck. Each card value and/or suit is linked to a specific encounter/location the heroes must face. When they earn a suitable number of Advancement Tokens (usually, between 8 and 16), they reach the "final" room. The duration of the rounds also helps you determine roughly how much time they have used for the exploration.*

This system is a little more complex than the previous, one but it has the advantage of providing a non-linear, virtually endless exploration system.

A good example of an abstract navigation system can be found in Beasts & Barbarians Heroic Tale #2: The Carnival of Nal Sagath, downloadable for free from the Gramel website.

THIRD CARD'S – VALUE PLOT TWIST

The best plots are the ones that are difficult for your players to predict. Twists and unexpected events drastically change the adventure and make it more interesting and fun to play. Remember: twists are made to astonish.

Deuce – Catastrophe. The villain's or the heroes' actions trigger a disaster of some type! Differently from the Big Event of the second card, the Catastrophe Plot Twist doesn't exist at the start of the adventure and poses an additional threat.

Three or Four – Change. As the game is progressing, change the Setting, Atmosphere or Adversary (or even all of them)! This can have amazing effects on the outcome of the adventure. For example, let's take the "find the kidnapped girl in the slums" situation and apply a radical change to its Setting, Atmosphere and Adversary. While looking for clues in the slums, the heroes are drugged and wake up hours later in chains, on a foreign ship making for a faraway land. Naturally, the kidnapped girl is on the ship too and the heroes must first free themselves and then rescue her.

Five to Seven – A Personal Matter. The scenario is about a personal matter concerning one of the heroes. The Villain might be an old Enemy returning from the past or he has kidnapped, cursed, or killed a party member's relative or love interest. Whatever the reason, from now on, the story gets very personal.

Eight or Nine – Nest of Snakes. As they proceed in the adventure, the heroes discover that the situation is much worse than they expected. Maybe the Villain is only the servant of a more powerful evildoer or the conspiracy has branched out so far that even people beyond suspicion are part of it. The plot is so complex that the party will need some extra help, time, and luck to get out of their predicament.

Ten – Helper. Some unexpected help comes the heroes' way. Maybe the sweet damsel in distress they must save turns out to be a diehard Amazon warrior. Or the barbarians chasing the heroes, impressed by their courage in fighting the great evil in the forest, join the party's side for the final battle. Or else, an evil character turns good and befriends the heroes.

Jack – Traitor. An ally of the party turns out to be an enemy! Maybe he has been working for the Adversary all along, or the heroes have done something that changes his allegiance. Or, as in Ten above, the Traitor is actually betraying the bad guy, becoming a friend and Helper of the heroes. Alternatively, the Traitor has simply made a terrible mistake, like not locking the back door of the palace, and now wishes to put things right. Remember, a good traitor can become so important in your plot as to obscure the main villain.

Queen – Things aren't What they Seem. The Setting, Adversary, a patron, an NPC or even the mission itself is not what it appears to be, and this has a serious impact on the story. Maybe the girl the party is going to rescue wasn't actually kidnapped, or the evil warlock is only a poor herdsman cursed by a relic, or the debauched nobleman who has been opposing the heroes throughout the adventure turns out to be a friend. Whatever your idea, this twist is based on the difference between appearance and reality.

King – Repercussions. The heroes' actions have major repercussions on the future of the campaign, or of the Dominions. These consequences can be positive or negative, but the party must live with them. If the group stops the dark ritual of a Nandal shaman, aimed at creating eternal winter in the northern lands, they might cause a terrible drought lasting for years. Or, if the anonymous Phalanx Officer the party has saved from the Valk riders is the legitimate son of the Emperor, they can gain a precious

friend. Actions have consequences, and some of them are lifelong.

Ace – Dilemma. The adventure presents a moral choice of some type that the heroes must make. If the heroes are hired by colonists to clear a ruined city of hideous monsters, but then they discover that the monsters are actually the original dwellers of the city, what is the right thing to do? Many dilemmas are of a very personal nature: if the evil warlock is a childhood friend or someone who once saved the hero's life, what will the hero do? It is up to the players to make their own decisions.

Joker – Weird. This card indicates a weird twist, like the party discovering they are working for an evil patron. Otherwise, you can draw two cards and mix their meanings. For example a Deuce (Catastrophe) and a Four (Change) might mean that, by interrupting a dark ritual, the heroes free a powerful demon that sends the whole city back in time, to a few hours before the fall of the Dread Star.

FOURTH CARD'S – VALUE CLIMAX

The fourth and last card refers to another crucial part of the story: the main scene, the moment of maximum tension when the Game Master gives his narrative best. The players will probably forget the rest of the adventure but they will remember this part. It is also important to decide at which point to play the climax scene. If you are running a single session, the best moment is in the middle of the game, so that the party has time to complete it and can feel satisfied at the end. If you are playing a multi-session adventure, you might want to include a cliffhanger at the end of the session, made to hook the players until the next game.

Deuce – Sacrifice. Someone, a hero or an NPC, is given the opportunity to sacrifice himself to save the day. For example, the princess offers herself to a demon to spare the life of a hero she loves. Or a character is given the chance to kill the mad king, at the cost of his own life. Remember, a sacrifice doesn't necessarily lead to a character's death but, when the players consider the opportunity, they must believe it to be so. Even when a hero stands alone against a horde of barbarians, unexpected help may come just in time to save him.

Three or Four – Unmasking. The story climaxes when someone finally drops his mask or something incredible is revealed: the goodhearted priest of the Divine Couple turns out to be the master of a sect of demon worshippers, or one of the heroes, who has always thought she was an orphan, discovers that she is the last heir of a powerful Tricarnian prince, or an old witch tells the hero that he cannot marry the princess because she is his sister. Remember, the revelation must always be very dramatic.

Five to Seven – Battle. A combat, such as a man-to-man duel in the arena or the clash of two massive armies, is the high point of the story. The clash of blades or of opposed wills will resolve the scenario.

Eight or Nine – Escape or Chase. At a certain point in the story, the party must escape from a dangerous situation, such as the collapse of an underground temple in which the heroes have killed a powerful demon. Alternatively, a thief has just stolen a treasure from under the heroes' noses and they must chase him along the rooftops. Remember, the fact that the main villain is gone doesn't mean that the adventure is over.

Ten – Impending Doom. The power of ineluctability, like in an ancient tragedy, characterizes the climax scene, and the heroes seem doomed to unavoidable failure. For example, the meaning of a grim prophecy is revealed or all the odds are against the party, making the situation desperate. But a strong arm, a powerful will and a good dose of luck can triumph even when all seems lost.

Jack – Race against Time. The heroes have a limited amount of time to complete the adventure and must hurry! Otherwise the Nandal horde will storm the city, or an ancient curse will kill the princess, or the poisoned wine the heroes have drunk will cripple or blind them for life. A Race against Time can be on a small or larger scale. In the first case, the heroes have been bitten by a demon and they only have a few minutes before being turned into hideous abominations. The situation will be resolved in a single scene. In the second case, the heroes only have ten days before their immortal souls, trapped by a sorcerer inside an hourglass, trickle down like sand, causing their eternal death and damnation. The situation requires a whole adventure to be solved.

Queen – Rescue. A hero truly feels lost without a damsel to rescue. The highest point of the scenario is a breathtaking scene in which someone is rescued or something is retrieved. For instance, the princess has been taken captive and is now bound to an altar. The party must free her before the big, ugly guardian wakes up and tries to eat the adventurers for lunch.

King – Reinforcements. When all seems lost, reinforcements come to the heroes' aid! They might be friends, trusted soldiers, or simply the cavalry. You can interpret this situation in the opposite way, too: when the heroes have almost defeated the villain, he receives fresh help, greatly reducing the party's chances of victory. When you introduce reinforcements, be careful not to shift the narrative focus from the heroes to the reinforcements. The players will feel left out if you make your NPCs (the reinforcements) solve the adventure instead of the heroes. The reinforcements should be strong enough to provide substantial help but they must not overshadow the player characters. In addition, remember that, in *Savage Worlds*, Allies are usually controlled by the players, not the Game Master, which makes them feel more in control.

Ace – Stand-Off. A classic in action movies, a stand-off is a stalemate situation lasting until someone takes the initiative and the story explodes, with dramatic consequences. A typical stand-off happens when two groups are studying each other, weapons drawn, but nobody acts. Another example is when the bad guy holds someone hostage, which prevents the heroes from acting. Remember, the stand-off is meant to be resolved: use it to reach the climax, and then let all hell break loose.

Joker – Weird. You can always try something very weird, or draw two cards and combine their indications into one climax scene. For example, an Eight (Escape or Chase) and a King (Reinforcements) can create a scene in which the heroes chase the Valk bandit who kidnapped the princess and finally corner him, but, when they are about to free the girl, a Valk horde arrives on the scene, making the heroes' task much harder.

MANAGING YOUR RESOURCES
When you prepare a scenario, it is important to effectively manage your most important resource: time.

The four most important (and time-consuming) activities when preparing a scenario are: devising the plot, flavoring the story, working out creatures' stats, and designing maps/making props.

When you have little time, you must choose what to concentrate on, dedicating a certain amount of time to each aspect.

Devising the Plot. *It is crucial. You should devote most of your time to this (50%).*

Flavoring the Story. *This aspect (see above) is also very important. It is the flesh and blood covering the bones of your plot. You should dedicate at least 25% of your time to this.*

Working out Creatures' Stats . *This is usually very easy in Savage Worlds. Don't waste too much time on it (10%), unless you are planning a very particular combat. Almost all the creatures can be created by taking a monster from the core rule bestiary and altering a couple of stats.*

Designing Maps/Making Props. *Before starting to draw a very elaborate map, ask yourself: will the players ever see it? Also, is a complete map of the current location really necessary, considering the heroes will visit only two or three places? If the answer is "no", avoid wasting time on maps nobody will see except you, use a map-less system (see above) and concentrate on other things. Props are a different matter: a good prop (which can also be a detailed combat map) can really enhance your game, but keep in mind that you need enough time for plot devising and flavoring.*

PUTTING IT ALL TOGETHER

Now that you have used inspirations from the cards and devised a rough plot, you are almost finished. You just have to work out the creatures' stats (unless you want to do that on the fly) and add some details to the locations and background.

Still unsure about how the whole thing works? Check the example below!

Plot Example: The Curse of the Great Biter

Sitting down with the Adventure Generator, I shuffle my deck of Action Cards and draw four, placing them in order on the table. They are:

1. Six of Clubs (Setting)
2. Ace of Hearts (Adversary)
3. Ten of Clubs (Conflict)
4. Eight of Diamonds (Reward)

The player characters are currently in the Kyrosian city of Chalat on the Sword River, so the adventure I generate will have to tie into that area.

The first card is Clubs and gives me a setting of "Ruins." I like the idea of an ancient temple of some sort. The second card is Hearts and gives me an adversary of "Schemer." I like the idea of a scheming, deceitful woman. The third card is Clubs again and gives me a conflict of "Nature." Giving this some thought I decide it will either be the woman's greedy nature, or some natural beast. Perhaps I can use both! The woman's motivation will be her greed, so she is after a jewel of some sort. There will also be a monstrous animal in the adventure. The fourth card is Diamonds and gives me a reward of "Fame." This is a tough one, but probably it will mean that the PC's only reward this time will be fame for their deeds.

For the fleshing out process, the first card is a six and gives me a hook of "Hired." I decide that the woman will use her wiles to "hire" one or more of the party. The second card is an ace and gives me an at-

mosphere of "Big Event." I like the idea of a big natural event and decide there will be an earthquake. The third card is a Ten and gives me a twist of "Help." I decide that the earthquake will actually help the adventurers somehow. The fourth and last card is an eight and tells me the climax will be an "Escape." The party will have to escape the crumbling temple as the earthquake topples it!

Now we must put it all together and add some background texture to it.

Hadiya, a beautiful but greedy courtesan, is a love interest of one of the heroes. During a night of love, she artfully whispers in her lover's ear about an ancient temple of Lythros, the Crocodile God.

"The cult practiced sacrifice and was driven out by the locals," she says, "and the temple was sealed. Some ships and fishermen vanished in the waters near the ruins, so people called it cursed and kept their distance. But the people also spoke of great riches left behind by the cult; particularly a legendary green gem called the Heart of the River, which is maculated like the skin of the Sword River alligators. Only those clever enough to avoid being ensnared by traps or killed by the evil creatures dwelling in the temple could make off with the riches."

But Hadiya tells her lover she's found another way into the temple. A wandering beggar who passed the temple one week ago just after a large earth tremor, told her of how the tremor had caused a temple wall to collapse and create a hole! Hadiya continues to convince her lover and his friends to take her to the temple in search of the jewel.

Inside the temple the party will have a few encounters with traps and some degenerate survivors of the cult, who have been living in the sealed temple for generations. In the depths of the temple is an underground pool with submerged tunnels that lead to a river within which lives an enormous crocodile - the Great Biter itself! This is what has fed on fishermen and ships that get too close to the temple ruins.

The pool hosts a small patch of rock in the middle where the altar of the temple stands and the precious gem, the Heart of the River, lies upon. The party will have to find a way to cross the pool, and while doing so will discover a cleverly concealed bridge-like platform below the surface of the water.

Possibly, in one of the previous encounters in the temple, they'll have found cryptic inscriptions hinting to "looking for the well concealed way" or something similar.

While crossing the bridge, they will be attacked by the Great Biter which will try to drag the adventurers in deep water and devour them.

At the end of the fight, the party manages to reach the altar in the center of the pool and grab the great jewel.

At this point Hadiya pulls out a tube containing a powder of a very deadly Lotus poison, and gloats how she will kill the entire party with its deadly cloud and take the jewel for herself!

Just then an earthquake will shake the complex and she will be crushed by a falling crocodile-headed statue. The party will then perform a daring escape from the crumbling temple to the surface, with the ceilings collapsing all around them, walls cracking, and the lake waters rising as the river pours in.

The party's only reward will be fame for ending "The Curse of the Great Biter."

EIGHT REALLY FAST PLOTS

The generator requires some time to be used. Even an expert user will need at least half an hour to design a plot. But sometimes you have to devise an adventure in very little time. In this case, you can use the following suggestions. The plots are deliberately simple and short, so that you can add to them as you prefer.

† *A girl is kidnapped by a hideous creature. The party must save her.*

† *The heroes are lost in a very hostile environment (such as a desert), their provisions are dwindling and they are desperate. Suddenly, they spot an ancient city, where they can probably find water and food, but the place is inhabited by a debauched, dangerous race.*

† *A patron orders the heroes to steal a precious item from an evil sorcerer in a very well protected mansion. Additional twist: the heroes' patron turns out to be worse than the sorcerer and tries to con them.*

† *The heroes are imprisoned by a mad villain who has a major obsession (gladiators' games, dangerous Lotus experiments, embalming beautiful girls,…). They must escape from his den before it is too late.*

† *A hero or a close friend is accused of a crime (usually murder) that he hasn't committed. The party has limited time to find the culprit.*

† *The party is hired to bring back a fugitive or to collect the bounty on the head a powerful criminal. This will require a dangerous journey in a wild region.*

† *At the start of the adventure, the heroes are being chased by a large group of evil NPCs (Cairnlanders, Valk riders, or similar). They find shelter in an old ruin, a cave or other indoor environment which the pursuers dare not enter because it is the den of an ancient evil.*

† While in a deserted, the heroes bump into an NPC, often a beautiful girl. She asks for their help because the cruel local tyrant has done her some wrong. But, they soon realize the girl was a specter, a restless soul looking for vengeance. Then, they meet the tyrant who is harassing another one of his subjects. If they decide to fight the cruel lord, the specter will help them.

BEASTS AND BARBARIANS

MONSTERS OF THE DOMINIONS

T his chapter presents some of the creatures players will find most interesting. It includes mounts, summonable beasts, and so on. It is not to be considered an extensive bestiary, but only a taste of the foul monsters one may encounter in *Beasts and Barbarians*!

MODIFIED MONSTROUS ABILITIES

The Demon monstrous ability, introduced in the *Fantasy Companion*, is slightly modified in the *Beasts and Barbarians* world, so it is reported below.

DEMON

• **Demon:** Demons are immune to poison and disease. They have a +2 bonus to recovering from being Shaken.

ANCESTOR'S GHOST

These ethereal creatures are the ghosts of men and women who lived thousands of years ago. Sorcerers evoke them because they are free from the constraints of existence and can perceive the world in a way that living beings can't.

DAUGHTER OF HORDAN

It sometimes happens that Hordan herself appears in the Dread Sea Dominions to answer the call of some very powerful sorcerer. When the evil Demon Lady arrives, she must be entertained. Giving her a proper mate, a man of great vigor and beauty, is the best way to appease her insatiable lust.

If she is satisfied, before going away she leaves a gift for the sorcerer who called upon her: a large, green egg, warm and pulsating like a heart. If properly cared for and regularly smeared with human blood, the egg hatches after thirteen days. The creature emerging from the egg is a six-armed baby-snake which will become a woman of terrible beauty, a Daughter of Hordan.

These creatures are secretly venerated in the dark temples of Tricarnia because they have both human and demonic features. The newly born being grows into an adult in thirteen months. During this period she has the intelligence of an animal because, despite her aspect, she lacks a soul. Yet, the devious Priest Princes of Tricarnia know how to make her blossom in all her glory. If a Daughter of Hordan kills and devours the raw heart of the man who fathered her, she acquires a soul and human intelligence.

Some sorcerers actually prefer to kill the father as soon as possible because an animal-like Daughter is a useful and faithful pet as long as she is properly nourished; while an intelligent one is cunning and seeks personal power. Indeed, there are tales of entire families of Priest Princes who become subjugated by one of these six-armed monstrosities.

Note: the following stats refer to an intelligent Daughter of Hordan. An animal-

Attributes: Agility d6, Smarts d6, Spirit d10, Strength d6, Vigor d6
Skills: Fighting d6, Intimidation d12+2, Knowledge (specific era) d10, Notice d10, Stealth d12+2.
Pace: 6; **Parry:** 5; **Toughness:** 5
Special Abilities
• **Anchor:** Ancestor's Ghosts cannot leave the place that they haunt or, if summoned by a sorcerer, cannot go farther than 12" from their evoker.
• **Ethereal:** Ancestor's Ghosts are immaterial and can only be damaged by magic.
• **Ghost Powers:** An Ancestor's Ghost can use these Powers, using Spirit for arcane skill rolls: *divination, detect arcana, darkness, fear, and telekinesis.* It has 15 Power Points and, when they run out, the ghost disappears.
• **Spirit Precognition:** An Ancestor's Ghost can perceive dangers as per the Danger Sense Edge.

like Daughter has the same stats as an intelligent one except Smarts (A), and she is a Henchman rather than a Wild Card.

Attributes: Agility d8, Smarts d8, Spirit d8, Strength d10, Vigor d8
Skills: Fighting d8, Intimidation d8, Notice d8, Persuasion d10, Stealth d6, Taunt d8.
Pace: 7; **Parry:** 6; **Toughness:** 8
Gear: Six bronze long swords (Str+d8), bronze helm (+2, only head).
Special Abilities
• **Claws:** Str+d4, but intelligent Daughters use weapons.
• **Constrictor:** She adds +4 to Grapple attacks.
• **Demon:** +2 to recover from being Shaken; Immune to poison and disease;
• **Otherworldly Temptress:** This creature is born of lust and is aware of her mother's seduction skills. She can use the Temptress Edge, with 10 Power Points. Only intelligent Daughters have the wit to use this ability.
• **Six Arms:** A Daughter of Hordan has six arms, so she can make three attacks per round without any multi action penalty, or six attacks with a -2 penalty.
• **Size +2:** The body of a Daughter is only slightly bigger than that of a human but, including her snake tail, her total size is comparable to that of a horse.
• **Snake Body:** This creature crawls. She is quite fast, but cannot run.
• **Supernatural Beauty:** A Daughter of Hordan is gifted with supernatural beauty and no mortal woman can compete with her. She has Charisma +6.

DEMONIC MASTIFF

These impressive beasts are dog-like creatures. They are the size of a pony and have a cruel beak and mane of black thorns. They come from another dimension and the wise men say they are the hounds of a terrible race of demons. Demonic Mastiffs are incredible hunters and can track any type of prey tirelessly, so sorcerers evoke them when they have to find a fugitive or guard a place.

Attributes: Agility d8, Smarts d6(A), Spirit d8, Strength d8, Vigor d8
Skills: Fighting d8, Intimidation d10, Notice d8, Tracking d10.
Pace: 7; **Parry:** 6; **Toughness:** 8(1)
Special Abilities
• **Armor +1:** Thick hide.
• **Beak:** Str+d8. Their saliva is acidic, so this attack has AP 1.
• **Demon:** +2 to recovering from being Shaken; Immune to poison and disease;
• **Mane of Thorns:** The Demonic Mastiff can shoot a volley of black spines. It is a ranged attack with range 3/6/12, dealing 2d6 damage in a Small Burst Template, and uses Agility as shooting die. The Mastiff can shoot up to three volleys each day.
• **Size +1:** Demonic Mastiffs are the size of a pony.
• **Supernatural Tracker:** The Demonic Mastiff ignores all Tracking penalties for bad light and old tracks.

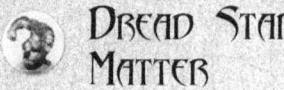

DREAD STAR MATTER

Some Tricarnian sages believe Dread Star Matter came to the Dominions on the Dread Star, and its home is the cold, endless skies. Others tell the tale about a mad sorcerer who created this as an experiment.

Whatever its origin, this creature is a mass of protoplasmic goo. It is almost mindless, but animated by insatiable hunger. It slowly crawls around, exploring its surroundings and enveloping any living matter it finds.

Dread Star Matter is virtually immortal and, as long as it finds enough food, it continues to grow.

Attributes: Agility d4, Smarts d4 (A), Spirit d6, Strength d10, Vigor d8
Skills: Fighting d6, Notice d4.
Pace: 4; **Parry:** 5; **Toughness:** 9
Special Abilities
• **Absorb:** If the Dread Star Matter hits with a raise, it absorbs its target! The victim is grappled and must win an opposed Strength roll (-4) to break free. While it is "inside" the Matter, he keeps suffering damage every round, as it eats the victim alive.
• **Construct:** +2 to recover from Shaken. Immune to called shots, disease and poison. A construct ignores Wound Modifiers.
• **Fast Regeneration: It** can make a natural healing roll each round, unless the damage is caused by its Weakness. This works also when the Matter is Incapacitated.
• **Pseudopods:** Str+d4. This creature can sprout one pseudopod plus one per each point of Size. Each pseudopod has Reach equal to the Size of the creature. So, Dread Star Matter with Size +3 has four pseudopods, each with Reach 3. The creature can attack using all its pseudopods without any penalty.
• **Size +3:** A very big pile of trembling slime, with Size varying from zero to ten.
• **Weakness (variable):** Various subspecies of Dread Star Matter exist, each with a different weakness (see sidebar). They suffer 2d8 damage per round when in contact with its weakness, and the damage ignores any Size bonus vs. Toughness.

DREAD STAR WEAKNESSES

The Dread Star Matter is an alien organism, so it is hard to discover its weaknesses. To determine which substance represents the weakness of a given specimen, the Game Master can choose any substance she likes or draw a card from the Action deck and check the table below.
A Lotusmaster can analyze a Matter sample in a small laboratory or, even better, make a Lotusmastery (-4) roll to discover its weakness. The necessary experiments require a full day of work. In case of a very unusual type of Matter, a specific quest/adventure is required to discover its weakness.

Card Value	Weakness
2-6	Fire
7-8	Salt Water
9-10	Alcohol and Spirits
J	Salt
K	Oil
Q	Any acid
A	Cold
Joker	Draw two cards and combine them.

FANGED APE

These giant creatures aren't native to this world, although some of them today live in the Lush Jungle and in various deep forests. They are the offspring of specimens that escaped from the control of sorcerers. They are big, grayish apes that are completely mute and have impressive fangs. They are very violent and magicians usually evoke them when they want to beat someone to death. Fanged Apes are also excellent climbers. A Fanged Ape can move with impressive ability among trees and even along the roofs of buildings.

Attributes: Agility d8, Smarts d6(A), Spirit d8, Strength d12+3, Vigor d10
Skills: Climbing d12+2, Fighting d8, Intimidation d8, Notice d6, Stealth d8.
Pace: 7; **Parry:** 6; **Toughness:** 10
Special Abilities
• **Fangs:** Str+d6.
• **Fists:** Str+d4. Fanged Apes usually attack by smashing their enemies with their massive fists. When they hit with a raise, it means they grab their opponent with both hands and give him a massive bite, gaining a free attack with Fangs.
• **Jungle Lord:** While among tree branches or on rooftops, the Fanged Ape can move like on normal ground, as long as it has something to grab onto (at most 3" from one branch to the next).
• **Size +3:** Fanged Apes are 12 feet tall.

Fighting Bird

This name applies to several creatures: combat and hunting hawks, giant crows, fighting vultures, and all the other small-sized birds used for hunting or war in the Dread Sea Dominions. They are sometimes evoked by sorcerers for defense, scouting, or delivering small packages. Fighting Birds evoked via the *summon ally* spell have Smarts d8(A) and can speak a rudimentary language that only their evoker can understand.

Attributes: Agility d10, Smarts d4(A), Spirit d6, Strength d4, Vigor d6

Skills: Fighting d8, Notice d10, Stealth d8.
Pace: - **Parry:** 6; **Toughness:** 3
Special Abilities
• **Flight:** Fighting Birds fly at a Pace of 12 and have Climb 2.
• **Size -2:** Fighting Birds are quite small.
• **Small:** Attack rolls against these creatures suffer –2 due to their diminutive size.
• **Talons or Beak:** Str+d4.
• **Threaten:** Fighting Birds are trained to fly around enemies to hinder and distract them. This counts as an Agility Trick with a +2 modifier.
• **In the Eyes!:** A fighting bird that scores a raise on a Fighting attack hits its target in the eyes. The target must make an Agility roll. In case of failure, he suffers the One Eye Hindrance. If he scores a 1 on the Fighting die, regardless of the Wild Die, he is affected by the Blind Hindrance instead.

Giant Scorpion

This monstrosity is one of the most dangerous beasts of the Red Desert. As big as a pony, it can be found wandering among ancient ruins or hunting in the deep desert. It is very aggressive but, luckily, quite stupid. Its almost impenetrable armor and extremely lethal venom make it suitable prey only for the most skilled desert hunters.

Attributes: Agility d6, Smarts d4 (A), Spirit d6, Strength d10, Vigor d6
Skills: Fighting d6, Notice d4.
Pace: 7; **Parry:** 5; **Toughness:** 9(3)
Special Abilities
• **Armor +3:** Thick exoskeleton.
• **Poison-2:** A Giant Scorpion's stinger delivers Lethal venom.
• **Size +1:** As big as a pony.
• **Stinger:** Str+d4, Reach 2.

Headless Zombies can be created with particular (NPC only) versions of the *zombie* Power.

Attributes: Agility d4, Smarts d4, Spirit d4, Strength d8, Vigor d6
Skills: Fighting d6, Notice d6.
Pace: 5; **Parry:** 5; **Toughness:** 7
Special Abilities
• **Claws:** Str+d4.
• **Clumsy:** A Headless Zombie is extremely uncoordinated. The Game Master cannot spend bennies on its rolls.
• **Head Control:** Any character with Arcane Background (Sorcery) who acquires the head of a headless Zombie can try an opposed roll between his own Sorcery and the Zombie's Spirit. If he wins, he takes control of the creature. In case of failure, he can try again after one day. In addition, a sorcerer controlling a Headless Zombie can use 1 Power Point to give the monster one of the following Edges: Berserk, Dodge, Fleet Footed, Sweep. The Edge lasts for the duration of a fight. When bestowing the Edge, the sorcerer must be within 12" of the Zombie.
• **Smelling through the Neck:** A Headless Zombie can inhale air through its neck and "smell" it. It is incredibly skilled and follows a scent trail as accurately as a bloodhound (Tracking d10).
• **Undead:** +2 Toughness; +2 to recovering from being Shaken; immune to poison, disease and called shots.
• **Weakness (Head):** Crushing the severed head of the Zombie (Toughness 3) immediately kills it, reducing it to a heap of rotting flesh.

• **Weakness (Eyes):** Called shots (-4) to the eyes are the only way to defeat its impenetrable armor.

Headless Zombie

Ancient, forbidden tomes explain how to create these vicious undead creatures, but they are only second-hand reports because the true masters of this disgusting practice are the Pygmies who probably learned it from their Keronian lords during their time as slaves.

A Headless Zombie acts exactly like a Zombie but despite its missing head, a Headless Zombie can perceive the surrounding environment much better than a normal Zombie by "smelling" it in a very peculiar and revolting way (see below).

The head of the Zombie is kept by the sorcerer who has created it to control the will of the undead slave.

Idol Dancer

The few travelers who dare pass through the Land of Idols tell stories of graceful shadows after dusk dancing among the statues of this desolate territory. They are called Idol Dancers and they are tall, naturally-armored creatures with strangely human faces.

Ferocious and bloodthirsty, it is hard to say if they are intelligent too. They use no tools and seem to lack any type of verbal communication, with the exception of bloodcurdling shrieks. Yet, they impale their victims on the idol statues and dance in a circle around them all night long before munching on them slowly as the sun rises.

Attributes: Agility d8, Smarts d6, Spirit d6, Strength d8, Vigor d6
Skills: Fighting d8, Intimidation d6, Notice d6.
Pace: 8; **Parry:** 6; **Toughness:** 7(2)
Special Abilities
• **Armor +2:** Thick exoskeleton.
• **Claws:** Str+d6.
• **Quick:** The Idol Dancers have extremely fast reflexes. They can discard any Action Card below 5 and draw another, but they cannot discard the latter.
• **Smell of Blood!:** Whenever an Idol Dancer is within 6" of fresh blood (as in the case of a wounded character or a victim Shaken by damaging effect), it gains the Frenzy Edge.
• **Speed of Lighting:** An Idol Dancer is capable of incredible bursts of speed. Once per combat, it can use the *speed* Power with Vigor as Arcane skill. The Power only has standard duration and, when it ends, the creature must make a Vigor roll or be Fatigued.

JATAKAL

The Jatakal is a demon summoned by the Valkyrie from the depths of hell. Its name means "demon steed" and it actually looks like a jet-black horse with fiery eyes and puffs of smoke spewing from its nostrils. Under its hair, the Jakatal's flesh is made of fire, and it is so hot that nobody, not even

a Valkyrie, can ride it. The Valk priestesses summon them before battles and unleash them on the enemy armies to cause panic and destruction.

For the purposes of the *summon ally* power, a Jatakal is considered a Veteran creature.

Attributes: Agility d8, Smarts d6(A), Spirit d8, Strength d12, Vigor d8
Skills: Fighting d6, Notice d4.
Pace: 10; **Parry:** 5; **Toughness:** 8
Special Abilities
• **Bite:** Str+d4.
• **Demon:** +2 to recovering from being Shaken; Immune to poison and disease;
• **Fear:** The mere sight of a Jatakal causes Fear.
• **Fiery Death:** Whenever a Jatakal is Incapacitated, draw a card from the action deck. If it is red, the beast literally bursts into flame. Any target within a Large Burst Template centered on the Jatakal must make an Agility roll or suffer 3d6 damage, and check if he has been set on fire.
• **Fire Breathing:** Jatakals breathe fire using a Cone Template. Every target within the cone can make an Agility roll at −2 to avoid the attack. Those who fail suffer 2d8 damage and must check if they have been set on fire. A Jatakal cannot attack with its bite and breathe fire in the same round.
• **Fleet Footed:** When running, the Jatakals roll a d10 instead of a d6.
• **Size +2:** They are as big as horses, but a lot more skeletal.

 # LHOBAN ICE DEVIL

This big, furry humanoid might be mistaken for a bear at first glance, but it is actually more similar to a giant ape. Its fur is white and its hideous black face is crowned with two long horns. Its razor-sharp claws are its deadliest weapon; they are deep blue and contain venom that can literally freeze a man's heart (see sidebar).

Luckily, these monsters are rare and solitary. They live only in the most desolate mountains of Lhoban and never come below the snow line. They hide in the deep snow and suddenly jump up to ambush travelers, who they then kill and drag to their dens. They are carnivorous and not particularly picky about their food.

The people of Lhoban believe them to be wretched souls fallen from the Path of Enlightenment. This is because the Ice Devils are terrified of holy monks who sometimes hunt them to obtain the gift of Cold Vision bestowed by their venom (see sidebar).

Attributes: Agility d6, Smarts d6, Spirit d6, Strength d8, Vigor d8
Skills: Fighting d8, Notice d8, Stealth d8.
Pace: 6; **Parry:** 6; **Toughness:** 7
Special Abilities
• **Claws:** Str+d4.
• **Fear of the Holy People:** A Lhoban Ice Devil cannot attack a character with the Monk (contemplative) Edge, unless the Monk attacks first.
• **Venom (-2):** The Ice Devil's claws contain Lethal venom which acts by lowering the victim's body temperature. If the victim survives and has the Enlightenment Arcane Background, he might obtain the Gift of Cold Vision (see sidebar).
• **Size +1:** A Lhoban Ice Devil is eight feet tall and weighs up to 300 pounds.
• **Snow Dweller:** A Lhoban Ice Devil's fur makes for perfect camouflage in the snow, granting it +2 to Stealth rolls in snowy environments. In addition, its large feet move effortlessly and it ignores Difficult Ground while on the snow.

THE GIFT OF COLD VISION

The Lhoban healers say that the Ice Devil's venom is always lethal. It slowly freezes the blood until the victim's heart stops. Then, if he or she is strong enough, the victim's heart starts beating again, overcoming the cold and escaping the grasp of death.
While their heart is frozen, some monks feel their soul leave their body for a brief moment and move to the next stage along the Path of Enlightenment. The body soon snatches the soul back but the monk retains strange "memories of the future". This is called Cold Vision.

In gaming terms, a character with the Enlightenment Arcane Background who is Exhausted or Incapacitated by an Ice Devil's venom is allowed a Spirit (-4) roll. In case of success, he gains the divination Power and 20 Power Points which can be used exclusively for the divination and don't recharge. When the Points are used up, the monk loses the Power.

Despite the greatness of this Power, very few monks dare hunt a Lhoban Ice Devil to experience the Cold Vision.

SHADOW BAT

Shadow Bats are huge beasts with a wing span of twelve yards. They live in abandoned ruins and wherever there is food (they are omnivores). Sorcerers sometime evoke them as mounts. A Shadow Bat can travel up to one hundred miles per night but must rest in a dark place during day. They can be evoked only outdoors and at nighttime.

Attributes: Agility d6, Smarts d4(A), Spirit d6, Strength d12+3, Vigor d8
Skills: Fighting d6, Notice d6
Pace: 3; **Parry:** 5; **Toughness:** 8
Special Abilities
• **Bat Sight:** Shadow Bats ignore all darkness penalties.
• **Claws:** Str+d4.
• **Spooky:** Characters seeing a Shadow Bat for the first time must make a Fear roll.

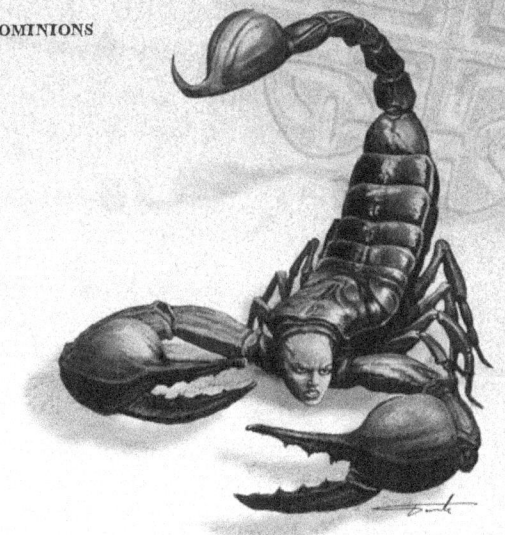

- **Flight:** Shadow Bats fly at a rate of 6", with Climb -1.
- **Size +2:** Shadow Bats are equivalent in size to a warhorse.
- **Weakness (Light and Sound):** Shadow Bats are very susceptible to strong sounds and flashes of light. They subtract 2 to opposed rolls against light or sound based attacks and have the same penalty to recover from Shaken effects caused by light or sound.

 ## Singer Demon

A totally alien creature, a Singer Demon resembles a giant scorpion, with a human face of incredible beauty and a strange, resonating stinger. Both sexes exist but males seem to be very rare.

Differently from normal scorpions, Singer Demons' stingers are hollow and make a strange hypnotic sound when shaken, like a snake's rattle. Singer demons are highly intelligent and love being surrounded by a plethora of adoring slaves that double up as a tasty snack when they are bored. Sorcerers are rarely willing to evoke Singer Demons, because these creatures always try to remain in our world and subdue their evoker.

Attributes: Agility d6, Smarts d10, Spirit d10, Strength d10, Vigor d8
Skills: Fighting d8, Knowledge (Arcana) d10, Notice d6, Persuasion d10, Stealth d6.
Pace: 6; **Parry:** 6; **Toughness:** 9
Special Abilities
- **Claws:** Str+d4
- **Demon:** +2 to recover from being Shaken; Immune to poison and disease;
- **Rattle:** A Singer Demon's stinger rattles, making an enthralling sound. It counts as the *stun* Power and uses the Demon's Spirit as arcane skill. The Demon can use the rattle any time he isn't attacking with the Stinger.
- **Size +3:** Singer Demons are the size of a horse.
- **Stinger:** Str+d6. The stinger of a Singer Demon contains highly toxic poison. Any character who suffers a Wound from the stinger must make an opposed roll against the Demon's Spirit or be controlled as for the *puppet* spell. The effect lasts until the Demon is banished or slain. A Singer Demon can control a number of creatures not higher than his Smarts die (so, usually ten). Extras who fail the Spirit roll aren't Incapacitated but only Shaken, and under the control of the Demon.
- **Supernatural Beauty:** Singer Demons have extremely beautiful faces and voices. They have +4 Charisma.
- **Tricky Creature:** An evoked Singer Demon actually *wants* to stay in the Dread Sea Dominions, so she tries in every way to break free of her evoker's control. If evoked for more days, she is allowed an opposed roll between her Spirit and the evoker's Arcane skill to free herself immediately after being summoned. She makes the same roll when the evocation ends.

Spirit of the Betrayer

According to a belief shared by many cultures, from the Cairnlanders to the Ivory Savannah Tribes, a man who betrays and kills a friend cannot find his way to the afterlife when he dies until he has saved the life of another human to repay his debts. Such creatures actually exist and appear as grayish humanoids dressed in ragged cloths and armed with old weapons, bearing insignia of forgotten realms. Sorcerers summon them to use them as bodyguards.

Attributes: Agility d6, Smarts d6, Spirit d8, Strength d6, Vigor d6
Skills: Fighting d8, Notice d6, Stealth d6.
Pace: 6; **Parry:** 8(2); **Toughness:** 7
Gear: Short Sword (St+d6), Large Shield (+2 Parry, +2 Toughness vs. ranged attacks).
Special Abilities
• **Guardian:** Spirits of the Betrayer can intercept a blow aimed at a friend within 3" from her. In this case, the Spirit suffers the damage instead of the original target. If the Spirit of the Betrayer suffers a Wound saving a friend, it is freed and disappears forever, his debt repaid.
• **Hovering Pace:** Spirits of the Betrayer don't really walk, rather they hover over the ground. So, they are never hindered by difficult ground and gain +2 to Stealth rolls;
• **Protector:** The Spirit of the Betrayer can use the Total Defense action to protect a friend within 3" of him. The action works as normal, but the friend benefits from the Spirit's Parry, shield bonus included.
• **Undead:** +2 Toughness; +2 to recovering from being Shaken; immune to poison, disease and called shots.

STEPPE PONY

An ugly, furry, but extremely resilient pony of the steppe. The favorite mount of Valk warriors.

Attributes: Agility d8, Smarts d4(A), Spirit d6, Strength d12, Vigor d10
Skills: Fighting d4, Notice d6
Pace: 8; **Parry:** 4; **Toughness:** 8

Special Abilities
• **Fleet Footed:** Steppe Ponies roll a d8 instead of a d6 when running.
• **Kick:** Str.
• **Run all The Day:** Steppe Ponies gain +2 to Vigor rolls to resist fatigue.
• **Size +1:** Steppe Ponies are smaller than normal horses.

SWAMP CAT

This beast, typically found in the swamps of Tricarnia resembles a crossbreed between an otter and a puma. Big, brown, and slender, it loves water and is an excellent swimmer. It can swim very fast without causing so much as a ripple, and stay underwater for more than eight minutes. Its favorite hunting technique consists of diving into water, swimming underwater to the riverbank, and then jumping out to snatch a helpless duck or, occasionally, an unlucky rice field slave. Its jaw, in fact, is strong enough to break a man's neck and once it bites, it rarely releases its prey.

When not hungry, they are curious and playful beasts. Some Tricarnian lords keep them as pets and enjoy unleashing them on fugitive slaves.

Attributes: Agility d8, Smarts d8(A), Spirit d6, Strength d6, Vigor d6
Skills: Climbing d6, Fighting d8, Notice d8, Swimming d10, Stealth d10.
Pace: 6; **Parry:** 6; **Toughness:** 5
Special Abilities
• **Aquatic:** A Swamp Cat can swim at a Pace of 6. It can also use Stealth while swimming without any penalty.
• **Bite:** Str+d6.
• **Iron Jaw:** Whenever a Swamp Cat hits with a raise during a Fighting attack, this means it has locked its jaw on to its prey and won't let it go. In gaming terms, the victim is considered grappled and suffers Str+d6 bite damage every round, unless he manages to

escape by winning an opposed Strength roll in which the Cat has +4.

TREE HORROR

Very few people have seen a Tree Horror and survived to tell the tale. These creatures are rotting trees with some vaguely human features. They are capable of movement and are driven by blind hatred for all living beings. They lurk in the thick, haunted forests of the Caledlands, and serve the Caled druids. According to ancient tales, only the druids know the exact ritual to create such abominations. It involves nailing several helpless people to the trunk of a tree, to awaken its soul and taint it forever.

Tree Horrors can be of various sizes, and the cost and requirements to awaken them depend on this feature (see sidebar).

Attributes: Agility d4, Smarts d4, Spirit d6, Strength d10, Vigor d6
Skills: Fighting d6, Notice d4.
Pace: 4; **Parry:** 5; **Toughness:** 10(2)
Special Abilities
• **Armor +2:** Bark.
• **Claws:** Str+d4.
• **Lethargic:** These creatures aren't particularly quick. When a Tree Horror is dealt a deuce, it must stay still, skipping its turn. If Shaken, it can roll to recover.
• **Size +1:** A Tree Horror is bigger than a man.

• **Undead:** +2 Toughness; +2 to recovering from being Shaken; immune to poison, disease and called shots.
• **Weakness (Fire):** Tree horrors are very vulnerable to flames, suffering +4 damage from fire-based attacks. They always count as very flammable targets.

TREE HORROR SIZE
The Tree Horrors come in various sizes, as detailed in the table below. Tree Horrors are exclusively summoned by Caled druids. If a hero wishes to use the ritual to summon one through the summon ally Power, he must learn such a ritual during the adventure (he cannot know it right from the start).

TSA-GARA

In the language of the Azambi, a tribe of the Ivory Savannah, Tsa-Gara roughly means Whistling Swordsman. In fact, this big, dragonfly-like insect makes a remarkable sound with its wings, similar to the faint whistling of man, and uses its powerful sting with the dexterity of a master swordsman.

These beasts always hunt in groups and are capable of elaborate dances to disorient their enemy. They live in underground nests, whose entrances are cleverly concealed and hard to locate.

Tsa-Gara swarms can hunt as far as ten miles from their nests.

Tree Horror Size Table

SIZE	SPECIAL ABILITY	STR	TOUGH.	SUMM. RANK
+1		d10	10(2)	Novice
+2		d12	11(2)	Seasoned
+4	Large	d12+2	12(2)	Veteran
+6	Fear, Large	d12+4	14(2)	Heroic
+8	Heavy Weapon, Huge, Fear	d12+6	16(2)	Legendary

Attributes: Agility d8, Smarts d6, Spirit d6, Strength d4, Vigor d6
Skills: Fighting d8, Notice d6.
Pace: 1; **Parry:** 7; **Toughness:** 4
Special Abilities
• **Insect Reflexes:** Tsa-Garas are very quick when avoiding blows. While flying, they gain +1 Parry, and ranged attacks targeting them have -1.
• **Flight:** A Tsa-Gara flies at a Pace of 6 and a Climb Rate of -3.
• **Size -1:** Tsa-Garas are as big as medium-sized dogs.
• **Stinger:** Str+d4.
• **Hunting Dance:** If two or more Tsa-Garas are attacking the same target, their coordination is so perfect that their Gang Up bonus increases by +1. The maximum +4 Gang Up bonus still applies.

TSA-GARA BLADES

Tsa-Gara stingers are sharp, long and remarkably strong, despite being hollow. The artisans of the Ivory Savannah treasure them and craft them into daggers, short swords or, rarely, long swords (only the bigger stingers, belonging to beasts of human size).

In gaming terms, a Tsa-Gara blade weighs only 30% of the same blade in metal but breaks like iron. They are Rare items and can only be found in the Ivory Savannah or the Verdant Belt.

After killing a Tsa-Gara, a Survival (-2) roll is required to correctly remove and preserve its stinger, while a Repair (-2) roll is needed to build a blade. Ivory Tribesmen can do this with two Common Knowledge rolls. They are used to hunt Tsa-Gara for weapons since younghood.

Consider the results of both rolls to determine the quality of the weapon, as per the table below:

Two failures. *The stinger has not been removed properly or crafted in the correct way. No useful blade is produced.*

Success in one roll. *A rough object is made. Consider it an Improvised Weapon.*

Success in both rolls. *A normal weapon is built.*

Success in one roll and raise in the other. *A very good weapon is built! It either has AP 1 or grants +1 Parry (creator's choice). It can be sold for four times the price of a normal weapon.*

Raise on both rolls. *A true masterpiece! The weapon has AP 1 and grants +1 Parry. It can be sold for eight times the price of a normal weapon.*

TWISTED SERVANT

Twisted Servants are primitive humanoids, somehow similar to Nandals, whose bodies and minds have been deformed and mutated by evil magic. They are the typical creatures summoned by sorcerers. The sages have a strange theory about them: they might have been ancient slaves of the Keronians, snatched from their age to the present era by the power of magic. Twisted servants aren't very intelligent, but they are perfect when the only requirement is killing people or doing heavy physical work.

Attributes: Agility d6, Smarts d4, Spirit d6, Strength d8, Vigor d8
Skills: Fighting d6, Intimidation d6, Notice d6, Stealth d4.
Pace: 6; **Parry:** 5; **Toughness:** 7
Gear: Stone axe (Str+d8).
Special Abilities:
• **Claws:** Str+d4.
• **Mutated Aspect:** Twisted Servants are truly hideous to look upon, so they have the Ugly Hindrance.
• **Size +1:** Twisted Servants are bigger and more muscular than men.

KERONIAN IMP

These small demons were kept as pets by great sorcerers of the Keronian Empire.

After the fall of the Dread Star, the rituals to perpetually bind them to their masters were lost, but they can still be summoned and controlled for a short time. Keronian Imps are servile and apparently respectful towards the master, but, in truth, they have a twisted mind, ready to betray as soon as the chance arises. They are perfect for spying purposes and they know a lot about magic and the old traditions of the Keronian Empire.

Attributes: Agility d8, Smarts d8, Spirit d8, Strength d4, Vigor d8
Skills: Fighting d6, Knowledge (Arcana) d8, Knowledge (Ancient History) d8, Notice d8, Stealth d8, Taunt d10.
Pace: 3; **Parry:** 5; **Toughness:** 5
Special Abilities:
• **Demon:** +2 to recover from being Shaken; Immune to poison and disease;
• **Flight:** Keronian Imps fly with leathery, bat-like wings at a rate of 6" with Climb 0.
• **Size -1:** Keronian Imps are quite small, the size of a cat.
• **Small:** Attack rolls against these creatures suffer −2 due their diminutive size.
• **Tail Stinger:** Str+d4.
• **Try to Impress:** Keronian Imps always try to impress their masters with their awesome abilities. For this reason, they have the Helper Edge.

War Buffalo

War buffalos are the most impressive battle mounts of the Dread Sea Dominions. Only the Buffalo Riders, brave warriors from the Ivory Savannah, are bold enough to ride them. The taming of a war buffalo starts by capturing a wild specimen, when it is only a calf, and the process lasts for several years. War buffalos are extremely intelligent and loyal to their master. They let nobody else ride them and, when the master dies, the mount usually follows his fate. They are trained to fight and attack

with their horns every round their riders do not perform a Trick maneuver.

Attributes: Agility d6, Smarts d6(A), Spirit d8, Strength d12+3, Vigor d12
Skills: Fighting d8, , Notice d6
Pace: 7; **Parry:** 6; **Toughness:** 11
Special Abilities
• **Faithful Steeds:** War buffalos have the Loyal and Death Wish Hindrances toward their master. If their rider dies, they stop eating and let themselves starve to death in 1d10+10 days.
• **Gore:** War buffalos charge to gore their opponent. If they can move at least 6" before attacking, they add +4 to their damage total.
• **Horns:** Str+d6.
• **Size +3:** War buffalos are very large creatures.

Zandorian Caretaker

Probably the biggest vulture in the Dread Sea Dominions, this impressive, black feathered beast has a maximum wingspan of six yards. It is a carrion bird but if it cannot find dead animals, it is intelligent enough to kill its prey by taking them to its mountaintop nest and making them starve.

According to the Syranthian sages, the Caretakers have prevented the great evil lurking in the Cairnlands from swarming into Zandor, since they mostly feed on undead creatures.

Despite their name, they are common throughout the northern Dominions and not only Zandor. However, the savage Cairnlords hate these birds and love hunting them which has greatly reduced their numbers.

The Zandorian Caretakers can be trained and are very loyal to their masters because like many birds, their minds work by imprinting and they obey the first living being they see after hatching.

A Zandorian Caretaker's egg can be sold for 1,500 Moon.

Attributes: Agility d8, Smarts d8 (A), Spirit d8, Strength d8, Vigor d8
Skills: Fighting d8, Notice d8.
Pace: 3; **Parry:** 6; **Toughness:** 7
Special Abilities
• **Beak:** Str+d6.
• **Claws:** Str+d4. A Zandorian Caretaker kills its victims by holding them with both claws and by smashing their heads with its mighty beak. If the Caretaker hits with raise using its Claws, it can immediately perform a free attack with its Beak.
• **Flight:** A Zandorian Caretaker flies at a Pace of 8 and has a Climb Rate of -3.
• **Low Light Vision:** This beast sees extremely well in the dark. It ignores the Dim and Dark light modifiers.
• **Size +1:** Six-yard wingspan, capable of carrying a man away.
• **Killer of the Undead:** A Zandorian Caretaker is a natural enemy of all undead creatures. It is immune to Fear caused by the undead and, when attacking a creature with the Undead Monstrous Ability, it has +2 to attack and damage rolls. Denizens of the Dread Sea Dominions

DENIZENS OF THE DOMINIONS

Although the world of *Beasts and Barbarians* is populated by terrible and hideous monsters, humans actually pose the greatest threat to our valiant heroes.

From slavers to pirates, from evil cultists to raiders, humans can be even more dangerous than demons summoned from the pit of hell. This chapter introduces 51 profiles of common (and not so common) human NPCs of the Dominions, which you can use in your adventures.

CUSTOMIZATION

Each profile also includes additional tweaks, allowing you to use the same stats for different characters. Do you need a tavern wench or a princess? Use the Damsel profile and tweak it a little. The tweaks presented here are only examples, and the Game Master is encouraged to create his own customizations.

AMAZON

While the Amazons of Ascaia are the only known culture of women warriors, individual women living an independent life do exist in the Dominions, and they can be easily depicted using the following profiles.

AMAZON WARRIOR

A trained woman warrior from Ascaia, the Amazons' Island. It isn't uncommon for the Amazons to be hired as mercenaries, as they are known to be very skilled and absolutely loyal, so this profile can also be used for such characters.

Customization: Mariner (Boating d8), Mercenary Bodyguard (Notice d6), Archer (Trained Thrower (bow), Shooting d8), Healer (drop Fighting and Shooting to d4, add Healing d8 and Healer).

Attributes: Agility d8, Smarts d6, Spirit d6, Strength d8, Vigor d6
Skills: Boating d6, Climbing d6, Fighting d6, Intimidation d4, Notice d4, Riding d6, Shooting d6, Throwing d6.
Charisma: 0; **Pace:** 6; **Parry:** 6 (7 vs males); **Toughness:** 6(1)
Edges: Amazon, Combat Reflexes.
Hindrances: Code of Honor (Amazons), Loyal.
Gear: Bronze long sword (Str+d8), light leather armor (+1), medium feathered helm (+2, only head), spear (Str+d6, +1 Parry, Reach 1, 2 hands), medium shield (+1 Parry, +2 Toughness vs. ranged weapons), bow (Damage: 2d6, Range: 12/24/48).

AMAZON COMMANDER

A rugged warrior woman and veteran of many battles. She is very skilled both on and off the battlefield.

Customization: Hawk Ship Captain (Boating d8, Knowledge (Battle) d6, Quartermaster), Ascaia Noble (Knowledge (Battle) d6, Noble, add Amazon Blade to gear), Ascaia Mercenary Commander (Command, Hold the Line!, Knowledge (Battle) d8), Wandering Warrior Woman (Trademark Weapon (long sword), Bikini Heroine, One hand and half, remove bronze armor and add bikini).

Attributes: Agility d8, Smarts d8, Spirit d8, Strength d8, Vigor d8

Skills: Boating d6, Climbing d6, Fighting d8, Intimidation d6, Notice d6, Riding d8, Shooting d8, Throwing d6.
Charisma: 0; **Pace:** 6; **Parry:** 7 (8 vs males); **Toughness:** 8(2)
Edges: Amazon, Common Bond, Combat Reflexes, Nerves of Steel.
Hindrances: Code of Honor (Amazons), Loyal.
Gear: Bronze long sword (Str+d8), medium bronze armor (+2), medium feathered helm (+2, only head), spear (Str+d6, +1 Parry, Reach 1, 2 hands), medium shield (+1 Parry, +2 Toughness vs. ranged weapons), bow (Damage: 2d6, Range: 12/24/48).

ASSASSIN

Killing is both an art and a profession in certain parts of the Dread Sea Dominions. When political, commercial or religious issues cannot be solved with talks, bribes or simple intimidation, a dagger in the dark or a cup of poisoned wine are often used to settle the matter.

THUG

The lowest of killers for hire, this individual can be found in the taverns or dark alleys of almost any city of the Dominions. He mostly kills to rob his victims but never refuses a request to dispatch someone, if a fat purse is involved in the transaction.

Customization: Crime Band Leader (Intimidation d8, Connections (crime band)), Ruffian (Persuasion d4, add club to Gear), Cult Thug (Combat Reflexes).

Attributes: Agility d6, Smarts d4, Spirit d6, Strength d6, Vigor d6
Skills: Climbing d4, Fighting d6, Intimidation d6, Notice d4, Stealth d6, Streetwise d6, Throwing d6.
Charisma: 0; **Pace:** 6; **Parry:** 5; **Toughness:** 5
Edges: None.
Hindrances: Greedy.
Gear: Bronze short sword (Str+d6), bronze dagger (Str+d4, range: 3/6/12).
Special Abilities
• **Dark Alley Cat:** When in his own area (a city quarter, road or similar) an Extra Thug receives the Wild Die on Streetwise and Notice rolls. A Wild Card Thug has the Wild Die increased by one step (usually from d6 to d8).

POISONER

This shady individual is the person you need if you are looking for very special and dangerous concoctions. For an extra fee, he can also deliver his poison to your chosen victim.

Customization: Master of Disguises (Persuasion d8, Stealth d10), Fallen Alchemist (Smarts d10, 11 Power Points).

Attributes: Agility d6, Smarts d8, Spirit d6, Strength d6, Vigor d8
Skills: Climbing d6, Fighting d6, Notice d6, Persuasion d6, Stealth d8, Streetwise d6, Throwing d6.
Charisma: 0; **Pace:** 6; **Parry:** 5; **Toughness:** 6
Edges: Connections (crime), Lowlife, Poisoner.
Hindrances: Greedy.
Gear: bronze dagger (Str+d4, range: 3/6/12), poisoner glove (Str), poisoner ring, blowpipe (Damage: poison, Range: 5/10/20), various poisons (see below), 5 doses of refined Lotus.
Special Abilities
• **Poison Resistance:** A wise poisoner takes small doses of the most common concoctions on a daily basis, to develop immunity. So, he has the Arcane Resistance Edge, limited to the *poison* Power and natural venoms (like snakes').
• **Poisons:** A Poisoner can use the poison power with Lotusmastery d8 and 9 Power Points. He usually carries the following concoctions, each costing him 2 Power Points per dose, but can produce different ones as needed: *Amber Lotus of Last Kiss* (very fast injection poison), *Colorless Lotus of Mercy* (normal time ingestion poison), *Smoke Powder of Dreams* (very fast nonlethal poison to be inhaled, costs 4 Power Points, -4 to the Lotusmastery roll).

MASTER ASSASSIN

This faceless man skillfully wields his blade in the dark. He can be a royal executioner, silently delivering the king's judgment, or the vengeful hand of a secret cult, or just a very costly professional, like a senior member of the Assassins Guild of Jalizor. Regardless of his background, he is extremely dangerous.

Customization: Strangler (Martial Arts, change Trademark Weapon to bare hands, Strength d10), Deadeye (Marksman, change Trademark Weapon to composite bow, Shooting d10, add composite bow to Gear).

Attributes: Agility d10, Smarts d8, Spirit d8, Strength d8, Vigor d8
Skills: Climbing d8, Fighting d10, Lockpicking d6, Notice d8, Persuasion d6, Stealth d10, Streetwise d8, Throwing d6, Tracking d6.
Charisma: 0; **Pace:** 6; **Parry:** 8; **Toughness:** 7(1)
Edges: Acrobat, Assassin, Lowlife, No Mercy, Thief, Trademark Weapon (dagger).
Hindrances: Vow (always completing his mission).

Gear: razor-sharp iron dagger (Str+d4+1, AP 1), poisoner glove (Str), light leather armor (+1), lock picks, tiger's claws, silk rope, poisoner ring, two lotus concoctions chosen from among *poison*, *smite*, *slumber*, *lower trait* (vigor, agility or strength).

Special Abilities

• **Sinister Hand of Death:** The Master Assassin is a professional of murdering, and if he gets the chance to strike, he rarely leaves his victim alive. Spending a Bennie, he automatically gains the Drop.

BANDIT

Sadly, bandits are a common plague in the Dominions. Hungry serfs, disbanded soldiers, slaves on the run, poachers, and other such individuals infest forests, hills and less traveled roads, ready to rob anyone that comes near them, pillage villages and farms, and generally take what they need to survive by force.

BRIGAND

The most common bandits are the highwaymen. They usually move in groups, know their surroundings well, and employ spies to scout for potential wealthy victims and approaching road guards, or other similar dangers. In many lands there are bounties on the brigands' heads.

Customization: Desert Robber (Riding d6, add pony or horse to gear), Poacher (Survival d8, Woodsman, always equipped with a bow), Rebel (replace short sword and small shield with spear and medium shield), Disbanded Soldier (replace light armor and small shield with medium bronze armor and medium shield).

Attributes: Agility d6, Smarts d4, Spirit d6, Strength d6, Vigor d6
Skills: Climbing d4, Fighting d6, Intimidation d6, Notice d4, Shooting d6, Stealth d6, Survival d6.

Charisma: 0; **Pace:** 6; **Parry:** 6; **Toughness:** 6(1)
Edges: None.
Hindrances: Poverty, Wanted.
Gear: Bronze short sword (Str+d6) or club (Str+d4), small shield (+1 Parry) or bow (damage: 2d6, range: 12/24/48), light leather armor (+1).

Special Abilities

• **Ambusher:** Brigands are masters at catching their victims off guard. If they have time to set an ambush and are in their territory, before the combat starts, draw a card from the Action Deck for every ten Brigands in the band and put it aside. At the start of each round you can decide to discard the Action Card the Brigands draw and replace it with one of the cards set aside.

• **Bandit Chief:** One in ten Brigands is a rugged leader who keeps the band at his heel. He has Strength and Vigor d8, Fighting d8 and is usually better equipped, with medium bronze armor, a bronze battle axe, and a medium shield.

 ## BRIGAND LORD

Large groups of bandits, like the infamous Good Brothers infesting the Iron Route, are led by well-known leaders, who are at times even more powerful than nobles or governors. Some are vicious brutes capable only of instilling fear, others are cunning tacticians who can easily fool the armies of the civilized kingdoms.

Customization: Brutish Lord (drop Smarts and Spirit to d6, raise Strength and Vigor to d10, Brawny, Brute, Improved Sweep, drop Level Headed, replace medium shield and long sword with great iron axe), Former Soldier (Knowledge (Battle) d8, Command Presence, Tactician).

Attributes: Agility d8, Smarts d8, Spirit d8, Strength d8, Vigor d8
Skills: Climbing d6, Knowledge (Battle) d6, Fighting d10, Intimidation d8, Notice d6,
Riding d8, Shooting d8, Stealth d6, Streetwise d6, Survival d8.
Charisma: 0; **Pace:** 6; **Parry:** 9; **Toughness:** 8(2)
Edges: Block, Command, Improved Nerves of Steel, Level Headed, Natural Leader, Sweep.
Hindrances: Arrogant or Overconfident, Wanted.
Gear: Iron long sword (Str+d8), medium shield (+1 Parry, +2 Toughness vs. ranged attacks), bow (damage: 2d6, range: 12/24/48), medium bronze armor (+3), horse.
Special Abilities
• **Ambusher:** Brigands are masters at catching their victims off guard. If they have time to set an ambush and are in their territory, before the combat starts, draw a card from the Action Deck for every ten Brigands in the band and put it aside. At the start of each round you can decide to discard the Action Card the Brigands draw and replace it with one of the cards set aside.

BARBARIAN OF THE NORTH

The lands of the North, including the Borderlands, Northeim and the Cairnlands, are populated by savage people. Despite being quite different from a cultural point of view, these rowdy warriors can be portrayed by using similar stats.

BARBARIAN WARRIOR

The epitome of savagery, this wild, fur clad warrior is the nightmare haunting the dreams of the rich and peaceful citizens of Faberterra. Barbarians tend to fight and behave in an individualistic way, lacking the military organization of the civilized races. They are very proud and accept only the strongest as their leaders.

Customization: Northlander Clan Warrior (Vigor d8, remove light leather armor), Cairnlander Raider (Intimidation and Riding d6, add Severed Head to Gear, remove Fear of Magic), Borderland Forts Archer (Shooting d8, Trained Thrower (bow), add medium bronze helm to Gear), Borderland Forts Infantryman (replace bronze battle axe with short bronze sword, and add medium bronze helm to Gear).

Attributes: Agility d6, Smarts d4, Spirit d6, Strength d8, Vigor d6
Skills: Climbing d4, Fighting d8, Intimidation d4, Notice d4, Riding d4, Shooting d6, Stealth d4, Survival d4, Throwing d6.
Charisma: 0; **Pace:** 6; **Parry:** 7; **Toughness:** 6(1)
Edges: Brute.
Hindrances: Fear of Magic (minor).
Gear: Bronze battle axe (Str+d8), medium shield (+1 Parry, +2 Toughness vs. ranged attacks), bow (Damage: 2d6, Range: 12/24/48), light leather armor (+1).

 CAIRNLANDER WARLORD

This rugged individual is either the Lord of a Cairn or he leads a band of Cairnlander warriors and pillagers. Impressive to look at, he feels the might of his Ancestors on his side.

Customization: Chief of Pillagers (Stealth d8, add horse to gear), Lord of the Cairn (Noble, Knowledge (Battle) d6, add scythed chariot with six goats (use mule stats from SWD) to Gear).

Attributes: Agility d8, Smarts d6, Spirit d8, Strength d8, Vigor d8
Skills: Climbing d6, Fighting d8, Knowledge (Battle) d4, Intimidation d8, Notice d6, Riding d8, Shooting d8, Stealth d6, Throwing d8.
Charisma: 0; **Pace:** 6; **Parry:** 8; **Toughness:** 7(1)
Edges: Block, Dodge, Command, Iron Will, Nerves of Steel.
Hindrances: Arrogant, Greedy, Mean.
Gear: Bronze long axe (Str+d8), medium shield (+1 Parry, +2 Toughness vs. ranged attacks), bow (Damage: 2d6, Range: 12/24/48), medium bone armor (+2).

 ## NORTHEIM HERO

The Northlanders are led into battle by strong warriors, capable of amazing feats of violence and ferocity, which are immortalized in song by bards and poets. The war leaders might also act as chiefs at times of peace, but many refuse this honor because they know that the skills that make a man a strong warrior are different from those that make a wise ruler.

Customization: Lone Wandering Warrior (replace Berserk with One Hand and Half, replace great bronze axe with iron long sword and loincloth), Clan War Leader (replace Berserk with Command, add medium bronze armor to Gear).

Attributes: Agility d8, Smarts d6, Spirit d8, Strength d10, Vigor d10
Skills: Climbing d6, Fighting d10, Knowledge, Intimidation d8, Notice d6, Riding d8, Shooting d8, Stealth d6, Survival d4, Throwing d8.
Charisma: 0; **Pace:** 6; **Parry:** 6; **Toughness:** 8

Edges: Berserk, Brawny, Brute, Loincloth Hero, Sweep.
Hindrances: Fear of Magic (minor), Overconfident.
Gear: Great bronze axe (Str+d10, AP 1, Parry -1, 2 hands), bow (Damage: 2d6, Range: 12/24/48), medium bronze helm (+2, only helm).

BARBARIAN OF THE SOUTH

To the learned people of Syranthia and Faberterra all those who cannot speak the imperial tongue well are barbarians. This applies to both the northern people and the savage tribes dwelling in the Ivory Savannah and the Verdant Belt.

IVORY TRIBES WARRIOR

A typical member of an Ivory Savannah or Verdant Belt tribe, this man is both a warrior and a hunter.

Customization: Verdant Belt Villager Warrior (replace Gear with war club or short bone sword and sling), Magombi Tribe Warrior (Throwing and Strength d8, Strong Arm).

Attributes: Agility d8, Smarts d4, Spirit d6, Strength d6, Vigor d6
Skills: Climbing d4, Fighting d6, Intimidation d4, Notice d6, Stealth d6, Throwing d6, Tracking d4, Survival d6, Taunt d4.
Charisma: 0; **Pace:** 6; **Parry:** 6; **Toughness:** 5
Edges: None.
Hindrances: None.
Gear: spear (Str+d6, +1 Parry, Reach: 1, 2 hands), tribal shield (+1 Parry, +2 Toughness vs. ranged weapons, +1 to Intimidation, Taunt or Persuasion rolls), 5 javelins with atl-atl (Str+d4, range: 9/18/36, 1 action to reload).
Special Abilities
• **Wise Warrior:** Every band of twelve or more warriors is usually led by an experi-

enced warrior or hunter. He has Fighting and Survival d8, Smarts d6, and the Command Edge. He is a Wild Card.

GAZELLE HUNTER

Very few of these men still dwell in the Savannah today. Graceful and slender, they all belong to an almost forgotten tribe, the Shalimi. These people are born to run and can outpace a buffalo herd, if they must. They hunt with skill and stealth, but today most of them serve the White King, acting as heralds and messengers of his will to the Savannah Tribes.

Customization: Voice of the White King (Persuasion d8, Charismatic, replace gear with ivory chackram (+1 damage, +1 Charisma toward Ivory Tribes, symbol of his charge), Wild Card).

Attributes: Agility d10, Smarts d6, Spirit d8, Strength d6, Vigor d8
Skills: Climbing d4, Fighting d6, Notice d8, Stealth d8, Throwing d8, Tracking d6, Survival d6.
Charisma: 0; **Pace:** 8; **Parry:** 6; **Toughness:** 6
Edges: Fleet Footed, Extraction, Savage.
Hindrances: None.
Gear: spear (Str+d6, +1 Parry, Reach: 1, 2 hands), 4 bone chackrams (Str+d4, range: 4/8/16, ignores 2 points of Cover modifier).
Special Abilities
• **Born to Run:** A Gazelle Hunter can run almost an entire day without getting tired. He receives +2 to Vigor rolls to avoid Fatigue.

BUFFALO RIDER

Even the heavy soldiers of Kyros or the slavers of Caldeia tremble when this warrior approaches on his impressive mount, his face painted in war colors and the scalps of his fallen enemies hanging from his neck.

Attributes: Agility d8, Smarts d6, Spirit d8, Strength d8, Vigor d8
Skills: Fighting d10, Intimidation d6, Notice d6, Riding d8, Throwing d8, Tracking d6, Survival d4.
Charisma: 0; **Pace:** 6; **Parry:** 8; **Toughness:** 7(1)
Edges: Born in the Saddle, Buffalo Rider, Dodge.
Hindrances: None.
Gear: bronze tipped buffalo lance (Str+d8, AP 2 when charging, 2 hands when dismounted), short bone sword (Str+d6), 5 javelins (Str+d4, range: 6/12/24), light leather corselet (+1), tribal shield (+1 Parry, +2 Toughness vs. ranged weapons, +1 to Intimidation rolls).
Special Abilities
• **Buffalo Charge:** The first time an Extra is charged by a Buffalo Rider, he must make a Spirit roll or be Panicked.

CALED

The Caleds are a primitive people living exclusively in Caledlands, an uncharted woodland area. The sages say that they are the descendant of slaves escaped from the Keronians when the Dread Star fell. They don't know metalworking and are very xenophobic, leaving their homeland only for war or on manhunts.

Despite their poor technology, they are feared by all the civilized races thanks to the amazing feats of their naked spearmen and the great supernatural powers of their druids.

NAKED SPEARMAN

The most feared warriors among the Caleds, these primitive men attack savagely, protected only by their own ferocity and some magical tattoos. The tattoos identify the various clans and are believed to bestow great power.

Customization: The clans place great emphasis on their tattoos (see sidebar). You can depict each different tribe by choosing a different tattoo or by inventing a new one.

Attributes: Agility d8, Smarts d6, Spirit d6, Strength d6, Vigor d6
Skills: Climbing d6, Fighting d8, Notice d6, Intimidation d8, Stealth d8, Survival d8, Throwing d6, Tracking d6.
Charisma: 0; **Pace:** 6; **Parry:** 7; **Toughness:** 5
Edges: None.
Hindrances: None.
Gear: stone tipped spear (Str+d6, +1 Parry, Reach 1, 2 hands, Range: 3/6/12), stone dagger (Str+d4).
Special Abilities
• **Clan Tattoo:** Choose a clan tattoo from among the ones in the sidebar.
• **Naked Hero:** Every band of twelve or more Naked Spearmen is led by a hero, a powerful Wild Card warrior with Vigor d8, Fighting d10 and the Command Edge.
• **Naked Warrior:** As long as he wears no armor, a Naked Spearmen has the Loincloth Hero Edge and can soak wounds even if he isn't a Wild Card (in this case, he rolls only the Vigor die, without the Wild Die). This ability doesn't work if the Spearman is under the effect of fear or has lost an Intimidation Test of Will during this fight, since his gods shun cowards.

 # DRUID

Druids are the priests of the Caled clans. They worship ancient, secret gods and are in deep communion with the Caled forest itself. Druids are believed to be among the greatest sorcerers in the Dominions, but their powers are strongly linked to their land. These stats represent a druid of medium experience. More powerful dru-

ids must be designed individually because their stats change greatly.

Customization: Master of the Dead Leaves (replace *beast friend* with *zombie*, give all the powers a necromantic trapping), Warrior Druid (replace *entangle* and *beast friend* with *warrior gift* and *armor*, raise Fighting d8 and drop Sorcery d8, equip with a spear).

Attributes: Agility d8, Smarts d8, Spirit d8, Strength d6, Vigor d6
Skills: Climbing d6, Fighting d6, Knowledge (Arcana) d8, Notice d6, Intimidation d10, Sorcery d10, Stealth d8, Survival d8, Tracking d6.
Charisma: -4; **Pace:** 6; **Parry:** 5; **Toughness:** 5
Edges: Arcane Background (sorcery), New Powers, Power Points.
Powers [25 PP]: *beast friend* (animal call), *boost/lower trait* (war paints/curses), *entangle* (animated branches), *shape change* (wolf or bear or hunting bird or snake), *summon ally* (beast king, tree horror, medium swarm).
Hindrances: Bloodthirsty.
Gear: stone dagger (Str+d4).
Special Abilities
• **Call of the Wild:** While in the Caledlands, a druid's *beast friend* power only costs him half the normal Power Points.
• **The Forest has Deep Roots:** While in the Caledlands, a Druid can benefit from the Rapid Recharge Edge.

CALED CLAN TATTOOS
Each Caled clan is characterized by a particular set of tattoos, which identifies them culturally. A complete set of tattoos can be given only to adult warriors, the Naked Spearmen, and only by the shamans, since the tattoos are imbued with the strong magic of the Caled forest.

Here is a list of some of the most famous tattoos, with their effects:

Howling Stars. *The Howling Stars clan has a particularly strong bond with wolves. Their tattoos grant the Beast Master Edge, and each Howling Star spearman has a wolf animal companion.*

Deepwater Trout. *The members of this clan are natural swimmers and it is said that a Deepwater Trout cannot drown. Their tattoos bestow the Aquatic Monstrous Ability with Pace 6".*

Bark Skins. *The Bark Skins believe that the sap of the ancient trees flows in their veins, and they feel no pain even when they are almost dead. When a Bark Skin is Incapacitated, he makes a Vigor roll. If successful, before becoming Incapacitated, he can act for an extra round without any penalty.*

Tree Cats. *Tree Cats can climb trees as gracefully as pumas. They can move along the branches as if they were on normal ground and make Climbing rolls only in extreme conditions.*

Narrow Shadows. *You cannot see a Narrow Shadow as long as he remains among the foliage of a Caled tree. While in the Caledlands forests, they have +4 to Stealth rolls.*

CALED BEAST KINGS

Caled Druids can summon a particular type of magical creature called a Beast King. Despite looking very similar to normal animals, the Beast Kings actually represent an idealized and supernatural version of their species. As humans have kings and princes, so do animals.

In gaming terms, a Beast King has the same stats as a normal specimen, except the following:

† *It is a Wild Card*

† *It is larger: Size +1*

† *Its Smarts is a step higher than that of a normal specimen and it is human rated (so, given that a wolf has* Smarts d6 (A), *the King of Wolves has* Smarts d8)

† *Can speak the Caled tongue*

† *Can use the beast friend power, limited to animals of its same race, with arcane skill d10 and 15 Power Points.*

† *For the summon ally power, it is considered two ranks higher (so, if a wolf is a Novice Rank creature, the King of Wolves is a Veteran Rank creature).*

CANNIBAL

The Dominions have rarely seen an age as dark as this, and appalling deeds are far too common. Cannibalism is one of them. Whether driven by religion or simple hunger, cannibals are wretched people, cursed by both men and gods.

Many tribes of cannibals exist in the Dominions, but the most famous are the ebony skinned populations of the Cannibal Islands, in the very south of the world. They periodically raid nearby lands to hunt their favorite quarry: man.

CANNIBAL TRIBESMAN

A savage, barbaric man eater.

Customization: Brain Eater (see sidebar), Ritual Cannibal (use the Cultist profile adding the Cannibal Special Ability).

Attributes: Agility d6, Smarts d6, Spirit d6, Strength d8, Vigor d8
Skills: Boating d6, Fighting d6, Intimidation d6, Notice d6, Shooting d6, Stealth d6, Throwing d6.

Charisma: –2; Pace: 6; Parry: 6; Toughness: 6
Edges: Combat Reflexes.
Hindrances: Mean.
Gear: War club (Str+d8) and small shield (+1 Parry) or bone tipped spear (Str+d6, +1 Parry, Reach 1, 2 hands), stone dagger (Str+d4), bow (Damage: 2d6, Range: 12/24/48, RoF: 1).
Special abilities:
• **Cannibal:** A Cannibal files his teeth in order to tear off large chunks of meat. He can bite his opponent, dealing Str+d4 damage.
• **Scary:** A Cannibal is a frightful opponent, especially when he grins. He has +2 to Intimidation rolls.

CANNIBAL TRIBE CHIEF

This horrible individual has grown large and muscular thanks to his hideous diet. He is never sated and always wants more!

Customization: Brain Eater (see sidebar), Ritual Cannibal Cult Lord (use the Cult Master profile adding the Cannibal Special Ability).

Attributes: Agility d6, Smarts d6, Spirit d6, Strength d10, Vigor d10
Skills: Boating d8, Fighting d10, Intimidation d8, Notice d6, Shooting d6, Stealth d6, Throwing d6.
Charisma: –2; Pace: 6; Parry: 6; Toughness: 8
Edges: Brawny, Brute, Combat Reflexes, Hard to Kill.
Hindrances: Mean.
Gear: Great bone axe (Str+d10, AP 1, –1 Parry, 2 hands).
Special abilities:
• **Cannibal:** A Cannibal files his teeth in order to tear off large chunks of meat. He can bite his opponent, dealing Str+d4 damage.

• **Scary:** A Cannibal is a frightful opponent, especially when he grins. He has +2 to Intimidation rolls.

BRAIN EATERS

Each cannibalistic group has its favorite food. Some like the heart and liver, others prefer the fleshy limbs, but the worst are the brain eaters. Despite its reputation as the seat of an individual's mind, the brain actually hosts several dangerous parasites, which can cause a peculiar disease characterized by uncontrollable laughter. This is why the brain eaters are also called the Laughing Cannibals.

A Laughing Cannibal is subject to the following modifications:

† *His Smarts drops by one step (if it is now d4, it becomes d4 (A)).*

† *Each combat round, he can make a free Intimidation attempt, which doesn't count as an action.*

† *Since he shakes uncontrollably, he has –1 to all physical tasks.*

COMMONER

A common man or woman; the following stats can be tweaked to represent specific individuals. When necessary, roll on the Allies Personality Table to add some characterization.

Customization: Beggar (Persuasion d4, Streetwise d6), Merchant (Persuasion d6), Noble (add the Noble Edge), Scribe (literate), Smith (Strength d8).

Attributes: Agility d6, Smarts d6, Spirit d6, Strength d6, Vigor d6
Skills: Fighting d4, Knowledge (one craft) d6, Notice d4.
Charisma: 0; Pace: 6; Parry: 4; Toughness: 5
Edges: None.
Hindrances: None.

Gear: Bronze Knife (Str+d4) or farming tool (Str+d6, Improvised Weapon).

CULTIST

In dark, forgotten temples and in the palaces of depraved nobles, men gather to worship evil deities and to summon demons and other supernatural creatures. Their gods have many shapes but all Cultists share the same fanaticism.

CULT MEMBER

This wild-eyed, crazy individual does most of the dirty work, such as kidnapping girls for sacrifices or immolating himself in suicide missions. Despite being quite unskilled, they usually assault the heroes in great numbers.

Customization: Cult Spy (Lockpicking d6, Stealth d8, Streetwise d6), Temple Guard (Strength, Vigor, Fighting d8, Brawny, replace short sword with long sword), Undercover Cultist (Persuasion d6), Wild-Eyed Cultist (Intimidation d8).

Attributes: Agility d6, Smarts d4, Spirit d6, Strength d6, Vigor d6
Skills: Fighting d6, Intimidation d6, Knowledge (religion) d4, Stealth d6.
Charisma: 0; **Pace:** 6; **Parry:** 5; **Toughness:** 5
Hindrances: Delusional, Vow (they must abide by the tenets of their faith).
Gear: dagger (Str+d4) or short sword (Str+d6).
Special Abilities
• **Fanatical Bunch:** Cult Members gladly throw themselves into harm's way to save their Cult

Master. Only while protecting their Master they can use the Fanatics Setting Rule. In addition, they willingly submit to the Sacrifice Special Ability of the Cult Master.

CULT MASTER

The real leader of a cult is the Master, an individual capable of making dozens or even hundreds of people worship demons and other abominations. A man doesn't need to be exceptionally pious, intelligent, or strong to become a Cult Master. What really matters is his magnetism, his ability to persuade others to follow the path of evil. Some Cult Masters are powerful sorcerers but, for the most part, they are only overconfident madmen meddling with things that Man Must Not Know.

Customization: Sorcerer Priest (Sorcery d10, Arcane Background (sorcery), New Power x2, Power Points x2, 20 Power Points, he can use the Unholy Gifts with Sorcery and his own power points or fuel them with the Sacrifice Special Ability).

Attributes: Agility d6, Smarts d10, Spirit d8, Strength d6, Vigor d8
Skills: Fighting d8, Intimidation d10, Knowledge (Arcana) d8, Knowledge (Religion) d8, Notice d6, Persuasion d12, Taunt d10.
Charisma: +4; **Pace:** 6; **Parry:** 6; **Toughness:** 8(2)
Edges: Charismatic, Command, Command Presence, Fervor, Inspire, Hold the Line!, Iron Will.
Hindrances: Arrogant, Delusional, Overconfident, Vow (they must abide by the tenets of their faith).
Gear: sacrificial dagger (Str+d4), iron tipped mace (Str+d6), medium bronze corselet concealed under ceremonial gar-

ments (+2), cult relic (+2 Charisma, see sidebar).

Special Abilities

• **Inflame the Souls:** The Cult Master's words can whip his followers into a religious frenzy. If he spends a full round speaking to them, he can try a Persuasion roll. In case of success, all the Cult Members in a Medium Burst Template centered on the Cult Master acquire the Berserk Edge and automatically go berserk (the Burst Template is Large if a raise is scored). However, if the Cult Master goes down, all the berserkering cultists must immediately make a Fear check or be Panicked.

• **Sacrifice:** The Cult Master doesn't usually have Power Points of his own, but he can temporarily acquire some by making a sacrifice. This can be done by delivering a fatal blow to a helpless victim or a willing Cult Member. The action requires a full round (no other actions allowed except chanting and praying). A slain Extra grants the Master 5 Power Points, while a Wild Card grants 15. These Power Points last for the current scene only and cannot be regained in any way.

• **Unholy Gifts:** The Cult Master receives powerful gifts from his demonic deities in exchange for his adoration. He can use *armor, barrier, bolt, fear, smite, summon ally* (demonic mastiff, twisted servant, medium swarm) with Spirit as arcane skill. The required Power Points are generated by the Sacrifice Special Ability (see above). All these Powers have the dark taint trapping.

CULT RELICS

The Game Master can decide that some cultist groups possess tainted relics, strongly connected to the unholy creature venerated. As a rule of thumb, the rightful owner of the relic (usually the Cult Master) receives +2 Charisma toward other members of the cult. Many of these objects are only worthless junk made to impress the cultists, but some can have truly dangerous powers, and finding or destroying them can be the goal of an adventure.

Here are some examples of these evil objects:

Purple Flame of Gurdajos. *This flame-shaped dagger is made of a strange reddish metal and really looks like a living flame. It is said to have been crafted with a spike from the collar of the great demon Gurdajos. Once a month, if used to stab the dead body of a victim sacrificed to Gurdajos, it brings her back to life, her eyes filled with flame, as a loyal slave to the owner of the dagger. The zombie has the same stats as when she was alive, but her Smarts is one step lower and she gains the Undead Monstrous Ability.*

Scourge of Nar Karion. *A two-foot-long blowing horn, inlaid with gold, silver and tourmaline. It must be sounded next to a body of salt water by a person of noble blood. Then, the individual makes a Spirit (−4) roll. In case of success, within 2d6 hours the Scourge, a Giant Water Snake, emerges from the water (use the Giant Worm stats from SWD, replacing the Burrow with the Aquatic Monstrous Ability, it is a Wild Card). If the Scourge eats the hornblower, it places itself under the Cult Master's control for an entire day. Otherwise, it attacks the cultists and then leaves. The horn owes it name to the fact that it was once used to destroy the coastal citadel of House Nar Karion of Tricarnia.*

Jalimandra. *An age-old mummy whose bandages are inscribed with ancient Keronian prayers. In life, Jalimandra was a powerful sorcerer and he never truly died. If his bandages are soaked with the fresh blood of a sacrificial victim, the mummy whispers forgotten secrets to the ears of the worshipper. In gaming terms, Jalimandra can teach the worshipper any Sorcery Power the Game Master decides. However, the worshipper must make a Spirit (−4) roll to avoid acquiring the Delusional Hindrance. The summoners of Jalimandra are usually mad as hatters, but know 1d4 additional Powers.*

DAMSEL

You can use the Damsel stats to represent any non-fighting girl or woman involved in an adventure. Her role usually consists in being saved by the heroes, but she may turn out to be of great help. Given that she screams a lot but never gets eaten by monsters (at least, if the heroes do their job), she is a Wild Card.

Customization: Farmer girl (Healing d6, Survival d6), Princess (Noble, Intimidate d6), Priestess (Priest, Knowledge (Arcana) d6), Seductress (Persuasion d10, Very Attractive, Temptress (6 Power Points)) Tavern Wench or Courtesan (Streetwise d6, Fighting d6).

Attributes: Agility d6, Smarts d6, Spirit d6, Strength d6, Vigor d6
Skills: Fighting d4, Healing d4, Notice d6, Persuasion d8.
Charisma: +4; **Pace:** 6; **Parry:** 4; **Toughness:** 5
Edges: Attractive.
Hindrances: Damsel in Distress.
Gear: bikini or fancy clothes.
Special Abilities
• **Good Lungs:** A Damsel tends to scream a lot, especially when the bad, ugly monster is about to grab her! She has a very shrill voice and any Notice roll to attract attention receives a +2 bonus, as long as the Damsel is within 12" of her targets. In addition, when facing certain monsters with very sensitive ears (Game Master's decision), her screams count as a Smarts Trick.

GLADIATOR

These bold warriors who daily risk their life in the arena are the heroes of the masses of Faberterra, Tricarnia and many other civilized and not-so-civilized people.

COMMON GLADIATOR

This fighter is a professional but certainly not a star.

Customization: Escaper (Extraction, replace Gear with composite bow and bronze dagger), Retiarius (Two Fisted, replace bronze short sword and small shield with spear and war net), Syranthian Tusk Fighter (Martial Artist, replace Gear with Elephant Horns (iron fists)), Tricarnian Blind Mauler (Brawny, replace Gear with maul, medium half-body bronze armor, medium blind helm (-2 Notice rolls)).

Attributes: Agility d8, Smarts d6, Spirit d6, Strength d8, Vigor d8
Skills: Fighting d8, Healing d4, Intimidation d8, Notice d6, Taunt d6, Throwing d6, Shooting d6.
Charisma: 0; **Pace:** 6; **Parry:** 7; **Toughness:** 7(1)
Edges: Combat Reflexes, Distract.
Hindrances: Arrogant.
Gear: bronze short sword (Str+d6), gladiator armguard (+1 Parry, Str+d4), light half-body gladiator outfit (+1).
Special Abilities:
• **Gladiator:** If he succeeds in an Intimidation test against an adjacent opponent, he receives a free Fighting attack. This attack does not incur a Multiaction penalty.
• **Stirring the Crowd:** Once in each fight in the arena, the Gladiator can make an opposed Taunt roll, modified by his Charisma, to stir up the crowd. It counts as an action and the winner immediately receives a Bennie.

 VETERAN GLADIATOR

This man or woman is one of the stars of the arena. He is both a deadly fighter and an idol of the people.

Customization: Escaper (Extraction, Fleet Footed, replace Gear with composite bow and bronze dagger), Retiarius (First Strike, Two Fisted, replace bronze short sword and small shield with spear and war net), Syranthian Tusk Fighter (Improved Martial Artist, replace Gear with Elephant Horns (iron fists)), Tricarnian Blind Mauler (Brawny, Strength and Vigor d10, replace Gear with maul, medium half-body bronze armor, medium blind helm (-2 Notice rolls)).

Attributes: Agility d8, Smarts d6, Spirit d6, Strength d8, Vigor d8
Skills: Fighting d10, Healing d4, Intimidation d10, Notice d6, Taunt d10, Throwing d6, Shooting d6.
Charisma: +2; **Pace:** 6; **Parry:** 8; **Toughness:** 7(1)
Edges: Combat Reflexes, Counterattack, Distract, Frenzy.
Hindrances: Arrogant.
Gear: bronze short sword (Str+d6), gladiator armguard (+1 Parry, Str+d4), light half-body gladiator outfit (+1).
Special Abilities:
• **Gladiator:** If he succeeds in an Intimidation test against an adjaced opponent, he receives a free Fighting attack. This attack does not incur a Multiaction penalty.
• **Famous:** The crowds adore him, he has +2 Charisma.
• **Stirring the Crowd:** Once in each fight in the arena, the Gladiator can make an opposed Taunt roll, modified by his Charisma, to stir up the crowd. It counts as an action and the winner immediately receives a Bennie.

Iron Phalanx

It is not a secret that the once mighty Iron Phalanxes, the military divisions that made it possible to create the Empire, are now a mere shadow of their former self. Reduced to small numbers and mostly holding defensive positions, their training isn't as tough as it used to be and their ranks are full of foreign barbarians, who no longer know what it means to fight for the eternal glory of the Empire. Nevertheless, they are still a force to be respected and feared. Today, a typical Phalanx includes 300-600 Hoplites.

Hoplite

The standard infantryman of the Iron Phalanx. Protected by heavy armor and a full body shield, he moves at a slow pace on the battlefield. He lacks speed but is certainly lethal.

Customization: Veteran Hoplite (Block, Vigor and Fighting d8), Barbarian Troops (Vigor d8, remove the Phalanx Spirit Special Ability).

Attributes: Agility d6, Smarts d6, Spirit d6, Strength d8, Vigor d6
Skills: Fighting d6, Healing d4, Notice d4, Shooting d6, Throwing d6.
Charisma: 0; **Pace:** 5; **Parry:** 7; **Toughness:** 8(3)
Edges: Hoplite Training.
Gear: one-handed iron tipped spear (Str+d6, reach 1, range: 3/6/12), short iron

sword (Str+d6), heavy iron armor (+3), large iron shield (+2 Parry, +2 Toughness vs. ranged attacks).

Special Abilities

• **Row Leader:** One in twenty Hoplites is a Row Leader, who gives orders and makes the Phalanx react. He has the Command and Command Presence Edge. The name derives from the fact that he is usually placed at the start or end of a Phalanx row.

• **Phalanx Spirit:** In battle, a Hoplite raises his shield to protect not himself but the man to his left. In the same manner, he is protected by the comrade to his right. This requires absolute trust among the soldiers and grants the Phalanx the ability to fight as one. Every time a Hoplite rolls 1 on the Fighting die, regardless of the Wild Die, while having the Gang Up bonus from a fellow Hoplite, he can reroll the die.

• **Rank Fighter:** A Hoplite is trained to fight in very narrow space, so his maximum Gang Up bonus is +5 instead of +4.

PHALANX OFFICER

This man is a high-ranking commander of the Iron Phalanxes. In the past only the best men reached this position and only after having shed their blood in many battles. Sadly, today it is no longer so: advancements are often bought and a Phalanx Officer is rarely worthy of his name. The Phalanxes retain some of their might only thanks to the Row Leaders (see Hoplite above).

Customization: Veteran Officer (Knowledge (Battle) d8, Leader of Men).

Attributes: Agility d6, Smarts d8, Spirit d6, Strength d6, Vigor d6
Skills: Fighting d8, Notice d6, Knowledge (Battle) d4-d10 (see below), Persuasion d8, Riding d6, Shooting d6, Throwing d6.
Charisma: +2; **Pace:** 6; **Parry:** 7; **Toughness:** 7 (2)

Edges: Command, Noble.
Gear: iron long sword (St+d8), dagger (Str+d4), medium bronze armor (+2), medium bronze shield (+1 Parry, +2 Toughness vs. ranged attacks), horse.

Special Abilities

• **Variable Training:** A Phalanx Officer's skills must be proved in battle. Unless he is a Veteran Officer, the first time an officer is involved in a mass battle, the Game Master should draw a card from the Action Deck to determine the actual skills of a Phalanx Officer:

Card	Result
2	Totally Inept. He bought his rank. He lacks the Knowledge (Battle) skill.
3-5	Green Officer. Knowledge (Battle) d4.
6-8	Ordinary Officer. Knowledge (Battle) d6.
9-10	Veteran Commander. Knowledge (Battle) d8
J-Q	Lucky Commander. Knowledge (Battle) d8, Luck, Natural Leader, Spirit d8.
K-A	Old Fox. Knowledge (Battle) d10, Tactician, Leader of Men.
Joker	Military Genius. Knowledge (Battle) d12,

PHALANX INSIGNIA

Every Phalanx has an Insignia, a special banner that is brought into battle. The Phalanx exists as long as it holds its Insignia. The oldest Phalanxes have iron or steel Insignia dating back to the Tricarnian Wars, while the Insignia of the newer Phalanxes are made of silver and gold, metals that are weaker, just like the Phalanxes of our days.

Any Hoplite will give his life to protect the Insignia of his Phalanx, since its presence on the battlefield greatly increases the morale of the troops. The Insignia bearer counts as having the Command Edge and a Command Radius of 30". If using the Mass Battle Rules, the presence of an Insignia gives +1 to Battle rolls and +2 to Morale rolls.

THE LOST PHALANXES

The Iron Empire was victorious in many wars, but lost many battles too. Its Phalanxes were sent to very remote regions of the world, like the Red Desert, the Ivory Savannah, and the dangerous forests of the Caledlands. As time went on, many Phalanxes were lost and their tasks and destinations forgotten. All that is left are brief notes in old ledgers kept in the Imperial Palace of Faberterra. What might have happened to the soldiers and their Insignia?

PRAYER OF THE HOPLITE

"Please Hulian, god of steel and iron, give us a leader who knows from where the sun shall rise today". This is the common Hoplite prayer before a battle in which the men will have to fight under a thus far untested commander.

LOTUSMASTER

Those who study the arcane properties of the Lotus can be deadly and very adaptable opponents. They create potions that can embolden the most cowardly warriors and cure illnesses of all sorts, or destroy your body with subtle poison, as the Lotusmaster watches you twitch in pain with an amused smile. But the most dangerous are those who try to improve the nature of man in the name of their blind gods, progress and science.

LOTUSMASTER

These stats refer to an average Lotusmaster, a man or woman trained in the use of the Lotus but with no specialization in a specific field. When creating a Lotusmaster, it is strongly advised to choose a Customization from among those listed below or to create a new one.

Customization: Alchemist Apprentice (Lotusmastery d10, Chemical Tradition, add *blast* (Dragon Breath of Gis) to Powers), Artillerist (Knowledge (Demolitions) d8, Repair d6, replace *poison* and *boost/lower trait* with *blast* and *burst*, all his damaging powers are Heavy Weapons), Enslaver of Minds (Persuasion d10, replace Powers with *boost/lower trait* (Spirit and Smarts only), *fear*, *puppet*, *slumber*), Healer (Healing d8, Healer, replace Powers with *boost/lower trait* (Vigor and Healing only), *healing*, *dispel*, *succor*), Guardian (Notice d8, Alertness, replace Powers with *barrier*, *detect/conceal arcana*, *dispel*, *invisibility*).

Attributes: Agility d6, Smarts d8, Spirit d6, Strength d6, Vigor d6
Skills: Fighting d6, Healing d6, Intimidation d6, Knowledge (Arcana) d8, Lo-

tusmastery d8, Notice d6, Persuasion d6, Stealth d4, Throwing d6.

Charisma: 0; **Pace:** 6; **Parry:** 5; **Toughness:** 5

Edges: Arcane Background (Lotusmastery), Lotus Reserve, New Power, Power Points.

Hindrances: Cautious.

Powers [15 PP]: *barrier* (Red Lotus of Burning Wall), *boost/lower trait* (various lotus concoctions), *poison* (various poisons), *stun* (Gray Lotus of Stony Limbs).

Gear: dagger (Str+d4), Lotusmaster bag, healer kit, 5 doses of Refined Lotus.

Special Abilities

• **Well Stocked:** A non-player Lotusmaster generally has more time to study than a wandering adventurer. This is why he can use the Lotus Reserve Edge twice per session.

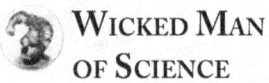

WICKED MAN OF SCIENCE

This powerful Lotusmaster has devoted his knowledge and intelligence to testing new Lotus concoctions on the best available guinea pigs: men! The death of innocents might, or might not, weigh on his conscience, but he obstinately perseveres in the name of science.

Customization: Gray Eminence Behind the Throne (Persuasion d10, Connections (Nobles, Crime), Noble, add *puppet* to Powers).

Attributes: Agility d8, Smarts d12, Spirit d8, Strength d6, Vigor d8

Skills: Fighting d8, Healing d10, Intimidation d8, Knowledge (Arcana) d10, Knowledge (Medicine) d10, Lotusmastery d12, Notice d8, Persuasion d8, Stealth d8, Taunt d8, Throwing d10.

Charisma: 0; **Pace:** 5; **Parry:** 6; **Toughness:** 8 (2)

Edges: Arcane Background (Lotusmastery), Improved Level Headed, Lotus Reserve, New Power x2, Power Points x2, Rich.

Powers [25 PP]: *barrier* (Red Lotus of Burning Wall), *boost/lower trait* (various lotus concoctions), *burst* (Everlasting Lotus of the Burning Phoenix), *poison* (various poisons), *stun* (Gray Lotus of Stony Limbs), *warrior gift* (various drugs of bestial warriors), *zombie* (Opaque Lotus of Awakening).

Gear: short sword (Str+d6), poisoned dagger (Str+d4, coated with a *poison* lotus concoction), poisoner glove (Str), medium bronze corselet (+2), Lotusmaster bag, healing kit, poisoner ring, 10 doses of refined Lotus.

Special Abilities

• **Abominable Creatures of the Lotus:** A Wicked Man of Science usually has a number of abominable servants at his service. These wretched creatures have been horribly mutated by his experiments (see sidebar). At least one of them is a Henchman, fanatically loyal to his master.

• **Well Stocked:** A Wicked Man of Science generally has more time to study than a wandering adventurer. This is why he can use the Lotus Reserve Edge twice per session. In addition, given his resources, he can use the Edge to create any concoction from the Lotusmastery Powers List, including the ones he doesn't know.

ABOMINABLE CREATURES OF THE LOTUS

A Wicked Man of Science has no problem twisting and torturing men and beasts for his evil purposes. These poor creatures are so subdued that they obey him in every way.

If you need a quick way to portray these creatures, you can use the Twisted Servant stats.

If you want something more elaborate, choose a basic creature profile (usually a human or an animal). Draw a card from the Action Deck (two if you want a really nasty creature) and find out which terrible mutation the creature has undergone. Unless the entry says otherwise, the creature also has the Ugly hindrance.

Card Value	Abominable Lotus mutation
2	**Giant!** *The poor creature has grown beyond measure. Every time this card is dealt, the creature receives Size +3.*
3	**Secret of Immortality!** *The Lotusmaster has made it! This creature is virtually immortal, having the Regeneration (fast) Monstrous Ability, but luckily it cannot regenerate wounds caused by either fire, steel or some other means devised by the GM.*
4	**Gills!** *This creature has developed gills and can survive in the water. It has the Aquatic Monstrous ability (same Pace as when moving on the ground) and an extra Vigor step.*
5	**Thick Hide.** *Every time this card is dealt, the skin of the creature becomes thicker, harder or with more scales, gaining +1 Armor.*
6	**Patchwork!** *This creature is the result of a weird experiment, made by combining the severed parts of different beings and brought to life thanks to powerful lotus concoctions. It has the Construct Monstrous Ability.*
7	**Wall Crawler!** *This abomination has sprouted suckers or similar devices and can easily move on walls and vertical surfaces. It has the Wall Crawler Special Ability.*
8	**Fangs and Claws!** *The poor being has razor sharp fangs and/or claws. It gains a natural attack causing Str+d4, and the damage goes up a die step (i.e. Str+d6, Str+d8,…) every time this card is dealt.*
9	**Fast!** *The creature runs very fast and is blessed with excellent reflexes. It has the Quick and Fleet Footed Edges.*
10	**Uh… Terrible!** *This creature is the Lotusmaster's greatest failure. It is so hideous and revolting it causes Fear. Any additional time this card is dealt, the Fear check modifier decreases by -2.*
J	**Wings!** *This creature has developed wings! It has the Flight special ability with the same Pace as when moving on the ground.*
Q	**Supernatural Intellect!** *The brain of this creature has been enhanced and its Smarts is raised by two die steps. So, the being has become aware of what the Lotusmaster has done to it. If a red card is dealt, it has the Vengeful Hindrance and is ready to betray its maker as soon as it gets the chance!*
K	**Death Defeated!** *The Lotusmaster managed to defeat his greatest opponent, death itself. This being was brought back to life, although it isn't exactly the same as before. It gains the Undead Monstrous Ability.*
A	**Incredible Beauty!** *The Lotusmaster did a work of beauty on this creature. It doesn't have the Ugly Hindrance, is supernaturally Attractive (Charisma +6) and can use the puppet power on members of the opposite sex with arcane ability d10 and 10 Power Points.*
Joker	**Deranged Creature!** *Draw another two cards and apply both results.*

MONK

The lonely figure of a wandering monk can sometimes be seen even in remote lands far from Lhoban. Not all monks are Jademen, because the doctrine of Enlightenment has slowly spread throughout the Dominions. Some monks are kind and humble but others follow twisted beliefs and are heralds of an ancient evil.

WANDERING MONK

A typical travelling monk. The same stats can be used for an Enlightened monk and for a Seeker of the Black Light.

Customization: Cela (Young Hindrance, drop Spirit, Agility and Enlightenment by one step, see sidebar), Corrupting Evil Monk (Persuasion d10, add a pain trapping to all his powers). Philosopher (Spirit d10, Philosopher, replace Monk (militant) with Monk (contemplative)), Temple Guard (replace gear with medium bronze armor and moon blade).

Attributes: Agility d8, Smarts d6, Spirit d8, Strength d6, Vigor d6
Skills: Climbing d4, Fighting d8, Healing d6, Enlightenment d8, Knowledge (Religion) d6, Notice d6, Survival d4.
Charisma: 0; **Pace:** 6; **Parry:** 6; **Toughness:** 5
Edges: Arcane Background (Path of Enlightenment), Martial Arts, Monk (militant), New Power.
Hindrances: Poor, Vow (religious tenets).
Powers [15 PP]: *boost trait* (moves of many beasts), *smite* (perception of the enemy's weak spot).
Gear: Three-piece rod (Str+d6, ignores shield Parry and cover bonus) or staff (Str+d4, +1 Parry, Reach 1, 2 hands) or reinforced prayer beads (iron fists: +1 unarmed damage).

DEMON HUNTER

A veteran in dealing with demons, this man has forged his own will and body to be a lethal weapon against the many abominations infesting the Dominions.

Customization: Chief of a small temple (Persuasion d8, Charismatic, Philosopher), Murderer of the Black Light (Stealth d10, Assassin, drop Demon Hunter).

Attributes: Agility d8, Smarts d8, Spirit d10, Strength d8, Vigor d8
Skills: Climbing d6, Fighting d10, Healing d8, Enlightenment d10, Knowledge (Religion) d6, Notice d8, Survival d4.
Charisma: 0; **Pace:** 6; **Parry:** 8; **Toughness:** 8(2)
Edges: Arcane Background (Path of Enlightment), Block, Brave, Demon Hunter, Martial Arts, Monk (militant), New Power x 2, Power Points.
Hindrances: Death Wish, Heroic, Vow (religious tenets).
Powers [20 PP]: *boost trait* (moves of many beasts), *deflection* (reading the opponent's intentions), *smite* (perception of the enemy's weak spot).
Gear: moon blade (Str+d8), medium bronze half-body armor (+2).

MONK MASTERS AND CELA
Many monks, especially militant ones, spend most of their lives travelling, because the doctrine of Enlightenment says that a man must find himself in the world. So, the more experienced monks (Wild Cards) often wander with one or more (up to five) inexperienced boys or girls under their tutelage. These young individuals are called Cela, which in the language of Lhoban means "disciple", and their level of experience may vary greatly. The Cela of a grizzled Demon Hunter can be a fully trained monk (use the standard Wandering Monk stats), while the disciple of a Wandering Monk is, in most cases, just a common boy or a girl (use the Young Monk customization).

NANDAL

Nandal is a Northeim word meaning "mute", because these primitive cavemen are incapable of human speech, given the particular shape of their throat. When communicating among themselves, they use a mix of grunts and gestures. They live in caves in the North but sometimes wander south, looking for food, mates, or simply warmer climates. This is why a surprisingly large number of Nandal colonies are found in the Iron Mountains. The Nandals are fierce and bloodthirsty.

NANDAL TRIBESMAN

An average caveman, with prominent jaw and small, sunken eyes.

Customization: Dog Master (Beastmaster, has d4 Nandal dogs with him, see sidebar), Fire Bringer (add flaming branch (Str+d4, +2 fire damage, chance of target catching fire) to gear, see sidebar), Tracker (Tracking d8).

Attributes: Agility d6, Smarts d4, Spirit d6, Strength d8, Vigor d8
Skills: Climbing d4, Fighting d6, Intimidation d6, Notice d6, Survival d6, Throwing d6, Tracking d4.
Charisma: 0; **Pace:** 6; **Parry:** 5; **Toughness:** 8(1)
Edges: Brute.
Hindrances: Bloodthirsty, Ugly.
Gear: reinforced stone war club (Str+d8), stones (Damage: str+d4, Range: 3/6/12), thick furs (+1).
Special Abilities
• **Grunting Brutes:** The Nandals grunt as one to get psyched up for a fight. At the beginning of a fight and before any Action Cards are dealt, a group of Nandals acting on the same Action Card makes a group Spirit roll. For each success and raise the group receives one Nandal Fury Token. At the start of each round the Game Master can use one of these tokens to let the whole group gain +2 on Intimidation, Fighting or damage rolls for the current round. Only a single token can be used each round for each group.
• **Size +1:** The Nandals are bigger than men.

NANDAL ALPHA MALE

A bigger, rougher and more savage specimen, usually the chief of a clan.

Customization: Fire Touched (causes Fear, Arcane Resistance only versus fire based Powers, see sidebar), Pillager (replace Gear with medium bronze half-body armor, medium shield, bronze battle axe).

Attributes: Agility d6, Smarts d4, Spirit d6, Strength d10, Vigor d10
Skills: Climbing d4, Fighting d8, Intimidation d10, Notice d6, Survival d6, Throwing d6, Tracking d4.
Charisma: 0; **Pace:** 6; **Parry:** 6; **Toughness:** 10(1)
Edges: Brute, Frenzy, Improved Sweep.
Hindrances: Bloodthirsty, Ugly.
Gear: reinforced stone war club (Str+d8), stones (Damage: str+d4, Range: 3/6/12), thick furs (+1).
Special Abilities
• **Chief of the Brutes:** A Nandal Alpha Male can use the Grunting Brutes Ability (see Nandal) using the Nandal Fury Tokens of a Nandal group within 12". A Token used in this way has only effect on the Alpha Male.
• **Size +2:** The Nandals are bigger than men. The Alpha Male is even bigger.

FRIENDS OF THE CAVE PEOPLE

The Nandals are primitive men, the equivalent of the real-world Neanderthals. They are slowly becoming more human and have recently discovered how to tame dogs and the secret of fire.
Nandal Dogs. *These beasts are ugly creatures, used by the Nandals to hunt and in war. Their relationship with the Nandals is stronger than that between civilized men and domestic dogs. Use the Dog/Wolf profile adding the Loyal and Ugly Hindrances.*

The Secret of Fire. *Fire fascinates the Nandals. It keeps them warm during the cold nights, turns raw meat into good food and keeps the terrors lurking in the darkness at bay. They consider it magical, so some of them use it in combat. They are the Firebringers, seen as something in between holy people and madmen. The craziest of them all are those called "Fire Touched", muscular warriors who throw themselves into fire to prove that nothing can scare them. If they survive, their scarred skin becomes so thick that even the hottest flame causes them no pain.*

PIRATE

A Pirate can be an ex-slave or simply a greedy sailor who has embraced a life of plundering.

PIRATE CREWMEMBER

Regardless of their past, these men are now the scourge of the sea.

Customization: Brown Sea Pirate (add spear and sling to Gear), Dread Sea Pirate (add bow to Gear), Helmsman (Boating d8, Quartermaster Edge, Man at the Rudder Special Ability, see below), Escaped Slave Crewmember (Strength and Vigor d8).

Attributes: Agility d8, Smarts d4, Spirit d6, Strength d6, Vigor d6
Skills: Boating d6, Fighting d8, Intimidation d6, Notice d4, Shooting d4, Stealth d4, Throwing d6.
Charisma: -2; **Pace:** 6; **Parry:** 6; **Toughness:** 5
Hindrances: Code of Honor (pirates), Mean.
Gear: Bronze short sword (Str+d6) or boarding axe (Str+d6), dagger (Str+d4, range: 3/6/12).
Special Abilities
• **Born on the Deck:** These men are skilled at risking their lives while boarding enemy ships. They receive +1 to Tricks while fighting aboard a ship.
• **Man at the Rudder:** Only for the Helmsman. He has a single Bennie which can be used only for ship-related tasks (boating rolls and soaking ship wounds as per the Quartermaster Edge).

 ## PIRATE CAPTAIN

Only the toughest scum can keep a crew of pirates at bay and this man certainly knows how.

Attributes: Agility d8, Smarts d6, Spirit d6, Strength d8, Vigor d8
Skills: Boating d8, Fighting d10, Intimidation d8, Notice d6, Shooting d6, Stealth d4, Throwing d6.
Charisma: -2; **Pace:** 6; **Parry:** 7; **Toughness:** 7(1)
Edges: Ambidexterity, Command, Two Fisted.
Hindrances: Code of Honor (pirates), Mean.
Gear: Iron long sword (Str+d8), dagger (Str+d4, range: 3/6/12), light leather armor (+1).
Special Abilities
• **Born on the Deck:** Like his men, he is skilled at risking his life while board-

ing enemy ships. He receives +1 to Tricks while fighting aboard a ship.

PYGMY

These very short jungle dwellers are isolationist and xenophobic. They hate trespassers and will do everything in their power to dispatch any stranger foolish enough to venture into their wet, dark lands. Sometimes the Pygmies leave the protection of their trees to attack travelers and raid villages in the Verdant Belt. They steal and murder but mainly they take slaves, especially beautiful, fair-skinned girls.

Nobody knows the fate of these poor souls, but many believe that they are sacrificed to ancient gods in crumbling temples deep in the jungle.

HUNTER

The most common Pygmy found in the Lush Jungle is a hunter, a skilled woodsman and tracker. Despite his small stature, he is bold, cunning and fierce – in a pygmy way, of course. The Pygmies don't fight in the open, they prefer a stealthy poison dart shot from the thick of the foliage, a trap concealed in the ground, and so on. Killing without being seen is the pygmy way of being brave, and this is why the civilized races say that a coward is "as bold as a Pygmy". But don't be fooled, the Pygmies are dangerous.

Customization: Bird Imitator (Taunt d10), Healer (he can use the *dispel* Power only against the *poison* Power, with Survival as arcane skill and 5 Power Points), Poison Savvy (Survival d12), Sentinel (Notice d8, Alertness), Spider Friend (Beastmaster, with a Giant Spider animal companion).

Attributes: Agility d8, Smarts d6, Spirit d6, Strength d6, Vigor d8

Skills: Climbing d8, Fighting d6, Intimidation d6, Notice d6, Shooting d8, Stealth d10, Survival d8, Throwing d8.

Charisma: -4; **Pace:** 6; **Parry:** 5; **Toughness:** 5

Edges: Woodsman.

Hindrances: Bloodthirsty, Small.

Gear: poisoned bone dagger (Str+d4, see poison master below), pygmy blowpipe (see poison master below, range: 7/14/28, see sidebar), stone hatchet (Str+d6).

Special abilities:

• **Jungle Dweller:** The Pygmies are excellent tree climbers. They can squeeze past gnarled roots and run through the dense undergrowth which carpets the jungle floor with perfect ease. So, they ignore Difficult Ground while in the jungle.

• **Poison Master:** Pygmies are known for their dangerous poisons. In gaming terms, while in the jungle, they can use the *poison* Power with 5 Power Points and Survival as arcane skill. In addition, both their daggers and blowpipes are coated with a Very Fast Injection *poison* (no Power Point required), which can either be lethal or only cause Fatigue.

TRAPPER

It is not a secret that Pygmies are fond of spiders. In particular, they love their ability to lure preys into their complex, invisible webs, and then eat them at leisure. A Pigmy Trapper's philosophy is being just like that. He loves luring his victims into traps and pits and, once they are captured and incapacitated, he finishes them.

Customization: Bird Imitator (Taunt d10), Trap Master (Survival d12), False Bait (Extraction, Fleet Footed, Taunt d6), Sentinel (Notice d8, Alertness), Spider Friend (Beastmaster, with a Giant Spider animal companion).

Attributes: Agility d8, Smarts d8, Spirit d6, Strength d6, Vigor d6

Skills: Climbing d8, Fighting d6, Intimidation d6, Notice d6, Shooting d6, Stealth d10, Survival d8, Throwing d8.

Charisma: -4; **Pace:** 6; **Parry:** 5; **Toughness:** 4

Edges: Woodsman.

Hindrances: Bloodthirsty, Small.

Gear: bone dagger (Str+d4), sling (Str+d4, range: 4/8/16), stone hatchet (Str+d6) or bone tipped spear (Str+d6, +1 Parry, 2 hands, Reach 1).

Special abilities:

• **Jungle Dweller:** The Pygmies are excellent tree climbers. They can squeeze past gnarled roots and run through the dense undergrowth which carpets the jungle floor with perfect ease. So, they ignore Difficult Ground while in the jungle.

• **Trap Master:** When a fight occurs in an area of the jungle that the Trapper knows well (like an ambush site or deep in pygmy territory), the Game Master secretly places up to three traps onto the battlefield. The traps can be devised by the Game Master or chosen at random (see sidebar). Each trap has the size of a Small Burst Template and can be spotted by winning an opposed roll between the Trapper's Survival and the opponent's Notice. It is possible to trade a bigger trap for a number of smaller ones (Medium Burst Template = 2 SBT, Large Burst Template = 3 SBT).

MASKED WARRIOR

Very little is known about the Pygmies' gods, but the spooky Masked Warriors must be somewhat connected to religion – or so the scholars say. Sometimes, among the other warriors, you can see one wearing a large, impressive mask. He is a Masked Warrior, a sort of paragon and very charismatic figure for the whole tribe. But there is more to this custom: the masks are considered magical, as they represent heroes from the past. When he wears such a mask, a Pygmy somehow turns into the mythological figure the mask represents, and is capable of incredible feats. No one knows if the masks truly affect the warriors or if it is just a matter of self-suggestion. Whatever the truth, beware: a Masked Warrior is a dangerous opponent!

Customization: See Pigmy Masks sidebar.

Attributes: Agility d8, Smarts d8, Spirit d8, Strength d8, Vigor d8

Skills: Climbing d8, Fighting d8, Intimidation d8, Notice d6, Shooting d8, Stealth d10, Survival d8, Throwing d8.

Charisma: -4; **Pace:** 6; **Parry:** 6; **Toughness:** 5

Edges: Command, Luck, Woodsman.

Hindrances: Bloodthirsty, Small.

Gear: pygmy holy mask (+3, only head) and related equipment.

Special abilities:

• **Jungle Dweller:** The Pygmies are excellent tree climbers. They can squeeze past gnarled roots and run through the dense undergrowth which carpets the jungle floor with perfect ease. So, they ignore Difficult Ground while in the jungle.

• **Masked Warrior:** Choose a Mask from the sidebar.

PAINTED SHAMAN

These men are powerful sorcerers and intermediaries between the tribe and its ancient, mysterious deities. They often paint their faces and comb their long hair in a strange way to look even more impressive and fearsome.

Customization: Headhunter (add *zombie* to Powers, always in the company of 2d6 headless zombies), Leader of the Tribe (add Command and Hold the Line!).

Attributes: Agility d6, Smarts d8, Spirit d8, Strength d6, Vigor d8

Skills: Climbing d8, Fighting d6, Intimidation d8, Knowledge (Arcana) d6, Notice d8, Stealth d10, Sorcery d8, Survival d8, Throwing d8.

Charisma: 0; **Pace:** 5; **Parry:** 5; **Toughness:** 5

Edges: Arcane Background (Sorcery), Improved Impressive Aura, New Power, Power Points, Woodsman.

Powers [25 PP]: *beast friend* (strange prayers and dances), *bolt* (throws poisonous spiders), *fear* (curses), *poison* (venomous gases and fogs), *summon ally* (giant spider, medium swarm, alligator)

Hindrances: Bloodthirsty, Small, Vow (religious tenets).

Gear: skull scepter (Str+d4, delivers touch attack like a Sorcerer's staff), curious headgear (+1).

Special Abilities:

• **Ancient Sorcerer:** The Pygmy Shamans worship unknown gods, so they can use a wider range of powers than traditional sorcerers (in gaming terms, from both the Lotusmastery and Sorcery power lists).

• **Jungle Dweller:** The Pygmies are excellent tree climbers. They can squeeze past gnarled roots and run through the dense undergrowth which carpets the jungle floor with perfect ease. So, they ignore Difficult Ground while in the jungle.

PYGMY BLOWPIPES

The Pygmies use sturdier versions of the traditional blowguns that are at least four yards long. These weapons require great lung capacity (Vigor d8 required), but have an increased range (7/14/28). They aren't usually sold.

PYGMY TRAPS

Whenever the Game Master needs a pygmy trap, she can draw a card from the Action Deck and check the table below. Note that Trap Skill refers to the skill of the trapper (usually his Survival die), while Trap Size refers to its area of effect, i.e. Small, Medium or Large Template. Typically traps are spot winning an opposed roll between the trapper's Trap Skill and the victim's Notice.

Spades - Pit. *A deep pit (at least four yards deep) concealed by moss or dead leaves, as big as the template of the Trap Size. Any victim failing the opposed Notice roll must make an Agility (-4) roll or fall in. He is automatically Shaken. If a face card is drawn, there are spikes at the bottom of the trap that cause 2d6 damages. Leaving the pit requires a Climbing roll.*

Hearts – Slashing Branch. *This trap uses branches or ropes and, when triggered, it targets a single victim. Stepping onto it (failing the opposed Notice roll) triggers the effect.*

If the card isn't a face card, the trap consists in a loop of rope that closes around the victim's ankle and hangs him upside down. He is automatically Shaken and must make an Agility (-4) roll to break free. While in this awkward position, he suffers -2 to Parry and any skill roll, and cannot move. Any friend can simply cut the rope with a single action.

If the card is a face card, the trap is totally different. When the victim steps onto the trigger, a branch suddenly slashes up, throwing one dart per Trap Size (max 3 darts) at the victim. The darts are shot at Short Range with Throwing equal to the Trap Skill and deal 2d6 damage.

Diamonds - Beehive. *A simple but very nasty trap! The devious Trapper has concealed a hive (of bees, scorpions or similar) in the ground! Stepping onto it (failing the Notice roll) enrages the beasts, which come out and attack! They are a Swarm of size equal to the Trap Size.*

Clubs – Falling Objects. *The Trapper has concealed something dangerous among the branches of a tree. If a victim triggers the trap (failing the opposed Notice roll), rocks, logs and other heavy objects rain onto him. Any target caught in the Burst Template must make an Agility (-2) roll to avoid suffering 2d8 damage (3d6 if the card dealt* is a face card). The Game Master can also decide that the falling object is a net. In this case, it causes no damage but the targets fall under the effect of the entangle Power.

Joker – Really nasty trap! This trap is truly devilish! Draw another card, check this table again, and consider that the trap deals +2 damage and has +2 to opposed rolls.

PYGMY HOLY MASKS

Pygmy Holy masks are powerful items. Each is unique but they have some common features. They are incredibly sturdy (Toughness 9) but, if broken, the Masked Warrior must immediately make a Fear Check (-4). In addition, they are cursed. If a non-Pygmy character acquires one and doesn't destroy or give it back to its owner within a week, he acquires the Bad Luck Hindrance.

On the plus side, each mask (with some exceptions) grants its rightful wearer (so, it works only Pigmies) two Edges (or a Monstrous Ability) and an Attribute raise, as in the examples below. Mask wearers are also traditionally equipped with some specific gear.

Many other Holy Masks exist, but the following are the most common.

Baj-Baj (black spider). *Wall Crawler, Poison Master special ability (as Pygmy Hunter), Survival d10. Gear: poisoned bone short sword (Str+d6, see poison master).*

Chagawaba (grinning monkey). *Acrobat, Distract, Taunt d10. Gear: club (Str+d4), throwing stones (Str+d4, range: 3/6/12).*

Dugga-Dugga (thunder in the forest). *Can use the pummel Power, with 10 Power Points, using Vigor as arcane skill, Strength d10, Vigor d10. Gear: bone war club (Str+d8), shield (+1 Parry, +2 Toughness vs. ranged attacks).*

Jagon (weeping slave). *Healer, Pacifism (major) Hindrance, Healing d10. Gear: healing kit.*

Kataruh (tiger's brother). *Beastmaster, Beastfriend, Riding d10. Has a Tiger (use Lion stats) animal companion. Gear: short bone sword (Str+d6), small shield (+1 Parry).*

Lam Nam (dancing snake). *Counterstrike, Improved First Strike, Fighting d10. Gear: spear (Str+d6, +1 Parry, Reach 1, 2 hands).*

Nalinaku (dead baby). *Iron Will, Cause Fear, Spirit d10. Gear: 2 handed bone meat cleaver (Str+d8).*

Rakateru (silent hunter). *Marksman, Poison Master special ability (as Pygmy Hunter), Shooting d10. Gear: poisoned dagger (Str+d4, see poison master), pygmy blowpipe (see poison master, range: 7/14/28, see sidebar).*

Socha (weeping woman). *Amazon, Improved Frenzy, Fighting d10. Gear: staff (Str+d4, +1 Parry, 2 hands, reach 1).*

Tulamulu (angry lizard). *Improved Sweep, Nerves of Steel, Strength d10. Gear: stone battle axe (Str+d8), small shield (+1 Parry).*

Za Zanga (bitten by a tarantula). *Ambidexterity, Two Fisted, Intimidation d10. Gear: twin bone hatchets (Str+d6), light human bone armor (+1, +1 to Intimidation rolls)*

PRIEST

Priests can be very different from one another, depending on their faith and personal attitude.

GENERIC PRIEST

This man or woman is a devoted worshipper of the gods.

Customization: Friar Priest of the Divine Couple (Persuasion d8), Midwife of Etu (Healing d8), Priestess of Hordan (Attractive, Bloodthirsty, Arcane Background (Sorcery), Powers [10 PP]: *boost/ lower trait, fear*).

Attributes: Agility d6, Smarts d8, Spirit d8, Strength d6, Vigor d6
Skills: Fighting d4, Healing d6, Knowledge (Religion) d8, Investigation d4, Notice d6, Persuasion d6.
Charisma: 0; **Pace:** 5; **Parry:** 5; **Toughness:** 5
Edges: Charismatic, Priest.
Hindrances: Vow (tenets of his/her faith).
Gear: staff (Str+d4, +1 parry, reach 1, 2 hands), vests.
Special Abilities
• **Curse of the Gods:** A non-player priest character can invoke a curse upon someone. To do so, the priest must make an opposed Spirit roll, applying -2 to his roll. If he wins, the target of the curse is affected by the Bad Luck Hindrance or the *lower trait* power (GM's decision) until the end of the scenario. If he scores a raise, the curse is permanent, at lest until the priest lifts it or the player atones in some way. The Game Master should use this ability only when strictly appropriate. It is never wise to anger a servant of the gods…

WANDERING SMITH PRIEST

This man or woman is quite different from the typical priests you find in temples, chanting prayers and bowing in front of altars. He is a secret follower of Hulian, Lord of Fire and Smith of Words. He is forced to wander through the Dominions, hiding his faith to the world to avoid the Imperial persecution, but this doesn't prevent him from continuing his silent and lone fight against the cruel sons of Hordan and other demons.

Attributes: Agility d8, Smarts d8, Spirit d8, Strength d8, Vigor d8

Skills: Fighting d8, Healing d6, Knowledge (Religion) d6, Knowledge (Arcana) d8, Intimidation d6, Investigation d6, Notice d6, Persuasion d6, Repair d6, Shooting d8.
Charisma: 0; **Pace:** 6; **Parry:** 7; **Toughness:** 8(2)
Edges: Brave, Elan, Improved Nerves of Steel, Improved Frenzy, Priest.
Hindrances: Vow (religious tenets), Wanted.
Gear: disguised steel long sword (Str+d8, AP 2), bow (damage: 2d6, range: 12/24/48), 1d6 steel tipped arrows (AP 2), medium bronze armor (+2), medium bronze shield (+1 Parry, +2 Toughness vs. ranged attacks).
Special Abilities
• **Know Your Enemy:** Whenever a Smith Priest faces a supernatural creature (with the Demon or Undead Monstrous Ability), he is allowed a Knowledge (Arcana) roll to discover one of its special abilities (preferably a Weakness, if present).

SAGE

Sages and learned men are all that stands between civilization and knowledge and their complete destruction. Whenever a hero needs to check a legend, find a clue, or something similar, a sage is the right person to turn to.

Customization: Inventor (Knowledge (Engineering) d10, Repair d10), Physician (Healing d10, Knowledge (Medicine) d10, Healer).

Attributes: Agility d6, Smarts d10, Spirit d8, Strength d4, Vigor d4
Skills: Fighting d4, Knowledge (any two fields) d10, Investigation d10, Persuasion d6, Notice d6, Taunt d4.

Charisma: 0; **Pace:** 5; **Parry:** 4; **Toughness:** 4
Edges: Sage, Scholar.
Hindrances: Big Mouth, Elderly.
Gear: robes, writing implements, tools of the trade.

SORCERER

In this decaying age, practicing the dark arts is seen as an easy way to achieve personal goals: power, pleasure, riches, respect. But meddling with Things that Man is Not Meant to Know always has a price. Sorcery, like many other aspects of life and culture, is deeply rooted in the traditions of the various races, so a Caldeian sorcerer is very different from a Dancing Witch of the Ivory Savannah or a Death Speaker of the Cairnlands. Specific sorcerer profiles (such as Valkyrie, Caled Shaman and Tricarnian Priest Prince) are detailed in other sections and the list below completes the overview.

WARLOCK

A generic individual practicing the dark arts. Although not a real master of sorcery, he is feared and respected by many people and can be a tough opponent.

Customization: Cairnlander Death Speaker (replace Powers with: *armor* (wailing specters), *summon ally* (ancestor ghost, spirit of the betrayer), *zombie*), Dancing Witch of the Ivory Savannah (replace Impressive Aura with Dancing Witch, Agility d8, replace Powers with: *puppet* (charming dance), *raise/lower trait* (dance of blessing/cursing), *stun* (hypnotic dance of the savannah snake)), Gis Soothsayer (Knowledge (Arcana) d10, replace Powers with: *detect/conceal arcana* (truesight), *divination* (sees the future in the stars), *summon ally* (ancestor ghost, Keronian imp).

Attributes: Agility d6, Smarts d8, Spirit d8, Strength d6, Vigor d6
Skills: Fighting d6, Knowledge (Arcana) d8, Intimidation d6, Notice d6, Persuasion d6, Sorcery d8, Stealth d4, Streetwise d4, Taunt d4.
Charisma: 0; **Pace:** 6; **Parry:** 5; **Toughness:** 5
Edges: Arcane Background (Sorcery), Impressive Aura, New Powers, Power Points.
Hindrances: Arrogant, greedy.
Powers [15 PP]: *bolt* (tendrils of darkness), *boost/lower trait* (corrupt), *deflection* (I am not there!), *summon ally* (Keronian imp, twisted servant).
Gear: dagger (Str+d4), vests.

 ## SORCERER

A powerful practitioner of black magic, who has spent much time studying arcane tomes and learning forbidden secrets from creatures not of this world. Some sorcerers have at least one apprentice (use the Warlock entry).

Customization: Immortal Beauty (Habit (Major - drinking virgin's blood), Very Attractive, Charismatic, Temptress, with a Binding Ritual she has permanently raised her Persuasion to d12), Master Summoner (add singer demon, bear, tiger, giant spider, jatakal).

Attributes: Agility d8, Smarts d10, Spirit d8, Strength d6, Vigor d8
Skills: Fighting d6, Knowledge (Arcana) d10, Intimidation d8, Notice d8, Persuasion d8, Sorcery d12, Stealth d8, Streetwise d8, Taunt d6.
Charisma: -2; **Pace:** 6; **Parry:** 6; **Toughness:** 7 (1)
Edges: Arcane Background (Sorcery), Improved Impressive Aura, New Powers, Power Points, Rapid Recharge, Binding Ritual, Soul Drain.
Hindrances: Cautious, Greedy.

Powers [30 PP]: *armor* (invisible shield), *bolt* (tendrils of darkness), *boost/lower trait* (corrupt), *deflection* (I am not there!), *invisibility* (You can't see me!), *puppet* (Your mind is mine!), *summon ally* (Keronian imp, twisted servant, medium swarm, fanged ape, shadow bat, spirit of the betrayer).

Gear: sorcerer's staff (Str+d4, +1 Parry, Reach 1, 2 hands), ritual bone dagger (+1), ensorcelled robes (+1), two Lotus concoctions chosen from among: *obscure*, *stun*, *boost/lower trait*.

Special Abilities

• **Corrupted by Magic:** The body and soul of the Sorcerer have become tainted by his prolonged use of evil magic. Now he has dark, elongated claws (+1 unarmed damage), and his body always smells of decay. He suffers -2 to Charisma.

• **Binding Ritual:** The Sorcerer has permanently bound a Wild Card Twisted Servant to his will. This individual acts as the Sorcerer's personal servant and bodyguard.

THIEF

Criminals thrive in the wealthy cities of the Empire. Burglars, roof rats, pickpockets, and money forgers are only some of the shady individuals who earn a living by stealing the fat purses of merchants or by robbing temples and noble palaces. Some of them work alone, while others gather in small bands or even well-organized structured guilds, like the famous Thieves Guilds of Jalizor.

THIEF

Despite his skills and experience, this character is considered small time, but this doesn't mean he isn't devious and dangerous.

Customization: Acrobat Thief (Agility d10, Climbing d8, Acrobat, Treasure Hunter, add tiger claws to gear), Guild Thief (Enemy (Rival Guilds), Connections (Guild), add bronze short sword to gear), Fence (Streetwise d10, Connections (crime)), Lock Breaker (Lockpicking d10, Repair d6, Treasure Hunter), Pickpocket (Watch Your Back!, Stealth d10), Swindler (Persuasion d10), Spy (Charismatic, Danger Sense, Persuasion d8).

Attributes: Agility d8, Smarts d6, Spirit d8, Strength d6, Vigor d6

Skills: Climbing d6, Fighting d6, Gambling d4, Intimidation d4, Lockpicking d6, Notice d8, Persuasion d6, Stealth d8, Streetwise d6, Shooting d6, Taunt d4, Throwing d6.

Charisma: 0; **Pace:** 6; **Parry:** 5; **Toughness:** 6 (1)

Edges: Lowlife, Thief.

Hindrances: Greedy.

Gear: dagger (Str+d4), sling (Str+d4, range: 4/8/16), light leather half-body armor (+1), lock picks.

Special Abilities

• **Dark Alley Cat:** When in his own area (a city quarter, road or similar) an Extra

Thief receives the Wild Die on Streetwise and Notice rolls. A Wild Card Thief has the Wild Die increased by one step (usually from d6 to d8).

 ## MASTER THIEF

This character is one of the best criminals in the city. He can be a highly skilled roof cat, capable of sneaking into the lord's palace without alerting a single guard, or a high-ranking member of a thieves guild, or he can work as spymaster for some important ruler.

Customization: High-Ranking Guild Thief (Fighting and Throwing d10, Improved Block, Noble, replace bronze short sword with iron long sword), Professional Burglar (Overconfident, Acrobat, Treasure Hunter, Danger Sense, add tiger's claws, silk rope and a *slumber* lotus concoction to Gear), Spymaster (Streetwise d12+2, Connections (any three), Rich).

Attributes: Agility d10, Smarts d8, Spirit d8, Strength d6, Vigor d6
Skills: Climbing d8, Fighting d8, Gambling d6, Intimidation d6, Lockpicking d8, Notice d10, Persuasion d8, Stealth d10, Streetwise d10, Shooting d8, Taunt d4, Throwing d8.
Charisma: 0; **Pace:** 6; **Parry:** 7; **Toughness:** 6 (1)
Edges: Block, Connections (crime), First Strike, Improved Level-Headed, Improved Dodge, Lowlife, Thief.
Hindrances: Greedy.
Gear: parrying dagger (Str+d4, +1 parry, usually used offhand), short sword (Str+d6), sling (Str+d4, range: 4/8/16), light leather armor (+1), lock picks.
• **Dark Alley Lord:** When in his own city, a Master Thief has the Wild Die increased by one step (usually from d6 to d8) on Streetwise and Notice rolls.

TRICARNIAN

The dwellers of foggy Tricarnia are a mix of very different people. There are large masses of slaves, both born in Tricarnia and brought from abroad, and a small elite of Priest Princes.

SLAVE SOLDIER

The bulk of the Tricarnian army and guard corps is made up of slaves. A mix of drugs, conditioning, and training keeps them docile, under the control of eunuch overseers. The Priest Princes see the rest of humanity, their slaves included, as little more than cattle, so they have adopted special breeding procedures to create very specific slave castes (see sidebar). The following profile refers to an average slave soldier, while the customization specs can be used for members of specific castes.

Customization: Iron Stinger (replace Gear with large shield, spear, and light leather armor), Mastiff (Loyal, Obese, Vigor d10 and Strength d10, Fighting to d8, replace gear with long bronze sword and medium shield).

Attributes: Agility d6, Smarts d4, Spirit d4, Strength d8, Vigor d6
Skills: Fighting d6, Intimidation d4, Notice d4, Shooting d6, Throwing d6.
Charisma: 0; **Pace:** 6; **Parry:** 6; **Toughness:** 6(1)
Edges: Combat Reflexes (painkilling drugs).
Hindrances: Habit (slavemush).
Gear: bronze plated mace (Str+d6) and small shield (+1 Parry) or war sling (Damage: Str+d4, Range: 8/16/32) and bronze dagger (Str+d4), light leather half-body armor (+1).
Special Abilities
• **Drugged Mind:** A Slave Soldier's daily diet consists in a mix of rice and meat or fish, the slavemush, spiced with Khav

and other particular types of Lotus that make him very obedient. However, if he can't get any drugged food for a week, he becomes riotous, very jumpy and wild, receiving -2 to Fear checks, as per the Yellow Hindrance.

• **Weak Morale:** The Tricarnian Slave Soldiers aren't famous for their courage in battle. Every time a group of Extra Slave Soldiers is dealt a deuce as Action Card but they do not have a clear advantage (e.g., they don't outnumber their opponents) or aren't within the Command Radius of an Eunuch Overseer, they must make a group Spirit roll of flee.

EUNUCH OVERSEER

The eunuch officers of the Tricarnian armies are referred to simply as Overseers, so that they don't think themselves above their status. They wear impressive helms and carry long whips to keep the slave soldiers at bay. There is usually at least one overseer for every twenty Slave Soldiers.

Customization: Gorgon Helm (Command Presence), Manticora Helm (Strength d10, Sweep, replace whip and battle axe with iron maul), Vulture Helm (Shooting d10, Marksman, replace bow with composite bow).

Attributes: Agility d8, Smarts d6, Spirit d6, Strength d8, Vigor d6
Skills: Fighting d8, Intimidation d8, Notice d8, Shooting d8, Throwing d6.
Charisma: -4; **Pace:** 6; **Parry:** 6;
Toughness: 6(1)
Edges: Command, Frenzy.
Hindrances: Bloodthirsty, Loyal.
Gear: bronze battle axe (Str+d8), long whip (Str+1, Reach 5), bow (Damage: 2d6, Range: 12/24/48),

monster-shaped helm (+3), light leather armor (+1).
Special Abilities
• **Fight or Die!:** The Eunuch Overseers are the real backbone of the Tricarnian army: they make the slaves obey in no time. In combat, they can use an Intimidation roll within their Command Radius to stop soldiers from trying to flee. The roll has +4 if they have killed a friendly unit during the battle.
• **Taste the Whip!:** An Eunuch Overseer can use his whip for a called shot (-2) targeting a friendly Slave Soldier to make him fight with more vigor. If the target is hit, he doesn't suffer any damage but receives +2 to his next attack roll.

PRIEST PRINCE

The title identifies a generic Tricarnian noble. It refers to a Priest Prince of average power, quite skilled in sorcery and extremely wealthy. Priest Princes are usually accompanied by a dozen slaves at least.

Customization: Astrologer Prince (Sorcery d12, New Power, Power Points x2, add *divination* to Powers), Lotusmaster Prince (remove Binding Ritual and the Demonic Guard Special Ability, replace Arcane Background (Sorcery) and Sorcery d10 with Arcane Background (Lotusmastery) and Lotusmastery d10). Powers [25 PP]: *boost/lower trait, burst, dispel, poison, puppet, zombie*).

Attributes: Agility d6, Smarts d10, Spirit d8, Strength d6, Vigor d6
Skills: Fighting d8, Intimidation d10, Knowledge (Arcana) d8, Knowledge (Religion) d8, Notice d6, Persuasion d8, Sorcery d10.
Charisma: +2/-2; **Pace:** 6; **Parry:** 6; **Toughness:** 6(1)

Edges: Arcane Background (Sorcery), Attractive, Binding Ritual, New Power, Noble, Power Points.
Hindrances: Arrogant, Bloodthirsty, Quirk (hedonism).
Powers [15 PP]: *armor* (word of protection), *bolt* (unleash the hungry spirits!), *stun* (secret name of Hordan), *summon ally* (Keronian Imp, spirit of the Betrayer, Shadow Bat, Demonic Mastiff).
Gear: ensorcelled bronze long sword (Str+d8, AP 2), medium bronze armor (+2), poisoner ring, three assorted Lotus concoctions.
Special Abilities
• **Demonic Guard:** A Priest Prince usually keeps a permanently summoned demon under the effects of the Binding Ritual Edge as pet or bodyguard. The most common Demonic Guards are Keronian Imps, Spirits of the Betrayer, Shadow Bats or Demonic Mastiffs.

TRICARNIAN WARRIOR

SLAVES CASTES

The practice of selective breeding among Tricarnian slaves has led to the creation of some physical models, formalized in the concept of caste. A slave belonging to a certain caste is selected at birth and undergoes specific training. The most common castes are:

Iron Stingers. The Tricarnians were impressed by the Iron Phalanxes of the Empire and tried to imitate their way of fighting with their own slave troops. They are called Iron Stingers, due to their pointed helms, but they are only a shadow of the Iron Phalanxes. Equipped with light armor, they rely more on numbers than on skill.

Mastiffs. These slaves are enormous mountains of flesh. Extremely strong and apparently imperturbable, they are capable of violent outbursts. The Priest Princes use them as personal bodyguards or shock troops.

Overseers. The Overseers are a particular type of eunuch slaves whose task is to lead the Tricarnian troops into battle. They are taken from all castes, and because of their "charge", they are more concentrated on war than on other things. Each overseer is ruthless and feared by the other slaves, because they don't hesitate to kill or mutilate a fellow soldier to have their orders executed. They wear impressive helms, a symbol of their caste.

VALK

These short, bowlegged desert nomads started invading the civilized lands less than two centuries ago and are the main cause of the decadence of the Iron Empire. The following profiles describe their most famous and dangerous fighters, the Riders and the Valkyrie.

VALK RIDER

The typical clan member of a Valk tribe is both a shepherd and a mounted warrior.

Customization: scout (add Stealth d8, Woodsman), warlord personal guard (Fighting d10, Block, Frenzy).

Attributes: Agility d8, Smarts d4, Spirit d6, Strength d8, Vigor d6
Skills: Fighting d8, Notice d4, Intimidation d6, Shooting d10, Riding d10, Survival d6.
Charisma: −4; **Pace:** 6; **Parry:** 6; **Toughness:** 6(1)
Edges: Born in the Saddle, Steady Hands.
Hindrances: Bloodthirsty, Greedy.
Gear: Bronze short sword (Str+d6), bronze dagger (Str+d4), Valk composite bow (Damage: 2d6+1, Range: 15/30/60, AP 1) boiled leather armor (+1), steppe pony.
Special Abilities
•**Hit and Run:** A Valk Rider is trained to fight from horseback till young hood. For this reason he is particularly adapt in hit and run tactics. While mounted, differently from the normal rules, he can move part of

his pony's Pace, do a Shooting attack, and then finish his movement. It is considered an action (so causing multi action penalty).

 VALKYRIE

The Valk hold women in very low esteem, except the Valkyrie. These blonde warrior priestesses are the leading force of a Valk horde. The strength of their visions and their incredible powers make even the strongest warriors tremble.

Customization Jalka Maiden (raise Fighting to d8, replace sorcerer's staff with spear and shield and pony with Jalka, see sidebar), Bringer of War (Knowledge (Battle) d6, add two Command Edges), Old Crone (Elderly, Ugly, remove the Attractive Edge, add two powers and Power Points x2).

Attributes: Agility d8, Smarts d8, Spirit d8, Strength d4, Vigor d6
Skills: Fighting d6, Notice d8, Intimidation d10, Knowledge (Arcana) d8, Sorcery d10, Riding d10.
Charisma: +2; **Pace:** 6; **Parry:** 6; **Toughness:** 6(1)
Edges: Arcane Background (Sorcery), Attractive, Born in the Saddle, Charismatic, Command, Fervor, New Power, Power Points.
Hindrances: Bloodthirsty, Vow (Valk religious tenets).
Powers [20 PP]: *bolt* (invisible strangling force), *deflection* (demonic wind), *fear* (hideous laughter), *summon ally* (fighting bird, demonic mastiff, jatakal).
Gear: Sorcerer's Staff (Str+d4, +1 Parry, 2 hands, reach 1, deliver touch), bone dagger (Str+d4), boiled leather armor (+1), steppe pony.
Special Abilities
• **Living Banners:** Very few Valk warlords use insignia on the battlefield. A band of warriors usually gathers around a Valkyrie, her long blonde mane acting as a banner.

The Command Radius of a Valkyrie is 15" when she is on horseback. For this reason, a Valkyria is sometimes referred as "Living Banner".
• **Visions:** Valkyrie are famous to have vision. Spending a Bennie, and doing a Sorcery (-4) roll, they can use the *divination* power without spending any Power Points. A human (or horse) sacrifice reduces by two the penalty. Every further use of this ability in the same lunar month causes an additional -2 to the roll. A Valkyria failing the Sorcery roll is Exhausted. Critical failures also require to roll on the Sorcery Critical Failures Table.

JALKA MAIDENS
A Valkyrie often chooses to summon a Jatakal, a sort of demonic steed (see page 149). A Jatakal can mate with a mare and a partly supernatural creature is born, a Jalka (see below). Very similar to horses, the Jalka are fearsome creatures. Only a young Valkyrie in her maidenhood can tame and ride a Jalka, then she usually leaves her clan and wanders alone in the steppe, living only in the company of her demonic steed and other evil creatures.

The Jalka Maidens are much feared and respected, even by the other Valkyries.

JALKA
A Jalka is an abomination born of a demonic steed and a mare. It has the same stats as a Henchman warhorse, plus the Demon Monstrous Ability. It feeds on meat, has razor-sharp teeth (Str+d6) and causes Fear the first time it is seen. It can be ridden only by a Jalka Maiden.

WARRIOR
This catch-all profile can be used any time you need a combatant type NPC not falling in other categories.

SOLDIER
A warrior with average experience and gear.

Customization: Archer/Slinger (Shooting d8, Trained Thrower (bow/sling), add bow or sling to Gear) Cavalry (Riding d6, add horse to gear), City Watch (Notice d6, Streetwise d6), Levy Troop (Intimidation, Shooting and Throwing d4, replace bronze short sword and light leather armor with spear), Mercenary (Intimidation d8, Greedy).

Attributes: Agility d6, Smarts d4, Spirit d6, Strength d6, Vigor d6
Skills: Fighting d6, Intimidation d6, Notice d4, Shooting d6, Throwing d6.
Charisma: 0; **Pace:** 6; **Parry:** 6; **Toughness:** 6(1)
Edges: None.
Hindrances: None.
Gear: bronze short sword (Str+d6), small shield (+1 Parry), light leather armor (+1).

EXPERIENCED SOLDIER

A very skilled warrior, a professional in his field.

Customization: Heavy Caldeian Bowman (Trained Thrower (bow), Shooting d10, add bow to Gear), Syranthian Cataphract (Riding d8, add bow, spear and horse to gear), Noble bodyguard (Fighting d10, Alertness), Veteran Mercenary Troop (Block, Greedy).

Attributes: Agility d8, Smarts d6, Spirit d6, Strength d8, Vigor d8
Skills: Fighting d8, Intimidation d6, Notice d6, Shooting d6, Throwing d6.
Charisma: 0; **Pace:** 6; **Parry:** 7; **Toughness:** 8(2)
Edges: Combat Reflexes.
Hindrances: None.
Gear: bronze long sword (Str+d8), medium shield (+1 Parry, +2 Toughness vs. ranged attacks), medium bronze armor (+2).

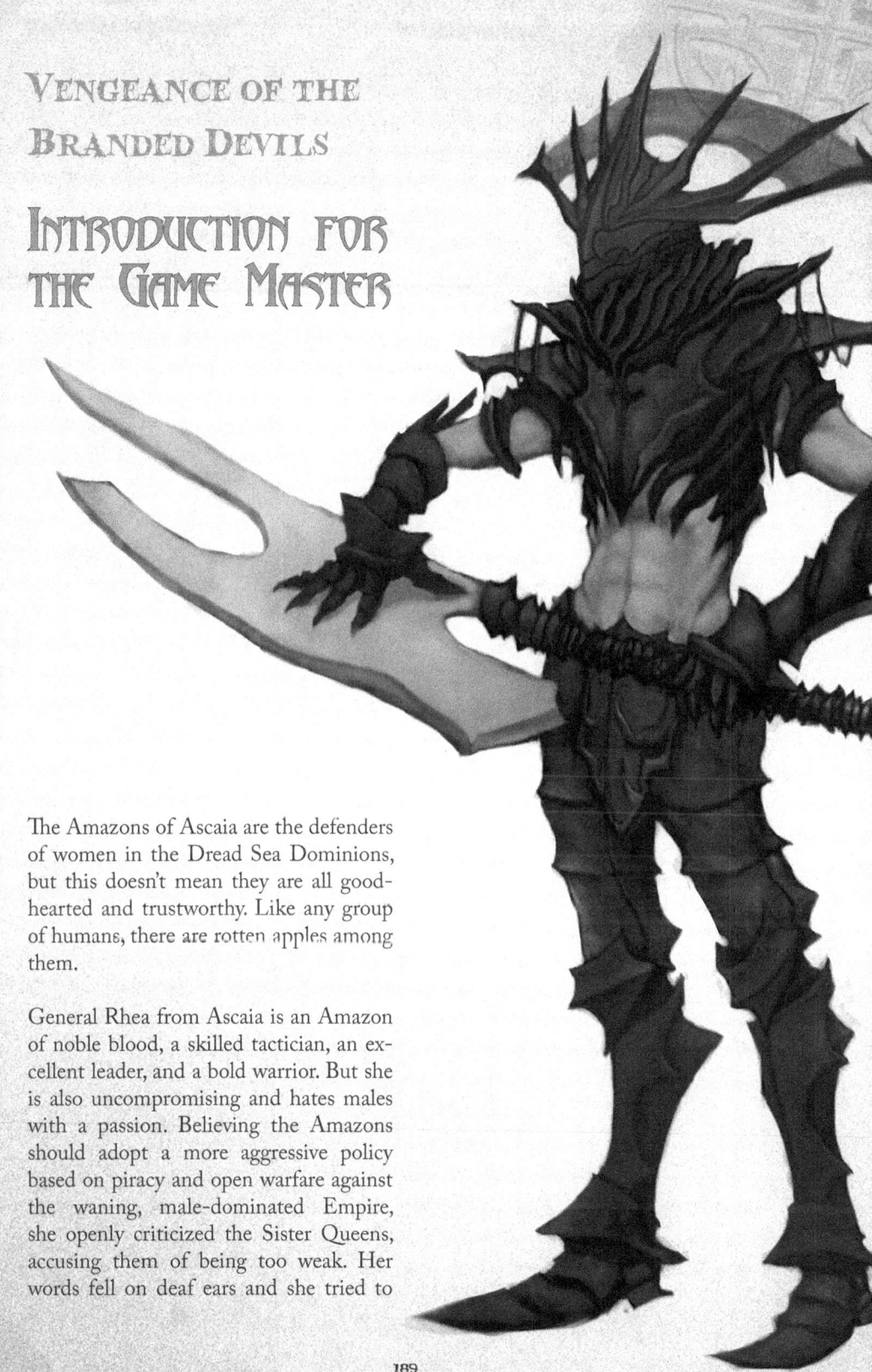

VENGEANCE OF THE BRANDED DEVILS

INTRODUCTION FOR THE GAME MASTER

The Amazons of Ascaia are the defenders of women in the Dread Sea Dominions, but this doesn't mean they are all good-hearted and trustworthy. Like any group of humans, there are rotten apples among them.

General Rhea from Ascaia is an Amazon of noble blood, a skilled tactician, an excellent leader, and a bold warrior. But she is also uncompromising and hates males with a passion. Believing the Amazons should adopt a more aggressive policy based on piracy and open warfare against the waning, male-dominated Empire, she openly criticized the Sister Queens, accusing them of being too weak. Her words fell on deaf ears and she tried to seize power, but her attempt failed. The Sister Queens knew Rhea's ideas had many supporters and, to avoid civil war, they showed mercy, exiling her and her followers. The traitors were branded with the Mark of Infamy and forbidden to set foot on Ascaia's holy ground.

The General became obsessed with returning to Ascaia to kill the Queens and take the crown. But she needed lots of gold to hire and train women warriors and buy ships and equipment. She set up a mercenary company, the Branded Women, who soon became renowned for their cruelty, especially toward men. Yet very few lords want a band of blood-thirsty women in their halls, and the Branded Women were forced to start escorting caravans from Valkheim to Jalizor, a lowly and poorly paid assignment.

During one of these journeys, the Branded Women exterminated a group of highwaymen. One of the bandits, Teggo, traded his life for a precious piece of information: he had once found a large vein of gold in the Vruun Hills, a desolate area in northeastern Zandor. He hadn't been able to hire enough men to mine the ore, which was also impure and would require a costly smelting process.

Rhea saw this as a sign her time had come. She knew where to get cheap, replaceable manpower. Her trusted companion, Ironfist, the finest smith in Ascaia, devised a new method to smelt impure gold. Now, Rhea needs to make sure the presence of the miners and Amazons goes unnoticed…

Not for Gold

The heroes are halfway between Jalizor and Zandor, resting at an inn along the Iron Route. The place is bleak: stale food, the booze smells of piss, and the resident dancer, Jeggah the Dancing Cobra, is… unattractive.

After sitting around the deserted hall for some time, two women in raggedy clothes come in. The women approach them hesitantly and, after a moment, finally find the courage to speak to the party. Danima, the older of the two, bows and addresses the heroes. If the party includes an Amazon, Danima addresses her directly.

"Honorable warriors, we have heard you are mercenaries and I, representative of the village of Gallan, want to hire you. We have brought money."

She opens a purse, containing the riches of the entire village: a couple of silver trinkets and some old silver coins, worth no more than 30 Moons in total.

Meager pay for the adventurers. If the heroes decline the offer, the woman drops to her knees and begs.

"It is all we have! Three weeks ago the Branded Devils came to our village, took our crop and kidnapped our men. Then they came again a week ago, stole more food and took away the elderly and younger men. They said they would be back for more food and our boys! We are ready to die for our children! We don't want you to fight for us, but teach us how to defend ourselves and what is left of our families!"

Some pleas demand to be answered, not for gain, not for gold, but because it is right to do so; this is just such a case. If the party still isn't moved by Danima's words, as a last resort she introduces the girl accompanying her. Jarra is her niece and the prettiest maid in the village. Danima offers Jarra and another girl from the village as slaves. This is a good opportunity for some interesting role-playing. The first player who decides to help Danima should be rewarded with a Bennie at the end of the scene.

When the heroes accept, Danima leads them to the village of Gallan.

GALLAN

Additional Information. Gallan is in a harsh, desolate part of Zandor, two days away from the inn. The trip is uneventful unless the Game Master decides differently. The party can use this time to retrieve additional information from Danima and Jarra.

The "Branded Devils", the women explain, are riders who wear black metal armor and horrifying demon-shaped helms. They speak in cavernous voices, brandish flaming weapons, and ride black horses. There are between twenty and forty of them and the people of Gallan believe them to be creatures from hell.

The Devils have visited the village twice, taking food and men, but no women. First they took the strongest and healthiest men, then the old and young ones. When they arrived, they had extra horses for those they took away and were extremely organized. They rode toward the Vruun Hills, where nobody goes, and disappeared as fast as they could.

After the first attack, the villagers tried to follow their trail, but the Branded Devils erased any trace of their passage.

The Village. Gallan is a very poor, out of the way place, no more than twenty flat-roofed houses huddled together like scared sheep. The fields are ravaged and deserted, except for a few women and young boys who stand around helplessly.

The village has no defenses: no walls, no fortification, no ditch – a perfect place to be raided. Its best defense had been its extreme poverty.

The heroes are taken to speak to Nara, Danima's grandmother and village elder. Nara is a toothless old crone, but her mind is clear and she is a healer (see sidebar). Nara tells them she is about to gather all the villagers in the granary so the heroes can explain what they plan to do.

SWEET TALK

When the villagers are all gathered, the heroes count no more than forty people. Most of them are women, the others are boys and a few very old men, and there is no one close to a real fighter among them. They are scared to death at the sheer thought of holding a weapon, and the great majority believes the heroes should fight in their stead. They must be made to collaborate, because the party cannot stand alone against the Branded Devils. Some courage can be roused in them with a persuasive speech (a Social Conflict); another occasion for the players to role-play. The heroes' main opponent is Yalirra, the potter's wife (Persuasion d6). For each two successes of margin of victory, the heroes gain a special Encouragement Bennie that can be spent only in Organizing the Defense (see below).

The heroes only have three days before the Branded Devils return, but many defenses can be prepared in such a short time. Naturally, they don't know when the attack will be and this add more uncertainty and drama to the whole situation.

As a rule of thumb, each hero can focus on a single task per day, but more heroes can team up with a cooperative roll. All the rolls receive +1 bonus for each Leadership Edge a hero has, and any skill can be substituted with Knowledge (Battle).

VILLAGERS' PERSONALITIES

The players' attitude toward the villagers of Gallan depends on how much they actually care about them. Here are some useful details about key individuals. Remember to use the Ally Personalities table as well.
Danima. *Thirty-year-old wife of the tanner. Often silent, she is bold and strong-minded.*

Jarra. *Danima's niece, sixteen. Not very bright, her main concern is finding a husband.*

Ranga. *Forty-year-old wife of the shepherd. Very muscular due to her work (Str d8, Brawny).*

Grandpa Four Legs. *A man so old nobody knows his exact age. He walks with two sticks, hence his nickname. He knows the area around Gallan very well, especially the Vruun Hills (Knowledge (local area) d10), but nobody pays attention to what he says. He has adopted Zot.*

Nara the Toothless. *Village elder and healer. She loves chatting about the good old days (Healing d8).*

Yalirra. *Potter's wife, thirty-five. Despite her efforts, she never manages to look attractive. She is very wary and easily scared.*

Zot. *A ten-year-old orphan, his face is always dirty. Insatiably curious, he dreams of becoming an adventurer and leaving Gallan (Agility d8, Young, Luck). Adopted by Grandpa Four Legs.*

ORGANIZING THE DEFENSE

Training the Villagers. Only five villagers are able to wield weapons (Motivated Commoners). Too few. With a full day of work, a hero can teach the other villagers some basic notions. Use the lowest of Smarts or Fighting. For each success and raise, five other villagers are converted to Motivated Commoners (up to a maximum of 20), or one skilled fighter is found (Fighting or Shooting or Throwing d8) at the hero's choice.

Getting Weapons. The Motivated Commoners are armed with farming implements (Str+d6, Improvised Weapons), but there is a small forge in the village and a good smith can turn simple tools into spears and similar weapons. The party can also ask some women to make arrows and other projectiles with a Repair roll. For each success and raise, the party can equip 5 villagers with bows or spears.

Studying the Battleground. The Branded Devils storm the village to take slaves and food, making it important for the party to know their surroundings. Each hero studying the battleground can make a roll using the lowest of Smarts and Notice. For each success and raise, the hero identifies a tactical feature of the area:

Granary. A sturdy building (8" by 8") with a single gate (4" wide, Toughness 8), which can hold up to forty people. It seems a good place for the dozen or so boys still present in the village to hide for an ambush.

Water Tower. This area of Zandor is arid, so a water tower was built in the center of the village (6" wide, 18" tall). From its top, archers (maximum 5) can target virtually any area of the village with +2 to their Shooting rolls.

Carts. Several carts (one per success spent on them) can be found in the village. Two people, including non-Motivated Commoners, can move them by a maximum of 3" per round to block a road or to grant Heavy Cover (Toughness 7, 3" by 3").

Fortifications/Traps. There is no time to build any useful fortifications. But on a roll with the lower of Stealth and Smarts, each hero working on this aspect of the defenses can devise one of the following:

Barricade. A wall 2" wide and 10" long, it grants Medium Cover (Toughness 6). The barricade counts as Difficult Ground and riders must make a Riding (–2) roll to jump over it.

Treacherous Ropes. Ropes stretched across a rider's path can be deadly. Each Treacherous Rope requires two people (can be Commoners) and is 5" long. An enemy rider can spot it with a Notice (–2) roll. Otherwise, the rider is hit across the neck, suffering 2d8 damage, plus other 2d6 for being unhorsed. A Treacherous Rope works only once.

Boiling Cauldrons/Falling Stones. The flat roofs of the village are an ideal place to put cauldrons of boiling liquids or various projectiles to be used against the attackers. During the battle, the heroes can decide to use Cauldrons or Falling Stones any time an opponent is within 6" of a house. The Cauldrons/Stones are considered on Hold and are manned by two non-combatants with Throwing d6. They deal 2d6 damage in a Medium Burst Template. If the Throwing roll fails, the Template scatters 1d4" in a random direction.

THE NIGHT OF THE BRANDED DEVILS

On the third day, two hours after sunset, the Branded Devils attack. They don't make any attempt at stealth; they try to scare the villagers as much as possible. They ride black horses and wield long burning poles (Reach 3, Str+d4, can set fire).

This battle scene can be played in two ways: on the tabletop or using the Mass Battle Rules (see sidebar).

The village is 48" by 48" and has fifteen 4" by 4" huts, plus the Granary and the Water Tower (see above). Arrange the houses along an imaginary main street (3" wide) going from north to south, with a square in the center.

The Branded Devils arrive in two groups, one from the south and one from the north. Each group is led by a Lieutenant and acts on a different Action Card. This time the Devils don't have extra horses, because they plan to take only a dozen or so boys and tie them to the backs of their saddles.

If the heroes and their troops are properly concealed, the Branded Devils must check for surprise. They don't expect any resistance. When they lose more than five members, they try to flee. If possible, they try to take their wounded comrades with them. Otherwise, they will finish them off to avoid leaving prisoners.

(M) Branded Devils (18)
(M) Branded Devil Lieutenants (2). Add Knowledge (Battle) d4 and the Command Edge to a Branded Devil.
(M) Motivated Commoners (5+)
(M) Commoners (10)

THE NIGHT OF THE BRANDED DEVILS: MASS BATTLE VERSION

Groups who prefer a faster approach to combat can run this battle scene using the Mass Battle rules.
The Branded Devils start with 10 Tokens. Their leaders have Knowledge (Battle) d4.
The Villagers start with 1 token per hero, plus one for each 5 Motivated Commoners, up to a maximum of 9. If any of the heroes has Knowledge (Battle), he can use it; otherwise, a party member must roll unskilled (d4–2).

The Villagers have +1 Artillery bonus for each Fortification/Trap devised by the party.
The Branded Devils have −1 Terrain disadvantage for each feature of the Battleground studied by the party.
The Villagers are ready at their positions and cannot retreat (+4 to morale rolls).
The heroes can take part in the battle as normal (see **Characters in Mass Battle** in Savage Worlds).
The Branded Devils automatically flee when they are reduced to 7 tokens or less.

THE FACE OF THE ENEMY

"Fall back!" shouts one of the Branded Devils, and as a single unit, the attackers retreat into the night.

Danima is standing next to you, her face dirty and her eyes wild with excitement. "I cannot believe it! We made them flee!"

A similar incredulous expression is on the face of all the surviving villagers.

Now it's time to find out who the Branded Devils really are. This can be done by removing the mask of one of the fallen enemies. They can also interrogate a prisoner, provided the heroes were lucky or skilled enough to capture one alive.

To their great surprise, the Branded Devils are all women as muscular as any male warrior. Each woman has an ugly mark in the shape of an "X" on her cheek, probably made with a hot iron.

Let the heroes make a Common Knowledge roll. Heroes particularly familiar with the Amazons of Ascaia roll with +2. Amazon heroines don't need to roll; they automatically know who the riders are.

With a success the heroes identify them as Ascaian Amazons. With a raise, they also

recognize the "X" mark as the Brand of Infamy, a punishment reserved for traitors.

If the party includes an Amazon heroine, draw a card from the action deck for each fallen enemy examined. If a Queen is drawn, the heroine knows the fallen Devil! She was exiled with some other rebels after General Rhea's failed rebellion. In this case, the Game Master can share some of the information contained in the **Information for the Game Master** section with the players.

Prisoners don't reveal anything. They will die rather than betray General Rhea.

TAKING THE INITIATIVE

Despite the villagers' enthusiasm, the war is far from over. The Branded Devils were surprised but they'll be back and it won't be easy to stop them a second time. In addition, there is no hint of where they are keeping the captive villagers. This time, however, the raiders had to flee in a hurry and weren't able to cover their tracks. If the heroes act quickly, they have a chance to find their camp!

The trail takes the heroes toward the Vruun Hills (see below). If she is still alive, Danima offers to accompany the heroes. She knows the hills well because her father was a huntsman and took her with him on hunting expeditions.

REPRISAL!

If the party waits more than two days, on the third night the village is attacked by the entire band of Branded Devils. They raid the village and burn it the ground.

The strike force includes:

(WC) General Rhea (1)
(WC) Ironfist (1)
(M) Branded Devils (36)
(M) Branded Devil Lieutenants (2). Add Knowledge (Battle) d4 and the Command Edge to a Branded Devil.

THE VRUUN HILLS

The Vruun Hills are barren, rocky hills, crossed by narrow passages. The vegetation is limited to leathery shrubs and weeds, and finding water is very difficult (–2 to Survival rolls). A small population of mountain goats is the only reason the hunters and shepherds from Gallan come to this area.

The hills owe their name to a mythical creature, the Vruun, which is supposed to live here. Very few people have seen it, but many claim to know someone who has, although no one really knows what it looks like. It is more of a legend.

In the past there was mining in the hills, but more than fifty years have passed and only Grandpa Four Legs remembers it.

ON THE TRAIL

Barren Creek. Following the Branded Devils' trail isn't difficult. The band stayed at the bottom of a narrow valley, but then took a side gorge and went deep into the hills. Spotting the turn can be tricky; the party must make a Tracking (–2) roll. If they fail, they miss it and wander aimlessly for four hours under the hot sun before realizing their mistake and coming back to the right path. Have the heroes make a Vigor roll to avoid Fatigue.

Enemy Camp. At dusk, the heroes find proof they are on the right trail. They come to what is left of a temporary camp, where the Branded Devils stopped to heal their wounded and rest the horses.

The party should camp here. It is a moonless night, and it can be very dangerous to wander the hills without proper visibility.

During the night, a terrible animal cry is heard, a mix of anger, loss and rage. It is so loud it wakes the entire party and echoes in the hills like thunder.

If Danima is with the party, she starts trembling and whispers:

"The Vruun! We must hide!"

Danima is right; the Vruun has been lured to the camp by the smell of the Branded Devils. The creature is huge, slow and ponderous, so the heroes have all the time they need to find shelter.

The Vruun (see **Creatures and NPCs**) enters the camp and starts devastating it, methodically destroying anything it finds. Then, with a last cry of rage, the creature breathes fire over the camp and leaves. The fire burns a long time before sputtering out.

If the party decides to fight the Vruun, the creature fights back, but doesn't chase them if they run away.

 Vruun (1)

Rain and Drunkenroot. On the second day, the heroes follow the trail until midday. They are close now, very close. But suddenly the sky darkens and a violent storm approaches quickly. If a few moments the rain starts pouring down, with lightning bolts striking the ground nearby. They must find shelter soon (Survival). If they fail, Danima spots a suitable place.

Next to a field of smelly brambles, there is a protruding rock, large enough for the party to huddle together under. A cold wind blows and the party is freezing, but it is impossible to start a fire during the storm. Each hero must make a Vigor roll or suffer a level of Fatigue. The level wears off after six hours or by warming up around a fire. If a 1 is rolled on the Vigor die, regardless of the Wild Die, it means the hero caught the flu and the Fatigue will last until the end of the adventure.

There's another way to make the situation less uncomfortable. The brambles near the rock are Drunkenroot, a plant with long thorn-shaped fruits which become white and very juicy when ripe. They are called Drunkenroot because they contain alcohol. Any hero eating a large amount of fruits feels warm (no need to make the Vigor roll mentioned above), but must check to avoid the effects of the plant (see sidebar). The heroes recognize the brambles with a Survival roll. If they score a raise, they also know about the potentially dangerous effects of the brambles. Danima knows them very well.

By mid afternoon the storm has subsided.

DRUNKENROOT: THE PERFECT CURE FOR THE FLU?

Except for the Alchemists of Gis, the peoples of the Dread Sea Dominions only know fermentation, not distillation. They can only produce drinks with relatively low alcoholic content. The natural alcohol of the Drunkenroot is far stronger and stays longer in the body. Any hero eating Drunkenroot must not overindulge or risks the consequences (Smarts roll required). If he fails draw a card:

Red Card – Bold. *The hero feels bold and handsome! He gains the Overconfident Hindrance until the end of the adventure. If he already has this Hindrance, he feels compelled to brag, acquiring the Big Mouth Hindrance instead.*

Black Card – Grim. *The hero feels sad, fatalistic and surly. He gains the Mean Hindrance until the end of the adventure. If he*

already has this Hindrance, the situation is much worse and he acquires the Death Wish Hindrance.
On the flipside, any hero eating too much Drunkenroot is immune to flu.

A Stroke of Luck. The sun shines again, but the rain has destroyed the trail they were following. Give the players time to realize the situation, and tell them there's no chance of finding the enemies now.

When they have lost hope, the group hears human voices nearby (no Notice roll required). The newcomers are two Branded Devils, standing at the far end of the Drunkenroot field! If the heroes are quiet (Stealth roll), they can approach the Devils and spy on them.

The two women aren't wearing their impressive armor, and they are busy cutting the Drunkenroot and piling it in baskets on the backs of their placid mules. Both women complain about the task; Drunkenroot is sticky and messy. The heroes notice the Branded Devils must have been here before because large chunks are missing from many of the nearby bushes. After filling the baskets, the Branded Devils leave and can easily be shadowed (Tracking roll).

If the heroes are spotted or decide to attack, the Amazons fight to the death. Even if taken alive, they prefer to die rather than betray their sisters.

A Reckless Beast. While the heroes are following the Amazons' trail or the Amazon themselves, they have another unexpected encounter. They first hear a low grunt and the ground starts shaking. If the heroes are shadowing the Amazons, the two women immediately start running. The Vruun has returned!

The beast is also trying to follow the Branded Devils' trail but, confused by the rain, can't find it. It angrily hits the ground with its beak, and then goes away. Puzzled by the beast's strange behavior, the heroes move on.

THE HIDDEN MINE

The heroes follow the women and come to a narrow canyon, a fissure splitting a rocky hill in two. At the end of the canyon they see the mouth of a cave.

Entrance. If the heroes are following the Amazons, they see the two women slow down and whistle a tune. The Branded Devils watching the entrance of the cave step out of the shadows and great their comrades.

(M) Branded Devils (4)

If the heroes aren't following the Amazons, they must make a Notice (–4) roll to spot the hidden sentinels. If successful, they can decide what to do, and maybe ambush them. The sentinels are considered active guards. Or the players can try to fool them by wearing armor taken from the enemies and by imitating the tune they heard (see sidebar).

If the sentinels are attacked one of them tries to run to the Large Cavern (see below) to raise the alarm. Stopping her can be handled as a short chase (3 rounds). If she manages to reach her sisters, 15 Branded Devils rush to the Entrance in 2d6 rounds and capture the heroes (see sidebar).

There is another way into the mine. With a Notice (–4) or Survival (–2) roll, a hero examining the rocks just above the cave's entrance spots a small fissure. The Branded Devils don't know about this fissure, which leads to the Glittering Passage below. A simple Stealth (+2) roll is required to reach it without alerting the sentinels.

Glittering Passage. This natural passage opens into a small cavern. If the heroes have a torch or another source of light they behold something marvelous: the walls of the passage are studded with glittering gold flakes! With a Notice and a Strength roll, a hero can pull off a small chunk of precious rock (value 2d6 x 50 Moons). The passage ends in an opening at cciling level of the Large Cavern.

An Agility roll is required to jump down to the Slave Barracks without suffering 2d6 damage.

DISGUISES

The suits of armor the Branded Devils wear are heavy but ideal disguises. An female hero with Vigor d6–d8 can wear it. Once in armor, a Persuasion roll versus the opponent's Smarts (or some good role-playing) is enough to pass routine questioning. Being male, having a Vigor out of range, or the Brawny Edge gives a cumulative –2 to the roll. So, a Brawny barbarian with Vigor d10 suffers –6 if disguised as a Branded Devil.

On the other hand, any man can easily pass as a slave, but this means wearing neither armor nor weapon and playing the part with a submissive attitude.

BEING CAPTURED

The Branded Devils are always looking for slaves. If they outnumber their opponents, they try to capture them alive by switching to Non-Lethal attacks. Subdued heroes are dragged to the furnace and start The Secret of Smelting scene as prisoners.

Bound and unarmed, they must free themselves (Strength roll required to break the ropes) and find weapons. There are lots of Improvised Weapons such as pickaxes and shovels lying around, and other weapons can be taken from any fallen Branded Devil. They can also retrieve their equipment, which is in the custody of one of the Branded Devils who captured them.

LARGE CAVERN

From outside it would be impossible to guess this hill conceals such a big cavern. It is as large as the Arena in Faberterra and almost as tall. There are several huts and buildings, but the main feature is a big furnace, constantly fed by slaves carrying baskets full of gold ore, while a few Branded Devils stand around brandishing long whips.

"The villagers!" whispers Danima, her eyes wide with fear and surprise.

The whole cavern resembles a busy anthill, with the slaves digging for ore in various side passages and corners and strictly supervised by their captors.

There are around thirty Branded Devils and sixty slaves. Despite the many torches, vast areas are poorly lit. Crates, sacks and piles of debris are everywhere, so sneaky heroes can explore the cavern but must be careful to avoid detection.

Any time the heroes move to a location requires a Stealth roll. A single hero failing the roll is enough to trigger detection by a guard. If the heroes are disguised (see below), they can try to fool her, otherwise she raises the alarm. If this happens, 4 Branded Devils rushing to the spot each round, up to a maximum of 20, until the heroes are captured or flee.

(M) Branded Devils (20)

The main cavern locations the heroes can explore are listed below:

Mining Tunnels. There are a large number of short tunnels all around the cavern. Whenever the heroes enter a tunnel, draw a card from the Action Deck. If the card is red they find four slaves and a single guard. If it is black, the tunnel is empty, but some digging implements are lying around (Str+d6, Improvised Weapon).

Slave Barracks. The slaves work two shifts of 12 hours each. At any time there are twenty slaves resting here. They are watched by only two Amazons, because they are usually too tired to cause any trouble. As an extra precaution, their feet are bound with a long chain.

The locks are easy to pick (one roll per person) but it takes a long time; each attempt takes five minutes. The other option is to get the key from Ironfist (see **Smithy** below). Once free, the slaves can be persuaded to aid the heroes in fighting the Branded Devils is they can be equipped weapons. Pickaxes and similar implements can be found in the Mining Tunnels, while proper weapons are available in the Smithy.

(M) Branded Devils (2)
(M) Slaves (20). Use the Commoner stats.

General Rhea's Quarters. This wooden hut is the best constructed in the mine. A pair of Branded Devil bodyguards always watch the door and anyone wanting to enter is thoroughly questioned and searched, even when wearing a full suit of armor. There is another way in; a small window on the left side of the hut.

The inside is luxurious, with a large bed, a table full of maps of the area, an armor rack, and a reinforced strongbox which looks very heavy. It has a complex lock and can be opened only with a Lockpicking (−4) roll. Rhea always keeps the keys on her person. All the ingots smelted in the furnace are kept in the strongbox. There are forty ingots in total, each worth 1,000 Moons and weighing 10 lbs. It is a valuable prize, but moving it will prove highly difficult (it weighs 400 lbs).

When the heroes enter Rhea's quarters, draw a card from the action deck. If red, the Amazon general is bathing in her bronze tub. She isn't afraid to use her great beauty to seduce any male fool enough to be deceived by her stunning appearance. She never lets her guard down and, besides her weapons lying outside the tub, she also has a dagger (Str+d4) in a leg scabbard, which she can use to get the Drop. After attacking, she'll shout for help, alerting the guards.

If the card is black, Rhea is somewhere outside inspecting the work being done in the mine, and the only occupant of the room is Dog.

This poor, emaciated man wears a cap and some filthy rags and is chained to a pillar like a dog. He is Rhea's favorite pet and she likes kicking him when she feels unhappy. Dog is actually Teggo, the highwayman who told Rhea about the mine. When she's around, he acts as an obedient slave doing whatever she wishes. If he ever got the chance, he would try to kill her.

(M) Rhea's Bodyguards (2). Use the Branded Devil stats, Fighting d10
(WC) Rhea (1)
(WC) Dog (1). Use the Motivated Commoner stats.

Smithy. This wooden hut is a fully equipped forge. Two half naked Amazons work under the supervision of a tall woman with a shaved head and a hammer in place of her right arm. She is Ironfist, second in command of the Branded Women. Any Ascaian Amazon heroine who has been away from home less than five years can make a Common Knowledge roll to recognize her (give the players some information about Ironfist, available in her stats).

The Smithy is full of weapons and half-finished suits of armor, including a couple of full Branded Devil suits. One is big enough to be used by a Brawny hero without penalty. There are also enough axes, long swords and spears to arm twenty people.

Ironfist isn't a fool and she knows her sisters very well; she has +2 to any Smarts roll to recognize disguised heroes. If she discovers intruders, especially males, she picks up a white-hot iron sword (Str+d6, +2 damage for flaming weapon, chance to set fire) and attacks with it.

If the heroes manage to dispatch her, they can take the key to the slaves' chain (see above) from her belt. Very smart and daring heroes might even manage to pickpocket her.

(M) Branded Devil Smithy Workers (2). Use the Branded Devil stats, Strength d8. Unarmored.

(WC) Ironfist

Branded Devils' Quarters. This long hut hosts several pallets and a central cooking fire. Although the Branded Women are renegade Amazons, this barracks shows they still follow a hard military discipline and keep everything in perfect order. There are always a dozen off-duty Amazons resting in the hut. Since they take off their armor while inside, the Amazons are wary of anyone who acts differently.

The door of the hut can be blocked from the outside, trapping the off-duty Amazons inside for at least three rounds, until they manage to break free.

(M) Branded Devils (12).

Vruun Puppy Pen. In a corner of the cave there is a pen surrounded by a thick stone wall. It is always guarded by two sentinels. If the heroes have managed to shadow the two Amazons gathering Drunkenroot up to this point, they see large piles of brambles stacked nearby. A constant grunting and occasional low yelps come from within the pen, which contains a young Vruun, a beast as big as a horse, which is extremely fond of Drunkenroot. The poor creature is required for smelting the gold in the furnace. If the party frees the Vruun, the beast goes wild and its shrieks attract its mother's attention (see **The Secret of Smelting**).

(M) Vruun puppy (1)

Smelting Furnace. The furnace is large and squat, and equipped with a sloping walkway for the miners to climb up and unload the ore. No fire burns inside, but its opening is blackened and scarred by some heat source. A small stone channel allows the melted gold to flow into an ingot mold. When the heroes reach this location (or are taken here as prisoners), they discover the Secret of Smelting and the last scene of the scenario begins.

THE SECRET OF SMELTING

The following text is written presuming the heroes come to the smelting furnace unnoticed and General Rhea, Ironfist and Dog are still alive. It also presumes the Vruun puppy is safely closed in its pen.

If necessary modify the scene below accordingly.

You are looking at the strange smelting apparatus, trying to figure out how it can work without fire, when two high-ranking Amazons, a beautiful woman wearing a red cloak (General Rhea) *and a muscular one with a crude smith's hammer in place of her right arm* (Ironfist), *approach the furnace and the inspect the ore level.*

"Bring on the beast!" the muscular woman shouts. For a moment the cave falls silent. Everyone stares in awe at the beast being dragged toward the furnace. It is a Vruun, but not the one you saw before, a much smaller one! It shouts pitifully, but the Branded Devils drag it to the smelter and, with nimble moves, tie its head to the furnace's mouth.

"Make him breath!" orders the red-cloaked Amazon.

The servants prod the beast's flanks and suddenly it releases a burst of flames into the furnace!

"Make it breath again! It isn't enough!" the one-armed Amazon growls.

The beast breathes fire once more, then it lets out a high-pitched weeping sound. To your surprise, a similar but louder sound echoes in reply!

You turn around and hear terrorized voices coming from the access corridor!

"Alarm! Alarm! The Vruun is coming!"

Like a devil straight out of hell, the mother Vruun you saw before storms into the mine. She is looking for her child and will destroy anything and anyone in her way!

Time for the party to intervene, lead the slaves outside, vanquish the Branded Devils and escape!

The battleground is the entire cavern (36" wide). The Vruun enters through the main entrance (6" wide). The furnace is in the middle of the cavern, surrounded by the other buildings (see below).

The Vruun puppy is tied to the smelter and cannot move until freed.

The Vruun mother reaches the smelter, destroys it, and frees her puppy. Then, the two beasts start attacking anything and anyone in the cave, picking the nearest target, until all the people are dead and all the buildings destroyed. Only at this point do they leave.

Rhea, Ironfist, Dog and half of the Branded Devils are placed within 6" of the furnace.

The other half start scattered around the cavern. After the first round, Rhea orders them to stand by the entrance to prevent the slaves from escaping; the entrance is held by a quarter of the total Branded Devils.

The fight ends when the heroes escape, or the Vruuns and the Branded Devils are dead.

(WC) General Rhea (1)
(WC) Ironfist (1)
(M) Vruun (1)
(M) Vruun puppy (1)
(M) Branded Devils (4 per hero)
(M) Slaves (20). Use the Commoner stats.

TERRAIN AND PROPS

Furnace: Place the furnace in the middle of the battleground; use a Small Burst Template. It has Toughness 9, Heavy Armor and it is full of liquid metal. The round after the furnace is destroyed, place a Medium Burst Template in the same position. Every character caught in the template must make an Agility roll or suffer 2d10 damage from fire. The second round the Template expands to Large Burst Template. If the fire spreads as far as any of the buildings, every round there is a chance the building catches fire. The smoke builds up slowly (the cavern is huge), so the Smoke inhalation rules don't apply until five rounds after the fire has started.

Other buildings: There are other buildings nearby: Rhea's quarters, the smithy, the slaves quarters, and the Branded Devils quarters. To keep things simple, the first two are 6" by 4", while the second two are 12" by 4". They have Toughness 7. Place them wherever you wish on the battlefield.

Dazed Slaves: The heroes should save the slaves and lead them outside. Divide the slaves into groups of four, and place them all around the cave. Each group of slaves must be at least 6" away from other groups. The slaves start the game Shaken, cannot move, and cannot recover from being Shaken as normal (they are too terrified). They need a hero within 3" of them to shout at them, push them, or order them to move. Making a Persuasion, Intimidation or Smarts (−2) roll Unshakes the entire group. From then on, the group of slaves is under the control of the hero, who should lead them out of the cave. Another group of slaves is chained in the Slaves Quarters (see above). If the heroes didn't free them before this scene, they are doomed to die in the devastation made by the Vruun.

Dog the Rebellious Slave: Dog, Rhea's personal slave, is kept by his mistress on a leash and acts completely subjugated to Rhea's will. During the battle, he does nothing and receives no Action Card until someone is dealt a Joker. When this happens, Dog acts immediately on the Joker (gaining all the benefits) and rebels against the cruel General.

AFTERMATH

The heroes should manage to leave the mine and save most of the captive villagers, while the Branded Devils, Rhea and Ironfist die fighting the Vruun or in the fire.

If the heroes save Dog too, he tells them of Rhea's treasure. Later, the heroes can come back to what is left of the General's hut and look for her strongbox. At the Game Master's discretion the gold might have partially melted (halve the total value). Either way, it's an enormous treasure.

What to do with it? The party can spend it on booze and courtesans, but the village of Gallan is in dire need —the harvest was lost and most of the food taken. Half of the gold would be more than enough to rebuild the village, buy food, and survive till next spring.

If the heroes decide to help the villagers, they'll be forever welcome in Gallan and benefit from the Luck Edge in the next adventure.

Without an alternative method to smelt the gold, the party and the villagers cannot extract any more precious metal from the cave.

CREATURES AND NPCS

BRANDED DEVIL

This soldier appears as a devilish creature with black, spiked armor and a demon-shaped full helm.

Some of these women are Ascaian Amazons, exiled from Ascaia as traitors and in the service of General Rhea and her second-in-command, Ironfist. Others are recruits the General has found in the last few years. All of them are proud of the Brand of Infamy on their faces and are ready to die for their leader.

The Branded Devils deeply hate all males, regardless of their race or age.

Attributes: Agility d8, Smarts d6, Spirit d6, Strength d8, Vigor d6

Skills: Climbing d4, Fighting d8, Intimidation d8, Notice d4, Riding d6, Shooting d6, Throwing d6
Charisma: 0; **Pace:** 6; **Parry:** 7; **Toughness:** 7(2)
Edges: Amazon (see Disguised below), Combat Reflexes
Hindrances: Loyal, Vengeful (males)
Gear: Bronze long sword (Str+d8), Branded Devil armor (+2, see below), medium shield (+1 Parry, +2 Toughness vs. ranged weapons), bow (damage: 2d6, range: 12/24/48)
Special Abilities
• **Branded Devil Armor:** These suits of armor were made by Ironfist, former master smith of Ascaia and rebellious Amazon. Made to impress as well as protect, they grant +2 armor (whole body, head included) and +2 to Intimidation rolls. In addition, a Branded Devil scoring a raise on an Intimidation roll immediately gains a free Fighting attack. The intimidation bonus and the additional attack don't apply if the opponents know she is a woman. A Branded Devil's armor weighs 30 lbs.
• **Branded Woman:** The Branded Devil is a member of the feared Branded Women mercenary company, famous for offering men no mercy. Whenever a Branded Woman Incapacitates a Wild Card, she receives a Bennie, which can be shared with any Branded Woman on the battlefield.
• **Disguised:** A Branded Devil is disguised under her armor. She cannot be recognized as a woman and men don't consider her a weak target. While in her Branded Devil Armor she doesn't benefit from the Amazon Edge.

COMMONER

A commoner from the village of Gallan; he or she would prefer to flee rather than fight. The following stats can be altered to represent specific individuals. When necessary, roll on the Allies Personality Table to add some characterization.

Attributes: Agility d6, Smarts d6, Spirit d6, Strength d6, Vigor d6
Skills: Fighting d4, Knowledge (one craft) d6, Notice d4, Shooting d4, Stealth d4, Throwing d4
Charisma: 0; **Pace:** 6; **Parry:** 4; **Toughness:** 5
Edges: None
Hindrances: None
Gear: Bronze knife (Str+d4) or farming tool (Str+d6, Improvised Weapon)

GENERAL RHEA

Rhea is an Amazon of Ascaia, born into a long line of warrior women who have never known the abuses of men. In her private life, she is quite fond of men, and is renowned for her many lovers. She believes her duty as an Amazon is to subdue males and extend Ascaia's dominion over the weak lands of the Empire. But it is all an excuse to justify her enormous lust for personal power. General Rhea is very beautiful and extremely capable of manipulating heroes. She is also a skilled warrior and tactician.

Attributes: Agility d8, Smarts d8, Spirit d8, Strength d8, Vigor d8
Skills: Climbing d6, Fighting d10, Intimidation d8, Knowledge (Battle) d8, Taunt d8, Notice d6, Persuasion d8, Riding d6, Shooting d6, Throwing d6
Charisma: +4; **Pace:** 6; **Parry:** 7 (8 vs. males); **Toughness:** 7 (2)
Edges: Amazon, Attractive, Bikini Heroine, Command, Counterattack, Hold the Line!, Quick, Noble, Temptress
Hindrances: Greedy (personal power), Vengeful (males)
Gear: Bronze long sword (Str+d8), bronze dagger (Str+d4), Ivy Marked Amazon Blade (Str+d6+1, AP 2, range:

6/12/24, see below), bow (damage: 2d6, range: 12/24/48)
Special Abilities
• **Disguised:** A Branded Devil is disguised under her armor. She cannot be recognized as a woman and men don't consider her a weak target. While in her Branded Devil Armor she doesn't benefit from the Amazon Edge.
• **Ivy Marked Amazon Blade:** Rhea comes from an ancient family of Amazons and she wields a blade that dates back to the Rebellion of the Sister Queens. This weapon is recognizable by a very delicate engraving on its blade, representing a strand of ivy. It is made of ancient bronze and Rhea keeps it sharp (it deals +1 damage). If returned to the Amazons of Ascaia, it grants the heroes the warrior women's friendship.

IRONFIST

This Amazon has a shaved head, impressive muscles, and no right forearm. She replaced it with a smith's hammer, hence her name. Ironfist wasn't born in Ascaia. When she was a girl a slavers' Hawk Ship took her there. She was so weak and ill they were forced to amputate her arm to save her life. Despite her mutilation Ironfist joined the Amazons with great enthusiasm. She became an impressive fighter and, later, a talented weapon maker, earning the title of Mistress of the Ascaian Forge.

Ironfist joined General Rhea in her rebellion and was also exiled. She nurtures a deep, indomitable hate for all males.

She made the Branded Devils' suits of armor.

Attributes: Agility d6, Smarts d8, Spirit d8, Strength d10, Vigor d8
Skills: Fighting d8, Knowledge (Metalworking) d8, Intimidation d8, Notice d6, Repair d10.

Charisma: –2; Pace: 6; Parry: 6 (7 vs. males); Toughness: 6
Edges: Amazon, Ambidexterity, Bikini Heroine, Brawny, Two Fisted
Hindrances: Ugly, One Arm
Gear: Long bronze sword (Str+d8), Iron Fist (Str+d8, AP 2, see below), smith's apron
Special Abilities
• Branded Woman: Ironfist is a member of the feared Branded Women mercenary company, famous for showing males no mercy. Whenever a Branded Woman Incapacitates a Wild Card, she receives a Bennie, which can be shared with any Branded Woman on the battlefield.
• Iron Fist: Ironfist built for herself the smith's hammer she wears in place of her right forearm. It is both a tool and an impressive weapon, dealing Str+d8 damage, AP 2. She cannot be disarmed.
• Mutilatrix: Ironfist is a reckless fighter and loves wounding and scarring her male opponents. Whenever she causes a Wound to a Wild Card, the victim must make an immediate Vigor roll. If he fails, he must roll on the Injury Table. The effect of the injury wears off when the Wound is healed.

MOTIVATED COMMONER

This commoner from the village of Gallan has decided it is better to die fighting for freedom than live as a slave. The following stats can be altered to represent specific individuals. When necessary, roll on the Allies Personality Table to add some characterization.

Attributes: Agility d6, Smarts d6, Spirit d6, Strength d6, Vigor d6
Skills: Fighting d6, Knowledge (one craft) d6, Notice d4, Shooting d6, Stealth d6, Throwing d6
Charisma: 0; Pace: 6; Parry: 5; Toughness: 5
Edges: None

Hindrances: None
Gear: Bronze Knife (Str+d4) or farming tool (Str+d6, Improvised Weapon)
Special Abilities
• Hurried Training: The Motivated Commoner has been briefly trained by the party and his stats represent more a temporary morale effect than a real knowledge of the ways of the war. After each week, a Motivated Commoner must make a Spirit (–2) roll or his stats revert to those of a standard Commoner. If he scores a raise, the Motivated Commoner has really learned something and he can retain the current stats permanently. The presence of the heroes at the village grants +2 to the roll.

 # VRUUN

Nobody really knows where the Vruuns came from, but today only a small family of these creatures remains in the Dominions. The Vruun is a four-legged creature, slightly bigger than a rhino, covered in a scaly hide. It has a massive head with a single horn and its mouth resembles a beak.

Despite its terrible appearance, the Vruun is a herbivore and usually tame. This doesn't mean it isn't dangerous. If threatened, the creature reacts wildly. It is large and strong enough to butcher a small army with a charge. Vruuns live exclusively in the Vruun hills where they can find plenty of their favorite food, an alcoholic shrub called Drunkenroot. They have three stomachs, and when the Drunkenroot is digested flammable gas is produced. By blowing the gas against its metal-rich teeth, the creature can breathe fire.

The Vruun has a long lifespan, up to three hundred years.

Attributes: Agility d6, Smarts d6 (A), Spirit d8, Strength d12+3, Vigor d10
Skills: Fighting d6, Notice d6

Pace: 7; **Parry:** 5; **Toughness:** 15 (3)
Special Abilities
• **Armor +3:** Scaly hide.
• **Fire Breathing:** The Vruun can breathe fire using a Cone Template. Every target within the cone must make an Agility (–2) roll to jump out of harm's way or suffer 2d10 from fire. Also, targets caught in the Template must check if they have caught on fire. The Vruun cannot attack by stomping in the same round when it breathes fire. After breathing fire, it leaves the smell of Drunkenroot in the air.
• **Heavy Armor:** The Vruun's hide is so thick and hard nothing except a siege weapon can truly damage it.
• **Heavy Weapon:** The Vruun's attacks are considered Heavy Weapons.
• **Large:** Due to its size, attack rolls against the Vruun are made at +2.
• **Size +5:** The Vruun is bigger than a rhino but smaller than an elephant.
• **Stomping:** Str+d6. The Vruun's teeth are blunt and the creature doesn't bite. It prefers stomping on its targets with its massive legs. The Vruun can attack all nearby targets as per the Improved Sweep Edge.
• **Weakness (Stomach Gas):** The Vruun is virtually impervious to any attack. Its only weakness is the gas in its stomach. Throwing a burning torch or something similar into the beast's open mouth requires accurate skill and timing (–4 Called Shot), but has a spectacular effect. The beast literally explodes, dealing 3d6 damage to any target in a Large Burst Template.

Pace: 7; **Parry:** 5; **Toughness:** 10 (2)
Special Abilities
• **Armor +2:** Scaly hide.
• **Fire Breathing:** The Vruun can breathe fire using a Cone Template. Every target within the cone must make an Agility (–2) roll to jump out of harm's way or suffer 2d10 from fire. Also, targets caught in the Template must check if they have caught on fire. The Vruun cannot attack by stomping in the same round when it breathes fire. After breathing fire, it leaves the smell of Drunkenroot in the air.
• **A Mother's Love:** If the Vruun puppy dies when its mother is present, the mother reacts wildly, gaining +2 to attack and damage rolls and suffering –2 to Parry, as per the Berserk Edge.
• **Size +2:** The Vruun is bigger than a rhino but smaller than an elephant.
• **Stomping:** Strength. The Vruun's teeth are blunt and the creature doesn't bite. It prefers stomping on its targets with its massive legs.
• **Weakness (Stomach Gas):** The Vruun is virtually impervious to any attack. Its only weakness is the gas in its stomach. Throwing a burning torch or something similar into the beast's open mouth requires accurate skill and timing (–4 Called Shot), but has a spectacular effect. The beast literally explodes, dealing 3d6 damage to any target in a Large Burst Template.

VRUUN PUPPY

This creature may be the only Vruun puppy in the world. The Branded Devils have fed it so well its fire breathing abilities are comparable to its mother's.

Attributes: Agility d6, Smarts d6 (A), Spirit d8, Strength d12, Vigor d8
Skills: Fighting d6, Notice d6

Index

Index

www.ingramcontent.com/pod-product-compliance
Lightning Source LLC
Chambersburg PA
CBHW050359030726
47503CB00006B/1931